WORD C

MW00966577

BILLIBU DADDINGS

Let me share a piece of wisdom I've picked up being the reviewer. You simply cannot go wrong reading anything Tee Morris writes. You won't find a better blend of action, humor, suspense, and romance anywhere else. Many genre authors like to mix the genres together to create a new flavor to their stories.

— The Dragon Page: Cover to Cover

Cynics will say that Glen Cook has already mined that concept about as deep as it can go with his Garrett P.I. stories but Morris has struck on a rich vein here. Morris cleverly plays the clichés of fantasy, detective, and gangster stories off of each other in a carefully plotted, subtly witty, action-packed thriller. I haven't enjoyed a cross-genre detective story this much since *Who Framed Roger Rabbit?*

— Michael Pederson, *Nth Degree*

The Case of the Singing Sword is the Holy Grail of reviewers -- the book you would never have found on your own but can't praise enough. There's not a single false note, flat character, or unbelievable scene. The pacing is perfect, the mystery is tightly constructed, and the whole thing is leavened with self-depreciating humor. Run do not walk to your bookstore and pick up this book!

— Linnea Dodson, *ReviewingTheEvidence.com*

Tee Morris has accomplished what is normally unimaginable – combining our own familiar world with that of fantasy and very real magic. Billibub Baddings is Sam Spade, Mickey Spillane and Joe Friday — all tough guys – combined with stories by authors such as Terry Brooks or J. K. Rowling.

— Alan Paul Curtis, *WhoDunnit.com*

Dragon Moon Press Titles by Tee Morris

MOREVI: The Chronicles of Rafe & Askana
(with Lisa Lee)

Legacy of MOREVI: Book One of the Arathellean Wars

The Case of the Singing Sword: A Billibub Baddings Mystery

The *Complete Guide to Writing Fantasy* Series

Volume I: Alchemy with Words
(contributing author)

Volume II: The Opus Magus
(co-editor)

Volume III: The Author's Grimoire
(contributing author)

The Case of The Pitcher's Pendant

A Billibub Baddings Mystery

By
Tee Morris

Dragon Moon

www.dragonmoonpress.com

www.teemorris.com

The Case of the Pitcher's Pendant: A Billibub Baddings Mystery

ISBN 1-896944-77-9 Print Edition
ISBN 978-1-896944-77-7

ISBN 1-896944-79-5 Electronic Edition
ISBN 978-1-896944-79-1

Dragon Moon Press is an Imprint of Hades Publications Inc.
P.O. Box 1714, Calgary, Alberta, T2P 2L7, Canada

Dragon Moon Press and Hades Publications, Inc. acknowledges the ongoing support of the Canada Council for the Arts and the Alberta Foundation for the Arts for our publishing programme.

The Alberta Foundation for the Arts
Alberta COMMUNITY DEVELOPMENT
Canada Council for the Arts
Conseil des Arts du Canada
COMMITTED TO THE DEVELOPMENT OF CULTURE AND THE ARTS

Printed and bound in the United States
www.dragonmoonpress.com
www.teemorris.com
www.jrblackwell.com

Save a Tree Program

At Dragon Moon Press, our carbon footprint is significantly higher than average and we plan to do something about it. For every tree Dragon Moon uses in printing our books, we are helping to plant new trees to reduce our carbon footprint so that the next generation can breathe clean air, keeping our planet and its inhabitants healthy.

Acknowledgments

In the Fall of 2004, *The Case of the Singing Sword* appeared in Dragon Moon's catalog and Amazon's listings. Its humble beginnings led to an Honorable Mention for *ForeWord Magazine*'s Best Fiction (that's *General* Fiction, not *Science* Fiction) of 2005, positive reviews on Fantasy and Mystery websites, and thousands of listeners in the "podosphere" when the title became a podcast featuring voice talent from around the world.

So…what's taken me so long in putting together Billi's next mystery?

The podcast of *MOREVI*, as some of you might know, led to my participation with not one but two titles for the popular *For Dummies* line. It was a very exciting opportunity for me both as an author and a podcaster, but I was reminded by many fans at cons and other book events that it had been some time since my last case with the Windy City's Dwarf detective. On finishing *Expert Podcasting Practices for Dummies*, I turned my attention back to my fiction, back to *The Case of the Pitcher's Pendant*. Working with Billi, Miranda, Mick, and Alphonse again was the reminder that while I genuinely enjoyed the *For Dummies* experience, fiction is my passion; and it feels great taking you all back to this Chicago of yesteryear.

As always, this book would not be happening if it weren't for Gwen Gades of Dragon Moon Press. While she doesn't "get it" with Billi's hard-boiled humor, she does not deny the Dwarf's appeal. I consider myself fortunate that Dragon Moon is making all this possible. While she is joining me for the first time as an editor, Gabrielle Harbowy is anything but a stranger to me. The two of us go back to my days at James Madison University, and it was a real thrill to work with a familiar face, and turn a good idea into a great mystery. This is a better book because of you, Gabrielle. And let's not forget the lovely Donna Mugavero a/k/a Ms. Information. Thank you for your help in making this book look so damn pretty!

Finally, there is my Muse. You know who you are. You opened my eyes, broadened my scope, and gave me the swift kick in the backside to get me back on track with my world, both Fantasy and Reality. You made an impression on this book, and something tells me you will be there for the mysteries yet to come. For everything, you have so much more than my eternal thanks.

Now, it's time to step back to a Chicago ruled by mobsters, snapping back from the Stock Market Crash, and facing hard times ahead. Batter up — someone is stealing First, and it's up to Billi Baddings to find out who's behind it.

Dedication

For 30 years,
you called him names,
showed no respect,
and from the stands offered free advice
on how to do his job.

You never did ask him why he did it.
It was always for the love of the game.

Dad, this one is for you.

Table of Contents

CHAPTER ONE

DIAMONDS ARE A DWARF'S BEST FRIEND

Chicago, 1930. You might think it's tough being a four-foot-one private dick in a world of six-foot-something thugs, but I got news for you—when hard times hit, we're all seeing eye to eye.

The name's Billibub Baddings, if you didn't check the book cover. Good chance if you zipped by the name, then you probably missed the words "*The Case of...*" which is your clue that I'm a private eye. So now that I've got your attention, let me explain how you come to find a Highlands Dwarf of Gryfennos working as a private detective in the cultural cradle of the USA—Chicago.

Now, I'm going to zip through the ugly, sordid details. Keep things on the sprite's time clock and all that. Try to keep up. But if I were to sum it up in a word: Orcs. Goddamn Orcs. Rotten, stupid, smelly Orcs. They had this idea that the world—well, Acryonis, which was *my* world only a few years ago—would be a nicer place if they were calling the shots. That's the part that makes the Orcs rotten. So the Black Orcs all gathered up in their mountain stronghold and worked out a pact with the Everlasting Darkness, which is, simply put, a prison for the darkest-down-to-the-core, baby-killing, puppy-burning, kitten-gutting evil. The realm Darkness called home makes Joliet Prison look like a summer villa in Miami, and *these* were the guys the Orcs thought would make great business partners. That's the part that makes the Orcs stupid.

And when you're this rotten and this stupid, the body odor just naturally follows you wherever you go.

It's one thing to go into business with evil, but you're really stepping across a line when you invite evil over for dinner and give it permission to put its feet up on the furniture and pick the lint out of its belly button in polite company. The Black Orcs were about to do basically this, by means of a ritual using the Sacred Talismans of Acryonis, and I was part of a fellowship that was sent to kick a little ass and finish this damn war once and for all.

We managed to get into the Orcs' stronghold and put a major chink in their plans, but here's where things got complicated for me. It was a mess—I mean, a real mess—that we had stepped into. Orcs, see, weren't big into books. The average Orc would look at a library and think, "*Fuel for fire.*" Somehow, though, they had read the right tomes in order to perform this ritual. The Talismans of Acryonis were all in the right place and the incantation was correct down to the last syllable. The barrier between realms began to tear apart; and the screams, shouts, and other ungodly noises coming out of the growing portal before us didn't make us feel any better.

Axes were cutting the air. Orc guts and arrows were flying every which way, and swords were getting up close and personal with one another. All the while, the portal was getting bigger and the folks on the other side were getting noisier. That's when I got the bright idea of taking the Talismans of Acryonis and tossing them into the portal. They were being used to open up this breech, so why not give these talismans a big goodbye and collapse that doorway in on itself?

It was a great idea that made a lot of sense to me. At the time.

The problem was that to do this, I had to get closer—a lot closer than I wanted to—to this portal leading to oblivion. No cleric, necromancer, or magister's apprentice had bothered to explain to me how "suction" works, especially on creatures as petite as Dwarves. And okay, I'll admit it—even if they had tried to explain the concept to me, I probably wouldn't have listened. I never really had a care or a liking for those magician-types. If their lips were moving, they were either spell-casting, or bullshitting me.

So, Billi got his ass sucked into this Portal of Oblivion, tried to remember those prayers you're supposed to say before you die, and hoped what he remembered was enough to get himself into the Everlasting Fields of Yearnese.

I woke up in a public library in Downtown Chicago. Who says the Guardians don't have a sense of humor?

So while this story isn't one I enjoy telling again and again…and again…I'm finding it easier to tell.

When I got here, it was 1927. By the time I figured out what a day, month, and year was, and that I wasn't going to be able to spend the rest of my long life in the boiler room of a public library, it was 1928. That spring I found a calling, worked to get myself on my feet, and went into business by the fall. In October 1928, it was official: the words "Baddings Investigations" were painted on the frosted glass of my office door.

If you would have told me everything was about to change a year later, I wouldn't have believed you.

1929 had a few surprises in store for me, everything from a lucrative case with one of the most prominent families of Chicago's upper crust to dinner with one of the most dangerous bosses of Chicago's underworld to a nostalgic reminder of Acryonis. The biggest surprise, though, came a year after I started Baddings Investigations. On October 29, the brakes were slammed on the party that was the Roaring Twenties. Overnight, princes became paupers, businessmen became beggars, and I was back to relying on the "Waldorf" routine.

Guess I need to explain that, too. This was one of the sordid details I had hoped I could zip by just a wee bit faster, but no matter how hard I try to keep "Waldorf, the Protector of Munchkinland" in the dungeons, that dink always manages to break out.

Before I could open up my office for business, I had to make ends meet. The best way for a Dwarf to do that *legally* was to work with what I had; and since I looked like I had stepped out of some children's bedtime story, I began a relationship with the Harvey Showenstein Talent Agency as "Waldorf, the Protector of Munchkinland." Seems there was this book—*The Wizard of Oz*—and its moving picture was a huge hit a few years back, so Harv's been playing me up for all I'm worth as the roly-poly protector of Emerald City.

Look, I ain't proud of it either, but my choices are this, ask for handouts, or break the law. I may be a son-of-a-bitch, but I'm a son-of-a-bitch who knows better.

When the fragile financial bubble burst, the demand for a private eye and his talents all but disappeared; but some fat cats managed to avoid the full sting of the Crash, even after November. The well-to-do set's desire to start up the party again was keeping the cash flow steady in February and March. Performing these events, though, proved to be a challenge. I had to make sure I wasn't wearing that self-satisfied smirk I knew I would conjure during moments of hypocrisy. I got the gigs because these rich dinks found me to be a novelty, thought I was outrageously funny, and I fetched drinks and snacks with a smile. If I flashed the smirk, my cover would have been blown and my girl Miranda would have been tightening the purse strings even more. This smirk would come when I would get the condescending smile or backhanded comment. Only a few heartbeats after the slur was delivered by some high society dink reveling in his own cleverness, I would catch a glimpse of the very same dink slipping an extra helping of cake or pigs in a blanket into his girl's handbag. Yeah, some of the fat cats managed to survive the crash. Not all of them did, however. Amazing how far people go to protect their pride.

With the weather finally settling into spring and May ushering in a false feeling of optimism over a dark year, the privileged fewer were really gearing up the festive gatherings, and Waldorf was in demand. I had two afternoon teas and then a bash at the Rothchild's. (I had to make sure my makeup was particularly heavy for that engagement. Never hurts to prepare for the worst.) A profitable but busy day.

Miranda was worried about me. Hey, what's new? It was my worrying about her that kept me so damn busy. I felt like I owed it to her to keep Baddings Investigations running, especially when she would start to say, "*We've always got cash in the kitty*," only to catch herself.

We were financially set after taking Julia Lesinger as a client, but neither Miranda nor I could have foreseen that one of the banks hit hardest by the crash would be ours. Our nest egg was gone. At least that was what the bank told us when they shut their doors for good. Now we were starting from the ground up, and I was determined not to have anything like that happen again. Some banks did manage to survive the bubble bursting, but instead of stashing all our remaining cash in someone else's vault again, I chose to keep half of it hidden. One Sunday, I met Miranda over at the office and declared the First Bank of Billibub Baddings open for business. Miranda kept this second kitty hidden in her desk drawer. Still, we had barely enough saved to be worth mentioning, so Waldorf was keeping the butter on the bread.

No, I wasn't particularly happy about it, but as I've always said—a Dwarf's got to do what a Dwarf's got to do.

I barreled into the office, still wearing rosy cheeks and overly-bushy eyebrows. The early afternoon tea was a huge success, and I even managed to drum up some interest for the munchkin appearing at a Bat Mitzvah, so things were looking up for the day, despite the Rothchild affair looming at the end of it. Then I realized I had forgotten the address for my late afternoon tea engagement. This detour to the office was going to be a severe cramp in my expected call time. If the traffic was forgiving and the tea room was close enough to my side of town, I would make it with just enough time to touch up the war paint.

"Heya, doll," I said playfully, "don't go weak in the knees now! I'm in full makeup."

"Billi…" Miranda began.

"I'd love to tell you about the rich saps I just performed for, Miranda, but I'm a bit pressed," I said, hopping into her desk chair. The strained creak it made under the weight of my armor made me freeze. I really wanted to keep office expenses to the barest minimum, and office chairs didn't come cheap.

"Billi…"

Knowing full well how Miranda loves her chair to be relaxed, I stood on the seat, keeping my movement slow and deliberate, in order to see her desk better. "C'mon, honey, can't you see I'm concentrating?"

"Billi!" she whispered tersely.

My head snapped up to finally make eye contact with her, and with the gentleman standing behind her, the two of them waiting for me in my office. Apparently, she had been playing the "*Mr. Baddings just stepped out, but if you take a seat in his office, I'll let him know you're waiting,*" card. This is what we do if I'm stuck in traffic, out to lunch, or on one of my Waldorf gigs. If the interested party is willing to wait ten minutes, Miranda knows they're serious, gets a number and a name, hands them my card, and then I do a follow-up when I get back.

I was okay with getting caught with my jerkin up, but it was when I got a closer look at who was waiting in my office that I lost my composure. My balance wasn't far behind.

Stars were now decorating the ceiling, and Miranda's voice sounded like it was coming from a few leagues away, across a vast valley. I think the helmet was screwing with my ears and making everything sound just a bit off, but with her voice mingling with the ringing in my ears I wouldn't have been surprised at all if she'd appeared as a wild wraith hovering over me, her outstretched arms spreading the tatters that covered her ethereal body like wings of a vulture soaring high above a battlefield of carnage. Instead of a vision of death and revenge, though, I saw an angel's face, her expression one of embarrassment, sympathy, and a hint of frustration.

If it weren't for the damn crash, Miranda, you'd be getting that raise today.

The groan I made when I returned to my feet reminded me of the chair. I glanced at it. The sucker was still intact, thank the Fates.

When the potential client spoke, the uncertainty was there. Clear as arctic crystal. "*You're* Billi Baddings?"

Okay, I was dressed in my old battle armor, my face covered with a light sheen of white makeup, ridiculous ruby-red dots painted on my cheeks, and the last touch to this look—a singular, bushy eyebrow easily mistaken for a *bogruthra* that had decided to park itself across my own brow. I looked like a complete and utter hayseed. This was not going to be an easy sell.

"Yes, Mr. McCarthy. Believe it or not, this uncoordinated but snappy dresser before you is Private Investigator Billi Baddings."

He nervously fumbled with his hat and then placed it on his head, "Maybe this was a bad idea."

First impressions are hard to erase, especially when they're bad. When they are as outrageous and ludicrous as the one I was currently making on Cubs Manager Joe McCarthy, they're unforgettable in the worst possible way. This was the kind of initial meeting that you share with the guys over a dinner table, the kind of story that no matter how many times you tell it, it just gets funnier (not to mention, crazier) with every telling.

I hated playing this card, but I needed the common ground. I also needed to save my detective face. "Mr. McCarthy, please. I'm doing what I can to pay the bills. It's tough times, and I've got people who rely on me—" I said, motioning to Miranda, "—to take care of things. If anyone understood how important that is, it's you, sir."

Miranda shot me a quick glare. Yeah, I was going to owe her for that little guilt trip. She knew how much I hated the Waldorf routine, and now I was using her the way a beggar uses the missing stump where a perfectly good leg once was, in order to score some coin.

"Alms for the stupid-looking Dwarf," I wanted to cry, *"Alms for the Dwarf."*

Joe McCarthy was a Pixie's heartbeat away from leaving, but those words made him think. I knew they would. Common ground.

Go on, Joe. Break the ice. Take a look at the pictures.

He cleared his throat again and then turned to the wall where my shrine to the pastime was. "I see," Joe spoke finally, taking his hat off, "that you're a fan."

"One of the biggest, Joe," I said, smirking. "Height not withstanding."

He chuckled as I picked up my helm and satchel. I gave a heavy sigh when I passed by him and started hanging my various props and costume pieces on a sturdy wooden tree. "Sorry about the get-up. It's tough enough being me, but right now, I'm something straight out of a bad batch of bathtub gin."

"What the hell is this get-up anyway?"

"A necessary evil," I said, a hint of loathing in my voice. "The Crash hasn't been a complete end-of-the-world for all the social elite, and there's a lot more demand for a novelty act than for a private dick." When I stripped down to the sleeveless undershirt and pants, Joe's laughter abruptly ended. I looked down at my body hair. Hey, Gryfennos gets cold in the winter. "Should I put the jerkin back on?"

Joe blinked. Apparently, that's not a term you hear in the Cubbies' locker room often. Well, not referring to clothes anyway.

"Um, no, no, Mr. Badd—"

"Billi," I interjected, stretching my arms casually. "You can call me Billi."

"Joe."

Poor guy nearly leapt out of his suit when the phone rang.

I glanced at the clock on the wall. Harv was such a creature of habit. "Miranda, let Harv know I won't be making the afternoon tea."

"He's not going to be too happy about that, Billi."

"He'll be a lot unhappier if I'm quitting." Over the angry ring of the phone, I continued, "I've got the Rothchild's tonight, the Abistair's tomorrow night, and the Loudon's next week. Remind him of that."

The echo of the phone's bell faintly lingered in the office after Miranda took the call. Minutes later, the sparring with Harv commenced. "Now hold on, Harv," I heard her say, "You know Billi's been reliable in the past. This is one of those—you know—unexpected things." She paused. "There's no reason to get snippy about this, Harv." Another pause, and then, "Now, Mr. Showenstein, I hardly think our discussion merits such language, nor do I think we are going to accomplish anything on a professional level if we continue such discourse."

Poor Harv. He thinks he can take on my girl Miranda. *You're charging into a line of Orcs armed only with a toothpick and a smile*, I thought with a snort. *Good luck, you dink.*

"You'd be talking to Harv instead of me if you wanted my Waldorf routine out at Wrigley for a few games," I started, partially closing the door to muffle Miranda's responses. Her words were not so quiet that I couldn't keep track of her progress with my agent. "But something tells me you're not interested in my Waldorf routine."

"I can't believe I'm here, to be frank with you, Billi." Again, he fiddled with the hat. "I don't know where to start."

"How about you start by taking a load off the loafers?" I suggested, motioning to the chair in front of my desk.

I climbed up the small crate in front of the sink and mirror, and started returning my face to something closer to the real thing. "Take a deep breath," I winced while removing the *bogruthra* from my brow, "and start from the top of your story. I'll be able to hear you over the magic I'm performing in this cauldron."

The warm water began to rush with a single slap of the faucet. I dipped my hands into the rising level of steaming water, working up a lather with the soap and vigorously applying the sweet smelling bubbles to my face. In the mirror I could see the deep red circles reducing to non-descript smears of pink, like blood soaking into your clothes when it rains on the battlefield.

"Well, it's early in the season and there's this team that's coming up in the league. They're out of Baltimore and they call themselves the Mariners."

"New team, right?"

"Yeah. For a first season, they're good."

I splashed water on my face, and gave a huff as I unscrewed my eyes open. "So what's wrong with that?"

"The problem is, they're *too* good." Joe didn't notice I was looking at him in the mirror's reflection of the room. He was blushing. This really was tough for him. "I'm going to sound like I've got sour grapes or something, but I just can't buy that this kind of talent has gone unsigned."

"What makes these Baltimore Mariners so good?" I said, giving my face another scrubbing as Joe continued.

"Their pitcher, for one thing. Never seen an arm like this guy's. If you're lucky, you catch a glimpse of his fastball. There's a rumor their catcher had to reinforce his glove with extra leather so he wouldn't break his fingers. When you watch this guy pitch, it's amazing."

Joe was right. This was sounding like a bad case of sour grapes. "Well now, I'm sure you've got scouts coming out of their cross-country tours who all have a lead on the next best player. From what I read in the Sports page, the Midwest is just a breeding ground for the next Lefty Groves, Willie Kamms, or Goose Goslins."

"It's not just the pitcher. The *entire team* is like this. I caught two of their games and spent both slack-jawed. I've seen outfielders catch what should have been grand slams. I didn't think it was possible to jump that high! Then there are infielders that make double-plays so fast even the umpires hesitate. And the batting averages, this early in the season, all promise to be record-breaking.

"I've been in this game for a while, and I've seen enough players and teams to know when something is just not…right."

Conviction is not easily faked. Sure, you can probably convince yourself that anything is true, especially if your team is flailing in the National League standings like a mermaid out of water. It's always better to blame something else—new talent, bad lineups, or sorcerers' curses—than to serve yourself up as the reason why the hometown team isn't meeting up to that previous championship season. (Yeah, so the Athletics managed to take the crown, but not without the Cubbies making the kind of final stand that heroes live and die for.)

What I initially thought was a sorry excuse to a somewhat lackluster start to the season, though, revealed that conviction. He was right, or at least he believed with every ounce of muscle that tensed in the bottom of the ninth, every drop of sweat shed in Wrigley during the hot, oppressive summers of Chicago, and every thought he put behind the batting and fielding lineups, that there was something fishy about this new team on the scene.

And with a name like the Mariners, how appropriate.

I gave my face another splash of soapy water, pulled the towel free of its rack, and dabbed at my face before asking, "So, why hire a private dick?"

"Because the owners, when I was discussing the possibility of having their people look into it, felt the same thing you did: That I was looking for a scapegoat."

Holy cow. That was direct. "Now wait a minute, Joe, I never—"

"Billi, you're a fan. You have to really love this sport—not the job, and definitely not the pay—to be a manager. It's not only a thankless job, but when the team does well no one gives you a pat on the back. I'm lucky if I even get a nod from the owners. And when the team can't seem to pull themselves out of the fire, the fans blame you after they finish blaming the guy they were cheering on in the last game."

Guilty as charged. I guess I never realized how much of a baseline commander I was. There'd been many a night that Mick and I praised the players in '29, and then last month we'd been bad-mouthing this man in my office for resting on his team's success as League Champs. Thinking back, I couldn't recall a moment where I'd said anything like, *"Well now, Joe really was thinking when he put together this lineup!"* It was like those rare, devoted generals who actually cared about their men; who came up with strategies that not only won battles but kept casualties to a minimum. Those were the generals I didn't mind spilling my blood for, and rarely did they get the credit they deserved. Meanwhile, most of the guys in the trenches only saw their own toil, only noticed when things went wrong. They never saw the bigger picture, or grasped the fact that the orders we followed were coming from someone who gave a damn about his men.

Fans can really be assholes. Present company included.

Miranda's voice snapped me back into my present world. She must have been getting a real earful from Harv, and I afforded her a smile when she said calmly, "Well then, should I remove Billi's other engagements as well? I'm sure you can find someone to cover. How many Dwarves do you have in your call books?" A pause, and I stifled a laugh as she replied, "Well, how tall are you, Harv?"

That's my girl, Miranda. Cooler than the Ice Queen of the White Mountains of Arctia, and just as deadly when challenged.

"For a while there, I thought they were right, but when I read about their last game..." Joe's voice faded away. I stepped off the crate and walked up to the side of his chair. He was torn about getting a private dick involved. This could cost him his job. But didn't he just say it wasn't the job? It was the game. It was all about the game. "I just know there's something odd about that team. Maybe the owners are thinking this is just me pointing fingers, maybe the commissioner is looking the other way because he doesn't want another Black Sox scandal, I don't know." He finally made eye contact with me. Pretty easy as he was sitting and I was standing. "I do know that right now, things are hard. On everyone. I don't know where people are getting the bucks together to even come to a game, but they are. This game means a lot to them. It means a lot to me."

I nodded. "Baseball isn't a game. It's a kind of magic, Joe. You know that. To an extent, so do I. I'm just a fan, I admit, so maybe I don't know all the ins and outs of the sport. Trust me when I tell you, though, that I know a thing or two about magic." I shot him a knowing wink and grinned. "And I'm here to tell ya, there is something magic about baseball. Something magical. Something sacred."

Joe turned his attention to the hat in his lap, his grin matching mine. Yeah, it might have sounded a little corny, but I spoke the truth.

"With the way things are," I started, "I'd like to see the Baltimore Mariners for myself, just to see if they're as suspicious as you claim they are."

He held up two tickets to Wrigley for Tuesday, May 13, and slid them next to my desk lamp. "They're going to be here for two games. Let me know what you think."

"My wages are $15 a day with a hundred and fifty down." I thought he would balk, but I had that nest egg to rebuild. "This commits me to two weeks of working with you, and you take care of any expenses, as well."

"Sure, Billi," Joe said, still staring at the tickets. "So long as you're not too crazy with those expenses."

"I'm a cheap date. Nothing to worry about."

His hat returned to his head, and after taking a moment to straighten it, he bent down to shake my hand. "Thanks for taking this on, Billi. I'm relying on your discretion in this matter."

"That's one of the things you're paying me for." Motioning to Miranda, I walked him to the door. "You can make your down payment and work out all the details with Miranda."

She was off the phone now, and her voice could not have sounded more pleasant. In fact, there was a delightful lilt to her tone with the manager of the Chicago Cubs. Only the bank calling to say, *"We found your savings!"* could have made her happier.

This was a step in the right direction. Don't think we weren't grateful. I gave the Guardians a "thank you" for two reasons: for giving Baddings Investigations a case while the bookings with Waldorf were strong, and for making it a case that involved baseball.

If there was magic in this world, it happened within sight of the three bases and home plate. All the gems in my world that decorated the walls and floors of dragons' lairs, the sword hilts of privileged princes, and crowns worn by emperors and kings, were nothing compared to the beauty and splendor of the diamond in Wrigley Stadium. It wasn't just a yard with dirt, chalk lines, bases, and a small hill in its center. Wrigley was a field of dreams. Dreams of eternal glory for the men who ran to the outfield, who took their respective bases, and prepared for battle against those who would dare enter their hallowed realm. Dreams for the kids in the stands, all wanting to don a uniform, kiss their moms goodbye, and wield their bats as enchanted weapons destined to knock the cover off the ball. And for the adults who had already selected their lot in life, Wrigley made the dreams of past innocence, lost wonder, and the promise that there was something inherently good still left in this world, come true.

Yeah, corny as hell. But all true.

I loosed another glance toward the clock. Rothchild's in a few hours. Enough time to get an early dinner at Mick's, get back here, and then catch a cab to the manor I wished I wasn't so familiar with. Eva was probably going to be there, and if I was lucky her head was thicker than a Troll's turd and she wouldn't recognize me underneath all the makeup. I had been cringing about this engagement all through April...

Then I tucked the tickets into the inside pocket of my coat. It didn't matter that much anymore. I had a client. I had a date with Miranda at Wrigley Field (whether she knew it or not). Just thinking about this case made me smile.

Baseball. I absolutely love this game.

CHAPTER TWO
The Things You Hear at Waist Level

The last time I set foot in the Rothchild Mansion, I was played for a sucker; and when Harv told me I would be performing here I was none too happy about it. But when Harv told me how much green I was going to collect from this one performance, I shut my mouth with a Troll-sized bite of pride pie.

That was before I scored the case with Joe McCarthy. A case with the Chicago Cubs—it was a fan's dream. Well, okay, so it wasn't an official job with Wrigley Field. If word got out that McCarthy was hiring private dicks to investigate other teams, the Sports sections of the *Tribune* and the *Daily* would blow it completely out of proportion and the higher-ups in the Cubs hierarchy would probably serve McCarthy his walking papers just to save face.

Keeping my involvement with the team as under wraps and low-key as possible was paramount. No lives were in danger, but a man's livelihood was on the line; and this livelihood was this man's passion. That's when I came to grips with the truth: my client wasn't the Cubs, but the pastime itself. McCarthy was going on a hunch, a deeply rooted concern for the sanctity of the sport. Baseball was doing its best, trying to make it through the hard times of 1930. If a terrific team suddenly hit a slump or if a favored team in a World Series were to get whipped harder than a pack beast on an incline, memories of the Black Sox scandal would no doubt spring into people's minds.

It was 1919 B.B. (Before Billi) when the Chicago White Sox faced off against the Cincinnati Reds in the World Series; and with the Sox infantry including foot soldiers like Claude "Lefty" Williams, Oscar "Happy" Felsch, and the great "Shoeless" Joe Jackson, there was no question that it would be a World Series for the Ages. It was also a healthy bet that Chicago would have a lot to celebrate come October, but it turned out to be a heartbreaker. The Reds won five games over the Sox's three. Not to say it wasn't a real nail-biter, at least from what I saw in the library archives, but the last game—at the Sox's own shire of Comiskey Park—seemed a little odd. "Odd" as in that sudden shift in the weather before a major battle, when that clear sky you were blessed with the morning you set up camp was suddenly swapped out for a fog bank thicker than split-*krea* soup come sunset. If you didn't have a really good wizard on hand to clear things up, it made for a long night, especially if the enemy attacked.

The 1919 Series opened with a score of 9—1 and a win for the Reds, and that raised a few eyebrows. It was the back-breaking 10—5 loss at the Sox's own field that got the wrong kind of people asking questions. The guy asking the loudest was a Sports scribe for the *Herald and Examiner*, Hugh Fullerton. He was the first to toss around the word "fix" in his write-ups, even in his post-season columns. Like many kings, lords, and nobles who tend to stuff their ears with fine silks on hearing rumors of revolution, team owners were trying to pretend that there was no possible way baseball could be so easily corrupted. As for the notion of someone fixing a World Series, it was inconceivable.

Fullerton's opinions didn't go away. Rumors in the 1920 season were now mentioning other teams taking a bounty for an error here, a poorly-pitched game there. Players were getting nervous. And before the '20 season concluded, a grand jury had convened to look into whispers and accusations against my beloved Cubs. What started with the Cubs ended with the Sox and a hard look at the 1919 Series. The scandal seemed to reach all the way up to that miser Comiskey himself (which got me to thinking: This dink was a former pitcher himself, and yet he treated his star players no better than castle slaves? What a prick!), but it was Jackson and pitcher Eddie Cicotte who stepped forward first and admitted everything.

Say it ain't so, Joe. Say it ain't so.

Even with Shoeless Joe and Cicotte spilling the beans like they did, nobody could really say who was involved and how deeply. The only thing clear as a prince's chalice was how interested the country was in the dirty details: the disgruntled players, the tightwad owners, and the opportunistic gamblers. Front-page news on every newspaper in my library's archives, and these were headlines from all across the States. The good news was, due to the lack of hard evidence, the Chicago Eight were acquitted of all criminal charges. The bad news: Kenesaw

Mountain Landis. (No, really…that *is* his middle name.) The club owners replaced the three-man commission overseeing baseball with this federal judge, making him into a supreme overlord and giving him the kind of power that would give an Orc a bulge in his breeches. With the proclamation, "*No player who throws a ball game, no player who undertakes or promises to throw a ball game, no player who sits in confidence with a bunch of crooked players and does not promptly tell his club about it, will ever play professional baseball,*" Landis banned eight players—regardless of the rulings of the court—from professional baseball. For life.

You could still start a tavern brawl by talking about the Black Sox. Some fans supported the overlord and his club-running minions, agreeing that there was no room in baseball for cheaters. But there were fan factions that sided with the players, especially with those who had been banned from the sport even though their roles in the conspiracy had never been clearly defined. The Sox delivered a pennant to Chicago, but Comiskey showed his appreciation with lousy wages, shitty treatment, and flat champagne. Could you really blame these guys—these eight incredible players—for giving into temptation? Yeah, it was a mess; and even after ten years and an economic crash, it was still a sore subject. I hadn't even been here for it and it got my codpiece in a twist.

A lot was riding on what I found out about this team, the Baltimore Mariners. If they were, in fact, that good of a team, then I would have to break it to McCarthy that he didn't need a private dick, but a charmed trainer and a better game plan. If other owners, managers, and team members were throwing games, this was going to be a real nightmare for the pastime, and the Great Depression was only going to get worse.

There was a growing tightness in my stomach as my coach-for-hire drew closer to the mansion gates. I took a deep breath and muttered something that, oddly enough, provided me with a hint of comfort. "Servants' entrance."

The cabbie glanced in his rear view and then slowed down. The fork in the road wasn't that far past the entrance gate, and if you blinked you missed it. I guess an obvious path for the hired help would be considered extremely poor taste, so the path was subtle enough for visitors to miss it, while the common folk knew where to look. Having it closer to the gate meant that the privileged would never see their staff making their meager way to the house. Serfs would just magically appear, ready to serve their lord and master with a stoup of wine.

Silently and methodically, butlers and maids in pristine white and black outfits filed into the mansion, giving a nod to the resident Jeeves as they did. I hopped out of the cab, grabbing the head butler's attention. Even with the hired help giving him the proper obeisance, Jeeves' eyes stayed on me.

The old boy's sneer grew more and more obvious as I approached. "How ya doin'? I'm the entertainment," I told him, presenting the Showenstein Talent Agency invoice that doubled as a work order for me.

"Yes." He sniffled. "Quite."

Oh, Jeeves, you really don't want to rub me the wrong way this early in the evening.

"I'm supposed to do my routine at seven, and then work the crowd until—"

"There is a water closet at the end of this corridor," Jeeves said, bringing his eyes back up to Human-level. "Feel free to make yourself ready there."

Hey, I've got my own can for a dressing room. I'm coming up in the world. "Thanks, bub."

The chatter didn't get any friendlier once I got into the lower bowels of the Rothchild Mansion. It was strictly business with the staff; and much like a military unit, the various foot soldiers were getting their assignments. The younger crew was cutting eyeteeth on this evening's festivities, so their posts were the farthest from the main hub of activity. The veterans merely nodded at their placements, duties, and priorities. It was nothing new to them. Keep the food hot and fresh, and don't blink at serving the bubbly to the odd senator or police commissioner, even though they made and enforced the laws that were supposed to prevent such libations from being available.

I had already checked in with my field commander at the door. I was the scout in this *soirée's* infantry, getting close with the enemy; so close I could smell their BO from a few hundred paces. Even further if I was downwind of them.

A soft *click* later, and I was alone with the toilet, bathroom sink, and a mirror far too high to make a difference.

After rummaging through my carpet bag of assorted costume pieces and makeup items, I found the small mirror that conveniently came with its own stand and propped it on the center of the lid. I had invested in this handy little contraption after one party too many where I couldn't find an adequate box to bring me up to Human mirror height. A handsome Dwarf smiled back from inside its frame. There was (as toilet lids usually allowed for) room enough for tins of makeup. White face. Rouge. And some black and brown makeup, depending on how severe I wanted to make the eyebrows.

"See you in a few, Billi," I muttered as I dabbed the white onto a small pad.

Apart from a heavy sigh, that was the last sound I made once the pale, stark paint began to cover my face. I had to get over this grumpiness because it would come through in my performance. Yeah, I had a case finally, but losing future Waldorf gigs would hurt my business more than I wanted to admit. I couldn't count on one case to pull me, Miranda, and the business through these tough times; so I needed to put on my best face (which got a grin out of me as I started to work on my first overly-rosy cheek) and make sure I was bringing home the mutton.

Painting the second cheek suddenly conjured an image of the Ice Witch herself, Eva Rothchild. Maybe it was one of those passing thoughts, wondering if she was somewhere in the mansion working on her own visage. I could have gone a lifetime (and that's a Dwarf's lifetime, mind you!) without seeing her again; but once I got to browning up the eyebrows, and unbraiding and bushing out the beard, I would barely recognize myself. Besides, with the limited attention span she was blessed with, Eva wouldn't wonder how many Dwarves there were in Chicago.

A few more strokes with the brush, and now it was time to hit the brows.

Oh, shit. I really must have been preoccupied. I'd forgotten to put my tunic on first. I was still in the street clothes I had changed into after heading home from the McCarthy meeting. I wasn't too worried about my dress shirt, but the tunic was one of those over-the-head jobbies, so I had to wiggle into it like a hot one from the Thieves' Guild. I always hated this dance; but at least this time, in my private water closet, I could do it alone with only my reflection in the handheld mirror mocking me.

"Welcome, welcome, one and all! Welcome,
welcome to this ball!
Now is when we dance and dine, revel in friendship
and times divine.
And on my charge shall I serve diligently
To protect you, the city's collected nobility.
So celebrate, eat, and tap your toes to song,
For this house will burn the tallow as ere the night
is long!"

All I wanted to do, at this particular moment, was vomit.

It was tough enough to somersault in light combat armor, but some of the things my clients wanted me to say added new depth to hokey. Then again, if my buddies from my old unit were to see me in this goofy makeup, reciting bad, silly poetry would be the least of my worries.

Now came the pride-swallowing portion of the evening. The sea of pressed trousers closed in, only a few of the waves parting for me, not out of respect but more to protect their expensive raiment from my face makeup. Eh, these guys were fine, unless they really pissed me off. Then, suddenly, I'd become the clumsiest son-of-a-bitch ever to wear light armor, and I'd take a strategic stumble into a particular pair of pants as I skipped though the crowd, lightly humming the national anthem of Munchkinland.

Alright, let's just put this to rest right now: Skipping is part of the job. I don't like it and I don't do it when I'm out of costume. I only skip, dance, or giggle when the price is right. Try and get me to perform this routine simply for your amusement, and I guarantee you'll be feeling some serious pain.

"Well, hello there, little man!" the man bellowed. This dink was so full of himself, especially when his friends reacted to the mocking toast. "So if I drink any more of this magic potion, what shall happen to me?"

I struck the pose of an actor from a silent film conveying shock and surprise. My outstretched hand turned to a quivering finger (not *the* finger, but I was tempted) pointing at his flute. "You drink the ancient elixir of Queen Illora," I said in my best trembling treble. "The more you drink of it, the happier shall you feel, but beware of its curse upon sunrise! And if you suddenly feel the sharpest of pains in your loins, you best follow the Yellow Brick Road and find salvation at its end!"

Another one of these high society types chimed, "So why is it a road to salvation, this Yellow Brick Road?"

Yeah, like I didn't see that coming. "Alas, it is marked so in the memory of those brave men who did not head the warnings of Waldorf!"

Applause. A raising of glasses. Then it was asses and backs to the Dwarf to resume whatever scintillating conversation they'd been enjoying before I showed up.

It was the image of Miranda standing in a breadline, or maybe doing something I wouldn't stand for one of my sisters doing to make some extra coin, that kept me going through the night. The contraband flowing in substitute of water didn't help matters much. The comments would get more and more abrasive. I would be expected to balance glasses on my head. It was always a roll of the bones as to how pleasant these elite would be when drunk. This was an older crowd, so at least the younger heirs-apparent were off keeping to themselves or hitting the harder stuff from poppy fields or South American jungles. They were usually the ones daring each other to slap said glass off my head. Damages would, of course, come out of the performer's pay.

That's it, Billi. Stay with the positive. You've got to, for Miranda's sake.

As I wandered through the collection of evening wear, I noticed an odd scent in the air. It wasn't overpowering, but had that subtle, lingering quality like the air in a kitchen just after someone's cooked a T-bone steak. The scent wasn't as pleasant or as mouthwatering as a T-bone; it was more earthy and stale, but it did have that lingering quality. When I caught wind of it again, I decided to follow it.

The source of the smell—the closer I got to it—now reminded me less and less of "overcooked T-bone" and more of "rotten eggs with just a hint of marsh". I never did like the assignments that would take me and my boys into the swamplands. It wasn't the variety of crawlies that would slither, swim, and slink their way around, but it was the smell. Nature's sewer, we Dwarves called the marshlands of Acryonis.

Stopping just shy of what I believed was offending my nostrils, I slipped into my routine before a small group of people. All of them were enjoying the bubbly with generous portions of party favors.

"Good and true nobles of the realm," I implored, removing my helmet and tousling my hair to make it look a bit more goofy. "May I impose upon you all and ask for your counsel?"

Never understood why these high society types all tittered and snickered more when I would speak like the Shakespeare actor-washout, but that's why Harv was paying me the big bucks: to keep these inebriated socialites happy.

"I have...fallen...in love..." And with a quick breath, I spoke timidly, "...with a lady in my court."

And here it came. The collected "*Aaawwwww...*" that never ceased to test my patience. How utterly condescending.

"Is she a tiny person, too?" one of the ladies, apparently fighting to keep her balance, asked me.

No, as a matter of fact, she's a six-foot redhead, with a great ass and tits that make babies tremble at the bounty of the feast.

Instead, these words left my lips. "That she is, my lady. A lady of minor nobility and I dare to court her; but I so need practice in my manners. I know how to use a fork and spoon, so that does me well!" Okay, I'll admit it: I think that's funny. I knew a few captains in my day that could barely grasp the concept of eating with their mouths closed. "There is something I would ask..." And here I made eye contact with the dipso struggling against gravity, "...of you, my lady. Might I practice a courtly manner by kissing your hand." Then I would start, and stutter a bit, and add, "*Just for practice!*"

Without the goofy makeup, there was no way these people would give me the time of day, but with me making a Goblin's ass out of myself and playing the Dwarf-in-love, I had charmed her enough to get an offered hand. Yeah, she looked at her date apprehensively as she did so; but still, I got the offer.

The lady in question was what I called one of those aging beauties. Not bad looking, but definitely not one of the younger fillies that could easily begin the celebrations at sunset, enjoy a good tavern tickle, and then return to the party and continue until sunrise. She was gracefully heading to the quiet life, or at least that was the image she was portraying.

The stench nearly knocked me over as I awkwardly took her hand and placed a soft kiss on her middle knuckle. I looked up and saw an elegant bracelet on her wrist, of what appeared to be emeralds and diamonds, exquisitely arranged. Quite an eye-catcher of an accessory.

I gave her wrist the smallest of turns and watched the stones wink back at me.

"Many thanks, my lady!" I exclaimed, giving a silly bow. I continued to speak while fumbling with my helmet, "So what do you think? Shall I charm my lady fair?"

"You're going to charm her short little socks off!" the lush replied, clumsily waving her hand around. "You are so damn cute!"

Her date put his arms around her, his own laughter growing less sincere and more awkward. "That's enough, Annie. I think the Dwarf has some other people to bother."

Ah, got it, pal. The wife's in her cups and making a spectacle of herself. The last thing you need is her drawing attention to herself and you. People might notice.

"Many thanks, my lords and ladies!" I exclaimed, straightening my helmet and giving another bow, "Eat, drink, and be merry."

Returning to the other guests, the smell subsided; but I now understood why there was something hanging in the air. Faint, and thankfully overpowered by the other aromas in the room. Damsel Dipso was not alone.

With an idea of what was causing it, I could now try and shut it out. The last thing I needed to make this evening complete was a headache akin to the ones brought on by the smell of the swamp. Another goofy routine or two, and then I could give myself a break.

A small group of salt-and-pepper shakers encouraged me to do a forward-tumble (probably to settle a bet to see if the short guy could move that well in armor). When I recovered from the simple gymnastics, I caught a glimpse of that unmistakable blonde hair, brighter than sunrise over the Shri-Mela Plains. I even dared eye contact with Eva Rothchild as I scrambled to take off my helmet and sink to one knee in honorable deference, though the slapstick nature of my gesture was hardly respectful. I didn't sink my head so low, though, to completely remove her from view. Her face remained just in my peripheral. Eva's only reaction was a turn of her nose upward, the angle of her head making it easier to polish off what remained in her glass, and then a quick swap with a full one that almost passed her by. Much like the other guests, she told me, *"Show's over, Dwarf..."* by turning her back to me, the dress brazenly dipping low.

Cute little temptress, ready to play. Yeah, that's my Eva. Beauty and the Bitch.

The salt-and-peppers were sympathetic to my snubbing, and they conveyed it with that collected *"Aaawwwww..."* I was dealt earlier.

A sudden flash in my mind of ripping out the battle cry of Gryfennos and taking my battle axe to everyone around me was what made me decide I was ready for a break. I was allowed one for every two hours. I was supposed to be part of the revels for three, so that meant at least one after the first hour and a half.

I glanced at the closest clock. Only forty-five minutes had passed. Now I remembered why I didn't include my battle axe as part of the costume.

Okay, so what could I do to check out for a moment without stiffing the host? Yeah, ol' Daddy Rothchild was watching, casting glances at me just to make certain I was worth the price tag. I don't think the hard times had hit him so hard that he was watching the pennies or anything, but I'm sure he didn't want to part easily with any of that hard-earned (and now, even harder-kept) fortune. Never quite understood why those folks who could afford to spend gold never did.

In the corner of my eye was a corridor leading to the East Wing of the Rothchild estate, and it appeared empty for the time being. A few minutes in the shadows, maybe fiddling with my armor, would give me the time I needed to clear my head of homicidal tendencies.

The hallway was still connected with the ballroom, but what a world of difference it made. A strange oasis of silence only footsteps away from a vast wasteland of privilege and vanity fair. I bent down in the shadows of a small alcove to adjust the laces along my boots. Not that they needed adjusting, of course. (First rule of combat: Lace your boots properly. Death on account of tripping over your bootlaces is something you really don't want on a ledger somewhere.) Still, playing the illusion of a "wardrobe malfunction" was an excuse to step away from the crowds and catch my breath.

"So, Miles, have you considered my offer?"

Maybe it was the lack of formal wear and stuffy attitudes in the quiet hallway that made this polished voice louder than its intended whisper, and maybe it was the echo of the corridor that made the intended whisper sound even cockier than it was. I merely continued to straighten my belt as Miles answered his friend.

"Bruce, if this was a different time, I would take you up on your offer, but I'm quite content with current arrangements. Besides, I have no reason to alter said arrangements, now do I?"

"But you are a friend; and if there is anything I am known for, it's looking out for my friends."

These guys were friends? This was a pissing contest of Orc-sized proportions.

Miles didn't seem phased by Bruce's insincere concern as he continued, "But my needs are covered, my business protected. It will remain as such, and provided you continue to do what you are currently doing, we will all benefit."

"Don't give me that shit, Miles!" Was that desperation I heard in Bruce's voice? "The Crash hardly touched you. Your investments were sound."

"I know they were. They were in my business, and my business still stands, tough times aside. I'm able to meet the needs of even my harder-hit clientele."

I straightened up and fiddled with my helm, to see if I had enough light to check these guys out. Miles had his back to me. The martini in his hand caught the light from the ballroom. Bruce was a good match with his pal, height for height. The tuxedo gave his broad shoulders an even sharper cut than normal, and while he wasn't poking Miles with a threatening finger, he was standing close enough to be pushing boundaries. Anybody getting that close to me in a tavern was looking to start a fight.

Usually, I would finish it.

Miles took a sip of his martini, holding his ground like a Dwarf unit standing against an Ogre charge. I almost admired Miles, but even in his confidence, he was an arrogant ass with a bull's-eye painted on his chest, just waving a banner over his head.

"Yes, it's true that you look out for your friends, especially at the tables, from what I'm told. If it weren't for your nasty habits, I think you would be an adequate businessman." The martini was polished off in a single gulp, and then Miles added, "Do you want to hold on to what's left of your family legacy? Then I suggest you sit back and continue to sign the papers that are put in front of you. Asking questions is a bad investment choice. Changing the arrangements is a far worse one."

Bruce took a moment. He was letting that last bit sink in. When he finally found his voice, that earlier cockiness was notably absent. "So you truly believe we're secure?"

"Even in what's left of our economics, I would dare say, yes."

Bruce gave a nod, scoffing lightly as he looked into the crowd. "I hope you're right. We're in uncertain times. Today's fortunes could disappear tomorrow."

"Not mine, Bruce. Not mine." Miles handed him an empty glass and gave his shoulder a light pat. "Be a chum and fetch me a fresh martini. I, for one, feel like celebrating tonight."

Miles had been doing so well, and then he'd gone and given Bruce a verbal kick in the nuts.

Maybe that was Bruce's problem: He was a working man's noble, still punching a time clock and not letting his subjects run the business. Maybe he was successful enough to run with the lead stags, but it was his personal demons that made him cursed goods. I started feeling bad for the guy, and made myself a promise to brush a cheek up against Miles' tuxedo pants before the evening was done.

A final deep breath, and it was back into the foray. I recalled the last time I'd worn this light armor in combat. I'd been surrounded by several garrisons of Dwarven infantry, screaming our heads off, with our halberds, spears, and *rølmstirks* (a pole-arm weapon unique to Gryfennos, and a pretty nasty weapon when in the right hands) all pointing the way to several ranks of Orcs, Trolls, and Goblins. By the time it was all over, a third of our numbers were on their way to the Everlasting Fields, and the rest of us were surrounded by a sea of stiffs.

A sea of stiffs. Huh, well, this party wasn't so different then.

The evening picked up its pace after my brief breather with Miles and Bruce, neither of whom I saw for the rest of the night. Good thing, too, because I really didn't need to explain to Harv why the client was charging us for a guest's laundry bill.

I did manage to have another passing with Eva, and afforded a smirk at the chatter I overheard.

"So, Eva, what's this I hear about your date at that merger party your dad thr—"

"He wasn't my date!" she snapped. I wouldn't have been shocked in the least if the glass in her hand had shattered. "I was just getting in a dig at Julie Lesinger."

"Huh," her date replied. If this dink was looking for a tavern tickle later that night, he apparently didn't intend for Eva Rothchild to be his intended. "That wasn't the story I heard."

"Really, Trevor?" Eva sneered, "And just what *did* you hear?"

Poor Trevor's face was looking mighty pale, matching the stark white of his tuxedo shirt. Then he did, perhaps, the dumbest thing you could do in such a spot. He spilled the beans.

"Well, I heard from Pamela that you met this...fellow...at the door, walked arm and arm with him..."

"How could I have done that, Trevor? He was a Dwarf, like that stupid circus clown my dad hired to be here."

"Well, yeah," he muttered, "but Pamela said—"

"Maybe you should have gone out with her tonight!" she spat. "Sounds like you two get along swimmingly!"

So I made an impression on her circles in my visit here back in '29. Now, there was something quite flattering in that. And from Eva's reaction to her date's curiosity, she'd been explaining herself ever since.

Nice to know I had gotten in the last word, after all.

CHAPTER THREE

Batter Up, Billi Boy

The sky was playing tricks with me. I could swear the cerulean blue expanse high above drew back further and further the longer I stared at it. There was enough of a spring chill that I wore a coat, but nothing so heavy that I would be suffering through the afternoon. If my seat was somewhere in direct sunlight, I probably wouldn't even need it. The light breeze, the crispness in the air, and that clear blue stretching upward the way Kiki Cuyler would when denying Buster Chatam that in-field homer the Braves so desperately needed for a win—it was that same euphoria I felt after stepping through an enchanted portico, emerging from between pillars into a realm leagues away from where I had been. This time, the portal was not made by the hands of Elves, skilled sorcerers, or even malicious warlocks, but by the hands of man. This was a day of days, and once in the embrace of Wrigley Field there would be no talk of the Crash. That world was gone, at least for the next nine innings. For the afternoon, reality was defined by a flawless diamond, the battlefield for gladiators of this realm and the far-off shire of Baltimore, their weapons crafted of wood, leather, twine and canvas.

Did I happen to mention that I love this game?

After a day of Waldorf gigs, this was exactly what I needed. (Actually, this was a dream come true—a case that required me to go to ball games.) The seats offered by McCarthy were a real treat. Fit for kings and queens, or at least high nobles, right along the base line. Sadly, Miranda had given me that look when I extended her the invitation. Suddenly there were things needing her immediate attention at the office.

It was her loss, and not just because she was missing out on the charming company that would have graced her afternoon. My vantage point was exceptional, close enough to see the afternoon sheen of sweat on Charlie Grimm's neck as he warmed up on First Base. That battlement was his post for the day, and I could catch the fierce glint in his eye that said he would defend his corner of the field right down to the final pitch. Sure, that should be every player's attitude before any game, but Charlie had that look my boys harbored before a charge. Catching glimpses of the players going in and out of the dugouts, I could see that everyone had that stare: the sharp, intense look of wanting—not planning or hoping, but a deeply-seeded *wanting*—to kill anything that got in their way.

I didn't think that my Cubs would be taking any lives today, but I ventured a safe assumption that they were determined to put the rookies from out east in their proper place. They were also probably looking for a spot of redemption. The Cubbies had just finished a four-day stretch with the New York Giants, three of those games ending in big, fat losses. Now they were facing the league's latest addition, the new team everyone was talking about. The Cubs weren't hungry for a win. They were ravenous.

"Hey, mac," the voice spoke from behind me, "you, uh, Billi Baddings?"

I turned around to see a pair of pages of the Wrigley manor, their outfits neatly pressed and clean, yet to be stained with the wares they would peddle throughout the day. Both were carrying sodas and hot dogs, the sight of the food reminding me that I was getting a little hungry. A pair of binoculars hung around the neck of the guy talking to me.

"Mr. McCarthy wanted to make sure you found your seats okay," he said pleasantly, handing me the dog and drink. He removed the binoculars and set them underneath my seat. "On the house, Mr. Baddings."

"I appreciate it," I said, tucking the drink between my legs. I glanced at the other guy still holding on to the unclaimed dog and drink. "Tell you what—on your way back up, pass that grand meal you got there to the first kid you see in the stands."

"Sure," the second page replied.

Yeah, any extra points I can score with the Fates are good points, if you ask me.

I went to tip them, but the lead page merely help up a hand and shook his head, "Like I said, Mr. Baddings: on the house. You're a guest of the

Cubs, and I was told to make sure you were treated like one." With a tip of the hat, he left me in my prime seat, the surrounding ticket holders asking me in silence, *"Who died and made you Emperor?"*

"What?" I barked at one guy who refused to break his stare. "A guy low to the ground can't have friends in high places?"

He blinked at me for a second before turning back in his seat to watch the Cubbies warm up.

My salivary glands exploded at the delightful taste of mustard, ketchup, and relish adorning the hot dog. This culinary delight of the Cubs was easily the equal of roast pheasant, honey basted and stuffed with cheese, wild rice, and assorted vegetables. The dogs of Wrigley Field, especially on game day like this, were a delicacy for the refined palette. Taking a swig of the Coca-Cola, I smiled and gave a little moan of delight. This was the only way to enjoy a ball game. A win for my beloved Cubs would make this day perfect.

There was a smattering of applause as the Baltimore Mariners took the field. On first sight, they didn't look all that imposing. They were sporting sharp uniforms with a fancy "B" monogram on the sleeve and the word "Mariners" in the same type arching across the chest. Very nice. These Mariners definitely had the look of a ball team with their act together. Their owner clearly loved the team and spared no expense.

I gave a defiant snort as I sat back and took another bite out of my hot dog. What was I thinking? Money ain't everything. You can't buy yourself a team.

The rumbling of the near-capacity crowd was now interrupted with occasional snaps of baseballs hitting gloves. I watched Charlie, Footsie, Doc, and Chick appearing to stretch out while they took stock of the visiting team. They weren't working very hard to conceal their interest in these rookies. They would stretch, then stop and stare for way too long. Stretch, stare for too long. Stretch, stare…well, you get the idea. If I hadn't known Joe's issues with the Baltimore Mariners, I would have thought that over half of the Chicago Cubs were pining for the visiting rookies.

The general banter crackled over the anxious afternoon crowd, introducing teams and making announcements. I was about halfway through my soda when I heard the call for Wrigley Field to stand for the playing of the *Star-Spangled Banner*. Hats off. Eyes on Old Glory. Maybe I'd not spilt any blood for this country; but I understood the honors, the presentation of colors, and the respect these ceremonies carry.

I was standing on my chair, but no one seemed to care or snicker over it. In fact, I think I caught a few nods of approval. "*The short guy just wants a better look at the Stars and Stripes*," they probably thought. And they would have been right. I could have seen the flag regardless, but I knew that by standing on the chair I would have a better look at it.

I was also given the opportunity to stare for myself at the ranks of the Baltimore Mariners, now lined up on Wrigley Field's Third Base line.

No different than any other baseball team. They had come ready to play. Something seemed to be missing in their collected poise, though. I didn't perceive that eagerness to get on the field and show their talents, the same desire to win. The home team was like barbarian warlords with the heads of rival generals spitted on the ends of pikes, ready for battle. The visitors came out to take the field like good servants reporting for work.

"*O'er the land of the free...*" Not a bad anthem. "*...and the home of the brave.*"

Then came those two words that got my blood going sent the crowd into an uproar: "*PLAY BALL!*"

The Cubs took the field, Guy "Mudcat" Bush taking the pitcher's mound. Joe was serious about giving the Mariners a good afternoon of ball playing. Mudcat had a terrific season in '29, and his start this year was nothing to dismiss. He had an arm better than a Black Orc catapult, and his fast ball might as well have been the one that gave the pitch its name. As far as Mudcat's slider was concerned, I swear he had some of the mage's blood in him. Already, this game was getting interesting and no one had even taken the plate yet.

I leaned forward in my seat, my Coke nearly done as I watched the first Mariner approach the plate. The rookie's name was Archie "Flyball" Randalls and he looked like he had cut school to play ball with the grown-ups. The first pitch Mudcat unleashed on him made his skin blanch to match the stark white of his uniform.

"*Striiiiiiiiiiiiiiiike*," the umpire called, his finger indicating "One" to the crowd.

Thank the Fates. An umpire who could see.

Archie tapped the plate and set up for another go. The second pitch made him jump back and lose his balance. The poor kid's uniform was now decorated with a smear of Wrigley brown, much to the amusement of Mudcat and the fans.

"Ball," the umpire barked.

Mudcat, apparently wanting to play with his food before finishing it, smirked as the ball returned to his glove. The garnish of dirt on the rookie's once-spotless uniform gave him extra satisfaction; but not enough for this little amusement to come to a close.

His leg cocked up and the slider I had seen before from first tier seats looked even better from my "special guest" vantage. The sudden *crack* earned a collected "*Ooooohhh!*" from the crowd (and even a small one from me) and the ball went zipping between Third Baseman and Shortstop.

Flyball didn't risk it. He hit First Base and stayed put.

"Shit, the binoculars," I swore.

The first thing to come into focus was Mudcat's face. He had just caught the ball, and turned to stare down Flyball on First. That pitch had been Mudcat's *famous* Mississippi Mudslider, one of the toughest pitches to hit in the league. Seasoned sluggers were annoyed by Bush's trademark pitch on account of how tricky it was, and rookies accepted the fact that it was impossible to hit.

But there, on First Base, was the rookie who had just achieved the impossible.

Mudcat didn't even try to hide it—he was pissed.

The pause was so long that I wondered why the ump wasn't calling a delay of game, but upon turning the specs to Home Plate I could see that even the man in black was a little dumbstruck.

Walter "Hound Dog" Hunt took his stance at home plate, and from the looks of him, I wouldn't have expected him to be a ball player. The guy was sporting a little grey around the temples and even in his pencil-thin mustache. He looked better suited to be a coach or a manager than as second in the batting line-up. I turned the specs back on Mudcat, and he looked like he was softening up a bit. Yeah, this old man was just probably living out his dream; only a new team would take him on at his age. Mudcat shook off the first pitch, gave a quick nod for the second, and fired off a curve ball.

It must have been the movement of my head, trying to keep up with the ball, or some trick of the light while following the pitch through binoculars; but it looked like the ball curved back into Hound Dog's bat. It was an optical illusion. It *had* to be. No curve ball flew in an "S" pattern!

The line drive zipped between the First and Second basemen. Kiki was hustling to try and stop ol' Walt from reaching Second. It looked for a moment like he was going to go for two, but instead it was Archie coming to stop at Third that had two bases touched. Hound Dog stopped himself and tripped back to First.

Two hitters up. One man on Third. One man on First. I didn't need the binoculars to know that Mudcat was about to explode.

The next Mariner, who from the looks of things didn't know he was to be the lamb for the slaughter, called himself Riley "Scooter" Jenkins. Mudcat shook off the first pitch. Then the second. On the third, he gave a quick signal of approval, cocked back and fired. The crowd murmured, gasped, and cheered at the speed of the fast ball. It was a blur, and ol' Scooter never even got a chance to flinch. In fact, all three of them—Scooter, Gabby, and the umpire, barely had time to reset before Mudcat fired in another burner.

The ump froze for a moment, then called out "*Striiiiiiiiiiiiiiike.*" His fingers signaled "Two" for the count.

Gabby stood up, shouting, "Time out!"

The catcher yanked his hand from the glove, flexing his fingers a few times before waving it lightly. In the binoculars, I could see Gabby looking at his hand with some concern. That last pitch probably stung harder than a rock wasp. He handed the ball back to Guy, and while I don't claim to read lips I'm pretty certain, "*What the fuck are you doing?*" was the first thing Gabby asked. They never got into the sharp gestures often seen in such heated conversations, but I could tell by the way Guy's head jerked back and forth that he was hopping mad.

All this, and we were just in the first inning. There were eight more to go.

A form stepped in front of my line of sight, and on lowering the specs I saw Joe emerging from the dugout, only to be shook off by Gabby. A blanket of silence fell over Wrigley, but the pitcher eventually nodded and tossed the ball in his mitt as Gabby made his way back to Home Plate. The crowd ripped that blanket of silence away with a riled-up roar, representatives of Chicago screaming out support for their Series-winning team.

Mudcat took a deep breath, cocked back, and let loose his Mississippi Mudslider.

The umpire yelled out, "*Strike Three!*"

I gave a gruff laugh on seeing Mudcat's smile. He enjoyed that. The crowd was with him. So he gave up two hits. Ancient history now. It was time to collect from these rookies, give them an idea of what they were in store for.

"Now batting for the Baltimore Mariners," came the gods-like voice, echoing through Wrigley Field the way a wizard's spell bellows from deep within Stone Guardian Valley, "Number Forty-One, Eddie 'Shadow' Faria."

The other Mariners, even the older ones, all seemed to carry themselves as rookies. Some of them were walking like they were the big cock of the roost, acting like they were already at Ruth status. Others still showed the wide-eyed awe of stepping into the grand arena, the roar of the crowd only making their smiles wider. Their dreams were being realized. Their innocence was strangely disarming.

Eddie Faria was very different. He was no stranger to the four-cornered battlefield, to the sand-sprinkled Home Plate, or to staring down the lone warrior on the tiny mound between him and Second. He had been here before. Eddie's face was calm, even. Underneath his expression, though, I saw something notably absent from his teammates: respect.

I turned my specs back to Mudcat and his expression had changed, too. The cocky smile was gone. Where once a firestorm of indignation had raged, his entire demeanor was now one of reverence, his eyes now soft. He leaned forward, signaling to Gabby that first pitch would work.

I zipped my eyes back to Home Plate and watched as the pitch came in with a hard, sharp snap.

"Ball," called the umpire.

The ball returned to Guy's mitt, then hopped back and forth between his pitching hand and his gloved one. I watched him look to both First and Third, weighing his options. Was he sizing up Walter on First, seeing if he was the kind of guy to make the break for Second? No. Mudcat kept looking back and forth between First and Home. Whatever he was considering, I didn't like it.

Finally, Guy took his customary stance, shook off the first pitch, and then gave a nod. With a quick jerk of his lead leg, Mudcat launched one of his sliders.

"Ball Two."

The common folk were beginning to turn, the protests and disapproval sounding like the rumblings a mob would make before storming the castle of a callous land owner. In my specs, though, Guy's expression didn't sway. The rebellious peasants might as well have voiced their discontent in a completely different shire. The pitcher remained content with his choice.

Eddie straightened up, his eyes never leaving Guy. He gave a slight smile and shook his head. Without the binoculars I wouldn't have noticed it; but it was enough for Guy to catch. I watched Guy give a nod—this time, to the batter—and then, when the catcher asked for the pitch, he fired in his fastball.

There was no surprise that it was a strike. Wrigley Field expressed its appreciation for Mudcat as if he'd pitched the strike just for them, like a noble tossing pocket change to the peasants. I, on the other hand, was reeling over that unspoken exchange shared between Mariner and Cub. Guy was holding back. Those first two pitches were "gimmies". Without trying, Eddie could have easily knocked them out of the park.

The real chiller for the spine was that Eddie knew it.

The next pitch was a knuckleball, and Eddie took a swing at it, hitting only air. The count was 2-2, but by the smile on the hitter's face you could see he was loving every minute of this now. The tip of his cap to Guy told Guy the same thing.

Mudcat cocked back and fired in another fastball. This time, Eddie's bat connected with it.

It was a high-pitched, broadsword-sharp *crack* that told everyone, "*Ain't no way anyone's catching this…*" and the ball sailed on one of those angles you'd see on sailors' charts when they plotted courses across the Oreani Ocean. It just kept gaining altitude. Higher, higher, and higher it climbed.

That ball had one destination—Canada.

Once I lost track of the ball, I turned back to Guy. Guy watched Eddie as far as First Base, and then looked in the direction of the ball that had cost him three runs. I thought he was going to be angry, but Mudcat was just the opposite. I focused my binoculars twice, and then a third time, just for good measure. He seemed oddly content, as if he had pitched his best. The hit was a well-earned homer, and Guy didn't seem to question in any way, shape, or form what had just happened. Yeah, he looked content, calm, and—strangely enough—honored.

Eddie Faria. There was something familiar about it. Somehow, I *knew* that name.

Several pitches and two outs later, the Mariners took the field. They fielded, hustled, and loosened up from their stay in the dugout. I switched my gaze over to the bullpen where a relief pitcher casually threw a ball back and forth with a teammate. Their manager's strategy appeared sound: Keep rotating the pitchers in and out, to keep the Cubs guessing. The line-up was being announced, but instead of making my usual notes I was watching the opposing team, looking for anything really outstanding, anything that would trip them up.

Then Shadow passed by the Third Baseman and Shortstop, breaking into a run for the lone mound in the center of Wrigley's diamond. I refocused my binoculars on the Mariners' pitcher and watched him warm up. Shadow's grin could have been easily misinterpreted for that same smug smirk that some of the other Mariners wore, but the binoculars revealed the depth behind it. Shadow loved the mound, perhaps one of the loneliest outposts a soldier could hold. With every pitch he threw, his grin softened. I would not have been surprised if he'd suddenly burst out into tears.

"Now batting for the Chicago Cubs," the unseen voice cheerfully announced. "Gabby Hartnett."

With the name "Hartnett" repeating until it finally faded into infinity, the voice of Wrigley began to rise like waves lapping up against the hull of a ship. Three runs down, the boys needed some encouragement, and their fans knew it. The bleachers exploded with exultation. *You can do this*, their collected war cry told Gabby as he dug into the dirt and sand surrounding Home, taking his stance. *These dinks are just rookies! You guys are the goddamn Chicago Cubs! Give 'em what for!*

The bat came up like a two-handed vorpal sword, and a nostalgic part of me believed the Louisville Slugger glowed with a magic only Gabby could call. The crowd's elation muted expectantly as the bat twirled ever so slightly in the batter's grasp.

It whistled. Even from where I sat, I heard it clearly. The high-pitched whistle was, in fact, the ball Eddie "Shadow" Faria fired to his catcher. At least, I'm *pretty sure* it was the ball, because I sure as hell didn't see it. Shadow's arm came around, and then there was the ball's shrill scream, still echoing in the air even after the hard, sharp *snap* of contact with the catcher's mitt.

Instead of the catcher whipping his hand free of the mitt the way Gabby had done earlier in the inning, the Mariner merely stood, threw the ball back to Shadow, and returned to his crouch. Business as usual.

Gabby kept looking back and forth between Shadow and the Mariners' catcher. I was getting the impression he was still waiting for the first pitch. A slight shake of the head—probably to clear it—and he finally returned his attention to Home, bringing his bat up and waiting.

The second pitch was so powerful, the ball whined this time. I know there's an expression *"Knock the cover off the ball..."* but could you possibly *pitch* it off? A second perfect fastball, provided you could see it.

Even the ump had to wonder about it. "Strike," he uttered, his voice possessing a slight lilt that almost made the call a query.

Then there was a shift in the wind, and that was when the scent tickled my nose: the sharp, acrid scent of copper baked by the noonday sun. The smell of electricity.

Magic. Somehow, Shadow Faria was practicing magic!

And it was working. The question was how well it was working.

The third pitch burned its way by Gabby. Not as fast as the second, but still as effective as the previous ones. Faria's incredible skill showed no signs of faltering on the second Cubs batter. Or the third. The inning ended quickly.

I lowered the specs and swallowed hard. "Hey, mac," I barked to the usher who had served me the pre-game meal. "Anyway I can get—"

"Whatever you like, Mr. Baddings. On the house."

"Another dog and Coke," I grumbled.

He gave his cap rim a touch and a pleasant smile. "Be right back, Mr. Baddings."

I watched the next Mariner, his smirk begging to be slapped off his face with the flat of my battle axe, take up the batter's stance. Mudcat's jaw twitched. He was grinding his teeth, and I caught glimpses of his bone-white fingertips clutching a baseball tightly.

It was going to be a long game.

Bottom of the ninth. Baltimore Mariners—11, Chicago Cubs—2.

Only the most loyal of fans and a few scattered optimists had remained, hanging on for this final inning. What had started off as a prayer for the day to last forever had turned into a lament to the Guardians for a quick and speedy end to this cruel and inhumane ass-kicking. The Mariners had only suffered a few moments where their game—and the magic that graced it—seemed to slacken; hence the two runs scored in the fourth. The pitching of the Mariners' Shadow Faria, on the other hand, never weakened. He was a machine, firing in strike after strike. Perhaps the mercy I'd silently begged of the higher powers had been granted in those innings where three Cubs had stepped up to the plate only to turn on their heels and take their seats back on the bench.

The magic being utilized by the visiting team appeared to be base enough to maintain them for the afternoon, but powerful enough to generate that signature smell that had tickled my honker. Sorcery tends to take its toll on the caster, and yet I'd not noticed any slips in the game or in the Mariners' performance.

"Ball four!" shouted the ump, snapping me out of my own personal Great Depression.

Chick Tolson trotted to First Base, not that there was a spring in his step or anything. He was just going through the motions now. Scoring nine runs at the end of the game would be nothing short of a miracle delivered by the Fates themselves.

Then I noticed Zack Taylor on Second. Shadow was slipping.

The Mariners' coach emerged from the dugout. The kid who had been periodically warming up in the bullpen now stood by the gate, just waiting for a nod.

Through the specs, Faria was looking tired. In the afternoon sun, the shadows of his cap made him look like a completely different person. It was a lot harder to catch his eyes or see his face entirely now that he kept his head down, presumably out of fatigue. The coach motioned for the fresh kid to take the mound, and a polite, respectful applause rose from the Chicago crowd. Visiting team or not, respect had been earned. Faria had pitched a hell of a game.

The Cubs could have taken the switch as an opportunity to go for broke and make a last push for a win…provided Faria had petered out in the fifth inning, the sixth at the very latest. This game was all but over, but my boys were at least trying to muster up the drive and strength to make this last stand a good one.

I sat back, taking a sip of the dwindling Coke. There was something poetic in those legendary last stands you sang songs of around the campfire. We were supposed to be inspired by those great military blunders.

Yeah, you heard me—blunders.

Any last stand meant that someone made a mistake. Otherwise it wouldn't be a *last* stand. I got into a lot of arguments with superiors when

I would refer to great last stands as the results of tactical errors. There was a good chance that was the reason I never made it past captain.

Now, watching my beloved Cubs gallantly giving it their all, my opinion on last stands started to wane. Poor intelligence and poor planning did lead to the downfall of many a champion, sure. But what about unexpected aces-in-the-holes, be they blades-for-hire, renegade warlocks, or that recently unearthed tome of forgotten spells? Magic wasn't supposed to be in this realm, and to the best of my knowledge, it wasn't.

Then again, that assumption had been challenged last year. When the dust settled I had one case solved, and a few unanswered questions about the new security measures in place at the District Attorney's office. 1929. Hell of a year, even before October.

So how were the Baltimore Mariners doing this? Could they have somehow found a volume of magic spells chucked into a Portal of Oblivion, evoked the Cooperstown Charm of Grand Slammers, and given themselves a one-way straight shot to their dreams? Doubtful. Since the Elves were the grand pooh-bahs concerning magic in Acryonis, the majority of spell books were written in Elvish script. Elvish is tough enough to read, but when it was written in that overly-decorated calligraphy, it looked like Dwarven runes scrawled after a three-day bender. Those few who were blessed with "the gift" *(HA!)* would face two options. The first would be to go and study with the Elves. This would mean going off to live, breathe, eat, sleep, and shit the Elven culture. While there are some awfully cute lulus in their realm, it's kind of tough to find a bed big enough for yourself, an Elven maid, and her Elven ego. Hardly worth the poke.

The other option: Wing it. You could study under another race, but no guarantees the magic would be as solid or powerful as Elven magic. It all depended on how ambitious the *gifted* ones were. The ones with serious *hubrimaz* would choose a residency at Arannahs. If they were lucky, they would be seen again a few decades later.

If they were lucky.

The idea of a book written in the Human tongue wouldn't be completely improbable, but highly unlikely. The magic contained within would be limited in scope and power, and it would be noisy.

Very, very noisy. Humans loved their magic decorated with all the gaudy baubles—you know, the wacky sounds, the bright flashes, and all the extra trimmings that would make the biggest Fourth of July celebration look like a string of firecrackers popping on a sidewalk. I never understood Humans and their approach to magic. It was one of the few things I agreed on with the Elves—subtlety. Elves kept their spellcasting slick, efficient, and subtle; subtle to the point of clever. I seriously respected that. The only hint of detection (that Elves didn't know we Dwarves could detect) was that smell of electricity. Granted, we Dwarves didn't know what "the smell of electricity" was, but we did recognize the scent of magic. When I would wake up on certain mornings after a particularly deep sleep, I would fire up the Vibro-Shave and absently wonder for a moment if Elves were about.

This was higher magic, possibly Elven, in the hands of a baseball team from Baltimore.

"Hey, Short Stuff," a familiar voice called from behind me, the cordial (and somewhat insulting) greeting decorated with a gruff, grunting laugh.

By the Fates, could this day possibly get worse? Apparently it could, considering the voice that chilled me through. I didn't need to turn around to see who it was. The insult was as trademark as his voice. The day could get a whole heaping mess of worse. If my friend, who no doubt was lumbering his way to my seat, gave a meaningful look to the Orcs that flanked him from sunup to sundown, I might find myself enjoying the comfortable accommodations of the Six Feet Under flophouse where no reservations were necessary and there was always a room available.

Seeing him was a surprise because I didn't expect him to be out of the Big House so soon.

"Hello, Al," I said, turning around to stare at the impeccably-dressed, cigar-smoking, doughy-faced killer, Alphonse Capone.

CHAPTER FOUR

TAKE ME HOME FROM THE BALL GAME

He took a seat next to me and the wood groaned in protest. If the planks had complained any louder, Capone might have ordered the Orcs accompanying him to reduce the seat to kindling. Luckily for the seats, there was no indication that the creaking bothered him in the least. Al Capone considered his appearance not "fat" but "imposing". It was also a collected sign of good living: excess, luxury, and wealth, even in these tough times. With those three blessings, power was inevitable. I had read about the "hard time" he served in the Eastern Pennsylvania State Pen, and about how he still possessed enough power to run The Business while he reflected on the wrongs he had committed in life. That was power only the strongest of warriors and mightiest of kings could dream to possess, and it belonged to this obese monster in front of me. A monster dressed in a tailored suit topped with a fine fedora.

"You a Cubs fan, Small Fry?" Capone asked pleasantly.

"I am. I mean, nothing wrong with the Sox. A Chicago team is a Chicago team, but I just seemed to have better fortune with the Cubs."

He laughed while pulling a cigar out of his coat pocket. "A bettin' man, too, huh? You're still full of surprises, ya little sprite ya."

Sure, he was baiting me. It was tempting to get snippy with Al, but I knew better. A quick glance at his Orcs told me that they were new and probably wanted practice at skillfully removing anything that bothered their boss. If I were to play my ace and use the "S" name on Al, his boys would likely take me somewhere up in the cheap seats and use me as a punching bag, or—since we were in Wrigley Field—batting practice.

I didn't care for the insults, but I really wanted to walk home from Wrigley instead of from the hospital. "I don't mind a friendly wager between friends, Al. I'm not enough of a gambler to work with your boys."

Capone had snipped off the tip of the cigar and he nursed a fine, warm glow as I spoke. A few puffs later he nodded, looking over the field. "I'm just surprised ta' see ya' here, Small Fry. I love dis game!" He motioned to an area closer to Home Plate, right up on the barrier between the fans and the field. I recognized that section immediately as the seats of privilege, normally reserved for baseball owners, politicians, and the local nobility. "Got some nice seats down there so I can make sure the ump is calling the game correctly. Great seats dere, but I never saw you's until today."

"I'm a regular, too, Al. My seats, though, tend to get a bit high up in the rafters," I said, motioning behind us. "My usual perch overlooks the Visitors side. It may seem far up and away from the action, but the wide view lets me catch those subtle choices coaches make during the game. It's a dance, Al, a real dance." I scoffed lightly, looking at him in disbelief, "And I'm so wrapped up in the game, I didn't see you take your seats among the Royal Boxes. Not sure why, but this is something I didn't expect—Al Capone, a fan of baseball?"

"I tell ya' sumptin', dis' game is all-American and I love dat. And when you come out on a day like dis', eh, ya' can fa-get ya' troubles and jus' enjoy da' game, enjoy life," he said proudly. It was inspiring. I could see in his eyes and hear in his voice the same passion that I nurtured for the game. "Yeah, sumtimes I like ta' get outside, get some fresh air with ma' kid. Pitch a couple. Maybe even get a few swings in with th' bat."

I nodded. "Yeah, Al, I have no doubt you're good at that."

He paused, then turned to look down at me, his mouth slowly pulling back into a smile that sent a shiver through my body. "I am pretty talented in dat respect."

A sharp dryness suddenly appeared in my throat, as if conjured by that subtle Elf magic I was just waxing poetic about. I figured this was a good time to make my exit.

"Where ya' going, Small Fry?" Capone asked me.

"Today was a great day for baseball, but a lousy day for the Cubs," I grumbled, clutching the schedule and program close to me. I was going to need some reference points for my homework on the Baltimore Mariners. "I figured a quick bite and then home, to sleep off today's disappointment."

"Well den," Al said cheerfully, "how's about I takes you home, huh? Cubs fan ta' Cubs fan? We's can commiserate on da' trip to wherever you were going ta' have dinna'."

Why me? Well, at least this time, Al was asking me face-to-face and not having his goons flashing their boom daggers at me, motioning to a car that waited to take me to parts unknown.

"Sure, Al. Cubs fan to Cubs fan."

I glanced around me, hoping beyond hope that someone with the press was taking pictures of this moment—Dwarf detective and Public Enemy Number One leaving together from a complete and utter massacre dealt by the Mariners. So long as there was photographic evidence of whom I was last seen with, someone would figure out the party responsible for my sudden disappearance. I did happen to catch a flashbulb bursting bright as Al and me ascended towards the exit, but my heart sank when I saw the tell-tale hat of a G-man behind the camera.

Great. Might as well have been a Forest Pixie or a Valley Gnome taking stock in where I was headed. G-men were about as gregarious.

We didn't have much to say as we walked through Wrigley Field. Hell, we didn't say anything as we walked to his car. I suppose I should have regarded this offer of a ride home as just that—a ride home. What had I done to piss off Al Capone, anyway?

"You know, Baddings, I took your advice while I was out of town. Stopped in Philly and treated myself to a movin' picture."

Aw, shit.

The memory slapped me harder than a cranky tavern wench.

"Headin' up t'Atlantic City. Business trip," Capone had told me on the steps of the courthouse.

"Make sure you don't work too hard. Give yourself a break. Take in a movie or something."

"I might jus' do dat," had been his answer.

"Really? How was the movie?"

"Eh, not bad..." he said with a shrug, "...until I got arrested in da' lobby."

I tipped my hat back, looking past the man's gut and up to that pudgy face of his, "Well, when I recommended you give yourself a break from things, I figured you wouldn't relax so heavily armed."

"It was a .38 I had. No big deal."

"Al, it was a gun."

"Fuckin' cap gun, Short Stuff," he sparred.

"Fuckin' firearm, Scarface!" I snapped back.

He stopped, raising an eyebrow at my tone. That was definitely a slip on my part.

I raised my hands in surrender, "Sorry, Al. I meant no offense."

He grunted several times. I think he was laughing. "Nah, nah, nah, no need ta' apologize, Small Fry. I see ya' point. I was probably asking fa' it."

An interesting reaction, and unexpected. There were whispers on the street that Al getting busted for the firearm charge was prearranged by Al himself. The details were sketchy at best, but word on the street was Al's business trip up to Atlantic City left a sour taste in the mouth of some other bosses. Word was that he knew this, so he set himself up to be arrested for gun possession.

Catching the smirk on his face, I also found it hard to accept Capone slipping up like that.

"Well, from what I understand, your stay in Eastern Pennsylvania was a working vacation."

"They took good care of me dere," he said.

"So I heard." I scoffed lightly at the thought that popped into my head. Why not share it with him? "And you could not have picked a safer place to lay low. Right, Al?"

His smile faded as we started walking again. "The view from my cell left a lot to be desired, Small Fry."

Well, at least he didn't hold me responsible for the arrest. Maybe a change of subject was at hand.

What had he said—Cubs fan to Cubs fan? "Tough game to sit through, huh, Al?"

"You ain't kiddin' dere, Short Stuff." Capone snorted, taking a drag on the cigar. He removed it from his mouth, and I could see the teeth marks in its tips were a little deeper than they had been a moment ago. "Never heard of dees guys, the Baltimore Mariners. I mean, what's a 'Mariner' anyway?"

"A fancy word for somebody who sails or navigates vessels at sea," I replied automatically. "Baltimore's one of those coastal towns. Maybe they're not right on the Atlantic, but they've got a pretty busy harbor."

"Eva' been dere?"

"Nope," I said, sighing heavily. "But I've read a bit about it."

We climbed into Capone's tank masquerading as a luxury ride. While it was heavily armored and probably the safest place with wheels in Chicago, it was hard to deny its creature comforts. Fully stocked bar, plush seats, enough room for a grand old *grundle'malk* in either the seat facing to or away from the driver. This was going to be one nice ride to Mick's.

"Where are we headed, Small Fry?" Capone asked.

"You know Mick's?"

He nodded, the smile returning to his face as he took a final drag of the stogie. The door slammed shut as the car rumbled to life, roaring like a dragon facing off against a brave slayer who should have stayed in bed.

The driver didn't have to ask where Mick's was. Everybody in Chicago knew where to get the best chili.

"So how did you get such good seats, Baddings? Where you's was sittin' don't come cheap."

Yeah, anybody passing by would have been able to figure out I was new to the first class view. It wasn't until the third inning I became aware of my face aching slightly on account of the goofy smile that had plastered itself there. Then there was my own private castle servant. His trips back and forth with topped-off soda, hot dogs, and even the indulgence I always looked forward to at Wrigley Field—Cracker Jacks—had caught the attention of the people around me. Why not Alphonse Capone on a glance down the First Base line?

"A case I'd worked on. A client was saying thank you," I said, keeping my eyes locked with his.

"Dat's some 'thank you' with the treatment you's was gettin'."

My head tipped to one side, and I felt a smirk form on my mouth, "You watching me instead of the game, Al? I don't know whether to be flattered or worried about that."

Capone wasn't smiling back. "I don't know either, Baddings. You an' me still got unfinished business between us."

"We do?"

"Yeah, we do," he repeated, a slight sting peppering his voice. "I'm still not sure what exactly happened dat night wit' you's and me and dat cockamamie Singin' Sword..."

"Speaking of that, how are your hands?"

Capone paused for a moment. My concern was genuine, but I was also curious. I wanted to make sure Capone wasn't suddenly sporting any new talents like moving things without touching them or turning into a Troll, though the latter wouldn't have been a far stretch for him.

"Not bad," he said, flexing his fingers back and forth. "Maybe when dat winta' wind picks up they get a little tingle, but I was taken care of by da' best. Only da' best."

The skin was healed as much as it could be; and while I don't think Capone's paws had been delicate and dainty-smooth before the night he discovered magic, his palms did appear to have a surface similar to parchment. To the untrained eye, the skin looked as if it knew a hard life, which I'm sure it did; but that night had been harder than any night he'd known in Chicago.

"So, what was I sayin'?" he asked, his full attention back on me. "Oh yeah, dat Singin' Sword...I was jus' about ta' say dat I may not be sure what I saw dat night, but I do rememba' leavin' you dere wit' dat bitch all glowin' and shit. Den the warehouse lights up da watafront, and we watch from da' car dis' fire dat we didn't t'ink no one was gonna walk away from. Come to find out somebody did, and dat somebody was you."

"So maybe I've got some sabertooth blood in my veins and eight more lives left."

"You wanna see if dat's true, Baddings?"

I took a deep breath, just letting that question take hold. Maybe claiming I had nine lives was kind of stupid, considering whose car I was getting a lift in. "Okay, let's say I'm luckier at escaping burning warehouses than I am at betting on Cubs games."

"So you can unda'stand my curiosity here. This is why I'm thinkin' we got unfinished business."

"That wasn't what you said at the courthouse."

"Nah, I didn't. I told you that I'd be watching you. And that was part of what I was doing ta-day—watching you."

I gave a chortle as I sat back against the comfortable backseat cushion, my legs now sliding up to fill the bottom seat. My feet were just at its edge. "Well, Al, I can't say that I blame you. Wasn't much of a game."

"Really? Den why did you stay for the entire t'ing?" He leaned forward, and then lightly tapped the tip of my shoes. "Might as well had a docta' attach dem binoculars to ya' seeing as how you used 'em so much."

Damn, Al, I was holding your attention. "You mean to tell me you weren't at all curious about the Mariners? Who these no-names were? Where they were coming from? Or more to the point, how they were playing ball the way they were?"

"Not really." Al flicked the sole of my left shoe, giving the balls of my feet a slight jolt. Didn't realize I needed to see the cobbler already. "And I don't think you need ta' be all dat interested in da' Mariners either."

You've got to be kidding me. "Hey, Al, I've been keeping tabs on these guys in the Sports pages and I have a tough time believing that they really are that good. Brand new team, breaking reco—"

"Hey, hey, *HEY!*" Al snapped, his face getting just a hint of that red that always meant trouble for the poor dink about to get an earful from him. "Baddings, I t'ink you lack faith in our boys." Capone's tone was now controlled, even, and that blush his skin took on disappeared, along with his anger. "I mean, dees are da' Cubs we're talkin' about, right? Dey still got anotha' game in 'em, and I'm thinkin' it ain't over yet. After ta-day, dose Cubs are gonna come back and come back with a purpose."

"Spoken like a true fan, Al," I answered carefully.

I wasn't too thrilled about Al encouraging me to look elsewhere when it came to the Mariners. I had thought my biggest challenge was going to be getting into the Wrigley dugouts or, more to the point, into the locker rooms; but now it seemed that Al himself wanted me to avert my eyes and ask no questions.

Suddenly, the gigs as Waldorf weren't looking so bad.

We turned a corner and the warm glow from Mick's bathed the street. The sun was hardly close to the horizon, but with the surrounding skyscrapers the evening shadows came a little earlier for that crazy Polack and his business, a business that was so deeply rooted in the community that he still managed to keep things running at the same level of quality even after that stupid glass bubble on Wall Street popped.

"Here we are, Billi."

Capone called me "Billi" for the first time since we'd met up at Wrigley. He did this to grab my attention. Oh sure, he knew what buttons to push with me, just like I knew which buttons—or *the* button, in his case—triggered that temper of his. Now he was using my name. He was a monster, sure, but he wasn't an idiot. Capone could see that the "Short Stuff" and "Small Fry" jabs had lost their power.

Not that I was numb to it. I just figured I would go down to the gym and get in a good workout on the bag. Every insult equaled a punch. Nice thing about a punching bag—it couldn't order other punching bags to take you to the outskirts of town and leave you there as a treat for the vultures.

Calling me "Billi" was a new battle tactic. And I admit—it worked. He had my undivided attention.

"The fact you're still walking—Hell, the fact you're still *breathing*—reminds me dat I'm keepin' you around for a reason."

"Not for the stimulating conversation?"

"I don't think so, Billi. We both know that."

I gave a nod. Capone didn't like to beat around the bush and he'd cut right to the truth of why I was still sucking up his Chicago air. He needed me. He needed me to lead him to the Sword of Arannahs, and he acknowledged the fact that me walking away from what happened on the waterfront meant I wouldn't be susceptible to the tried-and-true methods of persuasion.

I was a walking contradiction. I was the safest man in Chicago, the safest man living on borrowed time. I just had to make sure he never knew what happened to that talisman.

"Now you go pokin' around inta' business dat, quite frankly, ain't yours, even if someone's payin' you ta' make it yours. You keep dis up, an' my hand might be forced ta' revaluate our relationship. *Capisce?*"

"If you're worried about me getting in your way..."

"Dat's just it. I'm not."

Well now, if I didn't *capisce* before, I definitely *capisced* now: Jail had made him better at this kind of standoff. Best tell him what he wanted to hear. "I hear you, Al, and I'm listening to you as if you're a Siren's song."

He nodded. The expression on his face was one of satisfaction, like a grand master of a Thieves' Guild with the haul from a king's coffer spread before him. "I knew you would, Billi. I knew you would."

The sidewalk in front of Mick's never felt so good under my feet. I must have been a record-holder in some scribe's books: As far as I knew, I was the only man who had crossed Capone three times—twice on his terms and once on his turf—and was still able to tell the tale and not from a hospital bed or coffin. Yeah, that was me: The safest man in Chicago on borrowed time, and blessed with the Luck of the Forest Gnomes.

"Enjoy ya dinnah, Small Fry," he called from the back of his limousine, and one of his goons closed the door.

I stood by the curb, watching Capone's Caddie disappear down the street. It had been a nice ride in Capone's chariot, but it had been an even better ride because I'd made it to my destination intact. The Caddie disappeared in a sea of Fords and Chevrolets, and I felt that weight lift off my chest, that same feeling like when a yeoman would remove my breastplate armor after a march. Maybe I had been holding my breath longer than I realized, because that first breath I took on the street—the first one I was aware of—really tasted good, even with the smells of the city tingeing its Spring crispness.

The jingling of the bells seemed a lot louder than usual, and it didn't take long to figure out why. Mick's was quiet. Far too quiet, and not for the lack of customers. It wasn't the usual packed dinner crowd, but Mick who was behind the counter, the diners at the window tables, and even Mick's dutiful serving maid Annabelle, were all looking at me silently, some of them with their mouths hanging open wide enough that a sprite-bat could have flown in and made a cozy home. I almost barked, *"Yes, I'm short. Is there a problem?"* Between the disappointing game at Wrigley and my ride with His Majesty of the Crime Syndicate, I was short-tempered enough to really let loose. Hell, even some of the regulars who knew me were finding some kind of fascination with me and my stature.

Then my ego took a sword pommel to the gut. They weren't staring at me. They were staring at a guy who just got out of Al Capone's car.

"Billi, what the fu—"

"Mick," I interjected, making sure he didn't piss off any of the Norman Rockwellers enjoying their family outing. With the way times were, an outing to a restaurant was something special. They didn't need colorful vocabulary ruining it. "I'll have the usual, but spike it."

"How strong ya' want it?" he asked, still staring at me like I was suddenly growing to Human height.

Chances are, Mick didn't know half of what I meant in my hometown references, but he was street smart enough to figure out that Ogres, based on the way I used them in idle chatter, were big, ugly, and stupid. Ogres and Orcs were kissing cousins, which explains why they looked the way they did. Anyway, whenever I'd drop any of my Acryonis lingo on him, Mick was quick enough to figure it out. Ogre-strength meant "I want it to have some punch to it". Orc-strength meant "Make it mean; so mean that I got enough gas to get me to Pittsburgh and back".

"Give me an Orc and an Ogre trying to make a baby."

I heard a spoon drop with a clatter. Apparently one of the regulars had also figured out my idioms.

Mick whistled, then added, "I know times have been tough, but Jesus Chri—" The hallowed name caught in his throat, and he gave a slight wave to the priest pausing mid-bite in his Red Plate Special. "Sorry, Father Finelli."

I watched Mick go to the back, and from the pass-through where he or the odd cook or two were usually visible, I could see him reach up to the shelf above his head and pull down a fistful of spices. He disappeared from view for a few minutes and then reappeared with fresh produce in his arms. I could make out onions, three kinds of bell peppers, two varieties of hot peppers, and the tell-tale white caps of mushrooms.

Yeah, this chili was going to have plenty of moxie.

"So, Billi," my friend called from the kitchen, "you, uh, wanna give up the goods?"

"What are ya' talkin' about, Mick?" I asked, climbing up to my custom-built barstool.

"No, no, no, Scrappie, you're not playin' dumb with me tonight!" he answered, his dark blues seeming to go a shade darker as he waved a rather menacing knife in my direction, bits of onion and pepper still valiantly clinging to the flat of its blade. "What are you doing hitching rides with...you know..."

I gave a shrug, wearing the most clue-free look I could muster. I wanted to hear Mick say his name.

He gave a sharp groan of frustration and then said it again, "C'mon, Billi—you know...*him*."

"Him who, ya crazy Polack? I know a lot of people who I can associate with the word 'him' so narrow it down for me."

He mouthed the name with such exaggeration, a forced whisper with a heavy emphasis on the syllables was just audible over the scraping of the knife against the cutting board. That chili was going to be so thick, Elves could dance on it.

"Malone?" I asked, flashing Annabelle a smile after she dropped off a fresh iced tea.

"*CAPONE!*" he suddenly blurted out, the kitchen knife coming down on the other side of the pass-through with a sharp *crack!*

For a second, I thought he had cut off a finger; but when I saw both hands grip the rim of the pass-through, all fingers and thumbs present and accounted for, my sigh of relief became a belly laugh. Mick's eyes narrowed and finally he joined in my guffawing. Yeah, when I cracked that hardened exterior of Mick's, his square-jawed profile would soften, although working on his nerves might cost him a few more grays around those temples of his. Maybe he didn't care to utter the gangster's name in such a wholesome family place like his. Well, okay, as "wholesome" as it could be with us openly calling one another ethnic slurs. Not that we minded. So long as it was the two of us dealing the barbs.

"You crazy Scrappie," Mick huffed.

"The guy's a gangster, not some demon you summon up if you utter his name the night the Cubs lose at Wrigley. And that reminds me—" I placed a Lincoln on the bar. "This should settle our wager, right?"

Another two bucks slid next to my fiver, and I followed the arm behind the Washingtons up to the somber-faced man of the cloth. I was a Guardians-fearing man before I left Acryonis, but since winding up here with no way to go home, my faith's been a little on the rusty side. That didn't mean I went out of my way to spit on the stoop of a church. Far be it from me to even tempt the wrath of a deity, be it the Guardians or the God this priest worked for.

A warmth crossed my cheeks, and I cleared my throat. "Little vices, Father," I said, motioning to my cash on the counter.

He looked at his two bucks and sighed. "No need to apologize, my son. My bill, you see, was already paid up before you arrived." He gave a tip of his hat to Mick, who nodded back in reply. "Little vices indeed, my son, afflict us all."

I waited until I was certain the door was shut and Mick was back from the kitchen, on the other side of the bar, before asking "You're taking bets from *priests* now?"

"It was two bucks, Billi."

"From—a—priest!" I took a swig of the iced tea before continuing. "You're just asking for the Express L to the Underworld, ain't ya?"

Mick scoffed, tossing a dishrag over his shoulder. "Hey, Father Jay an' I are on good terms. I go on, give him confession, don't allow him to bet any more than five bucks, and we're good until next confession. The man's not allowed many—"

"That's not the Underworld I'm talkin' about," I whispered through clenched teeth. "What? Have you got Ogre balls for brains?!"

Mick furrowed his brow, then finally figured out my sudden, sharp tone. "Billi, a couple bucks from Father Jay, a fiver on occasion from you, maybe a few greenbacks between friends. It's nothin'."

"Until a bookie gets wind of it, and then that bookie goes to somebody and then *that* somebody goes to somebody, and we start climbin' the ladder."

"Capone likes my Chili and Rueben Special," Mick whispered.

"And you think I'm crazy for hitching a ride with him."

"Well that what separates me from you, pal. I just give the man's lunch to one of his goons and call it a day. I don't go ridin' around in the man's Caddy!" He considered me for a moment, and then asked me, "So how about you tell me why Capone was thinking he's your taxi?"

By the time I finished my exasperated sigh, Mick was back in his workshop, toiling over a bubbling cauldron and daring to look into my future, possibly seeing visions of my breath setting the walls on fire.

"Well," I finally began, "seems that Al and I—"

"Al?!" Mick barked. "You two on a first-name basis or something?"

That comment won Mick a smirk. I could hear Capone calling me "Short Stuff". I could hear myself calling him "Scarface".

I nodded. "Or something." One more sip of tea, and I continued. "*Mr. Capone* and I are both Cubs fans. He happened to see me at today's game and—"

He had just unscrewed a small jar of something and then froze. "You were there today, at Wrigley?!"

"Do you want me to tell this story or not? 'Cause, lemme tell ya, you're turning this campfire yarn into a bard's epic poem with these interruptions."

Mick pursed his lips and nodded, just before emptying the jar's rust-colored contents into the pot before him. My eyes managed to catch a glimpse of the label, or at least part of it. One word: Cayenne.

Yeah, maybe I asked for that.

"So anyway, I was there at Wrigley today, watching the Cubs get trounced. It wasn't pretty. I stuck around to the bitter end, even stuck around after the game. I wanted to get a closer look at these Mariners. I'm telling you, Mick, those guys were amazing!"

"Well, I didn't like takin' that bet, but everything I've read about them makes me believe that 'amazing' doesn't even come close."

Mick was right, but I couldn't go any further than that. He was just getting a hang of my Orc and Ogre references. How the hell was I going to explain to him that I had a honker that could smell magic?

Then I noticed my mouth beginning to water. That afore-mentioned honker was now picking up the "copulating uglies"-strength chili. My stomach gave a rumble.

"Let's just say there's something unnatural about the kind of baseball I was watching today."

"Unnatural?" Mick then poured a few generous ladles of the special chili into a deep, wide bowl, paused, and then asked me in an odd tone, "Or *super*natural?"

What kind of cockeyed question was that?

Mick was coming around to the bar and I still stared at him. When he presented me with the custom-made culinary delight, he shot his eyes repeatedly to the cash register. I followed the quick glance, and just visible—even with it wedged between the register and the wall—was the latest *Amazing Stories*.

This was another reason I wasn't too comfortable with the idea of telling all to Mick. He knew enough about me to know I wasn't from around these parts and that my background was, if anything, unique. Only my girl Miranda knew the whole story; and right now, I wanted to keep it that way. I wish I could tell you that choosing one friend to confide in was a difficult one, but Miranda was the best choice for two reasons. The first was that she's a pretty level-headed girl. Miranda didn't go flying off the handle concerning trivial stuff, although she did treat me to a bath in Buckingham Fountain for keeping a secret from her.

The other reason: Miranda didn't read *Amazing Stories*.

I never thought of myself as a connoisseur of anything in life. I was just a working class Dwarf doing my best to make a living for myself in this new world of mine; but when you're cooped up in a library, you tend to treat yourself to something new every night. I tried every kind of book out there, and when it came to Science Fiction I just couldn't wrap my brain around it. The whole notion of what these authors were pitching to me—time machines, invaders from Mars, trips to the Moon—I mean, were these guys serious? Alright, maybe Verne nailed the whole submarine idea, but that's a reach. Now we had *Amazing Stories*, taking some perverse pleasure in leading credibility on a long walk down the docks to where no one's around to hear the bullet. The stories and serials this rag sold to the American public involved ray guns, bug-eyed monsters, and all kinds of plots to take over the world.

Mick ate this stuff up the same way Chicago ate up his chili, and I couldn't help but harbor a sneaking suspicion that he believed the yarns *Amazing Stories* spun in their pages. By the Fates, how could anyone in their right minds take that Science Fiction crap seriously? Which is not to say I had anything against fiction. In fact, after the bowl of chili Mick was cooking up for me, I had a feeling that later tonight I'd be in for a long sit on the can with *The Mystery of the Blue Train*, turning the well-worn pages until Poirot nabbed his man.

I rolled my eyes as I looked away from the magazine and back to my wide-eyed friend. "Yeah, Mick. Why don't we call it supernatural?"

"Hey, there's a lot of weird stuff out there, Billi. You know? Maybe those Baltimore Mariners got something up their sleeves, something they ain't comin' clean about to the rest of the league?"

"Well, if they are fiddling with technology from the planet Crackofmyass," I scoffed, motioning with my full spoon to Mick's curled-up magazine, "I think that would be something hard to hide."

My first bite of dinner instantly opened up my nasal passages and even brought a bit of moisture to my eyes.

Mick took a lot of pride in my reaction. "How's that, Billi?"

I continued to chew, silently motioning to my half-full iced tea.

Before Annabelle left us, Mick stopped her. "Leave the pitcher, hon."

Well, I did ask for it; and boy those Orcs and Ogres were *grundle'malking* rough and hard, like wild dogs in spring.

"So," Mick began, a smug tone in his voice, "as you're thinking my Science Fiction don't know better, how come you think it ain't something otherworldly?"

"Well," I said hoarsely, taking a moment to whet my whistle before continuing, "have you read anything about a falling star hitting Baltimore?"

"No."

"Asked and answered." The second bite's kick was just as powerful as the first, but I didn't mind. Even at this strength, the chili was a much needed savior to a dreary (and, at one point, dangerous) day. I gave a smile at the crunch of fresh onion and bell pepper, and then paused before continuing my meal. "I will agree with you on this, Mick. There's not one of those guys I recognize from any other team. If this were a cream-of-the-crop collection of all the stars from both leagues, I'd believe *some* of what I saw. They were rookies, Mick. Even the older ones. Every last jack one of them. Chicago's got experience on their side, and nothing they did could turn the tide of this game."

"You thinkin' somethin's not jake with these Mariners?"

I popped the spoon in my mouth, cleaning it to a near spit-polish when I pulled it free. There he stood in front of me, The Would Be Detective of Planet Crackofmyass, ready to grab his 38-caliber ray gun, climb aboard his spaceship, and solve the mystery of the Baltimore Mariners: aliens from the evil empire of Fartinthetub.

The fresh vegetables crunched loudly for a few moments, and then I gave a sigh. My breath was potent enough to curl my mustache.

"Nah, Mick. Maybe I'm just a sore loser."

CHAPTER FIVE
Early Risers in the Windy City

A ripple of pain shot along my soles, a reminder of the Sorcerer's oath I took to make sure Baddings Investigations would be secure in our cash while surviving hard times. My body had finally caught up with me, and this morning I felt it all: double bookings as Waldorf, the excitement of going to a Cubs game, and the tension of sharing a ride with Al Capone. Yeah, I seemed to forget that I was no longer a Dwarf in my thirties and forties, full of courage for the missions, attitude for the higher-ups, and spunk for the ladies when I'd come home triumphant, when all this lust for life had been backed up with that unending drive of youth. I wasn't too worried about those three earlier charms slipping away from me the older I got, but feeling the aches and pains from head to toe, I knew now that in my youth I'd taken for granted that drive that got me up in the morning, gave my body the ability to ignore said aches and pains, and threw my fat ass into gear. *Hell*, I pondered, still staring at the ceiling, *I wonder if the youth of this world truly appreciates that enchanted fire inside of them. Do they truly realize—or even truly appreciate—the gift bestowed on them by the Fates?*

I mumbled some Dwarven curse as I sat up and scooted over to the edge of my bed. These self-pitying moments were becoming a little too frequent for my taste this year. It was probably brought on by the times, but this *melancholy*—a word that just makes me want to slap the shit out of bards and minstrels for thinking it sounds prettier when put to music—just chafed my ass worse than the muck mites found in the Eastern Swamplands of Acryonis. I didn't have to give into it, though. I could wallow in my self-pity all day until the dragons returned to their caves to roost, but what would it accomplish? Absolutely nothing.

Stop feeling sorry for yourself, Baddings, I thought. *You got a case. Make it a good one.*

My feet touched the small step by the bed and warned me with a few good throbs that they weren't going to touch ground without some sort of protest. I just ignored the pain as best as I could while crossing my apartment to the wooden step ladder that lifted me up to a Human's eye-level with the sink and mirror in my bathroom.

"Hey, Beautiful," I finally muttered out loud to the reflection. "How about we go get a coffee and a Danish somewhere? Start this day right?"

I was a particularly cheap date, especially when I was taking myself out. There were plenty of coffee shops within a few blocks that would deliver, and maybe a cup or two of java would blow the cobwebs free. Then I could hit the library to see if there were any back issues of the newspapers to shed some light on this new ball team from Baltimore.

With the water running and the rhythm of the bristles resonating in my noggin, I thought back to that night at the Rothchild's and the conversation between Miles and Bruce. They had really made an impression on me.

"Today's fortunes could disappear tomorrow," Bruce had said to Miles. Pretty profound, considering the source. Also carefully crafted. Was it a friendly warning, a threat, or both? *"Not mine, Bruce. Not mine."* Miles had answered as he handed Bruce his empty glass and gave his shoulder a light pat. *"Be a chum and fetch me a fresh martini. I, for one, feel like celebrating tonight."*

I didn't know this Miles character from a hidden passage in an abandoned keep, but in that reply he came across as a cocky son-of-a-bitch, stepping dangerously close to being an arrogant bastard. If a friend had ordered me to "go fetch" like some kind of well-trained hound, I would have done so, but not before adding in some kind of secret ingredient to that drink. What that secret ingredient would be, would depend on how much my friend pissed me off.

Well, those society dinks had a pretty convoluted idea of what a friendship was all about. I knew that. They didn't have friendships so much as they had mergers and professional relationships. The friendship was strong and unbreakable, provided both sides had something to gain. It sounded like Bruce wanted out of this business venture he'd agreed to with Miles, and Miles found their parting of ways an unacceptable condition to their arrangement. That assurance, or *promise*, Miles dealt kept haunting me, and I had to wonder how he could remain so assured considering the country's state of financial chaos.

Humans, though, liked to throw their words around, making people think their stones were bigger than they really were. That was a constant between both realms, but even more common on this side of the magic portal. The folks who actually made good on their claims were people who made the headlines, guys like Moran and Scarface. Maybe ol' Miles just loosed those words like an Elven archer, knowing that they would hit something somewhere.

I gave my mouth a good treatment of Listerine. On a morning like this, it helped me open my eyes a little wider. A few splashes of cold water and cologne, and this Dwarf would be hitting the wardrobe for threads that were far lighter than my Waldorf costume.

The usual double-takes, the usual snickers. I didn't really care to give anyone the cursed eye this morning, but I was feeling off-kilter. As a matter of fact, the *mea culpa* I'd endured while waking up was lingering. It was helping me get through the aches and pains of my feet, my back, and my sore arms. I always did regret the armored cartwheels, but the crowd loved them and they got me gigs.

This was one of those mornings when I couldn't afford to wallow in my self-pity. I needed to keep my eye on the prize; and with this case, there was a new brass ring to focus on.

Perhaps that was why I was noticing the looks. Most days, I could tune them out like a bad radio program, but today I felt the stares as heavy reminders that I wasn't from around these parts. *Stare all you like*, I thought with a sly grin. *We have more in common than you might think*. And that sly grin became a full-out smile as I made out the coffee shop only a block away. The java was not on par with Mick's, but they did serve some incredible pastries there.

"Hey, Billi!" called a familiar voice through the crowd. "It's my treat this morning!"

Now, this was a nice surprise. *Yeah, Jerry*, I thought as my stomach rumbled. *Your treat. This would be a morning for you to make good.*

Detective Jeremiah Flannigan worked for Chief O'Malley and Chicago's Finest, and yet he wasn't an asshole. This flatfoot actually had a personality. We got on great, and on occasion would work together on the odd case or two, much to the chagrin of O'Malley.

Jerry didn't hide the professional respect for me; and while the friendship was far from the one between me and Mick, he was a good guy. Somebody I knew I could trust. First off, his career was so spotless, so stellar that no one could hold his friendship with me against him. Even in that game of strategy and positioning for the throne, he played for keeps in being a good cop. Really couldn't figure out at times why this guy was working hard to keep ties with me.

Maybe it was because of that morning—a morning not too different from this one—when Beatrice and I had kept Jerry above ground.

The sweet cinnamon of a Danish was in my future that morning when the alarm bell cut through the usual Chicago din like a broadsword through leather armor. Its undulating chime made everyone freeze, creating a real-world still life with only the movement of automobiles down the street breaking the captured moment. When the third chariot passed by me, my eyes caught sight of the driver nervously tapping his steering wheel. He kept looking back at what appeared to be a closed-up pawn shop. I say "appeared" because the door was slightly cracked open but the windows and items displayed therein were hardly finished in their arrangement. The engine was running; and had I noticed this guy before the bell, I would have done my good deed for the day and warned him about straining those neck muscles.

The door flew open, and people still walking by the store scattered like infantry does when the missile launched from an opposing army's catapult descends from the skies. The car rocked as two guys hurled themselves into the backseat, one of them shouting orders to the driver. Over the alarm, an engine started to rev.

Here's when Jerry appeared in his police detective's best, his own boom dagger unsheathed. I'm not sure what he was shouting at that moment, but the boys in the getaway car weren't listening. I was going to perform my good deed after all, but it was going to cost me a few bullets.

Beatrice slipped free of her holster and loosed two rounds just as the Ford pulled out into traffic. Since I didn't want to complicate things at the precinct by adding a murder charge to my good deed, I wasn't aiming for the driver or the passengers. Both tires exploded, causing their chariot to list hard. Still the car barreled forward, determined to make Jerry a fine hood ornament.

Another shot rang out, but it wasn't from Beatrice. The driver slumped behind the wheel and the car jerked violently to one side, swinging its passengers against the door. The Ford smashed into a parked brother, and white-gray breath billowed from the grill. One of the robbers emerged from the backseat, shotgun braced and aimed for action. Jerry knocked him off his feet with a single shot to the shoulder.

Yeah, I forgot to mention that my pal Jerry was a crack shot. I'm telling you, this guy was the perfect cop. Well, almost perfect. Keeping company with me, from what he told me, wasn't considered good form from some of his colleagues, not that he gave a Goblin's ass about that.

Anyway, Jerry watched the shotgun bandit fall, and it was that hesitation that cost him. The other bagman, still in the car, lifted his own boom dagger. That bullet was aiming to make Jerry's morning even worse than it already was, and it would have done just that if my shot hadn't shattered the car window, and the bones in the bandit's hand.

I walked up to Jerry as he was kicking the shotgun away from the bandit he'd downed. I silently gave credit to this dink pressing his hand against his shoulder. He just groaned through gnashed teeth and took his wounds like a good highwayman. The ring of the alarm bell fading into the oncoming call of a police siren was more satisfying than a tight-bodiced tavern wench anxious to break in a new pair of kneepads.

Well, okay, maybe it wasn't *that* satisfying; but damn close.

When we saw the first car tear around the corner, I holstered Beatrice and said to Jerry, "Before I turn myself in, how about we get breakfast? It's my treat this morning."

Since then, "*It's my treat this morning,*" served as our greeting whenever our paths crossed. A brief reminder of how we met. Sometimes it was his treat, and sometimes it was mine. This morning, it really would be his treat, and with the "grumpixies" nipping on my ankles, I was going to let him make good on his offer.

"Morning, Jer," I said, looking up at the tall, imposing gumheel with a smile. "How are things at the precinct?"

He glanced at his watch before answering, "I wish I could say slow."

"No you don't," I grumbled, slowly wriggling my feet in my shoes. "You would hate the jobs you'd need to do to make ends meet."

"And that's the difference between you and me, Billi," Jerry said, his chuckle seeming to sing in harmony with the door's bell, "I get paid regardless. You're working client by client, right? I've been worried about you and Mindy since things turned south."

I could feel my eyebrow lift slightly. *Mindy?* I knew Jer was a single guy and pretty particular about what kind of maid caught his eye, but *Mindy?* Didn't take a detective to catch that clue. I wondered if Miranda was aware of the little soft spot Jer was nurturing for her.

"Yeah, *Mindy* is holding up okay, all things considered," I said, punching Miranda's newly-discovered nickname. "I make sure that when things are tight, I take the hit, not her. Call it that guardian angel in me." More like the cranky lycanthrope that guards the gates for some warlock. I'm a lot of things, but I'm no angel. "It's the odd jobs I take on to fill in those gaps. I'm feeling that service to two lords this morning."

As we waited by the counter for a pair of coffees and pastries, Jerry kept checking his wrist watch. It was just too early to be rushing this morning; but between his comment about wishing things were slow and the frequent glance at his time-keeper, Jer had another breakfast date closing in. Probably a sit-down with O'Malley. That would be a rough start to anyone's morning.

The two of us parked our duffs at a small table by the window that held the pawn shop within its frame. I didn't want to say anything about it, but I didn't feel too comfortable about the choice of seats. Not that I didn't understand why he chose this table. I understood all too well. He probably needed to step back to that time, just for a quick moment, to remind himself of how close he'd been to buying the shire. Moments like that keep you rooted. I know they do for me. Kev and I would sometimes linger over a battlefield after a skirmish, enjoying a pint or three and sharing a toast to having lived to see another day.

The problem with reflecting like that is getting stuck in the past. It's okay to pay homage to your brush with Death, but sometimes pitching pavilions and making base camp becomes too easy.

"Serving two lords?" Jer was still getting used to some of my hometown sayings. "How's that?"

"Eh, Monday was a Waldorf kind of day. Two performances. Still feeling it."

"Two? Didn't you tell me that two in a day was pretty tough?"

"Yeah, yeah, yeah, I did. But it had been a slow month so I needed to make up for it." I watched Jerry begin to slip away on me. Good thing I knew the quickest way to bring him back to the present time. "Monday wasn't a completely shit day though. I picked up a case."

"Really?" he asked, blinking quickly. "Something out of the ordinary?"

"Could be." That's it, Jer. Come back to your Real World. "Hell, I might even have some fun with this case."

"Then you really can't call it a job, can you?" Jerry snickered, smirking for a moment before taking a sip of his black coffee.

I returned the laugh before taking a bite of my breakfast. "It's the best kind of job," I commented in mid-chew. "This is a case where I can actually enjoy myself."

"Those are so rare. I envy you, Billi."

"Be envious over this beard that women can't resist." My hand slapped lightly against the side of my rotund stomach, "Be envious over this frame, a picture of solid health! Provided you're me, of course. But over a case? Nah. Even with the little moments of respite, a case is a case. A job's a job."

"Maybe you're right, Billi, maybe you're right."

Jer took an abnormally large bite of his pastry, his cheek swelling out from the food. For a second, I wondered if my friend was trying to get in touch with his inner bovine.

"Good Danish?" I asked.

"Mmmm…" Jerry grunted. He swallowed so quickly that I swore I could see the quarter of Danish work its way down his throat. Had it not been for its greasy texture and the icing drizzled on top, it would have gotten stuck on the descent. "Sweet," he finally said, checking his watch just before slurping his coffee.

"Jerry," I said, setting my mug down. "You're checking your watch more than a scout checks a strange wart on his hand that he picked up after brushing up against a patch of blue moss. Now if that wart starts spreading and you get a craving for raw tree bark dipped in ditchwater, then you've got a problem. So what are you worried about? Time traveling? Missed meeting? Otherwise, that watch of yours ain't going nowhere."

A second swig of his coffee and Jerry wiped his mouth clean, still working on a few bits of breakfast as he considered me from across the table.

"This is the problem with having a morning bite with a detective. You can only keep up a pretense for so long," he admitted, his stare never leaving mine. "I still think you should be working for Chicago, gumboot. You'd make a great addition to the force."

"C'mon, Jer," I scoffed. "Do you really see a Dwarf like me tearing through the Academy's obstacle course? I have a tough enough time getting my thirty-six inch waist out of bed, let alone over a seven foot wall."

Jerry spit his coffee back into his mug and then grabbed for a napkin, "You think you could wait to make comments like that until *after* I take a drink?"

Chicago's Finest had a point there. Coffee through the nose is never a pleasant thing.

Still, it's fun to watch.

"But yeah, Billi, I was hoping to catch you this morning, seeing at it was so close to the crime scene. I know it's a gamble asking you this, and hey, if you want to kick me in the shin, I deserve it; but I was hoping you would be...you know..."

"In between clients?"

"Yeah, Billi."

I savored another bite of the sweet breakfast (a much smaller bite than my friend was taking across the table), chasing it with another swig of java. "So why are my brilliant detective techniques needed on one of your crime scenes? You're no chump when it comes to this, you know that."

"I know that, sure. But there are those crime scenes that are just..."

"Weird?" I asked.

"Yeah, Billi," Jerry uttered. "Weird."

"We're talking a murder scene here, right? We got a dead body stinking up the place?"

"In a manner of speaking, yes."

In a matter of speaking? Yeee-ikes. What was at that crime scene? It was too bad Jer was so straight-laced. I think he desperately needed a drink.

"Well, since your stiff isn't in a hurry, how about we finish breakfast?"

Chicago's Finest weren't interested in keeping things low key. With the paddy wagon and two additional police cars on the scene, you would expect this place to be like an Orc's corpse, with the press covering it like crows enjoying a feast. Instead, there was not a public eye in sight. Chicago was still waking up, so the privacy and the convenience of manpower would be short-lived. The windows now looming over me displayed pedestals mimicking Human necks, fingers, and wrists. They were plain in their bareness, blending in with the ripples of crushed velvet surrounding them. Jewelry stores like this one, like all shops that indulged people in the extravagances of the Roaring Twenties, were considered true rarities now. Merchants of frivolous luxuries had started disappearing, and now these places were as uncommon as enchanted cloaks that granted their wearers invisibility or swords that could conjure fire. Rare treasures, indeed.

The temptation to try and pull a job on one of these stores, however, was all too common. In desperate times when people lost jobs and nest eggs disappeared, desperate measures were employed. Crime started to increase, and there was hardly anything anybody could do about it. Vendors like this rock-man here became bright, glittering targets to the would-be thief. They weren't always easy prey, though. Some of these places were rigged better than some strongholds and keeps I had seen.

Jerry stopped at the door and looked down at me. "Ready for the show?" While that was his trademark question before revealing a crime scene to me, the look on his face was a bit of a surprise. He seemed genuinely concerned.

"Listen, Jer," I said, snorting slightly at his handmaid-like behavior, "the concern is touching and all. I mean it. Gets me right here in the ticker, but don't worry about me. Regardless of what they're saying on the street, I'm a big boy and I can handle it."

"Okay, Billi. Come on in."

I walked into the jewelry store and immediately dropped.

CHAPTER SIX

All that Glitters...

Jer's hands wrapped around my arm, slowing my fall. I still felt the cold marble through my slacks and the slight sting from my knee striking the floor, but with my eyes screwed shut I didn't see a thing. Not that I needed to. The smell was that powerful.

"Woah-woah-woah, Billi," my friend whispered quickly. "You okay? You haven't even seen the body yet!"

"Yeah, Jer, I'll be alright." The reassurance didn't convince me, even though I knew it was my own voice talking. Nothing sounds convincing through clenched teeth.

C'mon, Baddings, you know what you've gotta do, I whispered silently to myself. And yeah, I knew what I had to do. I just didn't want to do it.

Because Dwarves spent a lot of time working in the dark, we've developed really talented honkers. We had to train ourselves to sniff out various gems, and the better we got at this skill the more we could use it in other ways, such as how to tell if someone was lying, sniff out the ingredients for black powder, or know if a woman was in the mood for a serious tavern tickle. You can understand how this sense of smell worked really well for me in this profession.

The only problem was controlling this talent.

Especially in sudden moments like this, overpowering aromas could easily knock me on my ass. I, like many of my people, had to not only develop my nose's abilities but also practice turning off this ability. Not easy in the least. I mean, how do you ignore or cut off one of your senses? We Dwarves discovered it was not so much ignoring the smell as it was acknowledging the offending odor and then focusing on some other aroma, no matter how subtle it might be. By concentrating on the second scent, we could—in a manner of speaking—filter out the nasty smell and be able to function. Farmers in particular had this down to an art form. (Hell, you would too if you were dealing with dung all day.) With Dwarves like me who started off in the mines, this safety valve was a little dangerous. Focusing on and filtering out certain scents, you could potentially discover a precious deposit of ore, a claim that would set you up for life. The only drawback: Your life would come to an abrupt halt as you died on account of bad air around your mother lode and yourself.

I was still teaching myself this "good air-bad air" trick and was finally getting a handle on it, but I wasn't ready for something like this. With a nod, I took in the stench, and I felt my stomach protest. *Find the other scent quick, Baddings, or you're shooting your cookies all over Jerry's loafers.* I took in a second breath, and caught whiff of the slightest hint of Burma Shave.

I'm really glad you're not a beard man, Jerry.

"Yeah, I think it's passing." Both my feet were now firmly planted on the floor. I wiped the tears away from my eyes and took in another breath. The Burma Shave was working, but barely. I could still smell that powerful stink all around us. "Sorry to give you a scare like that."

"What is it, Billi?" Jerry then motioned to the display cases on either side of us, "You allergic to the lush life?"

I gave a gruff laugh in reply, and was thankful my breakfast stayed put.

The morning sunlight was just coming into the windows and it was a really beautiful sight. From the looks of this vendor, the stones he peddled were from all over the world, from only the finest lodes that man had unearthed. I was eye-level with the displays so I couldn't see all of what this guy had to offer, but the stones in eyesight were impressive, even to me. I can't remember when I had seen such craftsmanship, such care put into presentation and setting of gems.

And the closer I got to the cases, the harder I focused on Jer's Burma Shave.

"As you can see, Billi, it doesn't look like anything's been taken."

This was going to be really difficult to prove without stepping on toes or ruffling feathers. I figured I'd just follow Jer's lead and keep my yap shut for now.

"Is that what makes this case weird, Jer? You come to a crime scene, but no crime is committed? I'd call that a lucky break."

His hand grabbed my shoulder and I came to a sudden halt. I was so focused on Jerry's scent that I didn't notice the cops and photographers around me. A pair of shooflies were snapping away, taking pictures of the ceiling. The other uniforms were craning their necks, all of them staring up.

My eyes went in the direction of their gazes, and I saw the poor sap. He was now part of the intricate décor, a décor now slightly cracked and crumbling from the force of his impact. There are ugly ways to die, and I'd pretty much seen 'em all in my days at war. I've seen beheadings, disembowelings, and even a few people torn apart.

I searched my noggin for a time I'd seen a man embedded into a ceiling. My brain was drawing a piss-poor hand, while the corpse above me held a Royal Flush.

"Okay, Jerry," I said, my eyes not leaving the macabre sight, "I'll give you this one: This is weird."

"Coming from you, Billi, that really is saying something."

I tipped my head to one side, narrowing my eyes on the body. "Any idea how he's staying up there?"

"We've been thinking about that," Jerry said, his hands pushing his coat open before coming to rest on his hips. "Either he hit the ceiling so hard that it somehow wrapped around him and is now holding him there, or..."

"Impaled on the sprinkler system?"

"That was our next guess," he groaned.

"And you're asking me, how did a grown man get all the way up there without the use of explosives, which would have left a calling card; or a catapult."

Jer shook his head as he looked around, his eyes pausing at a center case, the only one that appeared disturbed. A pedestal had been knocked over, its diamond bracelet cascading over it like a silver mountain brook winding down towards a valley. "I don't know, Billi. I know that O'Malley isn't one of your biggest pals, but you were pretty helpful on the Riletto case."

My bushy reds raised slightly. "O'Malley say that in his report?"

"Are you kidding?" Jerry peppered his question with a guffaw. "His report read like a Zane Grey novel, and apparently you weren't mentioned."

"Ain't that a shame," I huffed.

"No, actually, it was another detective. New kid, so he didn't know how big of a mistake it was mentioning you being invited to the scene. I still think the Chief left his door open so we could all hear the dressing down he gave him, just so we were all reminded the 'policy' when it comes to private dicks. Especially concerning the ones who make him look bad. I got a chance to see the report before he rewrote it."

"Before he rewrot—?!"

"Easy, Billi," Jer cut me off, casting a glance at the other officers who were still trying their best to examine the crime scene without a ladder. I picked up a few whispers about the coppers calling in a nearby fire company, but there was still the problem of getting the ladder into the jewelry store. Jerry turned his eyes back to me, and his voice was just above a whisper. "Look, there are a lot of things I don't really approve of when it comes to O'Malley. He's still the chief, though, and he's got a lot of loyal soldiers, okay?"

Glancing past Jer's waist, I made brief eye contact with a couple of uniforms. One of them happened to be motioning to me, and with a shake of his head and the frown he wore, I knew that I was a guest of Jerry's, not of Chicago's Finest. Word was probably going to reach O'Malley either in a report or over a pool table, but at least Jerry was untouchable. A spotless record, an impeccable performance in case solving, and the support of the press—Detective Flannigan could get away with this little indulgence. At least, for the time being.

"Anyway," Jerry continued, "this rookie was pretty grateful for your contribution, so I figured you might give me something—anything—I could take back to the desk."

I looked back up to the body. He looked pretty snug. "Watch him, Jer. If you see anything slip free, let me know."

The floor directly underneath the body was, more or less, undisturbed. No one really wanted to do any close-up examination until they were certain that body wasn't going to fall on top of them.

Underneath a thin layer of plaster and powered tiles I could make out scuff marks. Black.

"Jer, can you shed some light on our stiff's shoes?"

Jerry motioned to a pair of uniforms, "Any one shoe in particular?"

"Let's go with the right," I said to the uniforms now armed with flashlights.

Two tiny orbs of white slinked around the ceiling and finally met up at the victim's right foot. With the extra light, we could all see the polished surface of a high-end loafer glinting back at us. Black.

"What have you got for me, Billi?"

"You're not going to like it." I motioned to the scuffs in front of me while still looking at the lit shoe high above us. "The victim stood here, and it was probably a matter of bad timing, but he walked in on the perps and they took action."

"Took action?" Jer asked. "Are you saying…?"

"He was thrown up there." I walked out of the clearing underneath the body with a shrug and a sigh. "I said you weren't going to like it."

"Billi, come on, look at him!" Jer never did like a crime scene where something didn't make sense, but usually those problems involved something like a crook leaving behind fingerprints in an obvious location, a murderer stopping to change a flat tire, or some other form of sheer stupidity on the part of the criminal. This was the first time he'd had to deal with something completely out of his wide scope of comprehension, and he wasn't taking it well. "I have a corpse on the *ceiling!* A fully-grown male can't be picked up and tossed straight up into the air—this guy's got to be 250 pounds! But you're telling me that somehow—*somehow*—that is exactly what happened to this unsuspecting jeweler opening his establishment?!"

"No, Detective," a voice spoke from the doorway, "the jeweler was opening *my* establishment."

Whoever this guy was, his timing could not have been better. Uniforms were casting curious glances our way, Jer's volume gradually rising the longer he ranted. I just didn't have it in me to tell him that all the reasoning in the world, no matter how loud it was, wouldn't change my conclusion. Nothing would be gained by throwing Troll fat on this campfire.

The newcomer on the scene silently took stock of his inventory as he walked the gauntlet between the cases of precious stones, gold and silver creations, and precision timepieces. With a calm demeanor, he straightened his necktie, considered the two of us, and then looked upward.

"Davenport," he said, showing no indication of shock or surprise that his employee was on the ceiling. "The gentleman's name is Samuel Davenport, Detective, and it was his job to open and close my boutique."

"Samuel Davenport," Jerry acknowledged, jotting the name down on his notepad. "And how long had he worked for you?"

"Oh, I should say, eight years come this August." He looked up at the dead man again, and lightly clicked his tongue, as concerned as if he had just lost a button from his expensive suit. "What a shame. He was a fine manager. A fine manager."

"Your sense of loss is inspiring," I said.

The newcomer now gave me his full attention. I guess he was expecting there to be more to this public servant. Far be it from me to disappoint.

"I am a businessman at a time when staying in business is very precarious. I cannot afford myself to feel for every loss. I have to look at how my business is affected, and then show proper respects once I have the time. To be quite frank, I've not had the time lately."

Strike this guy off the list. He wouldn't have murdered his manager, on account of the damage it would do to his business.

"Well, I guess you've got to keep your priorities straight," I stated. "After all, times as they are, your business could disappear tomorrow."

"Not mine, Officer. Not mine," he replied.

Well now, slap me in the ass with a dragon's tail. If it wasn't ol' Miles from the other night.

"I'm sorry, sir," Jer chimed in. "Mr. Baddings here is not with the Chicago Police."

He had to say that. It was part of the job.

Miles granted me a slow nod, still contemplating who the hell I was and why I was in his shop. "Baddings?" he asked.

"Billibub Baddings. I'm a private eye," I said, offering him a card. "I'm here on my own dime though, so you have nothing to worry about."

"No, I don't." He then turned his back on me, leaving me there with the card still in my outstretched hand. A few of O'Malley's boys got a chuckle out of that.

All right, Miles. That's *another* black mark against you.

"I'm the head detective on this case. Detective Jerry Flannigan, sir."

"Ah yes, Detective Flannigan," Miles purred, his back now completely to me. "I've heard your name several times in the news. Superlative service you have given us all here in Chicago."

"Your name, sir?"

Miles straightened up to his full height, but then gave a dry laugh. "But of course, Detective, you probably don't know me on sight, as I'm certain we don't travel in similar social circles. Miles Waterson, as in B.D. Waterson and Sons. I'm the 'and Sons'."

Miles Waterson. Heir to the Waterson Jewelry Empire. Member of the Chicago Elite. Prick.

"Well, Mr. Waterson, as you see, we're trying to find out what happened here and discover if anything was taken. There are also some rather unusual circumstances surrounding your manager's death."

"And is that why you are here, Mister…Baggins, was it?"

"*Baddings*," I replied tersely. "And yeah, I tend to help out Chicago's Finest with the odder cases. But a man as educated and cultured as yourself should hardly be surprised by something like that."

"No, not at all." He looked up at Davenport, and then back to me. "So, what exactly have you discovered, Mr. Baddings, about the death of my best manager?"

"Quite a bit about his employer, but nothing that really pertains to this case." I heard a throat clear. I fired off a wink to Jer, letting him know I wasn't going to mortify him or his Chicago brothers. I also wasn't going to let this dink bait me into any kind of altercation that could prove embarrassing. "The investigation is still ongoing, and right now we've got more questions than answers."

Miles nodded. "You will keep me apprised of what you find, gentlemen?"

Jer handed Miles a card. Miles then turned to me, his hand open.

"My number's in the book," I said.

"Detective Flannigan?" a voice came from the back of the store.

All three of us turned to watch the uniform approach. He had a clipboard in his grasp, and a look of bad news plastered across his face like a *Tribune* headline.

"Yes, Officer," Jer said, accepting the clipboard from the uniform. "What have you got for me?"

"We found where the perpetrators broke in. It looks like they just came through one of the walls."

"How'd they do that? Through a window? Jimmie the backdoor?"

"No, sir, they came *through the wall,*" he answered. "There's this large gaping hole in the bricks, opposite of the rear entrance. Since they didn't trip the wires around the door, the alarm never went off. The manager must've also noticed this and went in thinking they lef—"

"What about inventory?" Waterson snapped. "Was anything taken?"

I have to look at how my business is affected, and then show proper respects once I have the time. To be quite frank, I've not had the time lately.

When it's your turn, maybe someone will make time for you.

"As far as we can tell, nothing was taken," the officer said. "It looks like the perpetrators were caught in the act, and then this—" He motioned to the body above them. "—happened."

Jer looked up from his clipboard. "That's it?"

The officer shrugged. "That's it, sir."

I was about to ask Waterson a question, then paused. I wasn't sure if it was the lighting of the crime scene or my senses playing tricks on me (blocking out those strong odors was not easy), but Miles looked as if he was going to pass out. Now he seemed—for the first time—genuinely upset. Over a *botched* robbery? I looked around and could see there were plenty of pieces which could have proven easy pickings to the common thief. Miles took a deep breath, and that seemed to steady him.

"You will keep me informed on the progress of this investigation, won't you?" he managed to say, although his voice came out rougher than a sabertooth's tongue.

"Absolutely, Mr. Waterson. I would suggest, as you're more familiar with your shop's inventory, that you and your staff run down the items. If anything is missing, you can let us know and then make a claim with your insurance company."

"Of course," he muttered. "Of course."

He tipped his hat to the two of us and walked out the door. By now the press was here and they were assaulting him with questions, questions that I don't doubt were the same as the ones bouncing around in my noggin.

"So what do you think, Billi?" Jer asked me, motioning to the damage around him, his eyes ending at the body still embedded in the ceiling.

"I'm thinking you and I ought to stay in touch, and when you can—" I cast a glance at Waterson, and then looked back to Jer, "—find someone who can do repair work on ceilings. Fast. I don't think Fat Boy's gonna stay up there for long. Try Michelangelo. Italy. Guy's a whiz with a brush and a bucket of paint, I hear."

CHAPTER SEVEN
JUST THE STATS, MA'AM

I always waxed nostalgic whenever I entered the Chicago Public Library at 78 East Washington Street. This was where it all began for me. Yeah, yeah, yeah, I know that when you're walking the mean streets in your deerskin loafers, trying to stay clear of the Trolls, the Orcs, and the Ogres all wanting to take a piece of you home to mount over their hearth like some kind of trophy, your time is best spent on the gun or archery range. However, the library is also a good place to be. Don't knock what you can learn from the right book.

Say you come upon someone who's not looking so hot. In fact, say the individual in question is stone cold dead. Take a whiff of their breath. If you're smelling almonds and you don't see any nuts around, then there's a good chance that person's a victim of cyanide poisoning. How about a priceless diamond that's under lock and key one moment and gone the next, as if conjured away by a wizard's spell. The only magic there is science and mathematics: mirrors can be angled just right to make something seem to be there when it really isn't. And if you ever feel like someone's ripping you off for your time, think about the why behind it; you just might find your business within tunneling distance of a bank. What appears as charitable work on the outside is indirectly making you a front man for a robbery.

No doubt, book smarts are just as valuable as street smarts. Capone's average foot soldier sure could learn a lot from one on how *not* to off someone, on how it's all in the details.

Then again, when your idea of subtle is a bullet to the back of the skull, you're not really going to care about the details.

Today I wasn't looking for distraction, nor was I diving into a reference. I was looking for the papers. I needed sports stats too current to be in any bound journals. By the time these scores appeared in books, the season would be done and the Baltimore Mariners would be bringing the pennant home to Maryland. So this meant heading over to my old stompin' grounds and tracking down a lovely lady who never failed to put a smile on my face, no matter how deep the dragon shit was for me.

"Gertie!" I said in an exaggerated whisper.

She looked over the horn-rims and her aura of concentration melted away with a smile that could stop a streetcar on its tracks. Gertrude deHavilland was not one for the makeup, the glam, or the glitz; and that's what made Gertie an enigma. If this librarian had wanted to, she could have headed out west and easily made a splash in the pictures. Even sans the glitter that starlets relied on to look good for the cameras, Gertie was a complete and utter knockout. She also had, aside from the sapphires behind the specs, a grace that others lacked, a poise that remained hidden behind the posture of someone quite comfortable in the quiet life found in libraries. There was also her outward sense of style: long hair that sported streaks of blonde amidst deep red, high heels that added a touch of flamboyance (and height) to her carriage, and a no-nonsense attitude from her native homelands that was neither flinching nor apologetic. She was not what I would have pegged for a bookworm, but I was not going to question her choice, especially since she was the sharpest tack on the corkboard when it came to finding anything filed and stored in this place.

"Billi." The smile disappeared as quickly as it had appeared, substituted by pursed lips and a scornful look that wasn't meant to be taken seriously. "Now go on. You know you don't have to—" And with the same exaggeration I showed in my greeting, she said, "—*whisper* here. Just keep your voice low and you won't get shushed."

A sharp and impatient "*Shhhh…*" came from a nearby desk. The old fossil stationed there was loosing on her younger counterpart the kind of cold death-glare that I'd seen in my share of stand-offs.

"Loosen up, Hazel," Gertie huffed, her volume remaining consistent.

"*Hmph!*" With a sniff, Hazel grabbed a stack of recent returns and headed off to the stacks.

"I swear," Gertie began, "that woman's a rock. Set in her ways, know what I mean?"

"I thought you meant she was just ancient," I quipped.

"Good to see you, mate," she proclaimed with that far and away accent of hers. Nothing less than music to my ears.

"A day when you're seen above the ground is always a good one in my book."

She gave a nod, setting aside the modest stack of papers in front of her. "And what can I do for you that will take up my afternoon?"

I smiled warmly. "How about reading out loud from a dictionary?" That earned me her endearing giggle, but it gave me a moment to think about her question. "And what makes you think I want to monopolize your important time?"

Gertie peered at me over the horn-rims, her eyebrow arching as she said, "Oh, Billi, don't start. It has been months since you came to a Snoopers meeting."

My hands were up now, held at verbal gunpoint. "I'm a busy guy. I've fallen behind in my reading!"

She clicked her tongue. "Your loss. Hammett's new book came up in the conversation."

Dammit, she knew this was my Athessia's Heel. "That's the one about the bird, right?"

"*I've* read it already," she gloated. "You could have heard my thoughts on it...last week...when we had our monthly meeting."

Much as I would have loved to keep the groan to myself, it got away from me. Gertie's to blame for this, too. When the Crash happened, I was getting really, really tired of the news, of learning who lost the fair fight with gravity in the financial district, and how many honest working types had kissed their savings goodbye. I was not in the best of spirits, and Gertie offered up something she thought I would enjoy. The book was *Red Harvest*, and it was a debut novel. Yeah, sure, I know people got issues with trying out new authors, but being a guy who believed in the power of giving someone the benefit of the doubt, I decided to give this writer a shot.

From that day on, I was Dashiell Hammett's cabin boy.

Don't get me wrong, now. Agatha and Sir Arthur were still my comrades in arms. I mean, they were the ones who got me into my chosen profession. But Hammett was the first writer to really *speak* to me. *Red Harvest* centered around a private dick who called himself "The Continental Op". (Catchy.) The guy who hires him dies before meeting with Op face-to-face, but that doesn't stop him from working the murder on his own dime. Turns out the stiff's dad is the town's lord and master, a guy who looks at something and before the day's end he owns it. (Hmm, did Gertie know how close this was hitting to my hovel?) Op's murder case becomes a job for the lord and master. On the surface, everything looks jake. On the surface. The more I read, the more I learned what a sneaky son of a bitch Hammett was as a writer. I loved him for that.

Gertie then shanghaied me into her book group, Snoopers. Bunch of blue hairs and bookworms that all had a passion for the mystery genre.

Being fans of the mystery, of course, made them a curious lot. "*So, Billi,*" one of the old Bettys asked as I was taking my seat that first night, "*what do you do?*"

"*Research,*" I had replied.

"*What kind of research?*" Eugene, the writer-hopeful asked.

Great. A bunch of mystery readers, and I was the big case to be cracked.

"*I solve problems for others,*" I answered carefully. "*I'm charitable that way.*"

Gertie came to the rescue, diverting attention to that month's read, *The Mystery of Edwin Drood*. Why that one? Well, it was Charlie Dickens and as it was December, people were all over *A Christmas Carol*. *Edwin Drood* was Gertie's Christmas present to all of us: an unfinished work by Dickens that was, in no uncertain terms, an unsolved mystery.

It was going to take me some time to relax around these amateur sleuths, especially with how we reminded each other when the next meeting was taking place. Didn't matter where we were in Chicago. If we happened to see one another, we were supposed to brush the tip of our nose with a single index finger. That was the silent signal.

Yeah, it was going to take me *quite* some time. Completely loosening up around my fellow Snoopers was out of the question, as I might slip and mention I was "on a case". That's a wizard's cauldron I did *not* want to stir.

The group did introduce me to some terrific mystery authors, I admit. It was also some quality time in the library, and a few extra stolen moments with Gertie. Financial demands were making my fun time scarce, though; and while I was continuously side-stepping what I did to pay the bills, I didn't care to share with the group my *other* little secret. I could have made one or two more of the meetings provided I showed up in makeup and costume.

No thanks.

This friction from Gertie, now that I was thinking more about it, was well-earned. Didn't mean I had to like it.

"Look, you know what I do," I pleaded. "Both jobs, I might add."

"That I do," Gertie said. Then a smirk crossed her face. "And how the group would love to know what you do. At least, the *chosen* profession."

Blackmail? "Gertie, you wouldn't."

"Wouldn't I, Billi?

This was payback. Cold, ruthless payback for being so anti-social over the past few months.

I unleashed the puppy-dog eyes on her. "Gertie, what can I do to get back into your good graces?"

"A sit-down dinner at Mick's?" she asked. "Just an evening with a good friend..." She paused and finally leaned in, giving me a librarian's stare. "...who is quickly becoming a total stranger."

I thought that would be the end of it, and this would be my cue to make a date for us.

I was wrong.

"A total stranger—" she continued, "—who waltzes in here, planning to monopolize my time for his own means."

Again, my hands went up. "Guilty as charged." Now it was my turn to lean in, giving her a look that was less cold than hers, more mischievous. "And being a lover of mystery, I would think you would show no hesitation in joining me on this little quest for knowledge."

She nodded. "I can't stay mad at you, and I can't say no to you, Billi." She stood at her desk, "Where are we headed?"

"Periodicals, and maybe the Archives." I said, following her deeper into the library. "I'm needing a look-see at some Sports pages."

She stopped, straightening up to her full height, which was not that much on me. No. Gertie wasn't a Dwarf, but she was no beanstalk either.

"Just a moment," she snapped. "We're looking up past Sports sections?"

"It's for a case." Gertie didn't move. "I swear!"

Her head nodded slowly, but the stare remained chilled like a windy Chicago winter. "We shall see, Mr. Baddings."

She called me "Mister Baddings". Ouch.

We continued to a series of tables and desks with scribes of all kinds hunched over books, magazines, and newspapers. Some were taking meticulous notes, others were cross checking periodicals with other tomes, and a few appeared to be reading just for the fun of it.

What were those precious few thinking? Lucky dinks.

"How far do you want to go back?" she asked.

"Not that far back," I said, standing up on my tiptoes as I could look at the newspapers hanging on rack after rack. "Just to last week."

"All right, how does..." Gertie said, scanning the library's collection. "...April 30 sound?"

"A good start."

The newspaper's fluttering resounded throughout the library, only a few readers disturbed by the two of us taking a seat at a vacant table. I scanned the Sports section, looking for scores. My finger finally found the Baltimore Mariners, playing the Brooklyn Robins. That game was not as harsh as the one I had seen, but the Robins were in the same encampment with the Cubs. Mariners—4, Robins—2.

"Let's pull a few more papers," I said. "And if you can pull out other cities—*New York Times*, *Baltimore Sun*, and *Philadelphia Inquirer*—that would be great, doll."

"Sure thing, sweetie," she replied cheekily.

I caught the warning. It looked like I was going to preoccupy her day, subjecting myself to her undivided attention, her wily charms, and that sweet accent of hers.

The things I do for this job.

Our afternoon's efforts were now spread across three of the library's larger tables, the previous occupants who were reviewing their books within earshot of us long gone. Some of those determined bookworms loosed dirty looks upon us before slamming their books shut and moving elsewhere to resume their study. In silence.

We had progressed back into April, close on the beginning of the season; and now with other publications at my fingertips, I was matching up game dates with host cities. Just as people expect carnage and destruction when Orc hordes are seen closing in on a shire like a black wave of death, Sports writers from each town made predictions of a complete and total trouncing from the newcomers to the League. From the looks of the scores, the Mariners did anything but disappoint.

In Brooklyn, the Robins' wings were clipped. April 28th, Mariners—11, Robins—1. April 29th, Mariners—8, Robins—3. April 30th, Mariners—4, Robins—2.

In Pittsburgh, the Pirates found themselves outgunned. April 25th, Mariners—9, Pirates—2. April 26th, Mariners—6, Pirates—5.

On their visit to Boston, April 19th, Mariners—3, Braves—0. April 20th, Mariners—6, Braves—1. April 21st, Mariners—2, Braves—5.

Hold on. The *Braves* beat the Mariners? The Braves winning a game against *anybody* was about as likely as domesticating a sea dragon. To beat a team as hot out of the box as the Mariners? Might as well as get a foot massage from a Goblin, and walk away with all your toes attached!

"Now, baseball—where I come from—is not that popular. If these were Rugby scores, I would probably have a fighting chance, but these are just numbers I'm looking at."

"Numbers can carry a lot of punch," I said with a chortle. "Ask anyone in the financial end of town."

"Well then, talk to me as if I don't know any better because…" She stopped as her eyes hopped from Sports section to Sports section. "…well, because I don't know any better."

"If I give you the details, I'm taking the chance that I spill the beans on my client, and you know I really can't do that and stay working. If I lost my job, I would probably have to apply here."

Gertie bit her bottom lip lightly and then gave me a curt nod. "Best you not tell me anything about your client, then."

"I can tell you this much without putting anyone in a bad place." I then motioned to the earliest Sports page open in front of us. "The Mariners, aside from the one game with—" I couldn't believe I was about to speak this team's name and refer to them as winners, "—the Braves, have been enjoying a very good premiere season. The team is a handful of rookies and yet they are all playing like seasoned pros."

"You know this from these scores?"

"Well, from these scores and from seeing them play yesterday."

Her brow furrowed. "Billi, maybe I am not grasping this, as I lack the same anatomy that you possess, but could this team just have an unanticipated stroke of luck? The right people, the right manager, and incredible timing?"

This would have been a great place to talk about the smell of electricity in the air. Luck? Well, if you consider working with sorcery as a way to guarantee your luck, then yes. Yes, this could be a team that got very lucky, continuing to control that luck from town to town, from game to game. I would have also agreed that it took a great amount of luck to somehow master this magic without any formal training, apply it to America's homegrown sport on a consistent basis, and not suffer any severe consequences from it. We could have wiled away the hours well into the next day, kicking around ideas of just how lucky the Mariners were as a team and how they were luckier still in having kept control of this major league spellcasting.

Yeah, I would have loved to chat with Gertie about this…

"Call it a detective's hunch," I said instead, my mind running through its collection of words. I needed to pick and choose carefully, "but I'm thinking 'luck' isn't their secret weapon."

Her eyes jumped again from newspaper to newspaper before she asked, "So, you're looking for some sort of pattern?"

"That, or maybe a Sports writer picking up on a detail that everyone else misses."

"Ah," Gertie whispered, "you're looking for another Hugh Fullerton."

Full of surprises, this librarian. "You know who Hugh Fullerton is?"

"Being a librarian who wants to know all the history of her new home, you tend to read up on a few names and their stories stick with you."

"But weren't you telling me just a moment ago," I asked, raising a bushy red eyebrow, "that your interests do not extend into the great American pastime that is baseball? Are you keeping secrets from your gumfoot friend?"

The specs slipped off her face, and her stare reminded me of an Elven archer's, narrowing her pair of peepers on a target before loosing that single arrow destined for an enemy's chest. "Let's try this again. These," she said, motioning to the open papers, "are just numbers and names to me. Nothing more. The stories behind these names and numbers, and the stories that bring about an effect on society, do hold my fascination."

The things you learn in a library.

I returned to the newspapers with Gertie serving as a second shadow. My eyes searched the commentary columns along with the scores, hoping to catch Fullerton's skeptical echo amidst the words of the true believers who heralded the Baltimore Mariners as the best thing to hit baseball since the Sultan of Swat. Early on in the season, there were articles from Ring Lardner that could be best described as biting. Humorous, I'd give him that, but humor that made you feel extremely unclean afterwards. Lardner's opinions were putting the greenhorn team under the magnifying glass while just south of him in New York the Mariners were being exalted and lifted into the higher echelons reserved only for legends. Grantland Rice, in his opposing commentary, called them "...the heroes of the emerald diamond, the return of baseball to its roots of innocence and wide-eyed wonder. When you watch the Mariners play, you remember why this sport is so great."

By the time I got to the present day newspapers, even Ring's voice softened up a bit, and that was speaking a kraken's roar. It wasn't too difficult to read between the lines that he had taken the Black Sox pretty hard, so for the Mariners to sway Ring only gave them legitimacy.

Maybe my client needed to focus less on the opponent and look more into the reason why the Cubs were falling short this season.

"Billi, you're looking as if you just lost your best friend."

I looked up at Gertie and managed a smile. Yeouch, that hurt. "I just got to realize something about my heroes. At the end of the day, they eat their dinner, piss in a pot, and sleep in a bed. Just like me." My groan reverberated throughout the library. "Sorry, Gertie, but I've been chasing my tail on this one, and I'm not happy about that."

"Apparently not."

Maybe I could salvage something out of this dungeon of disappointment. "So, I owe you a dinner at Mick's, don't I?"

She glanced at her wristwatch and smiled. "It's a bit early, but by the time we get there I think I'll be ready for the special." The paper seemed to take flight like a giant albatross, its gossamer wings spreading wide for an instant only to fold back and supplant its bird-like image with that of a flimsy banner waving in the breeze.

"Gertie," I said, catching a glimpse of the headline. "Put that paper back on the table for a minute."

She froze. A master sculptor could have used her as a model for a town square's statue. The newspaper fluttered back to the table, and Gertie replaced her specs back on her nose.

Her fingertips went to the upper corner of the paper. "Leave it alone," I said as I moved from chair to chair, to get next to her.

"What is it?"

"That," I said, pointing to the front page.

**THEFT AT RODIN MUSEUM BAFFLES POLICE
PRICELESS SKETCHBOOKS STOLEN!**

"I heard about this!" my chili-loving librarian gasped. "This museum finally opened to the public last year, displaying an impressive collection of Auguste Rodin sculptures. They have—sorry, had—a few of his notebooks, one of them containing the original notes and preliminary sketches of *Eternal Springtime* and *I Am Beautiful*. If I recall, the journal containing the ideas for *The Thinker* was also stolen."

"*The Thinker*? That's the one where it looks like—"

Gertie interrupted my words. "Yes, Billi, that's the one where the gentleman appears to be relieving himself." She shot me a stern look. "We might want to change our dinner at Mick's to an early lunch instead so that I can take you to a museum afterward. Get some *proper* culture in you."

I chortled, but then went quiet. "So long as the museum in question isn't the Ryerson."

Gertie shrugged. "What's wrong with the Ryerson?"

I grumbled, returning to the paper. "Another story, for another date."

In the corner of my eye, I swore I caught a hint of Gertie smiling.

The article pretty much said what Gertie had just relayed to me. This museum, while it could have been hit a lot harder, was picking up the pieces from a pretty serious heist that had occurred in the wee small hours of the morning. What was baffling to the Philadelphia cops was the lack of evidence. Guards didn't see anything. No alarms were tripped. Everything had been accounted for. The only thing the museum's hired muscle had noted as unusual were a few strong gusts of wind that seemed to sweep through the hallways when the museum was opened.

"I don't see the connection between baseball and a museum heist in Philadelphia."

"Gertie, Gertie, Gertie," I chided. "What do we say in Snoopers about mysteries and the clever dicks found therein?"

She rolled her eyes, her mouth twisting as if she were sucking on a really sour pomegranate seed.

"Open your eyes, listen close, and above all—take nothing for granted," she huffed.

"It's like my boy Sherlock says: When you have eliminated all which is impossible…"

Gertie chimed in as I finished, "…then whatever remains, however improbable, must be the truth. So, Detective Holmes, perhaps you can enlighten me on what you're seeing that I'm not."

"Well now, let's not put the cart before the pack beast, Miss Watson. One step at a time. This crime was in Philly, and it happened in the early morning hours of May 8th. Gertie, what does your paper say about the game on the 7th?"

"Well," she began, returning the paper to the Sports section. "On the 7th, the Mariners scored seven runs, and the Phillies nil." She looked up from the stats. "What the hell is a Phillie?"

"Make like a Kodak and focus, Gertie. What about the game on the 8th?"

She went to the other side of me, scanned the paper, and read, "Mariners—3, Phillies—2."

I looked at my own Philadelphia paper and the score from the May 6th game. Mariners—9, Phillies—2.

"Let's go to New York," I said, motioning to the papers across from us.

When I climbed up into the chair before the three newspapers, I heard a low growl. I thought for a moment that somehow a baby Troll had broken loose from its nursery. Gertie's hand moved to her stomach. I didn't bother to make eye contact. I'm sure she was letting me know with her gaze that she was going to be patient. For now.

We returned to Brooklyn where the Mariners were letting the Robins have it. At least, until the last game of their stay. April 30th, Mariners—4, Robins—2. I swallowed hard and closed the newspaper to take a look at the front page.

AMERICAN SAVINGS AND INVESTMENT BANK ROBBED DOORS CLOSED FOR GOOD

The headline story reported that American Savings and Investment had just managed to avoid the full sting of the Stock Market Crash, but there was a lot riding on this particular branch surviving in New York. If it prospered, then the business might live on through to the next decade.

That was before this robbery. On this morning, the vault was clean, its bones leaving no meat for any financial carrion. American Savings and Investment announced they were cutting their losses and calling their campaign done.

My eyes jumped to the closest newspaper, a May 3rd *St Louis Post and Dispatch* that reported a close shave for the Mariners: Mariners—2, Cardinals—1. As I had with New York, I returned to the front page to read the headline.

Gertie's gasp told me I had just earned a few more runs on her scorecard.

CITY ART MUSEUM HEIST!
PRICELESS RENAISSANCE OIL PAINTINGS STOLEN!

"Shall we make this a grand slam?" I asked Gertie. "Where to?"

Her stomach protested again, but she wasn't listening to it this time.

"Never been to Boston," she mused.

"Let's go," I said.

Back to Beantown. April 21st, Mariners—2, Braves—5. I closed the newspaper.

PRESIDENT HOOVER ADDRESSES
AMERICAN SOCIETY OF NEWSPAPER EDITORS

That would have been too easy. My eyes continued to scan the front page, and halted on another headline. Perhaps not as prominent as the President's talk, but news enough to get on the front page.

ADAMS SAVINGS & LOAN ROBBED
BANK STRUGGLES TO STAY IN BUSINESS

I motioned to the open papers. "Find me another close game with the Mariners. One they either lost or came close to losing."

Gertie leaned over the table, her gaze going from Sports column to Sports column until she found…

"Cincinnati. April 17th, Mariners—0, Reds—4."

I swallowed. "Close the paper."

FIRST NATIONAL BANK ROBBED
VAULT CLEANED OF CURRENCY!

"All right," Gertie spoke, her voice tight and dry, "I wouldn't call this coincidence anymore."

"It's anything but." Gertie was now looking at me quizzically. "I was on a crime scene this morning." I said, closing up newspapers.

Her head tipped down as she looked at me over her specs. "Come again? You were on the scene of a robbery?"

"Nope. Murder. And *attempted* robbery."

"Ah," Gertie huffed. "And you were going to tell me this…"

"Over our chili special, of course."

"Of course," she said, her eyebrow now stuck in a somewhat skeptical jaunt.

"I'm thinking I've got—" I took hold of Gertie's wrist and whispered a choice Gryfennosian curse. "—I've got tonight to figure out what the Mariners are casing."

"They have a game tomorrow?"

"Yeah, the end of a two-day stretch. Today was their break, and they appear to have bungled the burglary. If you and I have stumbled onto what I think we've stumbled onto, they're either making a play for the same mark or they're casing a new joint. I've got two days to figure out this bit of court intrigue before the Mariners head home."

She looked up from the paper closing in front of her. "Back to Baltimore?"

"Not if we can help it," came a third voice walking up behind us.

We both jumped out of our skins, but Gertie was the tenser of the two of us. The newspaper in her hands now sported a three-inch tear at its spine.

Detective Jerry Flannigan stopped in his tracks, wincing at hearing the paper tear. The natural echo of the library made it sound far worse than it really was, not that tearing paper in a library is really a good thing to begin with.

While Gertie was the responsible party, Jerry went pale as he looked over the damage done. "Oh geez, I'm—uh, did I just—?"

"No, no, no, no…" As I watched Gertie, I realized how much I really owed her on this one. I not only took up her afternoon and stretched her attention into the early evening, but I got her so wound up into this case that it cost the library a periodical. She took a deep breath, and that stopped the ripped newspaper from trembling in her hands. Gertie closed it as best as it would close, shot me a very quick, very deadly stare and then slapped a smile across her face. "No, not at all, sir. I tend to get too involved with my patrons and their research."

Yeah, she's talking about me.

"How can I help you, sir?" she asked Jer.

His pale complexion regained some of its color, and that color was red. "Oh, um, no ma'am. I'm here to see that guy behind you," he said pleasantly, pointing to me.

She now looked between us, and then looked at the papers strewn across the library's tables. "Ah, I see," she replied curtly. Her eyes came to rest on me. "Then perhaps I should clean this up while you two talk?"

Uh-huh, she really wasn't happy now. Another rain check for that date at Mick's. An unhappy librarian. Not good. It's like poking a basilisk with a stick and then running away. And yes, both basilisks and librarians have incredible memories.

"Thanks—" I started, but needed to clear my throat. I fought through the pain, and found my voice again. "Thanks for all your help, miss. I will make sure to give a donation to the library before I leave, considering all the time you have given me."

Gertie paused in folding up the St. Louis newspapers, and then resumed her duties while she said, "That would be lovely, sir."

That was sweat I was feeling on my hairy back.

"Billi?" Jerry asked.

"Yeah," I replied. "Sorry. It's been a long afternoon…"

"And evening," quipped a female voice from the opposite side of the table.

I didn't bother to look. Standing in the chair, I was eye-level with my fellow detective. "How did you find me?"

"Mindy told me you'd be here. I, uh…" Jer's voice trailed off as he watched Gertie for a second. "Sorry, did I interrupt something?"

"We were wrapping up," I said, ignoring the huff from behind me. "What's on your mind?"

"Well, this must be a case of great minds thinking alike. I heard you and the librarian here talking about the Baltimore Mariners heading back home."

"Yeah, I've been following that team pretty closely this season. Guess you could call me a secret fan." Sometimes, I hate this job, especially when I have to lie to friends. "I wanted to catch them one more time before they finished up."

"No need to rush and get a seat," Jer said. "We got one of the Mariners."

"Really," I chortled. "Guess they were celebrating a win today as well?"

"In the morgue."

The small gasp from behind caused me to turn this time. Gertie tore her gaze from Jer and locked peepers with me.

I reached into my coat and from my wallet dropped a few bills on the now-clean tabletop. "Like I said, Gertie. Rain check. I think I'm on the clock."

"You ain't kiddin', Billi," Jer said. "Just wait until you see the body."

CHAPTER EIGHT
STIFF COMPETITION

Beating the heat in Chicago isn't always an easy thing to do. You could go for a dip in Buckingham Fountain. No, perhaps it was not what the artisans expected of it and I'm not sure city officials intended the centerpiece of Grant Park to become a public swimming hole in a pinch, but what were the cops going to do? Arrest you for cooling off? I'm sure the flatfeet were thinking the same thing I'm thinking: it beats sweating like an Ogre dressed in full battle gear, and smelling like the underbelly of a pack beast. You could take a dip in Lake Michigan, but in the fountain you didn't have an undertow or shipping traffic, and—of course—you can see the bottom without a worry.

If we were to catch a glimpse of our Great Lake's bottom, we'd probably be inclined to change its name from "Lake Michigan" to "Mob Graveyard of the Midwest".

What the city didn't realize was that apart from taking a swim in Buckingham or risking your spotless record in the eyes of Lady Justice by stripping down to your underclothes, there was a third option if you needed to cool off: clock in some time at the city morgue. Yeah, nothing like stepping into the depths of Chicago's criminal crypt where its occupants are kept in cool comfort while those truly blessed by the Fates noodle through the cause of their deaths. Had Gryfennos—hell, had Acryonis—possessed the smarts on maintaining temperature in buildings, maybe clerics could have kept a handle on those plague outbreaks. I wished I could afford a creature comfort like air conditioning for the office or my flop, but that was a luxury reserved for the remaining upper class, and for businesses like printing houses, florists, and city essentials.

Sadly, with gangland crime the way it was, morgues were considered "city essentials". Stood to reason, of course. The last thing you wanted on a hot day in Chicago was to have the freezer here conk out. Health reasons aside, corpses were tough enough to stomach, but corpses left to their own time in sweltering heat? I'd continue...but I don't know if you're reading this over lunch, dinner, or a midnight snack. I really don't want to ruin your appetite, or kick up what you've already eaten.

So, while it wasn't a July or August heat, it was that kind of spring evening that reminded you summer was just around the corner. My coat was draped over my arm as I walked into the crypt with Jerry only a few steps ahead. I had to smile at the moxie of my pal, Detective Flannigan. The reactions were consistent: a nod to Jerry, then eyes dropped down to me—blink—and eyes returned to Jerry for a long stare. The expressions ranged from "*You remember what happened the last time you pulled this stunt?*" to "*You've got some nerve bringing* it *here*". It was sure money that some of those dinks were making a beeline for the "Snitch Line" the moment we passed, to let O'Malley know that I was here. Fucking shield-buffers, to think ratting out Jer would get them points toward something that mattered.

We weren't even past the first descending staircase when I had to put my coat back on. The sweat in my shirt was cold now, and I felt wide awake with the sudden chill against my skin.

"Just through here," Jer said, his voice sounding oddly out of place.

Maybe it was his own brush with death, but I picked up a slight waver in his voice. Not that he really wanted to be spending his early evening in the morgue. Apart from necromancers and dabblers in black magic (redefining stupidity with every incantation they mumbled), I don't know anyone who would enjoy clocking in some time in a place like this. Most of the staff here considered this job as a stepping stone to a loftier position in the criminal investigation hierarchy.

While we both dealt with death as part of the job, I felt a tightness in my throat and a welling in the pit of my gut as I entered the examination room where the covered body waited for us. If I'd been hungry when I got there (since Gertie and I had, more or less, worked through lunch), seeing the cold meat on the slab stopped my tummy in mid-rumble.

Hearing the chair legs grind across the floor and echo around us helped me realize what was so unsettling about the morgue. Death, as we dealt with it, appeared random or chaotic in some fashion. The blood splatters, the stiff's final efforts to remain standing before kissing the pavement, or the concluding act of defiance before taking one bullet too many—it didn't matter if the carnage was an organized hit, a crime of passion, or a last stand across a moor separating your nation from some seriously cranky Black Orcs, there would always be signs of disarray and rash decisions made in those final, fleeting heartbeats of life.

Not in a morgue. Here, death was diagnosed, catalogued, and tagged. Everything around the dearly departed was tidy, kept in meticulous order. The emotion forever caught in the face of the victims—innocent bystanders, soldiers, and marauders alike—was absent. The eyes were closed, the mouth turned down slightly. Neither forlorn nor peaceful, their expression—if you could call it that—conveyed nothing. That was what made death here so different than what we were accustomed to. Death, in this place, was just part of the daily grind, bereft of any thought, feeling, or purpose. The city morgue was truly dead in every sense of the word, and we were in the belly of this architectural beast.

Good thing there weren't any windows around to let us know it was night. That would have made this setting all the more uneasy.

Then Jer spoke. "Okay, Billi." His voice was probably far louder than intended, and perhaps it startled him a bit. The silence here was just too thick for my liking, and conversation served as another reminder that *we* were alive. It should have been assuring, yet everything felt wrong. The fact that we were alive in this very ordered, very particular place of death seemed a complete and utter mistake. We didn't belong here.

Here we were, nonetheless, taking our time to get to know a guy who was no longer in a hurry getting anywhere.

Jer asked more quietly, "Ready for the floor show?"

I shimmied on the chair. No wobble. A pleasant surprise. "So, what does a dead baseball player look like?"

He pulled back the sheet covering the stiff in front of us. "The ones from Baltimore look like this."

My eyes narrowed on what remained of this poor dink's face. The bridge of his nose was now bent, not to the left or to the right, but *inward.* His skin was an attractive blending of blues, violets, and blacks against a pale, pasty canvas, rivulets of crimson and brown dried against the surface and filling the deep folds of skin. Due to the face's concave condition, his lips were parted, locking his mouth into some kind of permanent snarl. His brow also remained furrowed, and I could only guess it was going to stay that way.

"Is this the best they could make him look?" I asked, wincing at every new grotesque detail I caught under the harsh light.

Jer's fingers were still on the sheet covering him. "That's just the warm up, pal."

The sheet continued to slip away, and I squinted at the sheen coming off the stiff. I should have gotten on the phone and called someone at Webster's, because a scribe needed to be there to redefine the term "shiner". This corpse was doing just that: Bruise after bruise after bruise all blended into one giant mass of swollen muscle and tissue. At a glance I would have believed him to be a victim of a dragon attack, or being at that point of impact where a trebuchet's flaming barrel had landed. I held my hand over the mass of bruises, and there was still warmth coming from the corpse.

"Yeah," Jerry said. "Folks here aren't sure how his body is doing that, but it's still not the weirdest thing about our guy here."

A bushy red eyebrow arched at that. "Really? A guy getting pummeled repeatedly until he resembles a Cro-Magnon isn't bizarre enough?"

Jerry took a step back from the stiff and took in a deep breath. He was noodling something through, and I could see he wanted to tread very gently with this. "Billi, take a look at the body."

"Do I really have to? It's already made an impression me."

"Look, I'm going with the evidence they're telling me here. So, look at him."

I turned back to the multicolored corpse. "All right, I'm looking at him." I tipped my Stetson to the guy's distorted face. "How you doing, Handsome?"

"Take a guess—how many hits to the body do you think it would take to do this kind of damage?"

Fisticuffs are important as a training tool, for grappling, for physical conditioning, and for self-defense. I'm a regular at the gym to keep those skills sharp. You've got to be able to make that right hook count in my business, regardless if you're going for a shot to the jaw or (in my case) the kneecap.

So, while I'm no boxing pro, I know that you can take a pounding and still not resemble this poor dink on the slab. To do this kind of damage would take a lot of hammer blows, or a few hammer blows with some serious strength behind them.

A vivid image of Kev, my pal from Acryonis' front lines, popped into my noggin. One of the bigger Humans I've fought alongside, Kev was a monster in my eyes. A monster who always was a hell of a lot of fun to be around. One night, he took a challenge put to him by a few of the officers in the Allied Races. There was a Black Orc refugee from the Arannahi contingent giving his all on the battlefield for the good guys. While the wild card's actions left no room for debate, there was lot of tension over him within the ranks. To show everyone that the Arannahi disciplines were deeply ingrained into this refugee—T'Kuras was his Arannahi-given name—the field commanders thought a boxing match between him and another member of the Allied Races would sate anxiety and apprehensions. Without question, Kev was the top choice, based on his massive size.

Another reason Kev was tapped for this bout—his record on the battlefield. His village had been wiped out in a Black Orc raid, leaving him the sole survivor. A sole survivor who carried a hell of a grudge, making him a blade with an impeccable kill record. If anyone could stand up to an Orc in the ring, it was Kev.

Everything started off friendly enough. Kev and T'Kuras put on a hell of a show; but in the fourth round things took a turn. The big palooka was tiring and his left eye was starting to swell up a bit. I shot a glance at T'Kuras, and he was only just starting to break a sweat.

"Kev, how about we make this the last round?" I whispered as he returned to his corner *"You're doing great, my fri—"*

"End this fight now," he hissed at me, *"and the next one will be ours."*

The crowd roared, ushering Kev back into the center of the ring. For T'Kuras, this was still a pleasant bout between allies. For Kev, it was quickly turning personal, as was evident when he let loose two quick jabs to the Orc's kidneys.

Okay, on a Human, where kidneys would be. Orc biology, as it goes with various races, is a little different from the average Human's. But still, who knew genitalia could exist anywhere but between the legs?

T'Kuras was still catching his breath when Kev leapt up, his fist cocked back behind his head. He brought it down as the Orc looked up. The sap's head twisted, and a string of black ooze that I knew was blood flew out like a bullwhip and caught the Arannahs Human in his corner.

We all knew it was a sucker punch and way out of the lines of a friendly spar, as was Kev's foot slamming into the bridge of T'Kuras' nose. When Kev loosed another two kicks to the Orc's ribs, only a handful of people were cheering. Things were turning ugly. We all knew that.

What we didn't know was just how ugly things were about get.

Kev's tribal cry tore through the unnerving silence that had fallen over us. He leaped and seemed to suspend himself for a moment in the air…

His descending fist was *caught* by another hand.

Kev hit the ring so hard that the surrounding earth kicked up. That earlier mirth and even the strangely charming smile T'Kuras had been wearing back in his corner were gone. When his ebony hand wrapped around Kev's thick neck, we all knew that T'Kuras was stepping back to his roots.

The first slap made Kev's entire body flinch to the left. The only reason he didn't fly to the opposite side of the ring was that he still remained in T'Kuras' grasp. His arms and legs were flung to the right by the force of the follow-up backhand. The Orc hoisted him up an inch higher, an undulating sound creeping from Kev's parted lips.

What suddenly struck me then was the silence. We were stunned into stillness, watching all this unfold. This couldn't be happening. Just a moment ago that monster was joking with the rest of us, enjoying a playful spar with…

Kev's body slammed hard against the ground again, snapping me back into the moment. Other Arannahi—four total—were stepping into the ring, surrounding their Orc and chanting something in what I guessed was their native tongue.

The Orc's chest was still heaving, but more slowly than when he'd been beating the shit out of Kev. We all watched T'Kuras' berserker gaze surrender to a realization, like dawn over a hilltop bringing a new day to a shire. As he started piecing together what he was doing, the rage slipped away from his face. That tower of black fur, muscle, and power collapsed to his knees and buried his scarred face into his own blood-stained hands.

The thing…was crying?

Just when I thought I had seen everything, the sun rose on a new day. When I went to pay Kev a visit at the healer's tent, I parted the flap and froze. Sitting next to my pal was T'Kuras. The Orc, with two Arannahi behind him, was applying a variety of ointments to Kev's bruises and scars. If Kev flinched, T'Kuras' own hands whipped clear of his body. The skittish behavior made both Human patient and Orc nursemaid chuckle.

From those few days, I took away three images I would not soon forget, even when setting up my farm on the Everlasting Fields. I saw an Orc cry, I saw an Orc play cleric to a Human, and I saw what someone looked like after getting into a fistfight with an Orc.

It was amazing what you could apply from my past into the here and now.

"Well, Jer," I began, playing that fight over and over in my head, counting the punches exchanged between Kev and T'Kuras, "whoever ganged up on this poor guy probably lost count while dishing it out. Maybe around fifteen swings with a bat, 'cause I don't think anything—*in Chicago*—could do this bare-fisted. I'm thinking you're looking at a guy or a group of guys with a lot of anger towards the Baltimore Mariners." I looked back at Jerry, tipping the Stetson further back on my head. "Considering the severe ass-kicking these guys gave our beloved Cubbies yesterday, I'm thinking you're looking at a suspect list thirty to fifty thousand deep. Where do you want to start? North Side, or South?"

My friend scoffed, shaking his head. "I wish it were that easy." He pointed to the darkest spot of one bruise the stiff sported by his left hip. "One." His index finger hopped to the stomach, again at the darkest point of the bruise. "Two." And so he counted, each time pointing to the blackest of the black-and-blue, his last gesture stopping at the guy's face. "Seven."

Lucky seven, huh? Not for this ball player. "You're saying whatever did this only landed seven hits on this guy?"

"That's not what I'm saying," he said, gathering up the sheet. "That's what the guys here are saying."

Jer went to replace the sheet, but I placed an open hand against his closest wrist. "Hold on a minute, Jer." I looked at the body again, and took a deep breath. "What I'm about to do is going to look weird."

"Between the body in the ceiling and this, I don't know how things could get weirder, Billi. Do what you need to do," he said, "so we can get out of here."

I gave Jer a final look, and then leaned in close to one of the bruises. The warmth was what bugged me. Even with the bruising, this body should have been colder than the summit of Death Mountain. The heat hinted to something not right with the true nature of things, and that kind of nature-tampering usually meant one thing.

Sniff-sniff. Yeah, there it was. Faint, but still there.

"Well, okay," I could hear Jerry say behind me. "That's something they don't teach you at the Academy."

I shrugged. Maybe the Academy graduates could learn a thing or two from this Acryonis war veteran. "Did the coroners narrow down a time of death?"

"Best they could give me was an educated guess on account of the bruises still warm and all, but within twenty-four hours." He nodded when I looked at him. "Yeah, that was my reaction, too, but they were going by the places where he had been left alone. The arms and legs were a lot colder than where he had taken these hammer blows."

So now I had magic at the ball game, signs of magic at a crime scene where a man was used as ceiling décor, and now here with...

"The shortstop," I finally said. "This is the shortstop for the Mariners."

"William 'Shuffle' Patterson. This team was his big break. First season in the big leagues, and the guy was not bad for a rookie. We've put a call into the Commissioner's office, asking to postpone tomorrow's game so we can keep the Mariners in town. If we get it, we've bought some time to investigate this murder properly."

All three events—the ball game, the attempted robbery at Waterson's, and this brutal murder—connected by magic.

"*All right*," Gertie had said, concerning the robberies and heists following the Mariners, "*I wouldn't call this coincidence anymore*."

I had a feeling—a *really bad* feeling—I knew where this magic was coming from.

Jer leaned in a little closer to me. "You okay, pal? You look like you just got some bad news."

"I did," I grumbled. "My past. It's catching up with me."

CHAPTER NINE

MURDER ... A NATIONAL PASTIME

Being part of a team—doesn't matter if it's on a battlefield or in a ballpark—creates a special bond. Especially if you got the right people leading the charge, the camaraderie can reach beyond cultures, sex, and race. The incredible ties that a team forges cannot be broken by spells, torture, or greed. It's a code, a code that is upheld without question or hesitation, even if you know what you're keeping a tight lip on is breaking so many laws that you keep seeing a condemned man trapped in your mirror.

Keeping this in mind, I knew it wasn't going to be easy questioning the Baltimore Mariners over William "Shuffle" Patterson. Trying to work through the Mariners "oath of honor" was going to pose a real challenge, especially as everything happening today was a reminder of their fallen teammate. His murder was the reason why they were practicing today instead of playing. (Looked like the League Commissioner was playing ball with the Chicago Police.) The practice was to get their minds off what happened to him, and the postponement of game was in memoriam, as well as a chance for local law enforcement to figure out what happened to the rookie player from out east.

William Patterson was nicknamed "Shuffle" on account of the quirky dance he would do just as the pitcher kicked back. I remembered snorting a bit at his skip, thinking the rookie must've had Vulkanos lava ants in his pants.

Then I'd watch him move when a line drive came his way. The kid's grace could have attracted scouts from the Chicago Ballet. His numerous double-plays possessed a fluidity about them, like watching a heavy potion drop and blossom into a crystal clear liquid, its stunning clarity consumed by a billowing opacity. His movements were effortless, poetic, and just another piece to this seemingly unending puzzle. This kid should not have been fielding for some new team of unknowns. Any scout worth his charmed armor would have snatched him up faster than a pickpocket liberating a nobleman of his purse, but instead he'd stayed undiscovered until the Baltimore Mariners appeared on the scene. I didn't know who was luckier; the kid for being blessed by the Fates with such talent or the Mariners for discovering him.

Then, as I descended closer to the field where the boys from Baltimore were warming up, I decided. His teammates were above ground. They were definitely the lucky ones.

"Excuse me!" I barked out to the bulbous individual chewing his cud like a cow.

The old man's tobacco-chewing paused, and then resumed slowly as his eyes narrowed on me.

"This ought to be good," he grumbled as I got within earshot.

"Comedy don't come any better than this," I said, producing my credentials. "My name's Billibub Baddings. I'm a private investigator."

The cud-chewing stopped. The old codger leaned over in my direction and spit a revolting wad of what appeared to be Goblin shit (only not as foul-smelling), which landed with a sickening splat by my foot. The fluid arms extending from the point of impact were just shy of my recently polished shoes.

I had a feeling this was a guy who, in his day, could pitch a fastball while in the heart of a tempest and still nail the strike zone without a worry or care. The wad was obviously the old man's opinion, if not a warning.

"I'm looking into—"

His chest puffed out as he talked, "My team wins their games fair and square. You dicks are starting to really piss me off."

So McCarthy wasn't the only coach hiring gumheels to look into the Mariners.

"Look, that's not why I'm here, Coach." I looked past him at the team swapping pitches and limbering up for their practice. "Sorry, I didn't get your name."

He looked me up and then turned back to the field. "It's in the papers if you want it. Now, if you don't mind, I'm busy."

I watched him chew his cud for a moment before giving my belt a tug upward and breaking the uneasiness around us. "I hope your mouth is the only place you put that tobacco, Coach, because if that shit's in your ears you'll miss the fact that I'm here about a player of yours—William 'Shuffle' Patterson."

"Good kid," he said, not even bothering to look at me as he spoke. "Hell of a shortstop."

Wow, Coach, try to keep it together. Your outpouring of emotion is overwhelming. I may join you in a good cry.

"Yeah, I know that. I was here Tuesday for the game. You all gave the Cubbies a run for the money."

"No we didn't," he said, before spitting another Goblin's turd out of his mouth. "We beat the pants off of you, is what we did." He turned around, and again his chest swelled, lightly jostling his crossed arms. "How about you go and tell that to Joe next time you see him?"

I didn't know how plain I had to make it to him that I was not grilling him on behalf of the Chicago Cubs. Yes, I was still on McCarthy's bankroll, but I was here now to do a hint of moonlighting for my friend Jer and (unofficially) for the Chicago Police.

"Coach, I'm more interested in what Shuffle was up to when he wasn't doing his shortstop jig. I'd like to find out why such a talented kid would meet with such an…" Unnecessarily violent? Bizarre? Grotesque? "…untimely death."

"My job is to coach these guys and lead them to a pennant. That's what they pay me for. I'm not their mommy, and I don't give a rat's ass what they do off the field until I get a call from the cops, and even then I've got to do what the owner tells me to." He spat again, and then his face contorted as he chewed in silence for a second or two. "If I had my way, I'd bus 'em back to whatever cornfield they were found in, pitching fastballs at scarecrows."

The crack of a bat tore my attention from the back of the coach's head toward the diamond. The Mariners' pitcher, Eddie "Shadow" Faria, was sending out pop flies to some of his teammates, and even in the casual warm-up exercise he presided with an authority. The look on his face struck me as nostalgic. Even something as simple as hitting pop flies to teammates brought him a peace, a comfort that you might find in a woman's arms. However, this joy was not as fleeting.

I felt a pair of peepers on me and noticed that the coach was looking at me over his shoulder.

"Coach, I'm here as a favor to a friend. I just wanted to find out what the story was with Shuffle. Whatever you've been dealing with in other cities, you're in Chicago now. We do things a little different here."

"Different, huh?" His eyes went from the top of my hat to my shoes and then back again. "I hadn't noticed."

Top notch coach and a comedian. The old man was just bubbling over with talent.

"Heads up!" Coach shouted, causing me to blink and the players to freeze. "Trouble, front and center!"

Practice resumed, save for four players that nuzzled their gloves against their forearms and trotted over to me. They were looking at one another, swapping a shared memory and a punch line to a joke only they understood. I recognized two of the four from the game I'd seen. Riley "Scooter" Jenkins and Archie "Flyball" Randalls. The other two were considerably older and, I would even daresay, a touch rougher in their demeanors. Still, they seemed to hustle with the young and showed no signs of their age. I could catch in their eyes, exchanged for Jenkins' and Randalls' arrogance, a history of experience and wisdom. Didn't make them any less cocky than the whelps. Difference was, they had the balls to back up the swagger.

"Alright, Trouble," the coach barked, referring to the four of them as one. "This guy is here asking questions about Shuffle and what he did with you all in between games. Tell the guy what he wants to know. The sooner you do that, the sooner he leaves."

Their voices replied over one another. "Got it, Coach," from Randalls. "Sure thing, Pappy," Jenkins said while the other two guys mumbled, "Yeah, Coach."

"Keep it simple, boys." Another spit, and then he loosed a smirk at me. "Have fun," the coach scoffed before leaving me with his players.

Yeah, this was going to be a real laugh riot.

"How you boys, doin'?" I started off, producing a notepad from my coat pocket. "My name's Billibub Baddings, I'm a private eye. Been asked to look into what happened to your buddy, Shuffle. I recognize you two from the game I saw on Tuesday," I said, motioning to Scooter and Flyball, before turning to the others. "Apologies for not recalling you two, but that was a long day for us Cub fans."

The four of them shared a chuckle at the mention of their victory, and I was willing to give it to them.

Then the biggest of them started in. "Well, I need to spell my name for you 'cause it's a little hard to pronounce, even for the pros in the press box."

"Sure," I said, poising the pencil. "Shoot."

"S-U—" was as far as my pencil wrote before stopping. My head slowly rose from the pad to look up at the broad-bellied man as he continued. "C-K-O-F-F-F-U-C-K-E-R." As the cronies around him tittered like an emperor's virginal harem, the big guy kept a straight face. "It's German."

I gave a nod and then resumed writing, "A-S-S-W-I-P-E. Yeah, I think I got 'Murphy' spelled right here."

Fat boy's smile melted away.

"Took me a second to recognize you from the pictures in the papers. 'Big Joe' Murphy, right?" I asked. Answered with nothing but the sounds of practice behind them, I turned to the last member of this cute little quartet. This guy was also big, but not portly like "Big Joe". This one was a stone shithouse with a guest room attached. "That leaves you, Sunshine."

Sunshine's reply matched the chill the remaining company of Trouble now sent my way. "Sam Saint."

"Sledgehammer Sammy?" I asked, my bushy brows raising slightly. "You got a hell of a batting average there, Sammy. I can see why they call you Sledgehammer."

"That's not the only reason, Tiny," he seethed, cracking his knuckles.

Yeah, like *that* was going to intimidate me.

"So you four are a pack called Trouble, huh? That's really clever, boys. And now one of your fellowship is down for the eternal count." I was expecting them to swap nervous glances between one another, but they just stood there, their eyes never leaving me. "You all seem as choked up as Coach Grizzly."

"Hey, watch your mouth, Shrimp!" Scooter fired off. That got everyone's attention. "Pappy deals with things on his time. We got to stay in the game right now."

"Easy, Scooter," Joe said, his gaze shifting from the younger player to me. "It's like this, Mr. Detective, we're all shook up about this because Shuffle was part of the team, and part of our gang here. We aren't wearing black and we're not crying in our gloves, because we got games to win. Chicago ain't making that easy what with the Cubs, and now the cops, working us so hard."

"Well, you know, when a friend—and a close one to you lot, I might add—gets himself turned into hamburger, I would think an investigation would make you all happy as fishermen catching a school of spawning mermaids. We're trying to *solve* Shuffle's murder here. We should be working together, right?"

"You deal with Shuffle's death your way," uttered Sledgehammer, "and we'll deal with it our way."

The only difference between these guys and cops: the uniforms. Different duds, same code of silence.

"I can respect that," I conceded. "Still, I'd appreciate some help here. How hard was it for Shuffle to live up to your gang's namesake? Did he get himself into any debts—?"

"You think we're gambling or something?"

"Big Joe" seemed to grow in front of me. No, this was definitely not the right avenue to pursue.

"I didn't say that, Murphy," I answered, my eyes narrowing on the posturing ball player. "Debt comes from a lot of things, and gambling is just one of them. I don't know how much you all like to live it up."

"Check the papers a little closer then, Shorty," Flyball snickered. "We tend to cover a lot more than just the Sports section!"

This punk was a true-to-life definition of "a singular wit", as he was the only one laughing. Instead of staring at me, Sledgehammer was shooting the visual frost at his whelp teammate. The sniggering slowed, and finally surrendered to a dry throat-clearing.

"I just might do that, kid. What can you tell me about Shuffle?"

Now the guys looked to one another and then Sledgehammer turned to me. "Maybe that jig he did was irritating as hell, but that kid could move."

"I mean, outside of the diamond. Out in the real world, what was he like?"

Sledgehammer bobbed his head back and forth, something I thought must have been pretty dangerous to the pea-sized brain that had to be jostling around in that big melon of his. "Well, he was dedicated to the game, you know? I mean, no matter the circle of friends you keep, someone's got to be a runt. I'm sure you know what I mean, right, Tiny?"

He got the crooked bushy red eyebrow for that one.

"Some people are leaders. Others follow. Nobody followed like Bill," Sledgehammer continued. "You told him to do something and like a good lapdog he did what he was told. I admit, I'll be missing that. A lot." He smirked and looked around the group. "One of you guys is going to have to be the runt now."

They seemed to suddenly slip into the midst of a shielding spell, effectively distancing themselves from me as they started a banter back and forth about who was the likeliest candidate for "Trouble's Pet Page".

Welcome to the other side of the ballpark, Billi.

This was the counterspell that silently nagged at me when I agreed to take this case. Professional baseball players were more than just grown-ups getting paid to play a game. These guys were icons of the time, heroes of legend and lore. The *real* heroes of the sport, they understood and respected the responsibility bestowed on them. Maybe they didn't want that responsibility, but they understood it was the price of the pastime.

These chumps were the *other* kind of baseball celebrities. They knew they were minor nobility and they reveled in it. If kids looked up to them, that was fine, so long as the little brats didn't keep them from getting to the closest speakeasy or brothel when the doors unlocked for the night. They considered themselves better than everybody else on account of a single ball and a crafted stick from Louisville, Kentucky.

Trouble—what was left of the Frivolous Five anyway—continued to cackle and guffaw. I waited until the jibes on Flyball, the youngest of the four, subsided. Eventually they honored me with their undivided attention.

"You girls done with your private tea party?" I asked.

I got a pair for a Dwarf, but that doesn't make me a complete idiot. One against four—I got a shot. I could pick a fight with these dinks and be confident I'd be walking away from it. Picking a fight during team practice, though, meant I'd need to tread gently. A scuffle between us could grab the attention of the team. One against four, sure. One Dwarf against the entire Baltimore Mariners roster? Not without my battle axe.

But like I said, I got a pair. "I mean, if you all want to head back to your little encampment, strip down to your jock straps and give each other rub downs, be my guest, but do it on your own time."

It's really funny when Humans try to look as if they're on the verge of a blood-rage. They wind up looking like Orcs in desperate need of ex-lax.

"We're going to give this another try." I said. "This *lapdog* was a friend of yours. I would think you want some retribution for this, and that's what I excel at."

Sledgehammer screwed his eyes shut, pinching the bridge of his nose. He finally looked at me, his expression curious in how pitiful it was. "Must be sad being so damn short, seeing as a lot goes flying over you. I'm gonna say it again—you deal with Shuffle's death your way. We'll deal with it our way."

Okay, this was getting me nowhere. "Fine. I will. You boys run along and play with your buddies, or play with yourselves, whatever you enjoy most. When you're feeling more cooperative—" I pulled out a business card and walked up to the wall. Extending up to my tiptoes would probably earn me a chuckle, but they were just watching me as I placed the contact info within their reach. "—here's my card. Call me."

The cover of my memo pad flipped shut before they took off to join the rest of their teammates.

A "lapdog" was how William "Shuffle" Patterson's best friends regarded him. I considered this as I made my way up the steps of Wrigley Field. Some friends. If this was the truth, then his death was even more tragic than it already seemed. To be beaten as he was, by sorcery, meant he suffered. I've been in full armor and punched by Humans, Orcs, and Trolls. I'll get the wind knocked out me, but the adrenalin and the moment gets me back on my feet. A punch spiked by magic, especially with whatever intent is behind the magic, can go through armor like a freshly-sharpened battle axe through warm butter. Okay, so it may cushion the blow to an extent, but you're not getting up. Not right away. You got to take a breath first, and if it doesn't hurt too much, take another one for good measure. If your ribs are bruised, you're getting off light.

A solid Chicago-tailored winter suit wouldn't have helped Shuffle. The first punch would have been enough to crack a few bones and keep him on the bench until the end of the summer. He had been hit *seven* times, and from what his corpse showed me, the magic had grown in its intensity with each strike. The last punch was probably the one to his face. I was sure he saw it coming. I was sure whatever was killing him made certain he was conscious enough to appreciate it. I was sure the last thing Shuffle felt was the sting of that last strike, before his nose and bits of his skull caved in and drove deep into his brain.

I was sure of all this because I've seen dark magic up close and personal. It doesn't do nice things to people.

The ball struck the seat next to me hard. It bounced between the chair and the back of its brother in the lower row, took flight for a brief moment, and then started falling towards me.

Slap, and I smiled at the tingling in my palm. If you catch a ball barehanded, you're running a real gamble. If a finger is too far inward, the ball's curvature will catch it and bend it against your palm, snapping it like a twig. Too far out and you might bend back a finger or two. Then you have the double pleasure of both needing your fingers reset and lousing up the catch. All this damage, of course, depends on the speed of the ball.

Then you've got the perfect catch, be it barehanded or with a glove. The hand forms a curve the ball can nuzzle into like a woman's body against your own in the throes of good *grundle'malk*. The point of impact is at that part of your hand where nerves are either conditioned (or deadened, depending on if you're an optimist or pessimist...) and can handle any velocity that canvas-covered sphere is sailing at. And when the ball comes to a stop, it's not you defying the laws of motion and making something stop, but it's you and the ball both ushering a state of rest.

The sting in my hand felt good. Really good.

I turned around and looked back at the field. Eddie "Shadow" Faria was staring back at me from the batter's box, Home Plate a pristine white just in front of his feet. His bat came to rest across his shoulders as he stared up at me. Faria was hard to read because he didn't look threatened, pissed, or even slightly perturbed. He was just standing there, content. Content because of the hit? It was a foul ball, you putz! Content that he missed me? Great. Trouble probably appreciated the gesture.

Content that he got my attention? Now there was a thought.

I started down the steps when I heard Big Joe call out, "Nice catch, Shrimp!"

The steps extended out, demarking a change in seating sections. It would be tight but I had enough room. I hurled the ball back into the diamond. The ball disappeared for a second, and then reappeared on its descent.

Big Joe would not have been a hard target to hit on account of his size, but it was how I wanted to hit him. The ball came straight down on that fat prick and bounced high off the top of his noggin. It had gained some speed after passing the apex I gave it. There was something satisfying about being able to apply some of that science stuff I picked up in the library while on a case. I didn't hear the rap against Big Joe's skull, but the impact had been powerful enough to drive him down to one knee.

I straightened my tie and coat, giving the Baltimore Mariners a quick once-over from my vantage point. A couple of the players were running to check on Joe while everyone else stayed put. They all shot me an Ogre's glare similar to Coach Pappy's, all of them save for Faria. He wasn't giving me anything to ponder on, outside of why he wanted my attention.

With a final adjustment to my hat, I continued up the stairs, making no indication that I noticed the card I'd left on the retaining wall was no longer there.

CHAPTER TEN

Dial 'B' for Billi

The office was the best place to catch a breath in the middle of a case. I'd take a stand on a stepstool and just peer over Chicago between the "Investigations" and "REDford 6500" painted on the inside of the window. Those Baltimore clowns were definitely putting up a good front for whoever was calling the shots. While it doesn't take a criminal mastermind to rob a bank, I didn't buy for a second that those dinks were savvy enough to know what to look for in the museums. From greenbacks to Rodin sketchbooks? That was quite a step up. They also didn't strike me as coordinated enough to do whatever they were doing while on the road. The difficult part was going to be proving how they were pulling these jobs completely out of sight. That was the part that made me most nervous. It was the part that most strongly suggested magic.

My eyes went to the hiding place of *My World Book*, and I gave a heavy sigh before taking a quick sip of my coffee. Maybe it wasn't time to bend the cover on that just yet. It was magic, I had no doubt. The smell of electricity still tickled my nostrils when I thought about everything.

I was just hoping it wasn't one of the Nine. Dealing with the one had taken a toll on me. It was hard not to look at the statue of Lady Justice when I passed Chicago's Courthouse. Seemed she was always looking down and grinning at me, as if she knew something I didn't.

There was a connection I was missing apart from how the Mariners were doing it, and the connection was the real brains of the outfit. It certainly wasn't Shuffle Patterson, since he was out of the picture on account of a severe case of death. The rest of Trouble could have been trying to throw me off by making him out to be a lapdog, but I didn't think they were that bright. Those four were answering to someone, and if I could find that reigning lord then maybe I could pull out that foundation from under them and make them fold like a bad card player at the gaming tables.

My train of thought was cut short by the buzz of the phone. A *click-click* silenced the dull tapping of clapper to bell, and then Miranda chimed in.

"Billi, McCarthy's on the line."

"Thanks," I replied, hopping down to the floor. I reached up to my desk and gripped the receiver. "Got it." With the horn now free from my chest, I spoke into it. "Mr. McCarthy? Billi Baddings here. How are things?"

"You saw the game on Tuesday," McCarthy grumbled. "We're still licking the wounds. I've never seen ball played like that before."

"I agree," I said. "I was pretty impressed by what the Mariners brought to Chicago, but not half as impressed as by what your boys dealt back. My Cubs played their hearts out."

"That they did," he agreed, a hint of pride just detectible under the current of regret, "but apparently it wasn't enough. Maybe that ball player getting killed was a—"

He caught himself before finishing the thought, but I took a huge liberty addressing it. "You're only human in thinking that, Mr. McCarthy, but I'd suggest keeping those passing thoughts to yourself."

"Geez," he swore. "This team is really working on me."

A moment or two passed before I spoke. He was calling me for a reason, not because he wanted to chat up an old friend and fan. I could only go so far in what I could tell him. "I don't want to get your hopes up, but I'm on to something with the Mariners. I know they've got one more game coming. I need a little more time to find things out."

"Okay, but that's your job, isn't it? Finding the time to take care of this?"

"Yeah, but I can't call up the Commissioner and have him further postpone your schedule for a few more days on account of a private investigation, now can I? Even if I were to get this past Landis and get him to sit quiet on it—which I doubt he would—"

"Good guess."

"I wouldn't want to risk the papers catching wind of it. We're trying to keep this all on the quiet. Careful as clerics, you follow?"

He paused. "Well, no, I don't. What the hell's a cleric?"

I shook my head and continued. "Phone up the Commissioner and ask for a few more days of mourning. Say it's so Chicago's Finest can score more time to go over the evidence, bring a bit of justice to whoever killed an up-and-coming player in the league. He'll love that, especially coming from the opposing team's manager."

"Yeah, he just might."

The conversation was now at a close, at least for me, but Joe cleared his throat. I knew he was waiting for something far more definite than I could give him at that moment, but I thought I would be okay as long as he didn't—

"So, Mr. Baddings, what do you think the Mariners are up to?"

Black magic. That could have been my answer, followed up with, *Oh yeah, and a series of bank robberies and upscale heists*. I could have revealed all that to a guy who didn't know what a cleric was.

Sorry, Coach, but I'm going to go for two bases on this in-field drive.

"It's too early to tell. But I can say with certainty that it's complicated. You'll just have to trust me when I say this is big, and I need time to see where it leads."

From the momentary silence, Joe understood. I didn't want him to worry, but he had every right to be concerned.

"Thanks for the candor, Billi," he spoke finally, his tone sounding a bit deflated. I knew he'd hoped I would have an explanation, but I couldn't give him one yet. "I'll be in touch after talking to the Commissioner."

"Thank you, Mr. McCarthy. Talk to you soon."

The *click* of receiver to cradle never sounded so loud. I looked up toward Miranda, but she was still typing up the monthly expenses on her Smith-Corona. She apparently didn't notice the click, so it was just me. What I had told Joe was not a lie, but I needed more information before I could start laying out the whole truth. At least, the truth that would make sense to a world that did not practice nor comprehend true magic. This was becoming complicated, involving a lot more than just the Baltimore Mariners. It could easily become a scandal that might wreck the entire season and maybe even shut down professional baseball as we knew it. Baseball had become a haven for many after the bubble burst. The dark shadow of Depression loomed overhead like a specter of Death, hovering over the damned until its time to reap. This sport had become the glue that held the country together.

Take baseball away from the masses and a reaping would indeed ensue.

My head jerked back to the phone as it rang out again. I was still by the desk. Hadn't moved since I hung up. I reached for the receiver, but my girl had beaten me to it.

"Billi," she called from the other room, "for you."

"Who is it?"

"Wouldn't say. Definitely a guy. Wanted to talk to you and only you."

Care for a little cloak with your dagger? (Now *there's* a saying that made some sense to me!) I picked up. "Got it." Back up to the ear and mouth. "Billi Baddings. Whadya hear? Whadya say?"

"Mr. Baddings?" The voice was male, with a gruffness from talking in hushed tones. "This is Archie Randalls."

"Flyball?" So he was the one who had picked up my card. The newly-appointed "lapdog" was looking for a friend to talk to, or possibly a way out. "Archie, I apprec—"

"I got to make this quick 'cause the guys are hitting the showers right now. I only got a few ticks, so just listen. You wanted to talk a bit about what happened to Shuffle. I can talk when we're not at Wrigley, so when can we meet?"

"Tonight."

"Meet me behind the Jefferson Hotel. Eight o'clock. I can probably duck out of the whoring tonight. You know the Jefferson?"

"A couple blocks from the park." I said, whipping my coat off the rack. "Behind the Jefferson. Got it."

"Thanks for leaving the number, Mr. Baddings. What happened to Bill…well, maybe what we were doing wasn't all that square, but that's just not right what happened to Bill."

"I agree."

"Eight o'clock. Don't keep me waiting, 'cause I won't."

A sharp click sounded in the receiver and he was gone.

Are you kidding, kid? I'll be there before you know or expect it.

My hat was on my head and my hand was on my office door when I paused. The kid was sharp. Had to be, to play ball like he did. Could he be crafty enough to be a doubleback, as we called them back in Acryonis?

Doublebacks were the worst kind of traitors. Whether you were in a full company or on a campaign with a group of eight, doublebacks were weak-willed saps tempted either by sex, druids, or rocks of gold. The easy lure of power—financial, primal, or elemental—it didn't matter to them. Usually the encouragement to turn on their brethren and the promise of the reward was their first taste of it.

Maybe in the Depression, hand-outs were not uncommon. Hell, in my world, hand-outs weren't all that uncommon. Troll-ravaged towns would need help after a raid, or some conjured plague. All charity aside, there was no such thing as easy booty. You had to earn that charmed weapon, either through hard work or by risking life and limb. If someone were to hand you power without test or question, you were either going to be called on to be a doubleback or you were being handed something loaded with a pain-in-the-ass curse.

From the sound of his voice, he was already wading deep in this mess the Mariners were making. What would he have to lose?

I considered this as I popped the clip out of Beatrice. She could do with a topping off.

CHAPTER ELEVEN

THIRD TIME'S A CHARM

Ace Taxis never let me down. No matter where I needed to be, my driver would have me there before the ink dried on his dispatcher's message. I had plenty of time to play, and that was exactly what I intended to do. Now that I knew where the team was staying in Chicago, I needed to figure out what floor they were on.

The Jefferson. Damn. This team was living large in the Windy City. Hopefully, the Cubs didn't know their visiting opponents were enjoying the lush life at one of the premier hotels in Chicago. A top restaurant, nice rooms, and all around royal service that could break a ball team owner's bank if the players got spend-crazy in their swanky flops. Maybe this was the way some team owners were compensating after skinflints like Comiskey caused the Black Sox Scandal, but putting a team up at the Jefferson was really raising the bar for everyone else.

I walked down the brightly lit alley, casually glancing around the loading dock. There was a delivery crew swapping crates of produce and goods back and forth for the kitchen, suggesting to me that the alleyway was going to change a bit once this delivery truck took off for the night. Keeping my stride wide and with a purpose, I slipped into the back entrance of the posh hotel and followed the skinny corridor to the kitchen where the early evening's repasts were being prepared. No stone hearths and blood-covered peasants impaling a pig on a spit here. Instead, the castle's cooking staff were dressed in starched white, bathed in bright light and surrounded by silver implements of all kinds. One thing that was no different from the kitchens of keeps I'd known was the shouting. Back and forth, orders were called across the servants' heads, and some would call back with an acknowledgment. There was some sort of organization to this chaos, but only the culinary infantry of this army understood its tactics. I was easily able to dodge and weave out of everyone's way. Their own missions kept them too preoccupied to notice me.

I stuck close to the shadows, employing those honed infiltration skills of mine…

Okay, maybe those "slightly rusty" infiltration skills of mine. From the number of double-takes I earned in my cross of the first kitchen, I wondered if I wasn't in need of some practice. I rarely afforded that many glances and furrowed brows.

The chef's office was finally next to me. I peeked over the windowsill and saw the office vacant, but with lights on. He was here, but probably somewhere gearing up the crew for tonight. With one more glance across the kitchen, I crouched low and hustled through the open space between my hiding place and the door. Once inside the office, I nudged the door closed. It wasn't shut, but it was closed enough to give me a semblance of privacy, fleeting as it might be.

My eyes quickly scanned across the desk for any kind of report from the night before. Hopefully he wasn't one of those creative geniuses who knew no equal in his element, but was a village idiot when it came to paperwork. I didn't have much time to rummage, and if he had things neatly organized for me, it would make my job that much easier.

I swallowed hard when I saw the mountains of parchment that overwhelmed his desk. A break would have been really nice.

Three stacks deep into this organized mess, I found the Room Service log, with a report from the assistant chef slipped carelessly inside the front cover. From the title of the form and the looks of the notes, the second to the Jefferson's Top Chef had resigned over Room Service.

The door swung open. "I told you to heat that oven to 425, not 375!"

Shit.

Since he was still shouting something to his crew, I was able to slip underneath the desk unnoticed, log in hand. Provided he didn't drop a pencil or take a seat and try to tackle some of his paperwork, I would be able to remain unseen…

…and wouldn't you know it? Like something out of a dock whore's day job, I was eye to eye with his crotch as he took the office chair. His knees were coming toward the desk. They paused just shy of me. (Thank. The. Fates.) Papers rustled back and forth.

"Dammit," he hissed. The legs disappeared from view and the chef's voice faded off as he bellowed, "Speddings! Where's the Room Service log from last night?"

Clutching the now sought-after log a bit tighter, I crept to the door, took one more peek around the corner, and then returned to the shadows of the kitchen and the access corridors.

I glanced at my watch and noted the time. 5:03. I might as well grab a quick look at the log now instead of trying to find a quiet spot. The servants would be returning from their duties, the loading dock would still have their crew on the last round of goods, and the kitchen staff—as I'd just seen—would be gearing up for the busy evening.

The Baltimore Mariners were staying at the finest hotel Chicago had to offer, but this did not necessarily mean they would be living the lifestyle of the wealthy and privileged. These guys were usually oat-fed workhorses. They had refined their talents for a game and turned it into their profession, but that didn't change their needs and wants to anything above their station. The clientele that usually stayed here would be set in their ways, and so would the Baltimore Mariners.

An order for a cheeseburger on the third floor, but only one. Someone's kid must have gotten hungry while Daddy was out at a business meeting. Nothing out of the ordinary on the following page, either. Then on the fourth page, another cheeseburger order, followed by a couple of steak orders. Another steak. Hamburger, hamburger, steak, steak...chicken.

Chicken? What was with the chicken?

Sixth floor. Even with the chicken, a lot of meat and potatoes were heading up to the sixth floor. I saw the servants' stairwell in front of me; but to make sure Speddings didn't lose his job, I waited for a chopping block to clear and slipped the Room Service log onto it.

My hand had just opened the door to the stairs when I heard someone behind me shout, *"Chef, found the Room Service log!"* Speddings would keep his job after all. Now it was time to keep mine, by getting a closer look at the sixth floor.

I took another glance at the watch. 5:32, and things were picking up on the Mariners' floor. There were a few door slams, a few playful shouts and dares coming from one side of the hallway, and the odd casual invitation out on the town.

Boy, they were all just shook up to no end over their fallen teammate.

The pen scratched across my memo pad as I tried to pick up any voices I recognized. In particular, I was listening for Trouble. My foot propped the servants' door open just wide enough for me to catch the quick quips swapped between teammates. As I waited for either Big Joe or Sledgehammer to pipe in, I considered the lack of remorse I was picking up from everyone. It may have seemed callous, but it was also reminiscent of how things were handled on a battlefield. Sure, we mourned our dead, but not until the end of the day; and some days were longer than others, depending on the battle. Maybe they were all setting that grief aside until they got home to Baltimore.

As if on cue, I heard a couple of guys passing by. "So, how long you think we're here?" came the question from the hallway.

"I dunno," the other voice replied. "Until we play that last game with the Cubbies and the cops say we can go?"

"And we stay here?" The voice chuckled. "If whatshisname was still kicking, I'd thank him."

Whatshisname? I continued to scribble as the two voices faded. Wow. Now there's a tight team!

Another *click-clack* of a door opening, and I clearly heard Sledgehammer. "Scooter's meeting us in the lobby."

Big Joe's voice came next. "What about Arch?"

"I think he's coming down with something. Hell, you saw him today. He was off."

"Can you blame him?"

Silence, and then Sledgehammer said, "Not here, Joe. Let's not talk about it here."

Oh, come on Sammy, let the guy talk. Make my job easier.

I slipped the mirror out of my coat pocket and angled it to catch a glimpse of them. While their room number wasn't visible, I did get a clear look at the number on the door *next* to theirs.

With their room locked up tight, their heavy footsteps resounded through the hallway. I was back in the concealment of the stairwell, watching their large forms blink out the sliver of light that shone into my hiding place. A single chime, and the gate between them and the elevator slid back. A second *clang*, its echo still lingering in the corridor, and the whine of an elevator's winch hummed lightly, carrying them away.

Beatrice was right next to my breast. I waited. Glanced at my watch again. Another door slammed, and I stepped into the hallway. All was quiet for the time being. The Mariners were either sleeping off what had sounded like a long practice, heading out for a night on the town, or just enjoying the comforts of the Jefferson. My enchanted lock picks were in my hand as I reached Sammy and Joe's room. The silver instruments easily slipped into the keyhole and waited for me to rap the tuning fork so they could get going.

I cocked my wrist back and paused. Against the doorframe might attract attention. I rapped the fork against the heel of my shoe instead, evoking a softer tone than I was used to. That was probably why the picks were working slower than usual.

Still, there was enough sound to make them work. Finally, I heard the catch. The bolt slid back. I looked to either side of me as I slipped the tools back into their wallet and stepped inside.

I'll bet that if Housekeeping worked their daily magic here, Sammy and Joe would have to take a step back and check the number on the door to make sure it was, in fact, theirs. It appeared, though, from the rumpled sheets and the unpleasant tinge in the air, that their room had been left alone by the hotel servants. Whatever clues might be hiding in this mix of dirty dishes, empty glasses, and discarded clothes were going to take a bit longer to find.

The overall smell, aside from the manly odor of locker room, suggested one of the ball players was a smoker. Cigarettes, but not Chesterfields or Lucky Strikes. I took another sniff. No, whatever the smoker was enjoying was of a higher-end tobacco blend. As for an actual brand, there was nothing useful in sight. The butts in the ashtray were keeping their names to themselves. Sammy had to be the human chimney since Joe's voice didn't sound like a smoker's, and he must have taken the pack with him. I took a few more glances around the room, my honker drawing a few deep whiffs. Nothing else of note, save for the pleasant trace scent of expensive tobacco.

Next to the phone, I found a small memo pad from the hotel and a pencil in need of sharpening. The top sheet of the notepad soon rested inside the wallet with my picks. The unkempt condition of the room told me nothing of what Trouble had been up to or what they were planning for tonight. I could deduce with a look at the suitcases, that either Sammy or Joe didn't seem to care if his socks and underwear were folded.

Both suitcases looked pretty worn from their time on the road. One of them appeared more "sentimental" than the other, its scratched and gouged surface decorated with various stickers. The more vivid, vibrant ones I recognized as cities the Mariners had visited this season. I flipped it open and reached inside the suitcase's inner pocket, and felt my stomach tighten as my hand touched some kind of linen. Clothing.

"Do I really want to know?" I asked myself out loud.

Pair of boxers. From the looks of their size, this was Big Joe's suitcase. The boxers, from what I could see and smell, were in need of washing. Strike One.

Sometimes, I just hate this job.

Since my hand was already sullied by the guy's undergarments, fumbling through Big Joe's pants pockets seemed the next logical thing to do. Specifically, I was looking for pants that still had the belt in them. Anything he'd recently worn. He struck me as the type of guy who would shove something in his pocket and then forget about it. Perhaps I might get a piece of the ball and earn myself First Base.

Nothing. Strike Two.

Time to move on to the other suitcase. Maybe I'd find—

My grip tightened on the open case lid as I stared inside it. "Holy shit," I uttered.

Military precision. The slacks, shirts, and even socks and shorts were folded and organized to an impressive grid-like pattern. The suitcase had taken a beating, but the contents looked like they had been pressed several times over, packed, and then pressed again. This was a lovely sight to behold.

It was also a trap waiting to be sprung. Anyone this organized would know right off that someone had gone through his stuff, and that would have ordered all of Trouble into a battle formation of the most defensive kind. I had to give Sledgehammer a lot of credit. For a ball player, he definitely had a lot of organiz—

The key slowly scraped in the lock, and I heard the bolt slide back. I darted for the bathroom, but then stopped short. Why do people come back to their hotel room after leaving? Sometimes, they've forgotten something. Sometimes their plans change and they turn in for an early night. Sometimes it's to answer Nature's most common of calls. Best not to dare the Fates and challenge Option Number Three.

I prayed the curtain was no longer billowing by the time they came into the room. Their footfalls were barely audible against the thick carpet, but I could tell it was getting awfully crowded in here. If two of the people I heard in the room were Sledgehammer and Big Joe, then they had a friend along for the ride. Scooter?

"Come on, Sammy, the cab's going to be here any minute!" a young voice cracked.

Yeah, that's why I get the greenbacks. From the sound of Scooter's voice, adulthood was still a far-off dream to him. He probably hit puberty at the doorstep of every gin joint.

"Hey, kid, how about you can it?" Sledgehammer barked back in reply. "I forgot my lighter."

"That stupid lighter of yours," grumbled Big Joe. "Fucking eyesore."

"Hey, it works, okay? And I like it."

"I don't think that is such a fair deal, though, for what we do," Scooter protested. "I mean, we're doing all the back-breaking and what have we got to show for it?"

"Kid, if you got a problem with how I'm running the show, then maybe you should think about hanging it all up, you know? The game, the lifestyle, the dames…"

"Running the show? You?" I nodded at Scooter's moxie. Unexpected, considering how he came across in my interview with them. "Yeah, tell me another one."

The quiet that fell across the room made my hand tingle, and the only thing that remedied that tingle was the feel of Beatrice. I was moving so slowly that no one would even catch a whisper of fabric against fabric. By the time I felt my girl in my grip, still in her holster, Sledgehammer chimed in.

"What's that all about, Scooter?"

The way Sammy used the nickname made it clear: Ol' Scooter was low in the batting roster with Trouble. Perhaps with Patterson down, that crack about being the "new runt" had hit far too close to home plate.

"Oh, come on, you think a fancy lighter from Europe and a pack of pricey smokes make you the big man in charge? Come off it, Sammy. What happened to Bill was—"

It was Joe who cut him off. "A hard lesson learned on Bill's part."

"Who are you kidding?" Scooter sounded terrified, but out of the bunch of them, he definitely seemed to have the best grasp on how bad this situation was.

"Quit shakin' like some Miss Nancy!" Sammy grumbled. "It's under control."

"That was a warning, Sammy! A warning to all of us!" Riley sounded scared, and in his fear he wasn't going to allow Sledgehammer to rap him on the nose like some disobedient pup. "You don't think it's a little weird Arch is so damn sick all of a sudden? He's scared!"

"You're exaggerating." Sammy's voice sounded unsteady. I could hear him by the bed, and then digging around on the nightstand. I guessed he was resuming his search.

"Am I? Didn't we have a job to pull when we got here? Huh? Has that job been pulled yet?"

"Hey, that wasn't our fault," Joe replied.

"Yeah," Sammy added. "Bad things happen. But everything's going to be jake. Arch gets over this bug, we take care of our business, and we're out. I don't see a problem."

"Is that all you got to say about it?" Scooter fired back.

Sammy paused in his search. "Shut up."

"No, I'm not going to shut up. We've always been open, talking about this ever since he—"

"I mean it, Scooter," Sammy growled. "Shut—up." He paused again, and I followed the sound of his footsteps moving towards...

I'd forgotten to close his suitcase.

My thumb immediately released the safety on Beatrice. She was now out of her holster, and I was just staring at the curtain, listening for anyone's approach.

"Hey, Big Guy."

Joe rapped something against the end table.

"Remember," he said, "you put it inside the drawer of the end table so nobody would mess with it?"

Movement, and then Sammy's voice came from the other side of the room, closer to where I had heard Joe.

"I don't like people messing with my things."

"Yeah-yeah-yeah, so you got your lighter and all the birds will be impressed..." Joe took a breath and then punched out, "...provided they're still around when we get there! Can we go now?"

Sammy was thinking about something, as that quiet had settled over the room again. Couldn't have been more than five ticks, but when you're hiding behind a curtain holding a loaded .45 with the safety off, every second feels like an extra year on you.

"Yeah, let's go." I heard both Joe and Sammy move, but then stop where Scooter's voice had come from. "And don't ever—*don't ever*—think I'm not calling the shots around here, 'cause I am. He's not the only one with connections. You follow?"

"Hey, hey, hey," Big Joe pleaded, "you know what this kid needs, Sammy? I think he could use something to eat. I mean, a really hot dish. How about a blonde?" The laugh that followed made me roll my eyes. Did Big Joe think he was *that* funny? "Get it? Something ta' eat? Blonde? Huh?"

Good thing you're a better ball player than a court jester, pal.

"Come on," Sammy finally replied. "Let's go."

There was a rustling of clothing, the door opening, the sound of bolt and latch closing. Even after the bolt slid shut, my breath was still in my chest. I splayed my fingers along Beatrice, took a strong grip of the curtain, and then yanked it back.

The muzzle pointed forward. I had a clear shot of the door. No one else was about.

Now, I exhaled. Twice in one night? The Fates were really watching over me.

I took a glance at my watch. 6:44. Time to make my appointment with Flyball.

The sun had just about set, maybe not across the horizon but definitely behind the Chicago skyline. A dull purple-blue hue surrounded me as I returned to the alleyway that served as the Jefferson's Servants' Entrance. On my descent from the sixth floor, I stuck to shadows and kept an ear out for any other footfalls above or below me. There was less activity now than before, and since people would actually be taking the time to pay attention to their surroundings, there would be far too many prime opportunities to spot a Dwarf. By the time I reached the loading docks, I had less than half an hour to scout around the meeting place to see if there was anything I needed to worry about.

Oh, there was plenty.

The delivery trucks had left behind a few towers of crates. Those temporary fixtures, along with garbage cans in desperate need of dumping, screamed out to me as prime ambush points. This setting didn't make me feel all warm and cozy about the upcoming chat Flyball and I were going to share; and considering the doubleback anxiety I'd had after his call, I didn't want to take any chances.

One tower of crates was empties from the kitchen, and would probably get picked up again by the grocers for refilling, if not by passers-by in need of cheap furniture. I myself could easily tip one back. As they were all stacked bottom-side up, this would be a great place to stash a boom dagger and have it on call when a Dwarf detective wouldn't be looking. Some of the other crates were still full. Those were fairly heavy and hard to move. Not as easily worked as these empties. So, behind the trash cans and full crates for surprise. Inside the empties for concealed weapons.

Beatrice was in my grip once more, and my trigger finger tingled lightly. I had owned battle axes and the odd mace or two that insisted on getting in some quality time on an opponent's skull if they were brought out to play. Beatrice was no different. She didn't like being out of her holster unless it was a serious situation that needed her undivided attention. I had loaded her up before coming here, so she knew I was expecting trouble. Now, it was her second time out—with the safety off, mind you—and I was alone.

No, I didn't presume to think the gun was charmed in any way; but Beatrice does have a personality about her. She was getting antsy.

The surrounding windows were dark, save one. A lookout could be up there, keeping a watchful eye over the alleyway, but it would be a real hassle getting word to Flyball without me catching it. The one lit window revealed nothing more than an empty room. Probably someone left a light on by accident.

With a tug at my tie, I checked the time. 7:32. Not enough time to run off, grab a cup of java, and get back before meeting time. Plenty of time, though, to holster my weapon, find a quiet place to lean, and enjoy a good bowl's worth of weed.

Pinching the pipe's bit in between my teeth, I packed what would do for a quick yet leisurely smoke. Through the scent of my freshly-lit match, however, came a coppery whiff I knew far too well. So much for enjoying a "leisurely" smoke. My hand remained over the flame, but while I prepared to light the tobacco, I shifted my eyes upward from the pipe's bowl.

Lights were flickering on from the street as that purple-blue of sunset was replaced by the dark inkiness of night. I was thankful to the Fates for the man-made illumination; because of it, there were few corners of the city that knew true, total darkness. The light around me and from the street was enough to reveal a silhouette standing in the open alleyway.

Cocky son of a *traulssa*. Didn't even bother to find a hiding place.

I fired up the bowl and started puffing. The plan was to create enough of a mask that Mr. Boulder Balls over there wouldn't notice me reaching for Beatrice.

I blinked as my mass of tobacco smoke shifted, and then returned to lazily hover in front of me. Peering through the wisps, I could see that the lone figure was gone.

He might have been gone, but I sure wasn't alone.

Beatrice was back in hand, and this time I wasn't sheathing her without loosing a round or two. Something then struck my wrist, moving too quick for me to catch more than a blur. The speed of the attack relieved me of my gun, and sent my arm bending in an unnatural direction. The shock wasn't enough to break bone, but it was enough to sting from shoulder to fingertip.

I also felt my balance give way. Instead of holding up the Jefferson with my back, I was now in the middle of the loading dock. Didn't matter if it was the Shri-Mela Plains in the heart of a battle or a loading dock in downtown Chicago, being out in the open was never a good place to be.

Before I could move to a better vantage point (which would have been *anywhere*, right now!), something slammed into my gut. Hard. Hard enough to relocate a few organs. I felt a sensation of weightlessness; nothing under or around me, but still I felt myself moving.

When this (literal) gut-wrenching trip ended, it wasn't going to be nice.

My upper back and shoulders took most of the hit. I crashed though a couple of empty crates, the wood splintering around me as I fell to the pavement. The impact knocked my innards back into place, but also knocked the wind out of me. I went to take a breath, and I seized up immediately. I had a severely bruised rib…if I was lucky. Easier now, I took a deep breath. It came out as a series of quick puffs.

Now would be a good time to get up.

I felt a stinging sensation around my neck, and then I was up in the air again like some damned winged unicorn. This time, it was into the trashcans. I was now working against a bruised—probably broken—rib, a necktie that reduced my collar by about two inches, and an oppressive smell of what had to be the garbage awaiting pick-up. This whole lack of quality air was not helping me in a fight I was losing, and losing with a lot of style. Then again, when your opponent is stacking the deck with dark magic, all your hands are going to suck.

My head wobbled upright and then turned sharply to the left. A moment later, another blow jerked it to the right. This guy was now slapping me, as if I was his own little tavern wench bought and paid for, to answer to his whims. His slaps might as well have been full-out right crosses; with how fast he was moving, I was feeling each blow down to the core.

Now I know how you felt, Kev, I thought through a haze of memory and consciousness.

My shoulder stung from hitting the alleyway, but my Gryfennosian pride kicked in and I refused to fall flat on my face. I worked my other arm, throbbing shoulder and all, underneath me and pushed myself up to my knees.

Yeah, to my knees. It was progress. Humiliating and degrading, sure, but it was progress.

I couldn't think of a clever way to get my ass out of this campfire—I was too busy trying to stay awake. The thought of bluffing my unseen opponent came to mind: Feign passing out, and let him think I was ready for a meat wagon. It sounded like a good plan for about five long seconds, but I really didn't like the idea of turning the light out for myself when some*thing* was using me as its personal punching bag.

What were my alternatives? *Come on, Billi,* I chided. (Even my thoughts were slurring at this point. Yeah, this was definitely a bad situation…) *What can you use, right now, against the dark magic kicking your ass from Al's South Side to Bugs' North?*

The flash made me bring my hand up to shield my face. At first, I thought the light was coming from headlights. Very big headlights. Then I wondered if I had been hit so hard that I felt no pain, or that maybe I wouldn't feel the pain until later. Or if this light was in fact the Great Crossroads, and I was on my way to those Everlasting Fields I'm always blabbering about. Considering those wench whacks, a full out punch would probably have knocked me right into the afterlife.

It hurt to blink. My face was swelling up. Still, I tried to grasp onto some semblance of awareness and reason. The light was white. Pure white. Pure white, touched at some point with…

This was magic. Someone was casting a charm. A protection spell.

My body swayed for a bit, and then I was back down, kissing the pavement. *Cast a protection spell, Billi,* I thought. *Good thinking.*

CHAPTER TWELVE

DETECTIVE, HEAL THYSELF

"I would tell you to stay in bed," the old man grumbled, "but we both know you won't listen."

"This time, Doc," I slurred through a swollen cheek and slightly puffy lips, "I actually might."

Okay, that hurt.

I tried to readjust myself against the pillows. That hurt. I looked back up to Dr. Roberts. *That* hurt. Miranda's hiss, followed by her grumble, reached my ears. And as you probably know the words by now, sing along. Yeah, it hurt.

"So if this is how you look, how did the street gang fare?"

Old Doc Roberts might come across more like a pain-in-the-ass than an experienced healer, but he really did know his medicine. When it came to patching people up, tending to battle wounds, and making sure that when you were on the mend, you mended proper, Dr. Ned Roberts didn't practice anything. He knew what he was doing. He was a true master of the healing arts. While our first meeting had been a visit of convenience (as Doc Roberts' office was across from my own), he had become the only guy I trusted to keep me going after the more perilous nights in a detective's life.

Last night had been one of those nights.

When I came to, I was in my bed. That was kind of nice, considering how uncomfortable the alley had been. I knew I had hit that asphalt hard. Now that I looked back on things, I had hit that asphalt repeatedly, bouncing across the pavement like a child's play-ball. My bed was a really nice follow-up to all that unpleasantness.

But the big question was how the hell I'd gotten from the Jefferson to my flop.

This was immediately followed by another question: How long had I been out? I could tell by how the room was lit that the sun was up and had been for a while, and I'd missed most—if not all—of the morning.

"I've set myself up on the couch, Billi," Miranda said. "If you need anything…"

"I do need something, sweetie, but it's back at the office." I took a deep breath, hoping that was going to ease up some of the pressure. Not even close. "Think you could go and get it for me?"

Miranda tipped her head to one side, that silent warning I knew oh so well.

"I swear, my ears are free of the dungeon muck. I'm not going anywhere, but I might as well preoccupy myself with some light reading."

"Billi," Miranda huffed, unwrapping a piece of Wrigley's and popping it in her mouth. The ferocity of her chewing reminded me of a pack of sabertooths enjoying an inept hunting party as fine cuisine. Yeah, she was upset, and she was going to let me know exactly how upset she was.

"If he's not going to listen to you, Miss Tanner, I can just give him something that will put him out of his misery faster," grumbled Doc Roberts.

"Reading." I screwed my eyes shut, groaning a bit as I shifted in my bed. "I just want to have something to read, something productive. I know I'm not going anywhere today."

"You might want to consider canceling your plans for tomorrow, as well. Since your organs are—well, they're not where they're supposed to be to begin with, I don't know what kind of internal bleeding you may have." He started packing his bag, thank the Fates. Didn't mean he went quiet, though. "I know you've got a few bruised ribs. Doesn't matter where your kidneys or liver are, those ribs need to heal."

"I would not presume to debate you on that, Doc," I agreed, giving a slight groan as I finally came to a stop among the mountain of pillows Miranda had built behind me. "But if I'm staying put, I should have something to entertain myself. My eyes aren't bruised or busted up, so I can read, yes?"

"I'm not moving in or anything," she blurted out, "but I *will* make sure you rest up during office hours."

I look at them both, and asked "Why does everyone think—"

"The Tennison Case," they both shot.

"Oh, come on," I retorted, my memory coming down on me like a sudden avalanche along Rancorsia's western face. "The Tennison Case was a pretty big deal."

"That muscle the perp hired was a pretty big deal, too," Miranda snapped. The pop of her gum made Doc Roberts jump. "He may not have done the number on you I'm looking at now…"

"Miranda, this case is different."

"Really?" she huffed. "How different?"

I glanced at Doc Roberts, and then narrowed my eyes (Ouch!) on the one woman in Chicago who knew everything about me and where I truly hailed from. Might as well let her know now where this case with the Cubs was headed. "*Very* different."

Miranda's gum popping stopped.

Doc Roberts closed up the bag and looked at me for a moment, snorted, and then turned to Miranda. "Make sure he takes it easy."

The bag was in his hand, clattering loudly as he removed it from my bedside table. A few moments later, his footfalls were echoing in the stairwell of my building, but Miranda just looked at me in silence.

She sat down on the couch, and softly popped her Wrigley's for a moment. Finally, she asked, "This has to do with you and your…past?"

"Miranda…"

"First, the weird phone call telling us where to find you. Then we get there, and Jer finds you still got Beatrice in the holster, fully loaded." She was now on her feet, pacing. "I shoulda known…I shoulda known…"

"Miranda…"

"I mean, why would someone attack you and then drive you to your office and leave you on the couch, huh? Yeah, just a little peculiar, don't you thi—"

"Mindy!"

That snapped her out of the tirade. From the look on her face it seemed only one person had permission to call her by that name.

"I need to take a look at a book I've got stashed in my office. It's behind the bookcase."

"What does it look like?"

It hurt to smile, but I did anyway. "It's the biggest one in that nook, and when you see it, you'll understand why I hide it." I thought about *My World Book* being out in the open, and added, "Carry it under your arm, and walk inside the sidewalk. Make sure the cover is facing into your body."

"Sure, Billi."

I was pretty certain that gum was still sitting in her mouth, inert.

"Look, Miranda, you wanted to know, so now you know."

She nodded, and then suddenly became aware of the wad of gum in her mouth. Miranda spit out the small, gray mass and tossed it into a waste bin.

Another slow wave of pain swept over me, but I knew it wasn't from trying to get comfortable. This was stress triggering a few bruised muscles. Nothing I could say would have helped. After the financial bubble burst, we hadn't found many opportunities to talk about Billibub Baddings, Captain of the Stormin' Scrappies. We hadn't talked about magic, the Nine Talismans, Black Orcs, Portals of Oblivion, or anything outside of the confines of this familiar world since that day in Grant Park. We had been focused on staying in business.

I had also figured she had never brought it up again because she really wasn't curious about it, but now I could see how far off the mark that guess had been. Miranda was not a Cleric Clapper, but that didn't mean she didn't go to church on Sundays. While she's got the kind of rack an inquisitor could appreciate, she didn't wear that crucifix of hers simply for looks. It meant something. Magic, and me just breathing her air, didn't challenge or test it, but it sure did bring up a few questions that neither volume of her Good Book covered in detail. She knew the truth about me now, and that was fine; but this was a case that forced her to really come to grips with that truth.

Truth, no matter where it comes from, carries with it a kind of responsibility. Miranda could handle that responsibility. Didn't mean it was easy for her to face.

"Is there any special latch that I need to worry about?"

"Nah, it should just open up if you pull hard enough, and you shouldn't have to pull that hard."

She took a deep breath. "Okay, I'll be right back."

"Thanks, Miranda," I said.

My girl didn't reply, nor did she look at me. She just picked up her purse, looked around my flop for a moment, and then headed out. I never wanted to complicate things for her. Miranda was a good girl. No, scratch that. She's a kind soul. One of the best apples I've known in either realm, and loyal to a fault. That's something I really appreciated about her, and now I couldn't help but worry that I was somehow taking advantage of that.

I was still staring at the door, my breathing the only sound in the room. Parts of my skin tingled, and not in a good way. Another twinge of pain. And then, completely unexpectedly, I saw in my mind's eye the light that consumed the loading dock of the Jefferson.

Fucking magic. It had saved my ass, and now it was putting my relationship with Miranda under a serious strain.

Thank you so much, Miranda, I thought as my eyelids began to close. *For everything.*

When I finally woke up, I saw Miranda curled up on the couch, with the remains of a day falling on her and a finished dinner special from Mick's. I had slept the entire day away. That meant I was probably going to be up all night. At least it wouldn't be too long of a night, provided Miranda had done what I asked her and…

I noticed that the lamp next to my bed was on. I took a deep breath and looked over the side, and there it stood on its spine. There was a slight twinge of pain when I smiled, but I didn't mind so much. Why, oh why, do I ever doubt my girl Miranda? Maybe it had been that cold stare that had penetrated through my deep sleep. She wanted me to rest up. Casework, in her mind, wasn't really rest. Delivering *My World Book* bedside was just contributing to the delinquency of a Dwarf.

Now, the hard part.

The act of reaching down shot pain along my left side, and then worked up my arm, threatening my hold on *My World Book*. My groaning remained at a soft rumble, but from the cold sweat that had broken out just from reaching down to heft the book off the floor and slide it across my lap, I knew I wasn't going anywhere anytime soon. I promised myself that the next time I ran into Trouble, I would make life extremely miserable for them. For all of them. I had really thought "Flyball" was going to be my guy on the inside, and then the whole thing wound up being an elaborate shut-out.

The book remained closed after the Herculean effort of getting it into bed with me. I really wasn't caressing its leather skin for any particular reason, just feeling the comforting sensation against my fingertips. Once more, my mind wandered back to the alleyway. I knew by the warmth, the scent (of course), and particular brightness of the light that my rescue had come from some kind of magic.

What was bristling my beard so much, though, was that I hadn't thrown the charm.

My fingertips paused between the cracks in the worn cover, the word *Chronicles* visible through parted digits in a language only I understood.

I never had figured out that locked drawer in the Assistant D.A.'s office. I did remember the spell, though, and a damn fine charm that was. Low enough level to be dismissed by most as just a particularly tough lock to pick, but a big enough dagger-in-the-side to make enchanted picks work hard for the treasure.

The charm that saved me in the alley, though, had been something else. It couldn't be mistaken for anything other than magic. That pitch had been out in the open, and the events at the Jefferson would have been a real problem for anyone not familiar with sorcery to explain away. I noodled through what might have led someone to throw such a spell. First, I was a Dwarf in Chicago, and I wasn't acting like a complete and total chump. No screams for God, no scurrying into the shadows in a panic, or the like. Hell, I had actually tried to fight back. It would have been clear that I was familiar with magic, and knew that magic was kicking my ass. Then there had been the unseen assailant using me like a party favor at some after-slaying bonfire. (Club the straw dragon hard enough, kiddies, and the sweets will pour out of his belly!) The offending party had obviously been using magic. That alleyway had been brewing over with alternative culture like a seer's cauldron left over the flame too long.

A locking charm in a Chicago courthouse, and now a protection spell at the Jefferson Hotel. Who was this third party casting these spells?

Thrum-thrum-thrum, my fingers drummed against My *World Book's* cover. Maybe an afternoon or two of watching the crowds heading in and out of the courthouse was in order. Teleportation portals were tricky to pull off and a lot higher in the realm of difficulty, so I was going to make an educated guess that this drawer-locker and protection-passer—whoever he was—was still using conventional methods like the L and good old fashioned sole-and-heel to get around Chicago. The book cracked lightly as it opened. I took a moment to remember where I had my pudgy nose buried in it last, back when I was tracking the Sword of Arannahs. Finding those familiar, overly-flowery Dwarven runes took me back to my old life, back to that life in Acryonis that I'd not given a lot of thought about until Julia Lesinger had hired me under false pretenses.

Yeah, she played me finer than a bard's mandolin, but it wasn't all bad. I had some fun before things turned black.

The grin melted off my face when my eyes fell on the script. Apparently, this portion of text had been handed over to one of the Elvish scribes. Lovely. This was not going to be the piece of pudding that I thought it would be. Maybe Miranda was right. I needed rest, and trying to work through Elvish was going to be anything but restful. I would probably be able to pull the basics of their grammar out of my backside, but as far as making sense of it, I might as well have been trying to solve the Riddles of Archeledya.

"Hey, Billi," came a groggy voice from the couch. I was so engrossed in the book across my lap that I hadn't noticed Miranda stirring. She was now sitting up, running fingers through her long, curly hair, taking deep breaths to clear her head. She blinked. "What time is it?"

I looked over to the clock. I must have been getting better, since I could turn my head to one side and not feel an invisible mace aerating my skull. "It's eight o'clock, sweetie." The slur in my voice reminded me that I was still not in the best of shape. "How about you get yourself home?"

"Nice try, Billi," she scoffed. "I'm going to make sure you stay in bed. Doc Roberts gave me the directions on what you should be taking and how much of it to mix in your food. You hungry?"

My stomach spoke for me. I returned my eyes to Miranda, who was already on her feet.

"I'm going to take that as a 'yes', and it just so happens I've got Mick's special in the icebox. I'll heat it up on the stove and get something in that stomach of yours."

True Guardians, Mick and Miranda, I thought as I listened to the clicking of the stove and the crumpling of paper bags. With the clatter of utensils and pots, the rumblings in my belly chimed in with their anticipation of the heated up lunch (or was it dinner?). This was definitely out of character for my girl, but so was me looking and feeling like a wad of chew-leaf ground into the sole of a combat boot. *Don't get used to this royal life,* chided that little voice inside my head.

So, back to *My World Book...*

The headache growing in my noggin started to subside as I concentrated on the Elvish script. Maybe it was just a trade-off of one headache for another. The words, grammar, and conjugations of this overly-complex language were finally starting to fall into place by the time the chili was heading my way.

Talk about lousy timing—either enjoy the realm's greatest chili, or save the world from a talisman of dark magic. Decisions, decisions...

Another protest from my stomach sealed the deal. The world could wait while I tried to eat. If anything would motivate me through the pain, it would be Mick's Chili of Supreme Healing.

More proof that the rest I'd gotten between Doc's visit and this warmed-up meal was already helping. Opening my mouth didn't hurt as much as it had before, and I could chew without too much pain. Miranda finally started breathing again when my spoon struck the side of the bowl. I wasn't sure what Doc Roberts told her, but I've...

Have I been worse? Maybe I've been in worse situations, but this kind of a beating was hard to call. That friendly protection charm, I won't argue, could not have happened at a better time. Another few slugs from whoever was clobbering me would have done me in.

With the empty bowl heading for the sink, I returned to *My World Book*. It was a line of script using the words "speed" and "strength" that had caught my attention, and now I needed to crack the rest of the passage. A headache was lingering in the back of my skull, but it was hardly an issue by the time I had the stanza figured out.

Lo, for 'twas upon the twilight of the Solstice that the Pendant of Coe was cast. While modest in its fashion, yet still bestowing reverence to the Nine, the Pendant of Coe grants unto those who wear it a strength and agility (Okay, so I thought "speed" and I was wrong. I told you my Elvish was a bit rough around the edges!) *beyond that of those not born of The Touched.*

The Touched. Yikes, did that bring up some bad memories and a few old grudges.

Elves called themselves Children of The Touched. Being born of The Touched meant that you were born of Elven blood. *Pure* blood. It also meant that you possessed spellcasting abilities. For the longest time, the Elves thought they were the only ones who could possess and control such power.

Yeah, you could say they carried a bit of the hinktyass air about them.

Then it was discovered that a few of the Dwarves, Humans, and even some among the not-so-cordial races were also born with spellcasting abilities. Suddenly, the Elves had some explaining to do to themselves. After all, *they* were The Touched. Granted, the entire Elven race was born with magic in them, while among the other races, it was only a select few. Elves took a few generations to reconcile this, and finally they settled on calling these rare spellcasters in other races The Beloved of the First.

Cute, but it was going to come back to bite them in their perfectly-formed asses.

These "Beloved" were invited to study at Elven academies, a gesture of respect and reverence. It seemed at first like a really nice mixing of cultures, but soon enough it was more than just the cultures that were mixing.

In pleasant company, Elves referred to these impure offspring as Outcast of The First. Between themselves, they came up with the slur "Crossblood".

Nice. Especially when The Touched discovered that quite a few Crossbloods possessed some seriously powerful magic.

Touché.

The Pendant of Coe knows no boundaries to what it blesses upon its bearer, so long as the desire is strong and no doubt lingers within. So shall the brothers and sisters within the bearer's reach—physical and spiritual—also rejoice in its power. It can, provided the confidence is true, also conceal those who possess it from adversaries. How'ere, those of The Touched shall see through the veil to the bearer's own nature true.

Speed and strength. Completely limitless. Not only to the wearer, but to those around them. And if the wearer was particularly savvy with the Pendant of Coe, he could disguise himself from the world.

Could the Pendant of Coe be the lucky charm for the Baltimore Mariners? It was high-level magic, not raw talent, that kept them in the Sports headlines. That much was a given.

The Pendant of Coe could also be what was keeping Trouble living high on the hog.

"Kid, if you got a problem with how I'm running the show, then maybe you should think about hanging it all up, you know? The game, the lifestyle, the dames..."

"Running the show? You? Yeah, tell me another one."

Scooter's unexpected display of balls made me smile again. I heard in his voice that same mantra the *blákora* (Dwarven word for greenhorns) would mutter for a full day before a charge. Work up that courage, and then let it fly at the call of the horn.

I was still nowhere closer to figuring out who was sponsoring the little outings by this troublesome quint—excuse me, *quartet*. That murder was a real question mark, too.

"What happened to Bill was—"

"A hard lesson learned on Bill's part."

"That was a warning! A warning to all of us!"

A warning? Or maybe a reminder of who was in charge? The headlines were showing a sudden shift from bank jobs—which, in this day and age, were truly a hit or miss—to high profile heists. Museums. Galleries. Jewelry stores. And the latter weren't random hits. Trouble, it seemed, were after particular items.

I grunted as I shifted in bed again. The chili had hit the spot, and my body was starting to settle in for the night, but I didn't want to go to sleep just yet.

"And don't ever—don't ever—think I'm not calling the shots around here, 'cause I am. He's not the only one with connections. You follow?"

Sammy had connections, did he? Connections big enough and tough enough that he had some sway over a killer, a killer not in the least bit disturbed over shaking up the sure thing that Trouble and the Baltimore Mariners were delivering. Whatever these dinks were into, possession of that pendant would make them unstoppable.

The Pendant of Coe knows no boundaries to what it blesses upon its bearer, so long as the desire is strong and no doubt lingers within.

Unstoppable.

Someone else *was* calling the shots. In fact, I was starting to see a web rivaling a Hurrenheim mountain spider's in artistry. Sure, Sammy was the lead Ogre, but Sammy didn't strike me as a purveyor of fine art. The silent party that they'd been speaking of, would be someone who understood art, or at least understood it well enough to know which pieces were valuable. This unseen partner would also be someone who understood criminals, or at least understood them well enough to be able to handle crooks like Sammy, Joe and Scooter. Then there was the control over these crimes. One score per city. No crime sprees or anything like that. Just the one big job, and then onward to the next stop on the game schedule. With that much power to tap into, why not enjoy it for everything it was worth? Why stop at one job?

Fighting the sleep was starting to hurt now, and I think Miranda could see it on my face.

"That's enough, Billi," she gently chided, removing My *World Book* from my lap.

I had forgotten she was there. The radio was playing, a single light was on by the couch, and the marker I had noticed earlier tucked in between her book's pages now rested on top of its closed cover.

"So, you finished it, huh?" I smiled, lifting my chin up ever so slightly. "Told you he was good."

"A role model for you, obviously," she scoffed while adjusting the pillows. "I'll be on the couch if you need anything. Okay, boss?"

"Miranda, you don't have t—"

"Yeah, I do," she said. "I have to because it's the right thing to do. So, get some sleep. This case isn't going away tomorrow. It'll be here when you wake up."

The Baltimore Mariners had one more game at Wrigley, postponed for now; but that sand was quickly filling the bottom chamber of the hourglass. Once the game was done, it was back on the road for the team. I was heading into the bottom of the eighth. I needed to get my pitching under control, or Trouble would send my next pitch out of the park.

And me along with it.

CHAPTER THIRTEEN

Dream a Little Dream

There's not a lot of difference between the perfect swing of a bat and the perfect strike of an axe. Slicing through armor can, if your swing is off, send you a pretty nasty shock. If the head of the weapon comes in at just the right angle, the impact is distributed evenly and you feel nothing. The poor sap on the other end, though, feels quite a bit. At least, for a moment.

A good hit against a fastball is the same thing, too. The crack of the bat sounds like the snap of a whip. You might feel the slightest tingle in the grip, but the sensation doesn't jar you. It's a bit like jumping into a lake early in the morning. You're invigorated. Reborn. Alive.

Then there are other kinds of base hits when you catch the "sour" spot of a Louisville Slugger. Folks love talking about the sweet spots of a bat, but rarely do you hear people talk about the sour ones. Those are the points where the ball connects and deals a bit of payback by sending a shock through the wood, the kind of shock that stays with you as you're hustling to First Base. No matter how tightly you ball your fists, the tremor is still in your hands, under your skin. Your legs are fine and all, but that shock can tap you somehow.

There's the real mastery in swinging an axe, just like swinging a bat: avoid the bad angles and you avoid the sour spots.

That was the real joy of brandishing an *enchanted* battle axe. There was no sour spot, no bad angle. The axe head just kept on cutting down opponents like the sharpened scythe of Old Man Death. Conventional battle axes were better against leather armor, but to go through anything metal required a solid swing and a lot of power behind it. Cast an enchantment, and the only way to avoid that blade was to not be in its path.

At least, that was the way it was supposed to be. Magic had a lot of rules around it, and things were just supposed to work without fuss provided you followed said rules. I was finding out that even if you followed the laws of sorcery to the final character of the spell, those rules had rules, too. It was one of those conditions that wizards and mages would tell you about just as the dragon shit was striking the chandelier. "*Oh yes, the blade will never need sharpening, but there will be those times when a spell corrupts itself. And that can happen at any time.*" Are there any warning signs to this sudden corruption? "*Sadly, no. It's just something that happens.*"

And people in my world wondered why I didn't trust magic.

In this battle, that whole "corrupt spell" kept crossing my mind as I cut through armor of all types. By the tenth kill, my hands were in some serious pain. I wish I could say they were numb from all the shock coming through the axe grip. No such luck. The shock was creeping up my forearms, and if it reached my shoulders I was going to be in a lot more than just severe discomfort. Still, when you and your boys are facing off with a line of Goblins, you have to fight through the pain. Otherwise, the Goblins will fight through you. Pretty strong motivator, if you ask me.

My teeth clenched so hard that I swore they were on the verge of shattering in my mouth like a fragile vase dropped from waist height. The shock was past my elbows now, the pain working under my skin and around my muscles with unseen tendrils that continued to contract. It was getting harder and harder to breathe. *Just keep swinging,* I thought as I knocked two more Goblins back. *Keep swinging!*

The pox-marked, wart-decorated face of the enemy rose up in front of me, screaming its fool head off. Like that was supposed to intimidate me or something? My axe came around and connected hard with the vermin's gut. If the enchantment had been working properly, it should have cut him in half. It did lift him off the ground, sure; and the blow got him out of my way.

What made no sense to me was how this Goblin was getting up.

Before I could see how it was keeping its entrails inside its body, I heard another one creeping up on my left. I delivered what should have been an effortless backhand, but that tingle of pain crept higher up my bicep. The Goblin fell, but his damn head was still attached.

Okay, now I was in trouble.

I twirled the bat in my hands and stepped—

Wait a minute. Why the hell was there a Louisville Slugger in my hands? This was the Battle of Shri-Mela Plains, and I was defending the home turf against a Goblin horde.

I heard the crunching of bone against bone, sickening snaps that were accompanied by the gurgling of blood and saliva as the Goblin I'd just clocked brought his lower jaw back into place.

"You haven't figured it out yet, Billi?" it asked me.

The bat, now apparently my only weapon in this fight, came up over my head.

Then the other Goblin held its mitts up, his armor not even sporting a dent from my earlier strike.

"Billi, look at what you're wearing," this one said with an incredulous shrug.

Armed or not, looking down at what you're wearing when you've got two Goblins within reach of you is pretty high on the "So Stupid You Should Die" List; and I'm an advocate for cleansing the particularly thick from the Waters of Life. There was something in the vermin's eyes, though—black as they may have been—that told me they weren't really going to take me down or even impolitely nudge me off my feet.

With instincts screaming against it, I looked down.

I should have looked up. I should have looked around me and asked why. I should have done something more than just stare at my uniform like a complete and utter mook. Even upside-down I knew that stylized "C" right away. The pinstripes stood out in sharp contrast to the stark white of the jersey and breeches. Sunlight breaking through the cloud cover above us struck the cleats laced snug around my feet, and even with the blood and grime all around me, the shoes were spotless.

The sunlight grew brighter, and brighter still, so bright that it managed to glare off the reflective surfaces of mud and murky rain puddles. I squinted for a moment, but a quick adjustment of my cap remedied the glare.

When my head came up, Shri-Mela was gone. Instead of metal against metal, I heard the quick *snap* of canvas against soft leather, the soft *crack* of bats sending out pop flies, and the occasional sounds of ball players shouting out encouragement or taunts to one another. Littering the outfield were dead Humans in thick furs, Goblins struggling to breathe with arrows protruding from their chests, and my own kinsmen limping off towards the visiting team's dugout.

I finally remembered the two Goblins and returned my attention to them. They were dressed as Baltimore Mariners.

The one with the loose jaw snorted. "Goddamn, Billi, you really must have been taken to the cleaners. You're hallucinating."

My bat started for it, but I stopped in mid-swing when the Goblin flinched.

"Some hallucination," I huffed. "You're not real, and you're flinching at an imaginary baseball bat."

"I know this may seem a little weird," the second Goblin said, his ungloved hand reaching down to scratch his balls. (I didn't know what was weirder—this whole dream, or the fact that this Goblin didn't know that Goblins didn't *have* balls!) "We're here to let you know, you should consider taking it slow. Rest up a bit, pal. Give yourself time to heal."

Now it was my turn to snort. "Really? Why, by the Fates, would my brain summon a pair of Goblins to one of my dreams and give me the advice to slow down? *Goblins?*"

They looked at one another, and knew I had them on that point.

Ballscratcher's brows cocked upward. "Okay, Sigmund, you tell us why we're here and what this dream's all about."

"Yeah," huffed the other one. He was wearing a glove on his right hand. A left-handed Goblin? Eh, it's a dream. "Are you taking a figurative or a literal interpretation here?"

My lips pursed together as I watched an Orc warm up in the bullpen. His pitch knocked the glove back into the catcher's chest, lifted said catcher off the ground, and propelled the poor dink through the wood barrier behind him. The Orc winced, looked at McCarthy, and mouthed with a shrug, "*Sorry.*"

"You know what all this is telling me, boys?" I asked after taking a good look around. "It's telling me that I'm noodling the case through, even as I sleep; and with what's around me I'm beginning to figure out a few things. For one thing, no one here—either from Acryonis or from Chicago—is wearing the Pendant of Coe. Otherwise, this dream would be less of a surreal look at how I'm putting things together and more like a replay of what happened behind the Jefferson."

"And how about the Jefferson?" asked Southpaw. "You still think Flyball's doublebacked on you?"

My mouth opened to give the affirmative, but then I paused. "He's high up on the list, sure, but I'm uncertain on the whys behind it. The kid wants out of this bad deal he's got himself into. I'm sure of that."

"Why?" countered Ballscratcher.

"He risked a call from the ballpark. I'm not thinking Archie's that good of an actor nor that cool a customer. If pressed, he'd probably fold, but he took a chance and called me the moment he was out of Trouble's ear-shot."

"Not bad, Billi," Southpaw nodded.

"Doesn't mean he's off the hook, though. If it wasn't Flyball, who was it?" I looked around Wrigley. The pitcher was also absent. "I'm also thinking that I'm not ready to stand toe-to-toe with Sledgehammer or Big Joe, but I'm good enough to make one last ballgame. If I catch that game, I just might figure out who's calling the shots, or at least who's got the Pendant. How's that?"

Snap-snap-snap-snap...

It was a purposeful, simple rhythm, coming from far behind me. One by one, everyone—Dwarves in battle armor, Humans both brandishing swords and Sluggers, and creatures and critters of all races—stopped where they were and looked in the direction of the sound.

I tipped my ball cap back, tilting my head toward the sound. *Snap-snap-snap-snap...*

No, it wasn't slapping. It was clapping. A pair of hands, clapping together in slow, mocking applause.

Clap-clap-clap-clap...

I removed my hat and turned to face the only spectator in the seats of Wrigley Field.

From between pudgy lips a stogie smoldered, light puffs drifting skyward as he nodded his head. I could tell by his smile and the way the flesh undulated around the layers of fat at his neck that he was laughing. He wasn't laughing at me, but he appeared to enjoy my dream-noodling. His hands continued their exaggerated clapping for a few moments, and finally stopped. The cigar came out of his mouth, as the other hand waved a beefy finger at me.

I noticed something stuck in between his pinky and his ring finger. What the hell was that?

"You...*yoooooooouuuu...*" Capone said, nodding slowly. "*Very* good, you. You never stop impressin' me, ya Brownie you."

Even in my dreams, Capone was going to make with the jokes on my height?! Unbelievable.

I caught another glance at what was stuck between his fingers, and that was when I remembered...

"Wait a minute! I do have a—"

A female voice calling my name compelled me to turn around, and the sun blinded me once again. I couldn't figure out where it was coming from. I thought it was at least noon, but for a moment everyone was gone. Turning my back on Capone felt about as safe as turning my back on the Goblins, but this was a dream—*my* dream—so I doubted if I was going to be facing any of those terrors you'd find in a Poe short story. No pits. No pendulums. Just Goblins playing for the visiting team.

The brilliance began to subside, and when I moved to block the sun with my hand, I felt the pain in my side. I gave a little growl and then sank back into the pillows behind my head.

"Billi! Calm down and lie still!" the female voice said. A blurry figure was standing over me. Blurry, but I could see hands resting on hips. "That'll show you for trying to move before you should."

Yeah. That'll show me. Thanks, Miranda.

With the sounds of a ballpark replaced by the sound of blinds being adjusted and the chiding from my secretary, I deduced that I was back in the Realm of the Waking. Now *that* was what I called a deep sleep.

Thank the Fates for vivid dreams that served as handy reminders. "Miranda, honey, do your boss a quick favor. Would you get me a plate and a pencil?"

"Hungry for a snack?" she quipped.

Sleeping on my couch was making her a bit grouchy. "Considering how you sound ready to gnaw through a sleeve of chain mail, I'd be afraid to ask for you to cook anything up for me. Hemlock isn't my favorite seasoning."

She gave a slight snort, shaking her head as she started putting together a pot of coffee. It's a good thing I hadn't covered up the word "coffee" with the Elvish labels I'd created in order to stay sharp in the lingo. "Looking at these labels now and knowing what I know, those odd quips of yours are finally making sense. Sometime though, you'll have to tell me a few stories about what you did in that place…what was it called again?"

"Acryonis," I said. "Sounds like Annapolis, only gives the tongue a bit more of a workout."

The percolator rumbled to life just as the plate and pencil reached me. "You're a doll. Now, in my wallet in the left jacket pocket, there's going to be a sheet of paper. It'll be a blank sheet from a Jefferson Hotel memo pad. Give me that, and then all I'll need is the java you're cooking in the cauldron."

Miranda crossed the room, "Seriously, boss, how are you feeling?" she asked over her shoulder.

"Well, when Doc Roberts was here, I was feeling like I had just gone fisticuffs with an Ogre."

"Uh-huh," she replied, reaching into my coat pocket. "Seeing as we don't have many Ogres in Leonard, Missouri, how about—"

"Remember the lummox you dated that first month you were working for me?"

"Who? Oh yeah…" From the look on her face as she handed me the paper, you would have thought she was sucking on a lemon. "Trevor the Caveman."

"Yeah, okay…about three Trevors are equal to one Ogre."

Her eyebrows raised slightly. "Billi, Trevor was a *big* man."

"Exactly." I groaned a bit as I shifted in the bed, then added, "Well, today I'm feeling like only a Troll roughed me up. Trevor's about the size of a Troll. Well, a scrappy one, anyway."

"Gotcha."

As I lightly rubbed the edge of the pencil's lead against the paper, I glanced up to Miranda. "So Trevor was a big man, you say?"

She shrugged. "Well, in height. *I* dumped *him*, remember?"

Yeeouch.

Words were now becoming visible through the dark fog bank of lead that now covered the center portion of the memo. I was just hoping that whoever was behind the chicken scratch—be it Big Joe or Sledgehammer—hadn't used cursive writing. I would have been just as happy trying to decipher Elvish script over sloppy cursive.

I caught a break on this one, and found that the words appeared to be in a standard, simple English print. Not too refined in the handwriting, but good enough to be legible through a light rubbing.

"How's this looking for you, Billi?" Miranda asked, looking at the note with me.

"Not too sure."

My eyes narrowed on the words:

Cog Hill
Sunday, 1:00 p.m.
Wear a tie!

"Looks like Trouble is hitting the links."

Miranda gave a little whistle. "Cog Hill. I'm surprised they're still open, with all that's happening."

"It's all in how you handle the lifestyle, Miranda," I grumbled. "That was made evident at that last party I worked."

"You mean that swank shindig out in the country?" Miranda's brow furrowed. "What about it?"

"Let's just say there was something in the air." Now her brow was really scrunched together. "In another life I was a miner. You got paid not only by the size but also by the purity of a lode. When you're working in the dark, you develop a nose for such things."

"Seriously?"

"Seriously." I chuckled and gave Miranda a wink, "So if a beau happens to give you jewelry of any kind, run it by me and I'll be able to give you an appraisal."

"I'll do that, boss," Miranda answered with a smirk. "So, you're telling me the high society types are keeping up appearances, huh?"

"As best as they can. Don't get me wrong—the rich are still rich. They are just not *as rich* as they once were." I looked at the note for a moment before continuing, "You get accustomed to the lifestyle; and when the rug is pulled out from under you, you try to figure out how to maintain that lifestyle, or at least the appearance of it. What carries more clout? The membership to Cog Hill, or the rocks hanging from your neck? Which one will offer you more of a chance to be seen, more opportunity to meet others that might benefit you? I may not be originally from around these parts, but there's a lot both worlds have in common. People are people, and pretense is everywhere. Not much you can say to debate against that."

Miranda suddenly shook her head, "Oh, yeah, I guess now's as good as any of a time to tell you."

With the exception of *"Billi, you're a great guy and I really like you..."* or *"We really need to talk about something...", "Now's as good a time as any..."* is perhaps the worst way to start a conversation with me.

My girl walked over to the coffee table and unfolded the newspaper. It was the Sports section, announcing the rescheduled game between the Cubs and Mariners: Tuesday.

"So, meeting on Sunday. Game on Tuesday," I said, looking up at Miranda. "Got my ass handed to me on a Queen's Platter Thursday night. Everything gets foggy from there. So all this makes today...?"

"Saturday afternoon, boss," she answered mournfully.

Damn.

"Since Doc Roberts said you needed to rest up, I let you do just that."

Cog Hill, Sunday, one o'clock in the afternoon. An extra day to heal would have been nice. Really, really nice. Instead, I had to pace myself, hope that Dwarven constitution would come through, and find the strength to walk upright tomorrow. The job Trouble was out to do wasn't going to happen until this meeting was over and done with. so this was a meeting I had to poke my pudgy honker into. Otherwise, the job would go down and Trouble would be heading for the next city. The next game. The next score.

"You should consider taking it slow. Rest up a bit, pal. Give yourself time to heal," Ballscratcher had told me in my dream.

I hate Goblins.

Setting the meeting reminder aside, I settled back into my blankets. "I'm serious, Miranda. You make sure I get up bright and early tomorrow, or so help me I *will* fire you."

Miranda chuckled at the threat, but the laugh disappeared when she noticed the stare in my eyes. The silence was awkward, uncomfortable, and downright nasty. "Yeah, sure, Billi."

My shoulders nuzzled into a really nice nook in the pillow, and I felt my eyelids close, only to have Miranda's voice bring me back. "You're going to pass on lunch?"

"Yeah," I groaned. "Going to try and get some more shut-eye. Heal up a bit."

There was that awkward quiet again. Sorry, kid, but tomorrow I can't afford to miss.

"I'll be around if you need anything, boss. Sweet dreams," I heard her wish me.

With visions of Al Capone dancing in my head? Shit. I hope so, Miranda. I really hope so.

CHAPTER FOURTEEN

Par for the Course

Very little green remained following Black Thursday, but the Cog Hill Golf and Country Club was one of the rare exceptions. The playgrounds for the rich were all taking a pretty hard hit, but Cog Hill seemed to maintain its membership, status, and stature as if the bubble had never burst. Two golf courses spread out and away from a gorgeous clubhouse. This "Nineteenth Hole" sported a massive dining hall of high ceilings and roaring hearths that doubled as a tribute to the artisans of stone masonry. This was the kind of palace that would make any prince's virginal betrothed tingle in all the right places and offer to do whatever it took to move in. Cog Hill's dining hall led to a smoking room, complete with hearth and Steinway, setting an atmosphere for pipe and stogie connoisseurs. This room, in turn, led to lavish guest accommodations, perfect for those golfers wanting another crack at the club record. And if you liked a bit of the sauce to add flavor to your weekend, a fully stocked bar greeted you in the foyer.

Yeah, it's Prohibition, but that's really for the common folk. At this place, you had the society's posh schmoozing senators and city councilmen alike. Nothing like a splash of bubbly to grease the wheels of progress.

Cog Hill was a reminder of the Twenties and the abundant good times enjoyed then. While the common man would sneer at the audacity this place showed by still running strong, you had to admire Cog Hill's *hubrimaz* for keeping its chin up through such financial dire straits. It was an accomplishment for such a luxury to be able to stay open when bread and soup lines were stretching around street corners everywhere.

Which was not to say I was setting aside my own hard earned greenbacks toward a membership. I'd clocked in enough time here with the Waldorf act to know I wouldn't last an hourglass here. Too many stuffed shirts and class struggles for my stomach to handle.

The cab was pulling up to the clubhouse, and I stroked my beard as the building grew in size. I was not dressed up in my gear this time, nor was I coming in through the servants' entrance. This time, I was here on Baddings Investigations business; but like I had told Miranda, I still didn't know *what* that business would be. All I had was a time, a place, and a reminder to wear a tie.

I straightened that tie for probably the fourth time. The suit was pressed and the shoes were polished, so I had no worries. Miranda, in her true form, was nothing less than a yeoman of sterling service; and even she admitted that while I looked like I'd been on the wrong end of a mace fight, I was walking well enough to get back on the case.

However, upon seeing myself in the mirror for the first time since the ambush at the Jefferson, I knew there was no other way to describe me: I looked like hell.

My face sported a shiner and a swollen jaw, and reviewing the damage after a few days of rest made me seriously consider how lucky I had been. Not just that protection spell, mind you. I got pummeled pretty hard, but I was only a few shots shy of Shuffle's fatal seven. My attacker had held back.

Lucky me, I thought, wincing as I felt my cheek.

So I looked bad. Like I cared. I was going posh today in order to put some pieces together in this case. How I looked really didn't matter.

The reaction from the valet opening the cab door for me, though, gave me pause. Maybe I should have cared. Looking like I'd just walked away from a tavern brawl might complicate things for me.

The doorman welcomed me (if you could call it that; neither his stare nor his mechanical movements came across as very warm or inviting) to the resort, and as expected I was bringing on the stares; more so than usual on account of the bruises and swelling across my face. A bell rang twice, and I could hear a quick scuffle. The din died down as I stopped at the bar and peered in the direction of the main dining hall.

A throat cleared from behind me. "Excuse me, sir, how can I help you?"

Here we go.

I turned around slow enough for even the clumsiest of Trolls to lumber up and drive its teeth into my noggin. The scarecrow towering over me was the one I'd caught sight of behind the desk, so he was probably the current shift's lord of the manor. His second was on the phone. The words *"I'm talking to the police right now!"* across his forehead in black ink would have been more subtle than his stares at us.

My shoulders dropped a hint after I let go of a deep breath, and then I looked up at the club manager. "Well, you could have been a huge help by not calling the cops on me, but with the way I look I suppose I shouldn't blame you." My lip was stuck in a curl on account of the swollen jaw, so I didn't need to work to give him a smirk. I was already there. "I will anyway."

The manager merely lifted his chin up in reply, giving the slightest of snorts.

I nodded. "Yeah, okay pal, here's my story—I'm a private eye looking into a murder. I was going to try and keep this visit as low key as I could, what with the height, and a face that would make a pox victim look like John Barrymore. Now you've gone and called Chicago's Finest on me, and that is going to complicate things. How can you help me, you ask? How about this—make like a demon at an exorcism. Scram!"

This tower of a man huffed and stormed back to the front desk, his mannerisms indicating he wanted the police here yesterday. As I had nothing to lose at this point, I proceeded into the dining hall.

Whoever was meeting Trouble here, he was willing to meet at peak hours for the kitchen. Interesting choice. I supposed the noon crowd might get too busy, but now with the minute hand at the forty-five, the place was at a lull. It would pick up again around one, and Trouble would be ushered to their seats without too much fuss, provided they kept to the dress code. They might be recognized if the interests of club members extended beyond the Stock Market and eighteen holes, but at first glance I could hardly picture these tea-toddlers and high society types kicking back with a dog and a soda at the top of the fifth.

The Maitre D' took one look at me and froze as if struck by a medusa's stare.

"Had a problem at the Front Desk. Don't worry. Cops are on the way." I sighed as I returned my gaze to the dining hall. "Just looking to see if I can say hi to a friend before heading back to town."

No, I really didn't know who I was looking for. I was thinking back to the dream, and Alphonse showing up. This didn't strike me as Al's typical battle attack plan. His approach was more like the land infantry at a full charge, hitting the opponent with all you've got. Coming in from a blindside to flank the enemy? Nah, that approach was too subtle; and the club itself was just too subtle of a place for Al to be keeping company.

Then my eyebrows perked up. I tipped my fedora to the host, and saw myself in.

It was easy to tune out the gasps and the snickers of the various tables I passed, so long as I kept my peepers forward and focused on getting to where I was headed. The top of my hat emulated a shark's dorsal fin, leaving in its wake a ripple of reactions. Probably would have served as a warning for my friend who sat waiting for Trouble to arrive for lunch. I could easily picture him suggesting, in the snidest tone he could muster, that Sledgehammer wear a tie.

I pulled a seat out and hopped up into it, and smiled at the table's lone occupant as much as my swollen jaw would allow.

"How you doing, Miles?"

Miles Waterson took a moment, and then his demeanor—snobby as it was back in the jewelry store—slipped back around him like a burial shroud across a dead prince. He looked around himself, daring to make eye contact with the people now staring at his rather odd, somewhat worse-for-wear guest.

"Mr. Baddings, if memory serves?" he asked me. "I almost didn't recognize you."

"Hey, thanks for remembering the little people, both figurative and literal."

He nodded, a slick and smarmy smile forming on his face. "As a businessman, it's good to have a command of names and faces, regardless of how significant—or insignificant—the person that you meet."

Charming. At least I was going to have a bit of fun this afternoon before heading back to Chicago. "I see." At our table were three additional chairs, complete with settings. "Expecting some friends around one o'clock or so?"

Miles didn't flinch at that. He was pretty good. "My business is my own."

"Unless it involves murder. Then it becomes my business and the business of the Chicago police."

"Careful, Mr. Baddings," he said, picking up his water glass. "I would hate to have my legal team contact you concerning charges of slander. Are you sure you would want to make such accusations in public like that?"

"Unless, Miles, *unless* it involves murder," I slurred. "Did I accuse you of anything? I'm just speaking hypothetically." I groaned, shaking my head. "You completely misunderstood what I meant, Miles. I was just trying to tell you that I only get involved in the business of others when murder is involved. Like what happened at your store. You know?"

"Yes, quite."

The tinkling of forks and knives continued around us as we stared at one another. Guess I needed to press a bit harder. I'm good at that.

"You know, Miles," I began, giving my coat jacket a slight tug, "I really don't like you, but I will tell you out of courtesy that whatever you're messing with is way out of your scope of understanding."

"That's quite a curious statement, Mr. Baddings," he replied, peppering his words with a slight chortle. "I wish I knew what it meant, but please continue."

"I don't know the hows and whys, but you are into some seriously crooked shit. What's worse, you're dabbling with forces of nature that will turn around and do a hell of a lot more than just bite you on the ass."

"Will they, now?"

The mocking tone just dared me to throw my hands up and say, *"Fine, pal, do what you like with dark magic; but when an* überwotch *bursts out from your chest, don't say I didn't warn you."* Maybe I didn't want to give in so easily to my temper. This guy was smart. I just hadn't found the right breadcrumbs to lead him. Yet.

"I think, Mr. Baddings, that you missed your calling. Instead of private investigation, you should have offered your services for children's parties. I think your gifts as a storyteller are quite extraordinary."

If you only knew, Miles. If you only knew…

"Eh," I shrugged, "the money's good there, too. Problem is I don't get to really use my noggin the way I do to catch chumps like you with their hands deep in the biscuit jar."

"Well then, seeing as you enjoy solving mysteries, perhaps I can give you a quick little problem to deduce."

Oh, he wants to try and play with me? Yeah, okay, you prick—let's play.

Miles began, "I know a gentleman—"

"A friend of yours?"

Miles arched an eyebrow as he kept his eyes fixed with mine. "More like a passing acquaintance."

"So he's not a *gentleman*, but more like he's a *guy*."

"Very well then," he conceded. "This *guy*—as you so eloquently put it—is apparently doing his duty to support the local Chicago authorities in their investigation of a robbery."

"Sounds like a stand-up guy you know there, Miles. You could do yourself some good in picking up a thing or two from him."

"Ah, but there's a problem." Of course there's a problem. There's always a problem, isn't there? "This guy, while gracious in his own cryptic warnings to me concerning things of which I am apparently ignorant, does not have any idea with whom he himself is tangling. This guy does not even begin to grasp what I am capable of, nor does he realize how close he is to finding out."

This is the best you can do for a threat, Miles? You are such a dink.

"So here is the puzzle for you to solve, Mr. Baddings: How long do you think this guy has, before repercussions befall him?"

"Gee, Miles, I wish I could give you the answer," I scoffed. Then I looked over my shoulder. "But my ride's here."

With the clamorous entrance they made, the uniforms might as well have been the fire brigade; I half expected to catch a whiff of smoke from the kitchen area. Chicago's Finest, though, had their beady blues set on me, so I knew I was on the last grains of my hourglass.

"I hope you miss me while I'm gone, Miles."

He nodded, his gloating smirk working away at what little patience I had left. "You sound most certain that we will be talking again."

"Call it a feeling," I said, raising my hands as I hopped out of the chair. I spoke over my shoulder, "You boys want to do this all polite and such? Or shall we do this—"

My wrists flew to the small of my back, immediately followed by the sharp pinching sensation that usually came with metal pressing too hard against bone.

"Easy there, fellas," I winced.

"Have a pleasant trip back to the city, Mr. Baddings," purred Miles.

"Be seeing you," I managed, just before a hand closed on the scruff of my neck.

The restaurant was going by me in a blur. If we hadn't been so far out of town, I would have sworn these boys were O'Malley's. It was a safe bet that the rough act was mainly for show. At places like this, it was all about the kind of display you could put on because you never knew who was watching. Hell, maybe one of these gumheels was bucking for a job at Miles' place. And though I could give them advice on just how dangerous it would be to work for a putz like him, I knew any warning would fall on deaf ears, seeing as I was the dink in the irons.

Looking up, I happened to make eye contact with three of Trouble. Riley, Joe, and Sammy took a step back on seeing me, and I shot them a crooked grin.

"Be careful if you complain about a fly in the soup here," I grunted as I passed them.

Back in those days of battle axes, broadswords, and bawdy wenches, there were plenty of nights when me and my boys—and when he was in town, my crazy Human pal, Kev—spent some sobering-up time in Acryonis' premier holding tanks. (I think there is still a watch at D'Hargoh Pointe with standing orders that if me or any of the Stormin' Scrappies come within a hundred steps of the town's borders, they're to shoot first, nock a second volley, and shoot again.) My pals back home would have smiled with pride to know that I'd not changed too much. Since the slip through the portal, I have spent the odd night or few in a Chicago lockup, due mainly to the fantastic relationship O'Malley and I have cultivated.

With both Chicago and Gryfennos jails as my basis for comparison, I could not deny that this was one of the nicest lockups I ever had the pleasure of visiting. No smell of piss. The meal I was given, an early dinner, was hot and home-cooked. Even the bunk was nice. It was a far cry from my own bed, but it still beat the muck mattress of Acryonis or the thinly padded (and thickly stained) ones of the Windy City.

The outer door groaned open, and I heard Wilbur call out to me, "Hey, Billi?"

"Yeah, Wilbur, what can I do for ya?"

"Someone's come to get you," he responded cheerfully. "See, I told you our phones worked out here!"

I craned my neck up from the pillow at the sound of keys jingling at my cell door. Even from this topsy-turvy vantage, I could still recognize my pal Detective Jerry Flannigan standing behind the scarecrow in the policeman's uniform.

"Jerry," I said, giving him a smile through a swollen jaw. "Seeing as how you're bailing my ass outta here, it's my treat this evening."

"Uh-huh," he grunted, "save that offer for after we get in the car."

Yeah, I had a feeling he was going to be a little grouchy about all this.

"It wasn't like I was causing trouble, now was I, Wilbur?"

The skinny snorted as he opened the door, "Nah, Billi, you've been great."

When I stepped out of the cell, I gave Jer a gentle tap of appreciation on his arm. His expression didn't change. "Let me see your wrists, Billi."

I grumbled a bit and held out my arms.

Jer stared at where cuffs had once restrained me, then spun on his heels to face Wilbur. My friend moved faster than a wyrd sister deep in a frenzy spell; and from the way Wilbur jumped, you would have thought Jer actually looked like one of those screaming harpies.

"Do you country bumpkins out here *think* before slapping cuffs on someone?" Jer barked.

"Relax," I huffed. "Wilbur and I are jake on everything. Right, Wilbur?"

The scarecrow waved dismissively at me. "Yeah, Billi. Except the thing about the cuffs. I think Bubba and Bufford were just a little excited to get a call, and they wanted to impress those city slickers. You know what I mean?"

True, there had been a bit of chafing left behind by the manacles, but these charm bracelets had nothing on the cuffs they used back in my stompin' grounds. "Don't give it a second thought." I managed a grin at Jer. "See, pal, everybody's looking for a ticket to the good life, even out here."

Jer shook his head, and then narrowed his eyes on Wilbur. "Next time, how about keeping a tight leash on your boys?"

"Well now, sir, when we got the phone call from Cog Hill, we were under the impression that Billi here..."

"Keep it by the book, Officer!" Jer snapped. "The suspect."

"The *suspect* was causing trouble and we needed to get out there as fast as we could, so we assumed—"

"Wrong, by the looks of things. I did a follow-up out at Cog Hill and it didn't look like there was anything amiss. In fact, they had forgotten about the suspect being there!"

They forgot I had been there? Damn. You sure know how to make a guy feel special, Jer.

"You got lucky here with Billi being a straight shooter and all," he continued. "All you would need is someone looking like this," he said, waving his hand around my face, "to make trouble for you."

Jer was not crazy about cops who let the power of the job go to their heads. He was also the kind of guy who sometimes got a bit overprotective of his friends, much like a mountain dragon protecting her newborns. If you so much as belch in a threatening manner, wings unfurl and villages are burning soon after.

My friend the police detective is a lot like that, just without the peasants on fire.

"Don't mind Detective Academy Top Graduate here," I interjected. "You guys have been great. I'll be even better once I get Beatrice back."

"You can pick it up out front, Billi," Wilbur said. He managed a smile, then glanced over at Jer, whose expression was as stern as the back of a pirate ship. He fought to keep the cheerful disposition. "Oh, and I didn't touch Beatrice, but I did clean your .38 'cause it was needing a little attention."

When Wilbur disappeared, Jer's more casual voice returned. "They offer to clean your guns here, too?"

"I'm telling you," I said, shrugging lightly, "they do things a little different outside the Windy City. Glad you could make it out here."

"You're lucky I got out here at all. We heard over the radio about a disturbance of the peace out at Cog Hill, and when the description came in, O'Malley was trying to cook up a reason to get a car out here while keeping an eye on me. He was ready to have my balls for breakfast when he found out you were at the morgue."

Was I right, or was I right? "Sorry about that, pal."

Jer just gave a heavy sigh, tipping his hat back right before opening the heavy iron door leading out into the modest police station. "Billi," he finally said while dragging a single chair up to the station's front desk, "what are you doing out here anyway?"

"Chasing down a lead." Climbing up on it, I signed for Beatrice and my effects, and continued my thought as I strapped on my girl. "A case I'm about to close."

"You found what you're looking for?"

"More like I'm kicking the wasp hive. Just need to make one more call, and then I've got two hot dates tonight." I looked up at Jer, "One of them's with you."

"Come again?" he asked.

"Yeah." I then called out, "Hey, Wilbur, I'm going to make a quick call, okay?"

"Sure thing, Billi," he replied.

As I dialed the phone, I looked at Jer. "After my dinner date, it's you and me, and we're going shopping."

"For what, exactly?"

I gave a shrug, "Something nice. Something sparkly. Something shiny."

CHAPTER FIFTEEN

No, Really, We're Just Friends

The jingle of the doorbell caught Annabelle's attention, and for that attention I was rewarded with a warm smile and a quick wave before she returned to bussing the table in front of her. Far different from my routine, I took a seat at one of the booths. I didn't really care for the way its table seemed to loom above and away from me, but I really needed the privacy. Fortunately, even though it was the dinner rush, I managed to swipe a pair of cushions from nearby chairs. Just for some extra elevation.

A quick glance at the watch assured me there was plenty of time before my second outing. I managed to grab some shut-eye on the ride home, and if this late dinner went fast I might be able to grab another satchel of winks before heading out again. Hectic as these long-ass days were, I did love 'em. Just love being busy doing what I want to do, you know? I thrummed on the table top, loosing a look at the door, then back to the watch. *C'mon, I can't afford for you to be late. Not tonight.* Hopefully, a problem hadn't come up between my call and now.

Tonight was a good night for Mick's, as usual. I thrummed the tabletop again, then fiddled with the napkin holder and salt and pepper shakers.

"Hey, Billi," came Mick's voice from the other side of the counter. His expression quickly changed when he got a full-on look at my face. "Jesus, Mary, and Joseph, pal, what happened to you?!"

That also caught Annabelle's attention, and she got a longer look at me. She gasped, and *that* made a few patrons turn their heads. I wished I had taken some time to learn a healing spell before going on that damn quest up Death Mountain.

"On-the-job hazards," I answered.

"Yeah," Mick scoffed, "if your job is hammering rivets in the Tribune Tower with your face!"

My fingertips tapped lightly together as I turned my attention back to the door. "No need to get your jerkin in a twist. I'm on the mend."

Apart from the murmur of Mick's customers, the quiet settled in; but it didn't last very long.

"Is there a problem with your usual seat?" Mick asked as he picked up a clean bowl. Some lucky individual was about to get a helping of the good stuff. "Do I need to make an adjustment or something?"

"Nah, Mick, I'm fine. Just needing a change of space. I'm meeting a friend for dinner. Can you whip up a pair of chili specials?"

His head jerked back a bit as if I had just told him I was following the Dodgers instead of my beloved Cubbies. "Hey, Billi, I'm down a man and you can see that the place is jumping."

"When's it not?" I chuckled back.

Yeah, this was also part of the joys of dining at Mick's. No matter how crowded it got at this Chicago institution, Mick made time for banter with the regulars. This repartee gave Mick's that personal touch.

Tonight was a little different. My friend's tone was leagues and fathoms away from playful. "Sorry, pal, but I'm a little behind, and I've got people in need of some food."

"Oh, come on, Mick," I groaned, rapping my knuckles against the worn wood of the table. "I've got a long night ahead of me, so if you could just keep it simple—"

"There is no keeping it simple, not tonight!" he shot back. (Now, Mick knows I don't like being cut off, so for him to do that means he's also got a lot of deliveries in the queue, too.) He motioned to the patrons along the bar, and a few of the tables. "I got a lot of orders to take care of before you helped yourself to that booth…and to my seat cushions."

Wow. He really *doesn't* miss a thing.

"Gerry and Albin both called in sick, and I'm not happy. I'll need one of them or something better to come walking through that door before I bump up your order to the front of the line."

The door jingling made both our heads turn. Gertie's eyes searched Mick's only for a moment before they landed on me. She arched her eyebrow and blew a rogue lock of hair out of her eyes before joining me in the booth.

"Sorry I'm late, Billi," she huffed. "Had to rearrange my evening just for—" And then, she got a good look at me. Those sapphires flashed concern as she gingerly touched my still-swollen cheek. It was like a feather brushing my skin, the gentlest of touches that carried with it a torrent full of emotion. "Good Lord, Billi, what happened to you?"

I went to answer, but then I saw Mick looking at me, then at Gertie, then at me again, and then back at Gertie.

"Okay," he said, clasping his hands together. His sudden smile was brighter than any Illumination spell I've ever seen cast. "Two chili specials, coming right up!"

What? But—oh, wait a minute…

Gertie's brow furrowed as she pulled out what appeared to be some sort of hard portfolio, her eyes watching Mick for a moment and then finally coming to me. "You know I'm probably breaking a half-dozen rules here. Checking out books is one thing, but if these photos are damaged in any way, shape, or form…"

"I swear, I wouldn't ask you to put your ass on the line if it weren't important," I said, flashing her that Baddings smile that won the ladies easily in Acryonis.

Her crooked eyebrow only rose higher. "Don't think for a moment, Mr. Baddings, that we are even close to being settled on our outstanding date. Tonight does not count."

"Now, is that what you think of me?" I asked. "Do you think I would stoop—"

And there was Mick, seeming to appear from the Mists of Trysillia with Annabelle right behind him. His dishtowel was draped over his forearm, and in one outstretched hand he carried a saucer with a small, fat candle burning from its center. Mick gingerly placed the far-from-usual centerpiece on the table as Annabelle slid the chili specials in front of us.

As this little bit of vaudeville played out, Gertie kept her peepers locked on me, that gaze of hers saying it all to me with chilling clarity.

"Dinner is served," Mick purred. Remaining totally oblivious to Gertie's reaction, he continued to play Maitre D' at Chez Miguel's. "Mr. Baddings failed to place a drink order with your meal, madame. What would you care for with your special tonight?"

"A Coke will be just fine," Gertie replied.

I pinched the bridge of my nose, screwing my eyes shut. He's my friend. He's my pal. He's really not helping out here one bit.

With a tip of the head, Mick glided away, leaving me under the drawn bow of a mad librarian, her fingers tapping on the table.

"You..." I started dryly, and then I cleared my throat. "You got something for me."

"As requested, with a lot of favors cashed in, I managed to get photos wired to me. Would you like to hear how long it takes to get photos wired to you, and would you like to hear how much longer it takes when you're having them wired to you under false pretenses?" I raised a hand, shaking my head slowly as Gertie continued, "I also managed to get photographs from the games at Wrigley. I specifically narrowed the photographs to ones that only featured the pitcher."

The photos of the Mariners' ace pitcher Eddie Faria, all taken from various angles, now formed a baseball fan's quilt. Five rows of pictures, three in a column. The wired pictures were nowhere near the clarity of the Chicago shots, but they would have to do. Somewhere in there was the last piece in this puzzle.

The Pendant of Coe bestows upon those who wear it a strength and agility beyond that of those not born of The Touched. While I still hadn't seen the blessed thing, my gut (and my dreams) told me one of the Nine Talismans was granting an edge to a baseball team of unknowns. I also knew, based on *My World Book*'s description and the fact that none of the Mariners wore an enchanted breastplate or were catching with a silver gauntlet, that the talisman had to be the Pendant of Coe.

This ended my certainty. Now I was going on my own deduction and a few hunches, some more confident than others. For one, the pitcher: somehow he was involved. The scent of magic really didn't hit me until the Mariners took the field. It was strongest when he was pitching those burners from mound to plate. When he was relieved at the end of the game, I had to search for the smell; and even when I caught it, the odor was merely a trace, an afterthought, like perfume hanging in the air after a viscountess crosses a grand hall to pay reverence to a king. How deeply was the pitcher involved with the Mariners' infamous Trouble? Faria seemed to keep his distance from the group of dinks that took a lot of pride in living up to their nickname. Smart guy...

...unless he was my boxing partner at the Jefferson.

Then came the heists. Could that have just been a strange coincidence? A headline crime in every town this team visited? (Well, in all save one town, and it took a visit from the President to trump it.) Hell of a coincidence, if it was. The crimes themselves, making a jump from simple bank jobs to museum heists, whispered of an outside influence. This player, probably not one from the Mariners' roster, understood the value of art. Currency can sometimes be worth less than the paper it's printed on, but sketches, portraits, and sculptures only increase in value. All this deduction continued to point to the smug prick that was Miles Waterson. Was one of Chicago's local royalty working this crew from Baltimore?

Throw in a botched heist at Waterson's own establishment, the death of a store manager, and the death of someone associated with these high profile heists, and you had a jigsaw puzzle. A stupid, fucking jigsaw puzzle. Did I ever mention how much I loathe jigsaw puzzles? And this was one of those puzzles where your dwarvlings have pinched the crucial piece and scooted away with it, raising your frustration level higher and faster than a dungeon's water trap. I knew that missing piece was in here.

The time had come to employ the two-handed broadsword of my trade.

Gertie watched me produce the tool from my coat pocket. "Billi?" she asked.

"Yeah," I said, peering at a Mariners-Pirates moment through its massive lens.

"Detectives *really* use magnifying glasses?"

I looked up, pursing my lips together. The stereotypes of being a Dwarf were enough for me to handle, but the whole "magnifying glass" thing with detectives bothered me a bit. Books, plays, and moving pictures would lead you to believe we were blind without the damn things. I was so put off by the question, I didn't even bother to thank Annabelle for the two drinks she brought to the table.

"My eyes are fine, Gertie," I grumbled, "but yes, some detectives—the *good* ones, thank you very damn much—use these to bring out some details that might otherwise go missed."

Gertie took a sip of her Coke. "Any idea what you're looking for?"

"Like I said, details." My lens bent and distorted the captured moment of Faria releasing a pitch that looked so fast, it had probably reached the off-camera catcher the day before. I couldn't see any glimpse of a chain or bulge of a token under his uniform. That was a stretch, I admit. A hope beyond hope that I would get a peek at the pitcher's pendant.

Huh. The Pitcher's Pendant. Worked for me.

The magnifying glass now pulled other players around the pitcher into view. William "Shuffle" Patterson at shortstop and Archie "Flyball" Randalls at Second, both of whom I knew as Trouble.

"What I need," I muttered moving deeper into the photographic patchwork on the table, "is that little detail I'm missing. That we're all missing."

"Somewhere in these pictures is the key to the Mariners fixing their games?"

"For starters." I looked up into the concentrated gaze of my lady librarian. "Remember that attempted robbery at Waterson and Sons a few nights ago?"

"The headlines and the scores?" Gertie tipped her head to one side as she dipped into the chili. "So you're looking in these pictures for…?"

"For the sign." I muttered, studying each image. "There had to be some kind of sign, like what we do in Snoopers, to let those involved know 'Tonight's the night'."

She looked over her glasses at me, "You're going to let a stadium full of people know that you and your friends are planning a robbery?"

I huffed, looking up from the glass. "Well, it's going to be something subtle. I'm not expecting any of the players to be wearing a sandwich board with big block letters spelling out, 'Hey, guys, how about we hit a jewelry boutique tonight!' or anything."

Her eyebrows bobbed. "Hmm." She cleaned her spoon of chili. "It has been a while since we've grabbed a bite together. I'd forgotten how irritable you get when you're hungry."

Dammit. I hate it when I get like this.

Waste not the gifts of the Master's toil, as my people's saying goes. Amazing how something as simple as Mick's garlic-cinnamon-tomato-pepper medley can clear your mind and give you a sense of purpose. The slow burn lingers under the tongue while the ground beef remains succulent in the surrounding sauce. My chili had cooled just enough to be ready for a mouthful, but enough heat remained to give the spices that kick. Bliss. Sheer bliss.

"Don't get too comfortable, Mr. Baddings," chided Gertie. "The chili's good, but you still owe me…and your bill is even farther from clear."

"Now come on. At first I was looking into something suspicious in baseball, and now I'm neck-deep in an attempted robbery and double-homicide. Think you can cut me some slack over there, Miss Thunder from Downunder?"

She froze, and her eyes seemed to go from bright sapphires to rich emeralds. "You didn't just call a Kiwi an Aussie, did you? Tell me you didn't."

My head cocked to one side. "There's a dif—"

The warrior's instinct—the one that controlled the defensive crouch in me—echoed loud and clear in my head: *Hey, Billi, if you value your balls, stop right now and change the subject.*

"Let me try again." I took a sip of my own Coke before continuing. "This started out as a discreet case for the Cubbies, but I'm finding out the hard way—as you can tell from the looks of me—it's a bit bigger than that." One more spoonful of Mick's best, and then I swapped the spoon for the magnifying glass. "I'm thinking there's a crew working in the team."

Gertie leaned in a little closer. "And that was why you were also looking at the robberies happening at the same time the Mariners were in each town?"

"Yeah. It just struck me as odd that high profile crim—"

"And continuing with WPOD's Evening of Romantic Classics," a radio crackled from across the diner, "the Chicago Philharmonic presents Pyotr Il'yich Tchaikovsky's sweeping masterpiece, *Romeo & Juliet…*"

When the music started, Mick upped the volume on his radio and turned around just enough to show off his profile, and the contentment glowing therein.

"Hey, Mick," I barked. "You know those two *died* at end of the play, right?"

Mick just snorted. "Love story's a love story."

I considered my friend for a moment, and then returned to the photos. Looking up at Gertie would reveal, no doubt, how hard my friend's good intentions were making me blush.

Then, as the music traded its sweet, caressing melody for the more dramatic staccato movement, I saw it.

"Hold on." I set my soda aside for a moment. "Let me see something, here."

My eyes swept across the patchwork again, and then I started shuffling the photos around. The dinner plates didn't give me a lot of wiggle room, but I was managing. Gertie, her concern divided between trying to figure out what I was thinking and being protective of the photos, watched me, her spoon slowly stirring her meal.

"You know, as entertaining as you may think it is when you're working in silence, I can give some critique on your one-man show." She slipped the straw from her Coke and chewed on it as she said, "Action's a bit slow."

My head popped up. Sometimes, when on the clock, I can be a bit of a chump.

"Sorry, Gertie. I tend to get a little…"

"Rude?" she quipped.

"Obsessed," I corrected. "Especially when I'm nearing the end of a case. I want this thing solved, and the sooner the better. When I initially laid these photos out, I mixed them up, so they're in no real order. Now I need them organized by opposing teams."

Now she *really* looked pissed. By the Fates, what did I do now?

"Billi, what is my job?"

What kind of question was that? "The bruise is on my jaw. My head is fine."

"I want to hear you say it," she insisted. "What is my job?"

"Fine, you're a—" Oh. Shit. That's right. "This night is really not going well for me, is it?"

"You want me to help you on this? It's going to cost you." Her eyes were back to ice-blue, and seemed to sparkle as her mouth turned into an extremely wicked smile. Far more wicked than I would have expected from a librarian. "Dinner at The Palms."

She wasn't kidding. I'd rather face a charging horde of blood-starved Goblins than the dinner bill at The Palms.

"You sure we couldn't do a few choice seats at Wrigley? Nice day. Terrifi—"

"A nice suit on you. I've got a lovely dress for the occasion. A nice appetizer." Ouch. "A lovely dinner." Oww. "And dessert." Ooofff. "That would serve as ample compensation, Mr. Baddings."

The last time I got hit this hard, it was at the loading dock of the Jefferson. "I'll have Miranda make the reservations."

Gertie loosed a curt nod, gently pushed me back, and started checking the backs of the photos. She was switching and swapping them out with the speed and skill of a tavern hustler. While dice games were the common gambling vice, cards—considered the nobleman's game—never failed to bring in some extra income for a few inns and pubs I frequented. It was more a matter of novelty than popularity with the cards, and the dealers in Acryonis who brought their games to the people were slick, quick, and skilled. You played card games for the privilege of playing, not to win. This was how Gertie handled the photos. She even gave a little flourish across the grid when she was done.

"The column to your left is the earliest, and you progress forward in dates as you go right." Gertie motioned to the head of each row. "Each row is a different city, or team, if you're going by what's in the picture."

By the Druids of Hadismill, she was good. Really, really good. "Um, I…wow, Gertie. So," I started, "which one—"

"This was the photo you were looking at. Pittsburgh. Third game against the Pirates."

I looked at the photo, and then my eyes slowly came up to meet hers. "Not bad, Gertie, considering you're not a fan of the sport."

With a wry smile, she picked up one of the wired photos and flipped it over, revealing a date, location, photographer's name, and what appeared to be a number for filing purposes, written in her delicate hand.

"The method to my madness, Billi," she said, winking.

I flipped through my notebook and found the scores I had jotted down with Gertie on my last visit to the library. With my eyes looking over Pittsburgh, I checked the scores. *April 25th, Mariners—9, Pirates—2.* Backwards. *April 26th, Mariners—6, Pirates—5.* Facing front. The other row was the Robins. *April 28th, Mariners—11, Robins—1.* Front. *April 29th, Mariners—8, Robins—3.* Backwards. *April 30th, Mariners—4, Robins—2.* Front. And finally, the Braves. *April 19th, Mariners—3, Braves—0.* Backwards. *April 20th, Mariners—6, Braves—1.* Front. *April 21st, Mariners—2, Braves—5.* Front. Now there were the photos from St. Louis...then Chicago...

"You found it, didn't you?" Gertie asked, her spoon returning to the chili.

"Yeah, I did."

She didn't ask (I really didn't expect her to), but the glass was out of my hand and in hers. Gertie slipped out of her side of the booth and pressed me against the wall as she slid into my seat. She was the quietest I've ever seen her, apparently determined to find the detail I had caught and she hadn't.

I'd be willing to chalk this up to librarian's pride, but I couldn't shake that feeling I got when Mick played Junior Gumheel with me.

My head tilted to one side. There are a lot of dames in this town. My girl Miranda is one of the serious head-turners and she knows it. Gertie, however, was the kind of maid that me and my boys always liked. When you'd see a girl like Gertrude at first, all prim, proper, and...well, let's just call it like I see it...book-smart, your demeanor would change. You tone down the bawdy quips, try to recall those basic etiquette lessons, and generally clean up your act.

Get a girl like Gertie to smile, and you'd catch the kind of mischief and madness that would take you completely by surprise, either in a drinking contest, a spirited debate over which cigar smokes best, or in a relentless tavern tickle. That was what I suddenly saw in Gertie when she had her "*A-ha!*" moment. Those baby blues behind the specs twinkled, a light of discovery dancing in her eyes.

But then, her heartbreaker of a smile disappeared. "So what does this mean?"

"It means I've got a long night ahead of me. A very long night," I said, casting a glance at the time.

My eyes jumped from the clock to Mick, who was standing just underneath it, grinning like the warlock who possessed the spell that would win him the day.

"You kids comfy?" Mick asked, turning up Il'yich's melodic tribute to the star-crossed lovers a few notches. "How about a nice dessert? On the house. Got a chocolate pie so rich I can barely afford to make it."

Tempting. With a dinner at The Palms so clear in my future a Seer could see it blindfolded, I knew I should take Mick up on the offer of free food.

Not tonight. "Sorry, Gertie, but I've got to go," I grumbled, gently nudging her to the edge of my booth seat. "I've got to make a phone call and cross my fingers that this case is taking the turn I think it's taking." I shoveled a few last spoonfuls of Mick's best and then slapped a fiver on the table. Not that Mick deserved the tip after playing Village Matchmaker. Isn't there a saying in this realm about the road to Hell and intentions?

I gave the tie a tug and the hat an adjustment before heading for the door. My hand hadn't reached its handle before I froze. The chill was reminiscent of an ice dragon's afterfrost.

An extreme cold. That's what I felt, and my outstretched hand balled into a fist. *Yes, Billibub Baddings, you are truly a Grade A dink.*

I turned around to where I had sat. Still in the booth, her profile visible over her shoulder, was my dinner date. She wasn't looking at me when she spoke.

"Wednesday," she said. Her smile surprised me. "Pick me up at 6."

Okay, dinner at The Palms, next Wednesday. I would either knock a hole in the kitty or pull a few more double-duty days as Waldorf.

My lips parted to say something, but she merely inclined her head. Odder still, her smile widened. "You're welcome, Billi."

This girl had some Elven Art in her veins. The ability to say, "*You're off the hook, Baddings…for now…*" and, "*I really do understand. Just go. Go, and do what you do,*" with three simple words. That was some real magic.

I gave a little chuckle in spite of myself and left for the streets of Chicago, the jingle of Mick's door chimes heralding my departure into night's embrace.

CHAPTER SIXTEEN

TOP OF THE NINTH

My new travel pipe wasn't as compact or as comfortable as my favorite one, but my biggest fan amongst Chicago's Finest had slapped that particular luxury out of my face at Benny Riletto's crime scene. I did possess a second Acryonis-made pipe, but on account of sentimental reasons I chose to leave it behind in the office. The last time I'd smoked that pipe, all hell had broken loose on Chicago's waterfront warehouse district.

I didn't feel like tempting the Fates tonight.

Jerry puffed his own smoke, letting the thick, acrid wisps race out from between his nostrils. This must've been something he'd seen one of his pals back at the station do with a bucket of finesse. Jer still needed practice, though, as he was suddenly hacking and coughing up a storm in the car.

I passed him a canteen of water. This wasn't the first time we had enjoyed one another's company in the wee small hours of the morning. I was prepared.

"So," my friend wheezed, "tell me again what we're doing here?"

"I told you," I muttered, reaching into my coat pocket for the flask. "We're shopping."

"Huh," he grunted. "So are there some special sales going on at two in the morning at B.D. Waterson and Sons that I don't know about?"

"Yeah," I said, removing the cap as my eyes narrowed on the boutique's main window. "A clearance sale."

My nostrils picked up the scent of the bathtub gin and I took in a few whiffs. Deep whiffs, as a matter of fact. This batch had taken a bad turn and was nigh undrinkable, but I'd needed to put it to some kind of use. The incidents both at the Rothchild Estate and here had gotten my brain working, and I'd come up with this as a practical application.

The fourth whiff caught Jer's attention and he noticed the flask, along with the sharp, unmistakable smell that it contained.

"Now, I am sure I'm gonna hear exactly why you got a flask of—" He leaned in, took a quick sniff, and recoiled. "—*really bad* bathtub gin."

"Medicinal purposes, my friend," I said. One more deep sniff should tide me over for the evening. I was about to give the honker another treatment when I saw the beam of light shimmer in the bottom left of the window and then disappear like a spirit retreating to shadows when a cleric closed in on it. "You see that?"

Click-clack was the cop's answer. Yeah, he saw it.

His door opened, but I grabbed him by the arm. "Pal, I know you're probably going to hate this, but I want you to cover my backside. I need to take point."

"Come again?" he quipped. "You want to take point with what? That thing?" he asked, motioning to the battle axe tight in my grasp.

The last time I'd had this old girl out to play was that earlier-mentioned night on the waterfront. While the travel pipe might have tempted the Fates, the axe was a good call. Maybe I would carry the Cleric's Blessings and not have a need for it.

The weapon gave a soft hum as I lifted it up with one hand, while I opened the passenger door with the other. "Trust me, Jer. This little Acryonis Slugger of mine packs a wallop. Let's go."

We crept across the empty Chicago street to B.D. Waterson and Sons, slapping an adjoining building with our backs. Jer looked across the street as he pulled a torch out of his coat and turned it on, then off. He waited for a second, and then repeated the on-off pattern.

From an alleyway across the street, another light appeared and then blinked out.

"Okay, we got ten minutes before backup hits the place." Jer whispered. "We're going through the rear, so if our boys try to duck out, it's covered." He glanced at the axe, his head tipping to one side. "You and that thing of yours ready?"

I spun it in my hand, earning a soft hum as the blade flickered, and then brought it to an abrupt stop. "Watch and learn, gumheel. Watch and learn."

Our strides were long and low, but we were slipping deeper into the alleyway like valley cats stalking their prey through the trees and rocks of claimed territory. I was taking point as promised, but trying really hard to keep it together, as I was currently down a sense.

I had to rely on the peepers and the hearing. And, of course, my judge of character. If this played out like I thought it was going to, our "master thieves" would be in for an off night. They would be played like a fine mandolin in the grip of a skilled bard.

Masons had effectively patched up the hole from the first attempt on Waterson and Sons. The back door was closed, but missing its cautionary padlock. No surprise there. Getting in had probably been a piece of cake this evening. The door only groaned a little as we pulled it back and slipped into the darkness of the jewelry store. Ahead of us we could hear the soft music of stones hitting other stones. Diamonds caressed their sisters within intricate arrangements. Sapphires struck emeralds in tiaras and ornate bracelets, and it was easy to picture rubies sliding free of their velvet displays and landing to rest against one another, clicking and clacking from the bottom of what could have been a simple sack.

The poor dinks didn't realize that the soft music their jewelry made was a bit off-key.

We watched the two shadows lumber a bit in the darkness, talk in sharp whispers, and then split up. I motioned for Jer to creep right while I swung around to the larger of the pair. With a final adjust against the grip, I took a breath and then stepped in between the display cases behind the preoccupied thief.

"I'm sorry, sir, but we're *still* closed for business," my voice cut through the dark, "even at this hour."

The shadows in front of me came alive, becoming the maw of some unholy beast conjured from a warlock's spell. It could have easily overcome me, but I swept the axe back and managed to grip a forearm with my free hand.

Never let the size of your opponent throw you, figuratively or literally. I was not so much a Dwarf at that moment, as I was a pivot point. I got a hold on the figure, and rooted myself into the marble floor with a simple bending of my legs and turning of my hips. The black hulk wasn't expecting this basic martial arts move; nor was it expecting the way its self-generated momentum spun it, sending it back in the direction it had come from. The shadow shattered an empty display case, with quite a bit of fanfare.

"Freeze!" I heard from behind me.

There was another shadow at the other end of the store, and it came to an abrupt halt.

Jer called out, "I got him, Billi."

The black blob in front of me was shaking itself clean of debris slowly enough that I was able to spare a few seconds. There was just enough light coming in from the windows to reveal Jerry rooting the second crook to the floor with the power of his gun's threatening muzzle. My eyes returned to my own hooded burglar, its attention jumping from its smaller doppelganger, back to me.

It charged again.

Still keeping that axe flat against my back (*Not yet, not yet...*), I bobbed, and then drove my shoulder forward. Connecting quite well with its groin, I pushed hard against the ground. The attacker didn't fly far, but did flip over me and crash into another display, this one still holding a few baubles and bangles.

I took a few steps back. (*Okay... now.*) The battle axe came out from behind my back, casting a small strip of light along the far wall. The gleam shimmered downward to stop on the burglar, its crumpled form surrounded by the glitter of necklaces camouflaged within shards of broken glass.

When the dark shape stood up again, I noticed the bag it was holding. A bag of stones would make an impressive weapon: a makeshift mace that could probably clock me so hard I would think I was back at the Giddy Galleon, enjoying their best brew.

When the thief's loot clattered against the floor, I tightened my grip on the axe. That dull clamor was going to serve as his death knell.

On the battlefield, hesitation can be lethal. Now, you can sit around before you hit the green, debating what you could do in the heat of battle; but when you have a front of hungry Trolls bearing down on you, the time to think about it is over. Act, or die. Even in a one-on-one standoff like this, hesitation doesn't work. I was only given a second to decide. In two seconds, a blade can find a gut, a dagger can cut a throat, a bone can shatter. So, ponder and plan all you like. Once in the arena, you're making decisions that will either have you walking out on your own, or have you carried out by four of your best mates.

The shadow's poor excuse for a battle cry confirmed it to be male. The guttural yell carried the tell-tale qualities of a deep bass voice and the gravelly undertones common to cigarette smokers. That and the mass of his forearm verified my guess as to who was hidden under this dark guise. From his clumsy run, I could see he wasn't feeling too steady. (Hell, crashing through a pair of display cases can do that to a guy.) I knew the battle axe could easily slice him open like a holiday pig stuffed to overflowing on a nobleman's table.

Considering all the mayhem these boys had caused, I could have turned this creep into a street beggar with one swing. Instead, it turned out that despite his botched robbery, it was going to be his lucky night. I was in a compassionate mood.

The flat of my axe connected hard with his nose, an easy target as it protruded from the cowl. Dark rivulets disappeared into the intermittent light creating a momentary web of blood in mid-air. The crunch of metal against bone made both Jer and his captive wince. The shadow, now upright, stumbled back two steps, struggled to move forward again, and then surrendered to gravity, toppling back like a mighty oak falling to the woodsman's trade.

By the Fates, knocking him out had been a hell of a lot of fun.

"You finished dancing in the dark?" huffed Jer. "'Cause I'd really like to get some lights on in here."

I straightened my tie and moved over to the hulk lying in the midst of shattered glass and expensive bracelets and necklaces. The cowl covering his head easily slipped off, and I bent down to get a closer look at the blood-decorated face of "Sledgehammer" Sammy Saint.

No, the broken nose didn't make him any prettier.

"Hey, Jer," I said, glancing up from Saint. "I don't know if you need more light on the scene to say hello to 'Big Joe' Murphy of the Baltimore Mariners."

Jer slapped cuffs on the shorter shadow-wraith, and then another removed cowl revealed my assumption to be spot-on. "Wow! 'Big Joe' Murphy. I wish I could ask you for an autograph," Jer snarled, clicking the cuffs a bit tighter, "but I lost a fiver on last week's game. Way to hustle out there."

Since Jer was preoccupied with the visiting team, I took the opportunity to look around. My eyes fell on a necklace sporting a stone the size of a giant's teardrop. This stone, with the smaller ones arranged around it, made a statement, all right: *I have money and you don't.*

As the piece slipped into my coat pocket, I smiled at the passing thought. *Maybe not on Miranda, but it would suit Gertie. Not sure how, but it would.*

There was a *tap-tap-tap* at the door window, and we saw the uniforms bathed in the pale glow of streetlamps. Calvary was here. Maybe they were late to the party, but they were still a welcome sight.

Good timing, too. The alcohol was beginning to wear off.

"Flannigan!" Chief O'Malley bellowed, probably loud enough to wake the dead. In Gryfennos. "I don't give rat's arse about yer record or yer service t' tha' city! I'm gonna bust you down to an Academy Freshman fa' this!"

Jer was getting a real dragon's breath worth of heat. First, there was the invitation to the crime scene at B.D. Waterson and Sons. Then came me beating the Chicago swelter with a visit to the city morgue. And now, at four in the morning, Jer and I sat in the Chief of Police's office, fresh from our late-night shopping spree at Waterson's. Across from us, O'Malley's thinning hair wafted around his head like a halo around a cleric's melon.

Yep. We'd gotten his fat Irish ass out of bed.

"You know," I piped in, "we did stop a robbery."

"Put a sock in it, circus freak!" O'Malley yelled. "I don't think any high-falootin' lawyer is gonna come ta' ya' rescue ta'nite. I've got you down fa' destruction of private prop'pa-tee, assault, and interference in a police investa'gay-shun." He snorted, and his smirk was well-earned. He had a point. To an extent. "As tha' day progresses, I'll see what else I can cook up."

Jer cleared his throat. "Chief, sir, it was Billi's idea to return to Waterson's tonight. He not only stopped what could have been a clean-out of one of Chicago's top jewelry dealers, but he's also delivered two suspects from the Davenport murder to us on a silver platter."

"I don't care for the private dicks, Flannigan, and ya' know that," the Chief snapped. "I especially don' care for tha' freaks of nature that fancy themselves above reproach!"

"Since when have I done that, O'Malley?" I shrugged.

His dark Irish eyes narrowed on me, and I won't lie—I was a little concerned. Any minute now, he was going to clutch his ticker and drop like a counterweight severed from a portcullis. O'Malley wasn't just inviting a coronary. He was setting up the banquet table, giving a play list to the minstrel, and lighting the hearth in anticipation.

"Are ya' sure ya' want ta' fence wi' me, Shorty?" He loomed over me now, and I could smell the night's crud and muck in his breath. *Jeez, O'Malley, you didn't even bother to give the pearly whites a brushing?* "I've been more than tolerant o' the likes o' you, showin' me up, makin' me look like a fool. Well, ta'night I'm done. Ta'night I'm gonna start wi' a clean slate, clean of the papers callin' me a Mick cop what's a showpiece for tha' City Hall." His beefy finger pointed to the phone. "Ya' see tha' telephone there, Shorty? I'll be calling Mr. Miles Waterson himself on that phone later this morning and I'm gonna tell him we stopped a robbery and cracked tha' case wide open for the murder of his worker."

Okay, O'Malley, let's see how long I can keep your attention before I need to switch the die. "You're going to call Waterson and tell him you stopped the robbery?"

"Of course I am!"

I gave a glance to Jer. "Told ya."

My eyes returned to the Chief, watching his attempt to be overbearing fail miserably. I shook my head and gave a long, slow sigh. "O'Malley, that is not going to do you any good...nor is it going to make you any friends in high places."

"Shit." Jer muttered. "Billi, what did I tell you in the—"

"I'm telling you," I said to Jer, "you got to trust me on this."

O'Malley's brows angled upward as he shot glances between the two of us. "Excuse me, but what are ya' two on about?"

Jer took his hat off and screwed his eyes tight. Here was the hook we had rehearsed. "Sir, we talked about this in the car and…" he took a deep breath. "Billi's got a theory—"

"Oh! *Does* he now?! The freak has got a better theory about this open-and-shut case of robbery-homici—"

"Actually, a robbery and *double* homicide," Jer corrected. He looked at me with a silent plea to just skewer him with a broadsword. Seeing as I didn't have one and that I needed to see this through to the end, he only got a curt nod from me. "And there might be a third body. Somewhere. Sir. Chief."

"A third body? Somewhere?" O'Malley needed to remember to breathe, or that vein in the center of his forehead was going to tear through the skin and wrap around the ceiling fan. He stepped away from us, seemingly considering the possibility that the body count in this case was climbing. O'Malley reached his city map of Chicago, and then spun around to address us both. "I take it this 'third body' is part of his *theeee-rrrie?* Tell me, this *theeee-rrrie* of yours, Baddings—why would it concern me and the phone call I'm gonna be making to Mr. Waterson?"

"Make that call, and it's going to tip off a series of events you don't want." More to the point, it was going to tip off a series of events *I* didn't want. I was only a step or two away from the Pitcher's Pendant, but if O'Malley, Jer, and Chicago's Finest didn't back me up on this one, the talisman was going underground. I couldn't afford that. "There's a bigger con going on here, and it's a con that's got a body count attached to it. If you don't follow my lead and follow it good, what you're seeing here in Chicago is just the warm-up in the bullpen."

"What are ya' on about, Baddings?" Great. O'Malley wasn't a fan of baseball. What a dink! "I donna' have the time—"

Roll those weighted bones, Baddings, I thought as I reached into my coat pocket. "Make the time, Chief!"

The lighting in the office wasn't designed for showing off expensive jewelry, but it was good enough to see that what I had grabbed was a sapphire. The glittering rock was so big that it not only made O'Malley's and Jerry's eyes bulge, but I thought I saw some of the cops out in the adjoining bullpen shield their eyes against its sparkle.

Settle down, boys. It's about to get interesting.

"Jesus Christ, Billi!" Jer said. "You lifted that from Waterson's?"

No need to lie about it, and definitely no need to worry about it. "I did."

O'Malley's expression was no shock either. "Bless tha' Virgin Mary," he whispered. His smile was as brilliant as a morning sunrise. "We can add robbery to the list of charges, and as it was a crime scene, tampering with evidence."

"Yeah," I said, lifting up the necklace. I gave a slight cough and held it out to Jer. "It's a beautiful piece, isn't it? I mean, I was just thinking how wearing this could make a girl worthy of a royal suitor's hand." I clicked my tongue and peered deep into the arrangement of smaller green stones surrounding the center piece, "But no, I wouldn't want to see this on a girl I knew. Not this."

"You're not going to see it on anybody because it's *evidence* in a robbery-homicide, you moron!"

Now *that* was a surprise. I looked up at my friend. He was no longer Jerry Flannigan, but *Detective* Flannigan.

And Detective Flannigan was pissed. "I trusted you, followed your hunch, allowed you on a crime scene—*twice*—and tonight you're lifting evidence—*expensive* evidence—from a crime scene?!"

"To prove a point," I insisted.

"My point, ya' mean!" barked O'Malley. "That yer crooked, just like any private dick, scrapin' 'is nickels and dimes ta'gether. Ya' saw it there and just couldn't say no, could ya?"

"Hey, I'm comin' clean, right? That's what this is all about: comin' clean and what we need to do about this, right?" I extended the necklace to O'Malley. "So how about we swap this necklace for a pair of bracelets? What do you say, Chief?"

The confession was making O'Malley's night. Well, okay, early morning. I wish I could say that what I was going to do next would break my heart; but even if it did, neither of them would have believed it.

My hand closed over the necklace and with a soft jingle, the jewelry hit O'Malley's office floor hard. He stepped back at the sudden explosion of stones scattering and dancing across the tiles. Neither Jer nor O'Malley moved, but both of them jerked upright as I hopped out of my chair and landed on the necklace's prize sapphire stone.

"Holy shit," gasped Jer. His eyes darted from the floor to me.

"It's okay, my friend." My Orc-smiting grin was added reassurance. "I didn't want to tip my hand all the way. Never hurts to have a dagger up the sleeve when your back's against the tavern wall."

I swallowed the bitter taste welling in my mouth and then tipped my head back, my own dark gaze peering into O'Malley's. "All right, then. Seeing as I have your undivided attention, how about you get those potatoes out of your ears—I know you got 'em in there—and you listen up? The clock is ticking, and we've got one shot at seeing just how far up the food chain this con goes. You in, O'Malley, or are you out?"

CHAPTER SEVENTEEN

Playing Hardball

The still nights always bothered me. The nights when the silence that was so loud it made your ears bleed. My boys in the Stormin' Scrappies unit would be moving low, moving slow, and with every rustle of grass, snap of twigs, and whisper of armor against earth, I would wonder if the silence was giving us away. The secret to being quiet was making sure that the sounds of the snapping twig, the whispering armor, and the murmuring grass were spaced well enough apart from one another that no one noticed them.

I would have been thrilled to be on one of those bothersome nights, but those kind of nights were spent in the company of Dwarves with covert military training. While I knew these cops were trained, and that their training was anything but a cakewalk, it wasn't the kind of training I was used to, and it definitely wasn't the kind of training suited for what we were doing right now.

Or maybe cops, on a whole, are a noisy bunch. Hell, I read somewhere that the cops in Canada rode on horseback. Yeah, that's really smart. When I think of stealth, I think, "*Hey, let's get on a tall, four-legged pack beast that makes a lot of noise when it moves and, oh yeah, doesn't mind voicing an opinion.*"

So there we were, staking out a very plain house located in the outskirts of Chicago. Well, it wasn't really a house. More like an upscale shack. It was apparent, even before the sunlight had died several hours ago, that though this dwelling was looked after, no one really lived there. At least, not for any prolonged period of time. This was the kind of house you stole away to when you needed to disappear for a while. Four hours outside of the city limits with nothing around? This was the definition of a safe house.

Yeah, I've done my fair share of stakeouts, both from the battlements of a keep overlooking a pass, and from the parked Ford (not mine, but easy pickings for a guy with my skills) sitting across from a perpetrator's known hovel. While I love the works of my girl Agatha, she never really explores the tedium of hours spent watching and waiting for something—anything—to happen. And it never bodes well for a stakeout when the biggest thing to happen to a place all day is you, the one supposedly laying low and observing all the activity.

First, the arrival out here might as well have been preceded by a herald flying a brilliant blue and lime green banner. I knew this was O'Malley's way of saying "My *operation, my way!*" when, as Jer and the parties directly involved all knew, the Chicago Police were moving on my word. This excursion almost brought back memories of me leading those beloved Stormin' Scrappies. Almost. With a truck full of coppers and two police cars tearing out of the Windy City, my nostalgia quickly slipped away like the memory of a dream. Fortunately, we were just acting on the initial lead. I hadn't gone into the finer details of this scheme of mine, and Chicago's Finest were following along.

For the time being.

O'Malley, upon arriving at the address provided, had his men fan out and surround the place. Now I got a hint of that Academy training, and while I guessed it worked adequately in the mean streets of Chicago, it didn't work so well out here. Downtown, there are plenty of places for concealment. Here, apart from high grass and a few trees, crouching down just made you look like a chump in a dark uniform, standing out like a Troll crashing a Pixie's family reunion. The Fates, however, were cutting us a break. There was no one here. Not a soul for miles. We were out in the farm country of Illinois, rural and remote.

My latest catnap had started while sunlight still hit the modest country house with its late afternoon glow. I woke up to find the house shrouded in darkness, its two kerosene lanterns the only light around us for miles.

"Coffee?" Jer asked, softly tapping my shoulder with the thermos' cup.

I took my eyes away from the soft glow coming from the one window, and now savored the aroma tickling my nose. It was Mick's brew, powerful as any potion of awareness.

A hand from the back seat knocked mine out of the way. Since I knew which of the two passengers back there was able to move unhindered, I didn't bother to go for my boom dagger. I knew who the hand (and the coffee that should have been mine) belonged to.

Without so much as a glance to Jer or me, O'Malley took the cup and sipped. His face twisted for a moment, and the gaze he tossed into the tiny cup showed that Mick's brew was little too potent for his sensitive Irish palette.

I didn't let the slur bug me too much. I couldn't afford to lose the Chief at this point. He could single-handedly botch this whole thing if his ego was challenged. It was best to humor him for now.

"So," O'Malley huffed. His voice sounded too loud for the car. "A day spent sitting here on our arses, starin' at a shack what's empty. This is yer brilliant plan, Baddings, for preventing another death and solving two murders?"

"Part of it, O'Malley," I answered, attempting to give him a subtle volume cue by keeping my own voice soft. "We secured the place. We made the call. Now, if my theory is right, we should be seeing something relatively soon."

He finally turned to look at me. "And exactly what are we going ta' see?"

I looked from the house to O'Malley, and then back to the house. "I—don't really know for sure—" The look on his face read like a witch's prophecy, foretelling him stepping out of the car and calling everyone in. I couldn't let that happen. My hands went up as I said, "—but just wait. Just wait, O'Malley. I'm thinking this is going to play out the way I expect. You just have to have a little patience and a little faith in the Dwarf."

His beady eyes went to Jer, then returned to me. "Ya' got half-an-hour."

"Come on, O'Malley. One hour."

"*Half-an-hour.* No more, no less." The car door's latch rang in my ears. Everything was so damn quiet around here. "You're lucky I don't call it off after I finish this piss."

He slammed the door out of spite. Why don't you just shoot your service piece in the air a few times, you stupid dink?

I shook my head at the rapid pitter-patter against the dry grass just outside the car. By the Fates, O'Malley, I know you don't like me, but please…a little decorum.

The sound was (thankfully) drowned out by Jer. "Billi, I'm getting a little concerned, myself."

"What's the time, pal?"

Jerry kept the torch down, so as not to let its light tip off that something was in the shadows. "Nine o'clock."

I nodded, giving my beard a slow stroke. "I know you're still trying to noodle all this through, too."

"Well, you could have let me in on a little more in the car. I know you said I had to trust you and all, but that stunt with the necklace—"

My bushy red eyebrows rose as I grinned. "It got your attention."

"Well, yeah…"

"And more important, it got O'Malley's attention."

"That it did." Jerry chuckled. His smile faded. "If this doesn't pan out like you're thinking, like you told me it would, O'Malley's going to drag you through the papers. Your name will only be good for fertilizing corn crops."

Dammit, I hate it when Jer is right like that.

"Baddings!" came a dry whisper, followed by a few choice swear words, and the sound of someone lumbering back to the car. I watched O'Malley wipe his hands on his pants and then the door groaned open and shut. "Behind us." He was still whispering. So nice he decided to play by my rules. "Headlights."

"Mind if I switch with you, Billi?" Jer asked me. "Give me a better angle on things?"

I slipped behind Jer, and remained standing in the driver's seat as I tracked the bright, twin orbs through the rear window. The road they followed only led to one place: our stakeout.

"All right," I muttered. "A good sign."

O'Malley shushed me. He was too engrossed by the sudden activity to see the glare I shot him. What an ass.

The tree we were parked behind would have appeared to be nothing more than a dark cutout against the night. The only way the driver could have seen the lone tree, or us parked behind it, was if he were to turn his car up the trail we had left behind, assuming that he noticed it. I was rolling the bones that he wouldn't. The night outside of the city was thicker than Orc blood.

O'Malley ducked down behind the driver's seat as the car passed. Jer and I shared a shrug at the Irishman's reaction and turned back to watch the car's progress. It rumbled by and then its engine surged again, working its way over the uneven earth. Light bathed the front of the house as the car settled into an even, rhythmic idle. Then there was silence, and the darkness was once more pierced only by the firefly-like glow of the lanterns.

O'Malley went for the flashlight, but this time I did the blocking, putting the torch in the driver's seat. "Not yet," I warned him. "We got to make sure this plays out."

His big, fat yap opened, about to launch into another one of his fits, but I had reached my limit. This was the Endgame, and I was going to be damned if this dink was going to screw it up for me.

My hand slapped around his mouth so hard that Jer winced. I was now touching my bulbous nose to O'Malley's. "I've been a good little freak all night, but now you're really working *past* my last nerve. According to your promise, I've still got about twenty minutes. So, if you don't want to see what I can do to you in *five* minutes with Jerry's thermos, I suggest you sit still, shut up, and watch!"

I released O'Malley, then reached past him for something in the backseat. The Chief recoiled—probably thinking about the thermos—but then relaxed as I came back with the binoculars. They probably looked bigger than normal in my hands, and that coaxed a snicker from the other side of the backseat. I silenced our guest with a look.

For you, pal, I'll only need two minutes.

Maybe this shack was in need of a fresh coat, but there was enough white left to make out the tall man stopping at the door. Dark suit and hat. That was all I could see.

No, wait a second. He had a small bag with him, shaped like the case Old Doc Roberts carried. It had to be the payoff.

The figure turned and looked across the field, seeming to take in the sound of crickets and assorted critters enjoying the night's solitude. *Look all you like*, I thought. *You're not going to see us*. I fiddled with the focus and caught the flash of a lighter. *Nice touch. Not for the thrifty*. His cigarette smoldered for a moment and then slipped back into darkness. The door opened behind him, and then the porch was empty once more.

I began, "Now we'll see if he takes the—"

Pop! We all saw the bright flash from the window, like lightning trapped between a wizard's hands. *Pop! Pop!*

Jer's dry whisper gave me a start. "Billi?"

"It's okay. It's okay. He's wearing a vest." Our man was fine, provided the guy hadn't taken a head shot. My binoculars went up again as the door opened. I watched as the tall figure walked down the stoop, took another long look around, and then got into his car.

"Shit!" I turned to Jerry. "Thermos, now!"

O'Malley was looking back and forth between me, the house, and the car now retracing its trip. "What hell are ya—!"

I passed the flashlight back to O'Malley while I took the thermos from Jer. "Signal the troops, O'Malley! Stop that guy!" I turned the key while working the clutch with the thermos. Being in the driver's seat was never part of the plan, but plans change.

The car lurched forward, and that momentum was all I really needed. My left hand steered while I pushed the thermos into the gas pedal with my right. I could barely see where I was going, but I knew I was headed in the right direction. I didn't want to waste time looking for the switch to turn on the police siren, so I leaned on the car horn instead.

"Billi, what the hell are you doing?" Jer yelled over the noise.

"Trying to get our man out of there. The bullets might have winded him, but he's got to get moving!" I looked over my shoulder. "The guy went in with a case. He didn't have it when he—"

The darkness disappeared along with the night's interrupted silence...and the shack.

What was causing that hum?

"Brake."

No, more like a high pitched whine.

"Brake!"

What was that, Jer? Did you say "Rafe"? Who the hell is Rafe?

The whine disappeared with a surreal pop.

"Brake!"

I'd never heard Jerry scream before, and I hope I never do again. It was a high-pitched shrill, like a Siren when she's having that "special time" that women have. (Oh yeah, not always is the Siren's song *that* sweet.) As piercing as his voice was, I was impressed his enunciation held out well enough for me to understand what he was screaming.

Granted, when I saw the raging inferno that the safe house had become, growing larger and larger by the second, I would have probably hit the brake anyway. The thermos slammed on the last foot pedal I hadn't tried, and I felt myself lurch forward. I heard a dull *thud* to one side of me while the car started to spin. The cab was starting to become brighter and brighter, and then the world outside decided to lurch a little, too. My grip tightened on the wheel, not that I thought it would keep us from flipping over. If we were going to take a tumble, we were going to take a tumble. I felt my stomach start to lift up in my throat. Higher. Higher.

The car changed its mind and slammed down on all fours, back to God's own Earth. My stomach finished its stay in my larynx and plummeted, and I was thankful I hadn't enjoyed the coffee Mick had provided. I think I would have lost it, plus anything else I had eaten before coming out here...

And that was exactly what was happening to O'Malley. Not quick enough to open the car door, he was spewing all over his urine-stained pants and the police cab's interior. The rest of us were slumped in our seats, watching the debris continue to flutter and fall from the sky. It was dark once again, but that heavy country darkness was competing with the illumination cast by the newly-created fire. We were close enough to feel the heat, but far enough away that we weren't in danger. Still, Jer was more than vindicated for the scream. Had I not hit the brakes when I did, we would have plowed into "the cannon's mouth," as Shakespeare would have said. Fire was indiscriminate that way. It didn't care if you were animal, vegetable, or mineral. You were fuel for it, regardless.

I heard the passenger door moan open, and O'Malley stumbled out into the field to survey the damage. Jer also got out, but walked in the direction of the oncoming reinforcements that barreled toward us. Maybe we'd gotten lucky and they had caught the tall assassin before he disappeared into the cover of night.

The flames dancing before us reached high into the night sky. It could have been a welcoming bonfire for travelers to a celebration or soldiers returning victorious from a great battle. Instead, this fire was someone's tomb. I swallowed and felt the dryness tear at my throat. If our man had been lucky, his killer was a professional through and through.

"So, have you seen enough?" I asked, turning toward the backseat.

With O'Malley's loss of faculties, it probably stank back there. Still, our other passenger was motionless, just watching the safe house burn. He hadn't bothered to make a break for it while the three of us were dazed from my driving. He knew the leg irons would have slowed him down enough for the cops to catch him. Again. "Sledgehammer" Sammy Saint was a real mix of emotions, part of his bottom lip now trapped underneath his top teeth. Since the first bank job, he had probably been thinking that he was the one calling the shots. After all, Sammy was one Trouble answered to. He was the Alpha Troll, the mountain of a man that was going to lead them to bigger, better, and brighter things, even better than being part of the unstoppable Baltimore Mariners. He was going to lead them to the best parties, the classiest dames, and all the right places to be seen.

That illusion was gone. Up in smoke, as it were. Sammy had never been a leader. He wasn't even a follower. He was just a stepping stone. A means to an end.

"Yeah." His voice was one of a man beaten. I wished I could feel sorry for him, but it wasn't going to happen. "I'll tell you guys everything."

O'Malley was now walking the perimeter of the fire, still checking for signs of life. I would never have pegged him as the optimistic type. Jer was flagging down the paddy wagon, no doubt hoping the same thing I was. Another hunch—and dammit, I really didn't like this one creeping into my noggin—was convincing me that the assassin had gotten away. Whoever he was, he had known exactly what he was doing.

"Well, Sammy, you almost got that right." I turned back to him, my eyes narrowing on his. "In the trunk of this car is my battle axe, and I've really not used it properly tonight. Seeing as you and I are all by ourselves, I think you're going to tell *me* everything first. Otherwise, I'm going to have to show you just how versatile that axe of mine is."

Sammy tore his gaze away from the fire. His head tipped back, and he looked down at me past the tip of his nose. "Is that a threat, Small Fry?"

"No," I replied.

The ballplayer-thief huffed. "Eh, what the hell do I got to lose?"

"When you talk to O'Malley and the cops—*back at the precinct*—you tell them everything, and it'll be jake with the lawyer types. Maybe not an R.B.I., but definitely a walk to First." I placed my hands on the top of the driver's seat, took a deep breath, and pushed back that growing anxiousness. "But I need to know the details now. Ya' follow?"

He cleared his throat, glanced one more time at the fire, and then turned back to me. "I got a record."

"Kinda figured you did," I answered. His eyes narrowed on me, and I shrugged. "Joe probably did the odd nickel-and-dime crime, but you? Your clothes, at the Jefferson, were orderly and immaculate, and you didn't like people touching your stuff. That's a different kind of behavior altogether. Either you were a military man, which I can usually spot, or you had done some hard time."

His face softened. "When I got out, I played ball because people didn't care about my record. They just cared about how I knocked the cover off it. I got lucky when a scout for the Mariners saw me. It happened to be one of those games where I *didn't* pick a fight." He took a deep breath. "If we had just kept it simple, none of this would have happened. You know, just kept it to the basics. Robbin' banks. You go where the money is. But I guess, when someone tells ya' you could be doin' better, you begin to think you can get away with just about anything." Now I was feeling sorry for Sammy. Murder had never been in the scheme he had cooked up for Trouble. I caught the remorse, along with the fire, reflecting in his eyes. "Just about anything."

Sammy kept talking. Told me everything. With every detail, I felt that anxiousness well up in me.

Regardless of what time I got back to Chicago, I had a lot to do. The night was still young.

CHAPTER EIGHTEEN

Strike Three, You're Dead

The cab disappeared into the darkness with a rumble, leaving me in front of the stone steps ascending to a tall door. The light coming from the foyer shone brilliantly through glass facets, giving the doorway an almost mystical quality. Well, okay, a somewhat *romanticized* idea of mystical. There was nothing magical or incredible about this brownstone, apart from the occupant that resided within. I began the climb up to the doorway, and that damn door kept getting taller and taller the closer I came to it. Optical illusions aside, the sweat I felt across my back didn't instill confidence in what I was doing, but time really wasn't allowing me to come up with a cunning plan. I had to act, hit my mark hard, and then get the hell out.

Then there was the other matter I needed to close, concerning the Pendant of Coe. I wasn't looking forward to that at all.

Now I was in front of the door, and I could easily reach the doorbell. Granted, I could also whip out the battle axe and make my own entrance.

There's showing *hubrimaz*, and then there's being a flat-out twat. Best to ring the doorbell.

My finger had not even reached the button when a shadow materialized on the other side of the door. Locks slid back, and finally the hatch opened to reveal the manor's butler.

No awkward reaction. No searching over me for a caller. Not even an "*Are you aware of the time?!*" His eyes met mine and the smile he gave me was especially cordial for half-past-one in the morning. "Good evening, sir. May I take your—?"

Now we had a moment of awkwardness.

"That's okay," I said, my grip tightening on the haversack. "I'm bringing my own to this shindig, and I'd like to keep the favors close."

"Very good, sir," this Jeeves replied. "If you will follow me, please?"

"No problem," I said with a nod.

Our footsteps knocked and clicked against planks of polished wood, shadows and faint reflections following us down a long corridor to the parlor. The connected arboretum made it easy to forget we were in the middle of the city. The brownstone was attached to a small courtyard, and this glass extension overlooked the modest sanctuary of green. I could make out the pale granite of a pair of benches, vacant now but patiently waiting for anyone that wanted to sit and enjoy some nature in the middle of a grove of concrete and cement.

Yeah, it was a beautiful setting promising some well-earned serenity from the hustle and bustle of the Windy City, but while the courtyard was serene, it hardly promised solitude. Anyone who stood in the glass encasement could watch any and all activity happening in the small yard. The arboretum was designed that way.

Seen this before. And because I knew it for what it was, I took a moment to look over the brownstone's extension.

The rulers of Acryonis—same shit, different race and culture when you got right down to brass keys—could not hide their true personality traits no matter how well they played political games. Your respective ruler can be judged by the company he keeps, and the keep in which he keeps himself. Arboretums such as this one, at first glance, were always a pretty addition to a castle, especially on the days where clouds were sparse, the sun so bright you winced at it even through closed eyes, and the sky an even brighter shade of blue. You would find the character behind the crown when you looked at the furniture. If the chairs were turned away from the windows, it was a sign of a benevolent ruler, a man or woman confident in their company and in their supreme guidance over the realm. Their atrium would be a place to mingle, a place to enjoy the warmth of the sun or marvel with a childlike wonder at rain or snow as it fell around them, their own person secure and safe from the elements.

My host was the *other* kind of ruler. His chairs faced the large windows, far enough from the glass that whoever occupied them would see anyone else entering the sunlit room. No furniture was arranged in an inviting social circle for friends to gather or share pleasantries. This was less of a sanctuary and more of a glass dais, built to watch people in the courtyard either overtly or covertly. The rulers behind this sort of setting wanted to watch their court and watch them carefully. If usurpers wanted to make a play for the throne, he or she would see them coming. It was part insecurity, part paranoia. Very *MacBeth*, if you will. Wouldn't surprise me in the least if that kooky Scotsman had his own atrium built shortly after taking the throne.

"Is there anything you need, sir?" the butler asked me.

Yeah, Jeeves, I could use a magic talisman handed over to me all polite-like. "Nah, I don't think so."

"Oh, come now," another voice said, entering from the opposite side of the parlor. "I'm sure we can find a beer, or do you care for something a bit stronger?"

My eyebrow crooked as my host entered the room, his hair slicked back and sharp as it was when I saw him at the country club.

"I think tonight, Mr. Waterson, I'm going to keep my wits about me." I was going to need every last one of them, I feared.

He stared at me for a moment, his smile a lot of things. Sincere wasn't one of them. "That you, Jeeves, that will be all. You can go home now. Enjoy your day off tomorrow, with my compliments."

The butler's name really was Jeeves?!

"Very good, sir," Jeeves said with a slight tip of his head. He was out of the room in only a few steps, leaving us alone.

"Please," Miles said, motioning to the couch that faced a high-backed chair, where he apparently held his own court.

I unbuttoned my coat. If I needed to move, I'd want the mobility. "That's okay, I prefer to stand."

Miles shrugged, then took that high-backed seat. "Suit yourself, Mr. Baddings." He considered me for a moment and then gave little chuckle. Apparently, I amused him like a court jester. "You are quite the enigma. And brazen, if I do say so myself."

"Brazen?" I asked. "Isn't that a nice way of describing me as pushy?"

Miles didn't flinch. "In some circles, yes." He laced his fingers together and cleared his throat. "Pushy, however, is not as attractive a trait. Brazen can have many practical applications in the real world, especially for an individual like myself."

Oh, was he going to make the play? This should be fun. "I'm not sure I fol—"

"I don't expect you to, Mr. Baddings, but I would be more than happy to explain my mind to you."

My grip slackened—not by much—on my haversack.

"It's a terrible time we're living in, and tough times require tough decisions and commitments made in order to survive. That is what this day and age is—survival of the fittest. The weeding out of the '*shouldn't* have's from the 'have's so that they are put back where they belong."

"With the 'have not's, I assume you mean."

Miles leaned forward, resting his elbows against his knees. "So you do understand my perspective? I suppose I should add 'intuitive' to your list of traits."

Yeah, I knew what he was saying, but I wouldn't go so far as to say I understood it. I've heard of people trying to purify a racial pool, but a financial one? That's a little odd. Despicable, no matter how you cut it; and with how this guy was handling things, it was a particularly disgusting form of despicable.

"So, what do you need me for?"

"Mr. Baddings, there are going to be some delicate matters coming up for me, and I will need a representative that will stand in my stead if I am otherwise engaged."

"You need a champion?" I asked with a chortle.

Another huff, and his mouth went crooked. "Hmm, perhaps… although 'champion' wouldn't quite be the word I would use."

"But Miles," I said, my hand casually slipping lower on the strap. "I would think you already have a guy in your corner, and a very reliable resource, if I may add."

"I'm sorry, Mr. Baddings?"

Oh, Miles, you shouldn't be planting this seed. You're not going to like the weed it grows. "It sounds like you're in dire need of someone to watch your back."

I know you're there, kid. That smell is in the air.

"I would be hard pressed to find a man of your talents."

I had to make this next shot count. For those not physically in the room with us. "With who is in your crew, I'm amazed you're even talking to me. If I'm reading the papers right, you took these guys under your wing and made them something more than just two-bit bank robbers."

"Mr. Baddings, a businessman like myself is always looking ahead, always looking to expand his resources."

"Expand? Or replace?"

Miles wasn't stupid, but it wasn't Miles I was trying to fish out. "In an industrial machine, everyone serves a purpose."

Gotcha. "And Big Joe—were you done with him once he served his purpose?"

"What happened to Big Joe?" a voice asked from a supposedly-empty doorway.

I didn't have to look to know who spoke. Besides, I wanted to watch Miles Waterson's face for his reaction. A muscle at the back of his jaw twitched, but he never broke his gaze with me.

"Mr. Randalls, I thought we were clear on your part in tonight's proceedings."

Flyball's suit wasn't fitting him well. Not that the ball players were pulling in the greenbacks like ol' Miles here, but they still made enough to get a decent suit. No, his threads were hanging on him. He was a fully developed coat hanger, and from the paleness he sported I wondered if the Mariners' fielder wasn't in need of a serious nap.

"You okay there, Archie?" I asked. "You're not looking so hot."

He asked again, "What happened to Joe?"

Motioning to the jeweler before me, I gave a slight shrug and answered, "Well, it's like this, Arch. Your big boss-man here is the one calling the shots, I think, so it's kind of inap—"

From here, my world became a series of Elvish epics, told in the blink of an eye.

Archie disappeared, or more like he became nothing more substantial than a blur. Suddenly, the air was knocked out of me by something slamming hard into my gut. I would have grunted in pain, but seeing as my liver was now up in my throat and I was gurgling bile, I really couldn't. The bitter taste in my mouth was quickly overpowered by the stinging in my back. That was the arm of the couch I found myself wrapping my spine around. My feet hit the floor, and the rest of me soon followed.

I gave a hard cough, and finally air was back in my lungs. That little bit of sweet pleasure was disrupted by the sudden lurch the world took. I had to take a moment and wonder why it felt like someone had pulled the brake on the Earth and I was spinning out of control, but then I realized it was *me* that had lurched and not the world. That attack left me a little woozy, and the strong scent of electricity in the air didn't help to stave back the nausea. I spit, and an explosion of violet-red spread out before me. The fact that I could still feel my jaw connected to my skull was reassurance that Archie's invisible mace had only succeeded in lifting me off the floor and dropping me back against the polished mahogany.

I smiled. I think I had spit hard enough to get some blood on the expensive couch I now leaned against. There were a few parties we Stormin' Scrappies had crashed back in Acryonis, catching tyrants and overlords off-guard in their posh palaces and garish boudoirs. Even with the odds against them, faced with starving masses and disenchanted generals armed with everything from pitchforks to trebuchets, these dinks would do their best to avoid a scuffle. Why? They didn't want to ruin the furniture. Blood's a real bitch to get out of fabric.

My smile widened as I dabbed my hand against my bloody mouth and then flicked it hard. Grab satisfaction whenever and wherever you can, I say.

"Okay," I heaved. "You want to know what's going on. I'll tell you what's going on. Coach Moneybags here is terminating your contract, just like he did with Big Joe and Shuffle Patterson."

"Nah, Bill was getting cold feet about this last heist. He was thinking about spilling the beans to the cops." Archie shook his head. "He was going to screw everything up for us."

"Try again. He was going to screw things up for your boss here." My gaze remained on Miles, watching him for a reaction. Still nothing. This guy either had Orc blood coursing through his veins, or one hell of an ace up his sleeve. "Miles had a real hum-dinger of a racket in mind, and unfortunately this lucrative campaign didn't account for you and the rest of your pals seeing your twilight years. You've served your purpose, and now he's cleaning house." I winced as I straightened up, giving Miles the once-over. "Apparently, he's doing it with a good amount of ammonia and bleach."

Archie's jaw twitched in the warm light of the parlor. I had his attention, sure, but his trust? I didn't think so. "What about Scooter?"

That was a good question. Scooter was still missing. Had to try for the bunt. "I'm thinking your boss here told you to lay low, right? You and the rest of Trouble needed to hide out somewhere, like a safe house, huh? Safe house on the outskirts of town? All you needed to do was come by tonight, do one more job for Waterson here, and then you were going to high-tail out to the safe house where the rest of Trouble was sitting tight, right? This was, after all, your last job."

Here was where Miles flinched. I'd struck a lode there.

"Miles," Archie began, his eyes finally switching from me to him. "What's going on?"

"Nothing I can't handle," he said, the smile on his face contradicting the look in his eyes. "I'm hearing a lot of conjecture but nothing of substance."

"You want substance?" I barked. "How about I gi—"

Without thinking I reached into my coat pocket, and again Archie moved with that unstoppable speed over to me. I felt my hand being slapped away—hard—and then a quick punch to the chest—harder—that sent me back into the couch. I bounced off its cushions, and was back on the floor.

Archie, now on the other side of the room, held an impressive diamond broach in his fingers.

"Nice, huh?" I wheezed. "Now, tell me you recognize it."

The stone twinkled in the parlor's light. It was hard to forget anything that impressive. "This is one of Waterson's. It was in the case the night of the first attempt."

"The first attempt when the manager unexpectedly showed up, right?"

"Well, yeah," Archie said, turning his eyes back to me. "Things got out of—"

"No, you were set up. Miles was counting on that survival instinct to kick in, and for you all to take care of a problem he had—a manager who knew."

Archie's brow furrowed. "Knew what?"

Now it was Miles' turn to shift uncomfortably. I was tired of being the only one doing so. (Granted, Miles was in less pain than me.) "Archie, we can talk about this later. If Baddings is here, the police can't be—"

When Archie spoke, his voice was a lot louder than it should have been. *"Knew what?!"*

"It's a fake, kid." I nodded to the stone in his hand. Damn, that thing stank! "That whole thing is a fake."

Yeah, little ol' Miles was starting to lose that ice dragon demeanor. He was looking more like a Goblin caught with its claw in the cookie jar. You know, the cookies that belonged to the Orc General?

"Archie, once we tie up this loose end," Miles said, motioning to me, "we can talk about this. You recall how we spoke about cooler heads prevailing in times of crisis?"

The broach slipped out of the ballplayer's hand and shattered at his feet. It was good as copies go, but unlike the real thing, these copies were fragile.

"Miles?" The hurt in his voice was a touch sobering. "What's going on?"

"Archie, I'll explain everything once we are out of here." Miles was on his feet. He gave his tie a slight tug and then pulled the Roscoe from his coat pocket.

I closed my eyes as I heard the hammer pull back, and then an acrid scent assailed my nostrils.

That bitter scent, my noggin quickly registered, was not gunpowder but electricity; and Miles was back in his seat, catching his breath.

The Second Baseman for the Baltimore Mariners was standing with his back to the window overlooking that quaint little courtyard. We both watched as the gun in Archie's grasp folded on itself. The lump that had apparently been the ace up Miles' sleeve fell to the floor with a dull thud, the hammer still pulled back but now unable to strike true.

"When did you start carrying a gun, Miles?" Archie asked.

"Now, Archie, I can imagine how this looks—"

"Really?" he snapped, a slight tremor cresting in his voice. His knuckles were growing as pale as the rest of him, his fists so tight I was expecting blood to come out of his palms. "Please tell me how this looks. *Please!*"

There went the voice again. What had *My World Book* said? *The Pendant of Coe knows no boundaries to what it blesses upon its bearer, so long as the desire is strong and no doubt lingers within.*

Yeah, I think this kid had no doubt he was being set up to be a sucker.

"I know that the private dick here had a piece you'd told us to pinch, and it's a fake. I know you told me that Sammy and Big Joe were meeting us outside of town at a safe house where we were going to come up with a better plan on hitting your place. I also know you had me take care of Shuffle because he was going to blab to the cops. And you wanted me to do the same thing to this guy here. That's what *I* know!" I flinched as he suddenly pointed at me. "I'm not some hired gun, you know? I ain't no killer."

"No, Archie, no you're not," Miles agreed as he slowly removed himself from his throne. His eyes were locked with the ball player's as he kept a wide berth between the two of them. "That's not what we all agreed to, but Mr. Patterson had become a problem, a problem that needed a decisive solution. The same can be said for Mr. Baddings here, and as you have relieved me of my gun, the responsibility now falls on you."

"Not until you tell me where the guys are!"

I heard the soft popping of stitches. I blinked my eyes hard once, then twice. I wanted to be sure of what I was seeing. Archie was looking pale; and considering what dark magic can do to you, this was no surprise. But he was also…*growing?* Yeah, I could now see some serious definition forming under his modest shirt and coat. His neck seemed to thicken like porridge left out to cool.

Miles' hands lowered to his side. He nodded, resigning to Archie's demand. His expression was tight, a combination of disappointment and frustration, but with a deep breath, he looked up at Archie. "Fine. You want the truth. Here is the truth of the matter: you *are* a killer. You killed Mr. Patterson as he was about to upset our opera. We live in desperate times, and what would happen to you in light of an injury? You wouldn't be enjoying the hospitality of the Jefferson, I assure you."

His fists slackened. The neck seemed to swell for a moment, then shrink. Miles was clouding the kid's confidence. How the hell did he know to do this?

"I had to secure all our futures, Archie, so we are killers together. I had met with Mr. Saint and Mr. Murphy on Sunday, informing them the operation was going to end here and now. When they refused to let this last job go, I had to take matters into my own hands. Now is the time to back out, and since they couldn't see things my way, I dealt with them."

Archie's stance faltered, and his hand braced against the smooth glass of the atrium. *C'mon, kid,* I thought, *you can't afford to lose it now.* "So Sammy and Big Joe..." and his voice trailed off. This was going to get bad. Really bad. "And what about—"

"Riley? Ah, yes, Riley..."

Riley? Not "Mr. Jenkins"?

"Well, Riley can see you through the window, and he's about to kill you."

Archie's hand and neck seemed to explode simultaneously, and his face twisted into an expression that was part shock, part confusion. His mouth opened, but only a pathetic hacking sound emerged. When he turned to look through the now-shattered window, its shards falling away as he pulled his ruined hand back, his head wobbled so unsteadily I half-expected it to drop off his shoulders. He strained to see across the way, and tried to take a breath. That took Archie back a few steps, and then he crumpled to the ground.

CHAPTER NINETEEN
DOWN, BUT NOT OUT

That's a rough way to go: The last thing you see is your *teammate* putting a slug into you. (Hell of a shot, though.)

My voice was back, but of the rest of me was keen on staying as still as possible. "That was nicely handled, Miles. You think fast on your feet when you need to."

He eyed Archie's corpse for a minute and then sniffed. "Yes, I think I did handle that well. Granted it was not how I planned it, but the end result was the same."

From a connecting room—what appeared at a glance to be a kitchen—came the crack shot, Riley "Scooter" Jenkins. "Nice way to keep Scooter here out of the way while you kept Archie in the dark," I complimented. "When were you going to let him know about all this?"

"Oh please, Mr. Baddings," chided Miles, "do you think for a moment I would have told him I was planning a getaway for just the two of us, Riley and myself?" He looked at Riley, and the look they shared...lingered...and then he sniffed again. "As you, no doubt, assumed, I was expecting you to come by, Mr. Baddings. I received word about the botched robbery tonight."

"You probably also heard about how only one guy showed up at the safe house, too," I added.

"That gave me pause, I must admit. My associate explained to me that Mr. Murphy showed up alone on account of you dispatching Mr. Saint at the boutique, so I should thank you for taking care of that matter. It was a safe assumption I would be entertaining you tonight. I allow Mr. Randalls to work his magic, and then tie up any remaining loose ends while over the Great Lakes."

I was finally able to prop myself up against the couch, really, *really* wishing for that healing spell I never learned. "Scooter" stopped next to Miles, the ball player's fingers splaying around the handle of his heater.

"So let me see if I got all the pieces put together here right, Miles. You seem like a smart guy, and a smart guy would have figured out that there was something to the Mariners and the bank robberies that followed them wherever they went. That's when you dug into the these ball players' pasts, found out one of them had a record, and that this ex-con was a front man of a group of ne'er-do-wells that liked to live way beyond their means."

"Miles, can we please go now?" Scooter insisted.

"Riley, the man is a detective," he cooed in reply. "Let him enjoy some job satisfaction."

With a slight snort, I continued. "So you passed yourself off as a fan, invested into the team, and then you approached these two-bit bank robbers because that's all they were—two-bit hoods. But you turned them into something special with the high priced heists, didn't you?"

"That I did," Miles stated. "With such power at their disposal what they needed was better management of their talents—"

There was my in. "And you needed a way out, didn't you?"

Miles probably hated being cut off as much as I did; but while he was hardly the pallid sight he'd been while Archie channeled the pendant, Miles did give that air of someone caught in a lie.

"How did you put it to your ol' pal, Bruce? 'Tough times aside, I'm able to meet the needs of even my harder-hit clientele.' Didn't make a lot of sense to me when I first heard it, but when I visited your store the morning of the murder, it clicked into place." Miles' peepers grew larger than Mick's Wednesday Hot Plate Specials. "You're right. It's a bad habit, eavesdropping."

The surprise yielded to a hard, dry laugh. "You were the munchkin at the Rothchild party?"

Okay, Miles, if I live through this, I'm going to have to kill you. You know too much.

"You needed an out when your manager, Samuel Davenport, brought to your attention that one of the store's premier pieces looked a little dodgy. He'd been with the company for eight years, no doubt worked his way up the ladder to manager, so I bet he had developed a keen eye for the rocks. You got a lot of high profile clientele, so it's a safe guess that they don't want some whelp taking care of them. They want you. If they can't get you, they get the manager.

"That master plan of yours, swapping out real stones for fakes and selling your needy clientele high quality Troll crap was brilliant. If any of your folks discover you're selling them shit, they're faced with a dilemma: admit to purchasing and wearing fakes without knowing any better, or keep up appearances. Your clientele is all about appearances."

The hammer pulled back on Scooter's gun. It was time to roll the bones and hope they didn't come up Medusa's Eyes.

"You guys were a convenient happenstance, Riley. Timing was everything."

His finger was around the trigger now. I hate being on the opposite end of boom daggers, I really do.

"Miles?" Riley swallowed hard, his eyes never leaving me but his words definitely intended for someone else. "What's he on about?"

There was something about that tone. It was unnerving me, but I couldn't really put a finger on it.

"Miles?"

At that, I didn't put a finger on the reason so much as I suddenly ran my fist through it.

Yeah, I knew that tone all too well from my *grundle'malking* days. Some dames were understanding that a soldier's lifestyle did not lend itself to settling down, siring the dwarvlings, and buying a few acres of farmland. Enjoying a tavern tickle was all about the moment. If the maid wanted you to carry a lock of hair, a small wreath of heather, or a token for luck in your breast pocket, that was mighty sweet; but simply put, a kiss was not a contract.

The harpies that seemed to miss this facet of the pre-battle boff, we called "Battlefield Biancas". These broads would give you a hell of a *grundle'malk* the day before you set off for the front. When you got back from the battlefield, you would learn that falling to an Ogre's club or a Goblin's short sword might have been a better fate. These Battlefield Biancas would be waiting for you at the city gates, latch themselves to your arm, and decide to enjoy a "Welcome Home" celebration with you. It was all good until you were about to head out with the boys afterward…and that's when the joyous tone in her voice would suddenly be swapped out for, *"Just where do you think you're going?!"*

And that was the tone coming out of...*Riley?*

"Oh, come on, Miles, are you kidding me?" I asked. I was going to call this pitch like I was seeing it. "You're holding out from your betrothed, here? You didn't tell him about the necromancer's scheme you cooked up?"

"I believe that is enough job satisfaction, Mr. Baddings," Miles said curtly.

"Miles, you didn't answer me," Riley insisted. "What's he on about?"

"We can talk about it on the plane," Miles answered, checking his watch. "We're on borrowed time here, so kill him and be done with it."

The gun then turned on Miles. Riley slowly backed between us, inching his way towards Archie's corpse.

"No, we'll talk about it now." He motioned to the body behind him. "If we need to get across town, we can move like jackrabbits with the necklace, right?" No answer. His arm straightened, extending the muzzle towards Miles. *"Right?"*

I wasn't much of a threat, slumped and leaning against the couch for support. That, and my haversack of weapons was over by Archie.

"Talk," Riley barked at me.

"Sure thing," I said. "Davenport—the guy you all murdered—probably picked up on a fake brought into the store. Miles assured Davenport he'd personally look into it, but Miles was actually putting him off. I bet you the farm, tavern, and family mule that Miles was even clocking in some extra time at Waterson and Sons just to make sure he could curtail any more questions and concerns from his 'fine manager'.

"Then he figured out there was something about those Baltimore Mariners. What perfect timing! So he concocted a con that would set himself up nicely. Give you guys a bit of direction, all leading to a hit on his own store as the final score. I assumed he confided in you that his store was full of fakes and he was intending to swindle his insurance company for millions?"

Riley nodded. "Well, yeah, that was the real plan, sure."

"And with you keeping an eye on Trouble for Miles, the two of you schemed out how to wrap everything up once this job was done. I just bet you two were going to take off for somewhere a little more tolerant of your lifestyle. Europe, perhaps? With the settlement check reaching your port-of-call, it would be just the two of you happily ever after. The baseball star and the well-to-do jeweler."

Riley's eyes jumped between us, and he finally muttered, "Canada."

I had hit the mark, and Miles' voice, peppered with a pinch of panic, confirmed it. "You have two choices here, Riley: Shoot this circus freak and come with me right now, or talk with the police. I'm certain, if you plead guilty to murder, you will merely earn life in prison." He cast a glance to the corpse. "But seeing as how you shot him in the back: premeditation. You may get the chair. Come now. Shoot him and let's go."

I chuckled at Riley, ignoring Miles' rising panic. I had to keep the kid's attention on me. "Really? Got your passport?"

It took a moment for the kid to answer. "Miles took care of it."

Now I had to laugh. (Shit, I hoped that wasn't a broken rib I felt.) "Have you *seen* it? You might want to go over the details, in case you're flying incognito. You're part of the Baltimore Mariners. You think no one's going to no—"

My head flew to one side, thanks to the mean mule's kick Miles planted. More blood on the fine couch, but Miles wasn't coming back here. That was a given.

"*That's enough!*" Miles shouted. "Kill him and let's go!"

"Gun's still cocked, Miles," Riley said, his head tipping to one side. So *that's* how a guy looks as a lover scorned. "I wouldn't move too quickly. Considering the nights we've spent together, you of all people know how jumpy I am."

Okay, push back that vision conjured before me. Please, for the love of the Fates, push it back. Back. Back. Got to stay focused here.

The ice in Riley's voice helped me focus. "Where's the passport, Miles?"

"It's waiting for us at the airport, in the charter plane, packed with the rest of our things, Riley." His eyes narrowed on the young ballplayer's. "And don't think we're not going to talk about this further when we're in the air!"

Riley shook his head. "Actually, we should address this now. If you've packed up my passport where I can't get to it, it'll be a little complicated getting into Canada. Won't it?"

It got way too quiet for my liking.

"I got a lot of reasons to pull this trigger, don't I?" Riley asked Miles. Or maybe he was asking me. "But I'm not gonna, because you're needed. So I'm going to help myself to the pendant, and then we'll head on out. All three of us."

Come again?

"Come again?" Miles stuttered.

"I figured you'd drive, and the detective and I would talk on the way. If what he says is true, then you were planning to off us all, so we can get rid of him however you planned for the rest of us. If all this winds up a lie, we can still send him for a swim once we're in the air." He took a few steps closer to Archie. "I'm just gonna grab the pendant, and then we can discuss our future together. Oka—"

The simple question suddenly erupted into a scream accompanied by a hard crunch, the grinding and snapping of bones mingling with a sound of something thick tearing apart. Miles probably didn't know the cacophony of gore, but I did. I could have gone my whole lifetime without hearing it again.

Riley toppled and fell to the ground, the gunshot ripping through the momentary silent shock that had fallen across the room. The echo didn't linger for long as a howl erupted from Archie, the sound nudging a few paintings off their hooks and rattling the glass in its panes. Turning towards the sound also meant turning towards the smell, the smell of fresh blood and exposed flesh.

Archie's mouth was stretching open so wide, it resembled an insect's mandibles. The jaw muscles stretched his lips to form a square orifice, the delicate skin there splitting under the abnormal strain. There was no blood to fall from these numerous slits as his heart was no longer pumping, but still his mouth dripped with it. Blood. Bone. Sinew. Meat. His open maw showed all this, and none of it belonged to him. It had once belonged to Riley. The unnatural bite had torn completely through Riley's ankle, too much for Archie to consume in only three chews.

Not bad for a guy who'd been dead a few minutes ago.

The Pendant of Coe knows no boundaries to what it blesses upon its bearer, so long as the desire is strong and no doubt lingers within.

The Pitcher's Pendant knows no boundaries. It seemed this included the boundary of death. Archie's desire to know what the hell was going on and who it was that had played him like a centaur's lyre must have been strong. I'd make a wizard's wager that the desire for payback when he learned his pal, Riley, had killed him, was even stronger.

Miles was trying to keep it together, but failing miserably. I was willing to give Riley a wave-along as he had good reason to fall apart. He only needed to look over his shoulder to see his right foot still remaining where he had been standing. Riley's sweat-kissed brow wrinkled as he stared in fascination at how the bones of his lower shin just reached up to nothing. It wasn't every day you got a chance to see what your skin encased, and for Riley this was a last-in-a-lifetime kind of experience. Both of them, though, were seeing something that I had hoped I wouldn't see in this world: a creature of the undead.

The undead, I had noticed in my ventures through the library, were a reoccurring theme in this world's "scare the piss out of folks" literature. Problem was, no one was really getting the undead right. At least, that had been my opinion until last Halloween when I had dared Gertie to find me a good scare. (Bit of advice: Never dare anyone from New Zealand to anything. They play for keeps.) From the library archives, she unearthed six magazines that had rolled off of Gutenberg's gadget a few years before I arrived. The "publication" (using that term loosely) looked no better than those silly rags Mick reads.

Gertie wasn't letting me judge this particular story by its cover. This six-part tale was entitled "Herbert West, Reanimator". It was written by some guy named Lovecraft.

I didn't sleep a wink that night. Or the next.

Ol' Howie P. didn't miss a beat. In particular, there was one aspect of the undead that other horror authors glossed over, but that Lovecraft nailed harder than spikes into a coffin top: The undead's penchant for violence. He had quite effectively captured what happens when a rational being is reduced to the most primal of states. Had he my experiences, he would have added two more details to West's serial. The first would be speed. It was a misconception that the undead walked heavy-footed, with eyes vacant and mouths agape, wandering as the eternally damned in search of fresh flesh. Try again. The undead, because they *knew* they were eternally damned and wouldn't be getting back to their dirt nap for quite some time, were cranky, hungry, and ready to make a ruckus. That kind of motivation makes you move. Fast. The undead were some of the most fleet-footed opponents on the battlefield.

The undulating sound coming from Archie's throat reminded me of those sabertooths that Goblins occasionally used as battle-cats. Riley looked numb with an over-abundance of memories, sensation, and fear as the pallid, deformed thing he once knew as Archie leapt from its corner of the sitting room, easily spanning the distance in one bound. It landed on top of Riley, pinning him to the floor by his shoulders. Riley would have probably preferred to go into a stunned state of shock, but instead he was retching from the putrid stench that wafted from Archie's abnormally wide mouth.

I wished the second bite, the one that took the right half of Riley's chest, had finished the job. It hadn't. It was Archie snapping Riley's neck that finally stopped the screaming.

Miles must not have been too broken up to see his sweet little buttercup lose a portion of his rib cage, because he summoned up the courage to reach for Riley's piece as Archie's head rocked back and forth, working the heart out of its nest of muscle, arteries, veins and nerves. He braced the gun in his grip, drawing a bead on the dining undead.

Archie's head rocked slightly as the slug entered into his scalp and exploded out the right temple.

Archie went still for a moment, and then the head craned back to consider Miles Waterson. A strand of blood, textured with bits of muscle and artery, dripped from his chin and drizzled a strange pattern on a small clean patch of Riley's dress shirt.

Yeah, good job, Waterson. You just pissed off the undead.

This was the second detail Lovecraft would have captured, if Lovecraft knew the undead as well as I did. The undead, as I'd mentioned before, were cranky, hungry, and fast, reduced to the most base of instincts. If your undead is re-animated soon enough after its demise, though, the intellect will sometimes stick around. This means you'd have an undead killing machine that was cranky, hungry, fast, and sporting a terrific memory for names and faces.

Especially for the dinks who had double-crossed them.

"*Mmmmmmiiiiiiillllllllllleeeeeeeesssssssssss*," Archie groaned, his benefactor's name ending as a serpent's salutation. "You look upset."

Miles pulled the trigger again. This time, he took out an eye, the force of the gunshot snapping Archie's head back. It didn't stay snapped back for long. Archie craned his head from side to side, as if to work out a kink.

"I'm sure we can talk about this," Archie's grating voice said assuredly. "You know, get those pesky details in order so we're all working together to the same goal. You remember saying that to us?"

Another gunshot. Square in the chest.

Archie took two steps back, Riley's fresh corpse threatening to topple him. Instead, he righted himself and asked, "What's wrong, Miles? Cat got your tongue?"

He knelt down and pried Riley's mouth open. We both heard something rip, and then Archie stood up again, offering Miles what covered his open hand.

"Here. Have Riley's. He doesn't need it anymore." And then the bloody Undead Archie smiled.

When the undead smile, I want to hide. There wasn't anywhere for me to go right now, but I wondered for a moment if I could blend into the furniture. Archie's beef wasn't with me, and for that I was thankful.

Then again, once he finished snacking on Miles, there were no rules saying I wasn't going to be the after-dinner mint.

Keeping that thought in the forefront of my mind, I made my move toward my haversack. The world suddenly tipped over, and I was lying face down against the floor. It's not like I was dizzy from the smell of gore. Hell, I had plenty of adrenaline going through me to keep me wide awake and alert. Not even a pot of Mick's strongest could snap me awake like this. No, I had tripped on something.

I looked back. Correction: Something had tripped me up.

Riley's hand was now locked around my ankle, and he was trying to lift himself up into something like a sitting position. I was going to take a guess the missing organs, ribs, and muscle made finding his center a little difficult. Just in leaning up, he groaned, spitting up blood that was in his mouth on account of Archie's recent desecration.

So shall the brothers and sisters within the bearer's reach—physical and spiritual—also rejoice in its power.

Great. Just great.

"Ooooooohhh, look at what I did," Archie grunted, motioning to Riley. He looked at the tongue in his hand, shrugged, and tossed it aside. "Now here's a thought, Miles. You fucked me over, but only as a business partner. With Riley here, it's a bit more literal." His entire body convulsed as he chortled. "I think he's going be a lot angrier than me, so I'd better not kill you. Not right away, anyway."

Riley tugged at my ankle. He wasn't necessarily pissed at me, but that didn't change the fact I was the closest thing he could grab for a quick bite. He was now rocking back and forth, attempting to rock on top of me, maybe so he could chew on my thigh as easily as a king would sink his choppers into a turkey leg.

I wriggled on to my side so that I was able to see him. My other leg was free, and I cocked it back as I saw the mutilated head and torso begin to roll toward me. The sole of my shoe connected with his face. His hold on me tightened and he came in for a second try at my leg. This time, I caught him just under the chin. His head slowly came back to look at me. Again, my foot shot out. With each kick, I repeated a mantra to give my leg a bit more power.

Fuck. *Kick!* You. *Kick!* H. *Kick!* P. *Kick!* Love. *Kick!* Craft. *Kick!*

My shoe was just stomping into ground beef that once was a face by the time he finally let me go. With my ankle free of the stinging vise-like grip, I pulled myself over to my haversack.

I heard another gunshot. Six. Miles had just bought his last bit of time.

Riley was moving for me again, but instead of falling on my leg he fell toward the head of my battle axe. He was still not able to control his center, so his free arm flailed in a pathetic attempt to either stop his fall or knock away my axe. It didn't accomplish either. My edge connected with his forehead, slicing through the skin and skull like a cook's knife through tender lamb. The bottom half of his brain splattered out against the floor while the top hit the couch.

Wow—that damn couch was ruined now.

Click. Click. Click.

Miles was staring at the pistol trembling in his grasp. *Click. Click.* He kept looking between the gun and Archie, trying to will bullets into the cylinder.

Undead Archie stopped advancing for a moment, crouched back, and then slipped over to Miles' left. "Boo," he taunted.

Miles let out a little scream and tried to pistol-whip Archie, but he was gone. Archie now appeared behind Miles, giving a soft brush of his fetid, stale breath against Miles' nape. This time when the .38 came around, Archie was waiting, smiling that seriously creepy smile that made me want to hide.

The wet crunch ripped through the sitting room. Miles Waterson had some power in those arms, some stock in that frame of his. Maybe he wasn't as hard as a seasoned warrior, but he had enough power in that swing of his to knock Undead Archie off balance.

This was Miles' chance to make a break for it, his moment to bolt for the door. While the undead were a pain-in-the-ass to kill, it was possible to give them enough of a whack to disorient them. Miles didn't know that, of course, but he should have recognized his chance for flight regardless.

When he finally did recognize it, it was too late.

Undead Archie grabbed the back of Miles' neck, lifted him off the polished marble, and planted the jeweler square in front of him. Miles was trying desperately to breathe, but what he was looking at defied reason and rationality. Hell, it was just plain wrong. Archie's head was now resting with an ear against his shoulder. Again, my ears filled with the wet, gurgling sound of bones rubbing and snapping against each other as this head righted itself, to glare eye-to-eye at Miles.

"Ow," Archie grunted. "That stung."

You think that hurt, pal, I thought as I let fly my battle axe, *This'll leave a mark.*

The axe was spinning laterally, cutting through the air as a discus would. Its whine was getting louder the more it spun, its glow growing enough to cast faint shadows behind Miles. Archie's abnormal mouth had opened once more to its widest; but as he heard my weapon, he turned—or at least started to turn—to the sound. His head was suspended in mid-air for a moment, its end-over-end tumble interrupted by the rest of his body. Somehow, it remained standing.

I heard Miles Waterson's high pitched scream over the whine, and then heard it end abruptly.

The weapon's chocolate-leather handle clocked the jeweler so hard on the temple that it knocked him out cold. Good thing, too, as he landed next to Archie's headless corpse.

I stared at my trusted weapon now buried deep in the far wall. An aching ripple passed through me as I realized how much effort it was going to take to dislodge it. I slumped down to my knees. With a slightly lower perspective, I could now take in the carnage surrounding me. Riley had been hacked up worse than a prize buck by a butcher's apprentice. Archie was hardly in any better shape. He had five slugs inside of him; the first having been the one that had killed him, while my axe had finally taken him down.

And there was Miles, out cold, sporting a knot on his temple that would be looking mighty angry come this afternoon.

I took a deep breath and pulled myself back on my feet. When I finally closed this case, I was going to sleep for a year.

Since there was no neck to keep the chain in place, the Pitcher's Pendant was now between Miles and Headless Archie. It was a real shame: Miles was finally within reach of all that power. Swing and a miss. Strike Three. I picked up the blood-stained talisman and caught the whiff of electricity now mingling with another coppery scent. Looking at it up close like this, I was treated to a memory of that night on Death Mountain. Faces, names, and voices now seemed to echo in my head. I wondered what that kid Sirus was up to. Hopefully, he'd started that forge like he said he would. And that Elf. Kiah was her name. She was a dish. A redhead, skilled with both bow and blade. Nice tits, too.

Turning the pendant over, I was treated to an etching of sunrise across the Shri-Mela Plains. Yeah, that's right, Plains Humans forged this talisman. On the human-settled end of that Acryonis expanse, Coe was a village dedicated to the control of magic, attempting to discover the nature of sorcery. How did it corrupt souls? Could the corruption be reversed? Was Light truly in equal opposition to Dark? My eyes studied the etching, and sure enough, I could see the clouds moving and the sunlight disappearing into their patchy embrace. I'd forgotten how beautiful the sunrises were back home.

Something tickled my cheek. I reached up and wiped away what I thought would be blood. When I looked at the pendant again, the etching was still. Goddamn magic inside this trinket was picking up on my own needs and wants. It knew within moments of my touch. Goddamn magic.

What really bothered me was that I knew I was going to need its power. I took another look around me, and nodded for my own sake, for my own validation.

"Okay then." I held up the Pendant of Coe so I was eye-to-talisman with it, "but let's get something straight: I'm calling the shots here. Not you. We do this tonight, and then we find someplace better suited for a trinket like you."

I glanced at the clock showing the wee small hours of the morning, then turned to Miles Waterson. "*We're on borrowed time here…*" he had said earlier.

"Let's see if I can't pawn this pendant here for just a few minutes more," I muttered to myself.

CHAPTER TWENTY

For the Love of the Game

A ballpark is a beautiful place to visit on a warm, summer afternoon, especially if the breeze is strong off the Great Lake and the sky is clear. Those days reminded me of many a pleasant trek through Acryonis. Me and my boys would be on our way to carry out some assignment, a gentle, steady wind sweetly kissing our faces. We would make record time to our night's camp, rest easy, and then at daybreak, do what we were hired to do. Those were great days to be alive.

Today, though, was the *other* kind of day.

I got out of the cab, and the rain was still coming down. It was heavy. It was miserable. It had effectively rained out the final game between the Mariners and my beloved Cubbies, a final game that, at this rate, would never be played. The brim of my hat bobbed up and down as pellets of water struck it hard, but I looked defiantly upward, daring my Stetson to fall off my noggin. With a featureless grey sky behind it, Wrigley Field looked more imposing than inviting. Even though I could hear in my ears the cadence of raindrops against my raincoat and hat, I didn't like the quiet. Not at all.

Days like this, when dressed in infantry armor, battle axe at the ready, soaked clothing adding a few more stone to your weight, tended to make you cranky as hell. When you're cranky and facing a platoon of Ogres, the smart money is on the cranky Dwarves. This added ferocity is not for Emperor, for the lands and loves of Gryfennos, or even for Family Name. It was knowing that the sooner all this shit was taken care of, the sooner a pint of the brewer's best and a raging fire in the hearth awaited you at My Friend's Cousin. That was the tavern of choice for the Stormin' Scrappies; and when the brewer was at the top of his game, the keg's bounty rivaled that of the Emperor's Private Stock.

And let me tell you, the brewer at My Friend's Cousin was always at the top of his game.

Days like this one made me homesick for my stomping grounds. Especially when I could feel that oppressive tension in the air.

The pounding deluge was amplified in the entranceway of the prettiest diamond in Chicago, a diamond too big to fit on a dame's finger. I wanted to find that comfort I always felt when I came here for an afternoon's diversion, but it wasn't going to happen today. I wasn't a stranger to this place, but I was hardly used to the seats I was heading to. My feet scuffed against the stairs as I started my climb to the private office, an overlook that I could tell would offer a particularly breathtaking view of the ball field. It would also, I had no doubt, give a good view of the bleachers, so one could get a bird's eye view of how many backsides were taking up space. An informal method of keeping an eye on the peasants, making sure they were still interested in the games and the gladiators involved therein.

I knocked on the door, and a few moments later, a suit answered it.

"Down here," I grumbled.

I did mention that being soaked by a downpour makes me cranky, right?

"Ah, Mr. Baddings," the page said in a tone much too pleasant to be sincere. "Mr. Wrigley and Mr. McCarthy are expecting you. If you would please follow me?"

My coat and hat were gathered up by another page, and the gesture along with the unexpected coziness of the office coerced a smile from me. Nothing wrong with a little primping, I suppose. Maybe to these guys, it was just the custom when you have visitors to court; but I liked the special treatment.

The clock was the first thing I noticed when the pages opened the door that linked the receiving room to the warm, luxurious study. The repetitive *tick-tock-tick-tock* should have given these dim surroundings a relaxed, perhaps even tranquil, feeling about them. Instead it only seemed to amplify the impending doom that was to come. Two of the people I expected to see were standing here, and the third man was seated behind the desk.

Then there was the other fellow, looking out the office windows. I couldn't recognize him with his back to me, and in the intermittent shadows I could only see the snowy white of his hair cutting through the dark. When expecting a hunting party of four, it's unsettling to find an unexpected guest in the line up. I stared at the mystery man for a second, took a breath, and then proceeded forward into this arranged meeting. Whoever this uninvited dink was, he must have been a guest of the man behind the desk. I didn't want to start off proceedings by questioning the host's judgment.

William Wrigley was the man I supposed should receive a swift punch to the jimmies for Miranda's broadsword of behaviors: gum popping. The guy was doing so well for himself in the business that he bought my beloved Cubbies and had this stadium built for them. The guy struck the ransom of a king's only son, and from the build of the throne that surrounded him, he was enjoying the juicy fruits of his labors.

My client, Joe McCarthy, nervously tapped his fingertips together. I was sure that telling his boss he had hired a private dick to look into the visiting team hadn't been an easy feat to pull off with clean trousers, but I knew this was going to be a really complicated matter to explain. I wanted to make sure nothing got lost in the translation. I didn't doubt McCarthy's ability to communicate to his boss that there was something fishy about the Baltimore Mariners, but in this case the demon resided in the details. This meeting was reassurance that there was no question as to who had done what, and why.

That was why I had told McCarthy to not only call up his boss and get him into the office on a rainy afternoon, but also to call up Mariners' coach Barry Barton, too.

Coach Barton huffed. "Goddamned private dicks."

"Good to see you too, Coach Barton," I said. He blinked quickly. I gave him a shrug and replied, "I took your advice and looked up your name in the papers."

"I am to assume," came the voice from behind the desk, the man's eyes considering me. What had to be running through his head as I stood there, all the confidence in the world behind my bruised and bandaged four-foot-one frame? Something that did strike me a little odd was the soft nature of Wrigley's voice. The guy was the owner of the Chicago Cubs and namesake of this stadium. I was expecting a bit more *hubrimaz* when he asked, "Billibub Baddings, Private Investigator?"

"Yes, Mr. Wrigley," I said with a nod. I then turned to the grey-haired geezer staring out the window. "But if you don't mind, sir, I was hoping to keep this conversation to all the concerned parties of this investigation."

That was when the fourth man turned around, and the confidence in his voice caused me to straighten up a little. "When it concerns the National Baseball League, I am a concerned party."

Last time I remember flinching like that, a general had dropped in on me and my boys for a surprise inspection of the Stormin' Scrappies. Unfortunately, we had been celebrating a lieutenant's bachelor party the night before, and the girls we had…contracted with… were still in our tent.

When the mystery man stepped into my light, though, I wished I was facing five of those pissed-off generals.

"Since Judge Landis was available, I thought his presence for this meeting would be…" The word caught in Wrigley's throat for a moment, but with a quick look to Landis, he turned back to me and uttered, "…helpful."

Yeah. So would a hot poker against my testicles if you wanted me to stay faithful to the miller's daughter.

Federal Judge Kenesaw Mountain Landis was, according to a lot of the Sports writers here in Chicago and elsewhere, proof that tyranny was alive and well in the land of the free and home of the brave. This guy should have been the one sitting in Wrigley's throne, the scepter in his hand no doubt a gold Louisville Slugger encrusted with pearl baseballs. His Honor and Royal Eminence Presiding was the man brought in to clean up baseball when the Black Sox Scandal tore down the sport's outer battlements. I had read up on this guy while researching my newfound passion; and I had read that he was, according to some, a guy who believed in the sport and what it represented at its heart.

That was a beautiful sentiment I could get behind, but beautiful sentiment didn't necessarily make you a stand up guy. (Remember the Orc with the bulging breeches?)

Landis was approached to be part of a watchdog group that would preside over the League. He had accepted the appointment under one condition: that he would serve the National Baseball League as *sole* commissioner, granted unlimited authority over the game, the players, and the owners. It was a hell of a triple play, and the judge knew he could make it.

The decisions of the Baseball Commissioner's Office were made "in the best interest of the game" regardless of how miserable the interested parties would be in the end. Landis was "independent and impartial" as long as you agreed to do things his way.

"Very well then," I said, motioning to nearby empty chairs. "Gentlemen, please have a seat."

McCarthy and Barton took a pair of seats in front of Wrigley's desk. Landis didn't move. I don't know what he had been told to get him here, but he was definitely hot under the hood. He was going to be a hard sell.

Wrigley pushed the morning's *Tribune* to the edge of his desk. "I am assuming you are aware of this morning's headline?"

BUSINESSMAN BUTCHERS BALLPLAYERS!
WEALTHY CHICAGO SUCCESS PLEADS INSANITY!

Yeah, a night I would be thankful to forget, and forget soon.

"I am more than aware of the headline. It ties in directly with my investigation into the Baltimore Mariners." Coach Barton grumbled something about my mother and something I would be doing to her if I changed my name to Oedipus. I continued, "You might have to dig around a bit, but you're going to find out that a deal was made with one Bruce Halsbrook. Halsbrook, from the Baltimore area, was posing on paper as the owner of the Baltimore Mariners. He wasn't."

Barton now looked at me, the hand that his head was leaning against now falling into his lap as he sat up in his chair. "Then who the hell was—"

"Miles Waterson. He was signing the checks that kept the team financed. I'm sure at one time, the Mariners were owned by Halsbrook, but I'm also certain that Halsbrook was not planning on being hit so hard by the Crash. After all, it takes a lot for a new team to be established in the League, doesn't it, Commissioner?"

Landis didn't say a word. In fact, I didn't even think he was paying attention to me.

"Check Halsbrook's records, talk to him, and try talking to Waterson. Provided Waterson is able to string together anything coherent, you'll find out he was helping Halsbrook with some cash flow issues. The original plan was to use team members to smuggle rare antiquities out of host cities and get them to Baltimore."

"Baltimore?" Coach Barton asked. "Why Baltimore?"

"It's that much closer to the Atlantic and the European Market," I said. "But that was the scheme—to use the Mariners as a ways and means of getting stolen merchandise out to connections on the East Coast."

Joe McCarthy cleared his throat. Yeah, Joe, I was pissing pretty hard in my pants, too. Right with you, brother. "But Mr. Baddings, when I hired you, it was to investigate the Mariners to see if they were rigging their games. Was something odd going on?"

In my mind, I could hear the *clickity-clatter-click-click-clickity-clack* of die striking die, as if I was conjuring Mistress Luck in between my cupped hands. I had to be careful here. I was going to tell them the truth, yes, but I had to put it in terms they would understand.

"Yeah, something very odd was going on. I think Waterson was also into something a little more devious with the Mariners. Along with fencing stolen goods, Waterson was exploring one of his interests—pharmacology."

"Pharmacology?" scoffed Landis.

"Yeah. Oddly enough, this starts with a relatively harmless little libation: Coca-Cola. Had a secret ingredient, once upon a time, that gave people a lot of pep. Turned out that secret ingredient was slightly detrimental to your health, so the company took it out of the drink, but for a while people used it to improve their energy. Waterson was also interested in 'improving' athletes."

"Hold on a second!" Barton was ready to pounce on me. "Are you saying I was telling my boys to take it in the arm?"

"No, Coach, I'm not saying that at all. I am saying you all need to know that the group known by the moniker of 'Trouble' was actually getting into a lot more than boozing and whoring." I held up a hand before Landis could speak. "This morning, Your Honor, you ain't working for the Feds. You're the Baseball Commissioner, so keep the robes hung up for now.

"The team was boozing it up because they were a new team on the scene, and a new team to be reckoned with. No denying that. What I'm saying is Waterson was also using Trouble—Riley Jenkins, Archie Randalls, William Patterson, Sam Saint, and Joe Murphy—to try out a few 'tricks' that might help them perform a little better on the ball field. That's how the Mariners were able to perform as they did."

"Using drugs to make you a better ball player?" Landis huffed. "That's disgusting."

"It wasn't the whole team, and Coach Barton was unaware this was going on. My investigation is clear on that. It was these five play—"

"Might as well have been the entire Mariners roster!" Landis snapped.

I glanced at Wrigley. He was grinning slightly. McCarthy couldn't seem to look either Barton or his boss in the eye. Landis was focusing on the wrong element here, and not helping the situation one bit.

"Gentlemen, please." I was glad I had paid attention to those Elven arbiters. Sometimes, the little gimmicks they used to calm down a table of pissed-off delegates came in handy. "I've brought in all the concerned parties to offer a solution to a scandal."

Dropping the "S" word, I knew, would win me back the Council Chambers if I lost them...or get me their attention in the first place if I started without it. Baseball was still under a lot of scrutiny, especially with "Death" Mountain Landis calling the shots. I had to get everyone's focus back to why I had called this meeting...and how I intended for this matter to be handled.

"This is a mess, I think we can all agree on that," I began, "and if you read the stories about Waterson and the Mariners' Trouble, you know this could eclipse the Black Sox Scandal on a level that would make the Gideon Joust look like a bad day on the Lists."

My analogy was lost on this crew.

"Let me try again," I huffed. "It's attention and publicity no one wants and the sport definitely does not need. The thing we got to accept here is that it wasn't the team at fault. It was its owner, its interim owner, and five guys that figured they would set aside a little easy money for themselves. The papers, provided this is handled properly, wi—"

"Mr. Barton," Landis began, "how long have you been a coach in this sport?"

My baby blues immediately went to the Commissioner. Bad enough he was cutting me off, but the fact he was calling Coach Barton "mister" didn't fill me with optimism.

"Been in the sport for thirty years," he barked back. "I've seen a lot of things happen in this game and in this league, Commissioner."

Landis' chin raised a hint at the comment. "I see. And I'm sure you thought the Baltimore Mariners were your ticket, didn't you?" His eyes narrowed on the man. "Shall I inquire into your background over those thirty years? Find out if you were even in the major league, or just looking for an opportunity? Still, in that time, you come to know the sport. You know the people who play it and why."

I didn't like the direction of his questioning at all. "Commissioner, if you would ju—"

"Three decades of playing the game, Mr. Barton," he continued, not even giving me a glance after cutting me off. A *second* time. "You didn't know any of this was happening under your nose?"

Landis took a step forward, and I recognized the stare. I'd seen it before. He was deliberately closing the door in my face. In His Honor's eyes, I didn't exist. My purpose was done, and now I was mute.

"I find that hard to believe," Landis added.

Coach Barton must have figured he had nothing to lose at this point but his pride. He rose from his chair, intending to go for one final stand. "Oh really? You think I was in on all this? Fencing stolen property? When did I have time for that shit? While the boys were enjoying the good life, I was stuck in my hotel room putting together rosters, working on the next team, trying to understand how they played the game." The finger Barton was jabbing into his own chest now turned to point at Landis. "Who the fuck are you? A fan with a title! You never played the game. You just watched it from the bleachers!"

McCarthy watched his peer silently and I saw the camaraderie there. Yeah, they were on the opposite sides of the diamond when the umpire called "*Play ball!*" and yeah, McCarthy had hired me to do a little digging into how the Mariners were doing what they were doing. That didn't change the fact they were both ball team managers. They were both part of that brotherhood, and they were equals. Joe was watching in awe and terror at the raw defiance pouring from his colleague.

"I've known this game a lot longer and a lot more intimately than you, pal! You're not the savior you think you are, and maybe you would figure that out if you pulled your head outta your ass!"

"You're making this decision a lot easier for me, Barton!" Landis bit back.

"Like you didn't have your mind made up before you walked in here? Before this dick here told you what he had found out?"

Barton was not backing down, and I admired his *hubrimaz* for voicing opinions other managers and owners probably felt but didn't dare express. When you're talking to a guy described by many as *"an autocratic czar, relegating final decisions to his totalitarian will,"* you tend to keep those passionate opinions close to the doublet.

The Mariners' coach took a breath and then dared another step forward. He was well within slugging distance, but he merely clenched his fists as he spoke, his voice now low and controlled. To a point. "Let's face it—I was fucked the minute you read the papers this morning. Blackball my team first. Give them the same treatment as the Sox. Then blackball me. Make me some kind of criminal mastermind or something, right? I'm supposed to be all-fucking-knowing, right? That's my job, after all. And you, someone who didn't have the strength or the guts to be part of this game, you're going to do all that, ain't ya?"

Landis' mouth pulled back. I think it was a grin. "With pleasure," he replied.

Tick-tock-tick-tock-tick-tock-tick-tock...

I wasn't sure how much time had passed, but now I became acutely aware of the damn clock. I could not imagine working in this office with that racket.

"Gentlemen," I began, "if you would plea—"

"Bill," Landis said, turning his back on Barton to face Wrigley, "I need you to—"

"HEY! I'M TALKING HERE!" That made even Landis step back. Every eye in the room was now on me.

I'd not barked like that since my Acryonis days. It was good to know I still had the pipes.

My voice returned to that Elven Mediator level. "Gentlemen, if you all would please give Commissioner Landis and myself a moment." I never realized those moderators had to work so hard. Now I felt a slight pang of guilt for every time I'd acted like a Troll's ass while those guys were trying to keep the peace between the Dwarven Empire and some other race. That pang of guilt dissipated when I saw the expression on Landis' face. "Mr. Wrigley, if you please. It will only be a moment's inconvenience."

The Cubs owner sized me up (and as I'm four-foot-one, it was a quick sizing up) and apparently didn't find me imposing. (Your first mistake, Mr. Wrigley.) He then gave a nod to Joe. McCarthy cleared his throat, probably to just break the heavy tension in the air, and then followed his boss into the waiting area.

Barton was still staring at Landis, who had returned to his view overlooking the rain-soaked diamond.

"Coach," I spoke gently. "Come on. Just a moment."

The old man's head whipped around to glare at me. *If it wasn't for you poking your nose into my team's business…* his icy gaze said. I had no way to tell him that it was just my job, and with times the way they were, I needed to be the best at my job or I'd be stuck permanently in the Waldorf gig.

He gave a snort, looked at the back of Landis' head (probably considering the best place to plant a mace), back at me (and where to hit me as his second target), and then stormed out of the room. He was the last man out, and the door slammed shut.

Tick-tock-tick-tock-tick-tock-tick-tock…

I walked over to where Landis stood. I judged distances, what was around us, and then stepped back to the chair that McCarthy had occupied earlier. With a grunt, I angled the chair to face Landis. When I turned back to Landis again, I caught him peering over his shoulder at me. I heard a few sniffs coming from him.

Yeah, he was laughing at me.

I gave the tip of my nose a quick pinch, straightened up, and returned to the Commissioner's side. "Sir, if you wouldn't mi—"

"Son, I don't know what you are intending to say or do right now, but if your intention is to change my mind I'm afraid you're only talking to air."

Not yet. "Commissioner, if you would please have a seat," I replied, motioning to the chair. "I would like you to consider—"

"What? A compromise?" he barked, still looking at the ball field. "Perhaps you are not aware—nor do I expect you to be aware—of something about me: I don't compromise."

Eye contact was out of the question. Still, not the time. "Actually, Commissioner, I'm not going to ask you to compromise. Not at all. Please, have a seat," I said motioning to the chair with one hand and gently placing the other on the sleeve of his coat.

Landis wrenched his arm back as if my touch was covered in slug bile. A nerve caused his face to twitch lightly as he looked down on me. Finally, I had his attention and he was facing me. "Whoever you think you are, don't presume to lay hands on me! I'm a Federal Judge and the commi—"

Now.

My fist thrust forward, connecting square with his balls. As he was a commissioner and not a player, I thought the odds were in my favor that he was not wearing an athletic supporter.

When the Mountain crumbled, I lent him my support and spoke gently, "How about you take that seat now, Commissioner?"

He managed to catch his breath just as he flopped into the comfortable chair, the seat probably retaining some of Joe McCarthy's warmth. Landis' eyes flicked open. His skin had turned quite pale from the shock of what just happened. His gaze, though, was dark and smoldering, promising a wrath of apocalyptic scale.

"I know you're about to explode, Commissioner, but before you find your voice I suggest you set your prejudices aside and you listen to me because I'm about to tell you how you're going to handle this whole mess. I know this isn't something you're accustomed to, but this is an extreme situation and as you've just noted, I'm a guy of extremes. Nod if you—" I considered what I was going to say, and then shook my head. "Nah, screw it. Just nod so I know you can hear me."

Landis took another breath, his hands still cupping his crotch, and with a soft groan he nodded.

"Commissioner, you are going to make a formal announcement that due to the underhanded business dealings with Miles Waterson and Bruce Halsbrook and the deviant behavior of the Mariners' players known as Trouble, you are removing the Mariners from the

League's records. Coach Barton and the remaining team members will still be allowed to play in the Minors, and they will all be eligible for advancement to the Majors..."

Landis took in a deep breath, his nostrils flaring. In response I lifted my index finger and repeated, "And they will *all* be *eligible* for *advancement* to the Majors. This was not their problem. Never was, and nor should it be now. The games the Mariners played and subsequently won will not even appear as forfeits. You're going to erase them from the standings. The only hint of their existence will be a few newspaper snapshots and a few headlines. That's it. The season continues as if nothing happened. If the players prove their worth in sovereigns, then maybe they'll find themselves a spot on the Reds, or even the Giants."

"And why," he wheezed, "would I even consider doing this?"

I leaned in close. Landis didn't like that. I knew he wouldn't. "You heard Coach Barton. You're a fan with a title, and because you're a fan you're going to do this because it's the right thing to do."

"The right thing to do?" It was time to give Landis some room. His composure was back. "This coming from *you*?"

Okay, he had me there. I could see some of that ire he was sporting right before I punched him in the baby bagpipes. "You may not approve of my methods, but you needed to be reminded why we are told not to interrupt others. Rude things happen to rude people."

He was out of the chair and towering over me. "I don't have to sit here and take—"

My arm swept behind his calves, sending him back into the leather chair.

"I'm afraid you do." I said. My buffer of courtesy was gone. He could squirm for all I cared. "I want you to seriously think about the judgment you're planning to pass. Is that the right thing to do? According to the laws of the land and the rules of baseball as set up by the League, yes. But is it the right thing for the sport, and the right thing for the country?

"Open your eyes, Judge. Look past the headline," I said, motioning to the *Tribune* on Wrigley's desk. "Our corner of the world is spiraling down into a maelstrom of hurt, and the Black Magic of Black Thursday is kicking all of us in the ass. It's not even been a year, and yet you open your eyes and take a look—we're not doing so good. It's going to get a hell of a lot worse."

"And your point?" he grumbled.

"Did you ever stop to ask yourself why, with all the shit that is being stirred up from the bottom of the moat, people still come to ball games? The good times of the Twenties came to a screeching halt in October, but when the season opened they were there, dogs of war merely waiting for their master's hand to snap and let them go.

"Maybe you are a fan with a title, Landis, but you *are* a fan. You make an example of the Baltimore Mariners and baseball will be nothing more than a dragon with a broadsword in its gut. People won't trust its players or its managers. Owners will probably be regarded as the Capones and Morans of the ballparks. The sport will die and it won't die gracefully. When baseball dies, a lot of hopes and dreams die with it. The guys will still play. I'm not worried about that. They'll play for the love of the game. But if you do what you're thinking about doing, it's all gone. The prestige. The poetic beauty. The belief in something that's still worth believing in."

Tick-tock-tick-tock-tick-tock-tick-tock...

Goddamn clock. If my axe were within reach, I'd be making time stop. At least, for this office.

After staring at me for what felt like a few solid years, Landis got up and returned to the window he had been staring out when I first entered the room. He was mulling it all over, or at least that's what I was hoping. Landis wasn't howling for my head on a pike like some berserker in the midst of a blood-rage, so I was going to regard his pensive demeanor to be a good thing. No, he didn't compromise, but I wasn't asking for him to settle on anything. I was telling him—a Federal Judge and Commissioner of Baseball—to do as he was told. The only way I could make this argument stick was to appeal to that fan, to that passion that we both shared in common. (Not that he would admit to having *anything* in common with me.)

What Landis asked me came out of Left Field. Seemed appropriate. "You are a private investigator?"

"That's my chosen trade. I'm pretty good at it, too, as you see."

"Then you have an understanding of the law, of what is right and what is wrong?" He looked down on me, the hard lines in his face appearing to reach deeper into whatever was warring in his soul. "At least, you should have."

"I'm supposed to dig into people's lives and impartially surrender the facts discovered to my clients. That's how my business works."

"My business is a little different," he said, before returning his stare out to the ballpark. "I am supposed to uphold the law, the rules that govern our great country. When I took on this role as commissioner, I swore to uphold the sanctity of this great pastime, because that is what this sport is to me. Sacred."

He cleared his throat and bowed his head for a moment. When it came back up, his eyes nursed a soft sparkle that resembled the raindrops striking the glass. He knew. He knew, and he hated it. "You're asking me to go against everything I practice in my sworn duty as a judicial officer of the Federal Courts."

"No, I'm not, Commissioner. I'm asking to you think about what will happen if you handle everything as a judicial officer of the Federal Courts. This call you have to make is not going to decide who's taking home the pennant, who's losing the season opener, or even if two teams head into extra innings. Approaching this with the same absolute judgment that you did with the Black Sox will backfire. Why? Because the first time a scandal hits, it's a shock. The second time a scandal hits, credibility that was once thought rebuilt is questioned, or worse—dismissed. I don't envy you, Your Honor." Figured he would like to hear that title. Inflate that ego a bit. Make him feel good about himself. "You're at a crossroads. Do you follow the rules, or do you do what is truly best for the game?

"Baseball is something more than a game," I was rounding third. Now I had to beat the ball to home. "This might sound like I'm sprinkling Pixie dew, but there's no other way I can put it. This sport's got a kind of magic about it. A genuine, sincere magic. Destroy that and you destroy something more. You plant a seed of suspicion concerning all things in here," I said, tapping the center of my chest.

My heart wasn't located there, but if I had pointed to where it was, it would have ruined the point I was trying to make.

His smile took me by surprise. "Are you certain you're not running for office?"

"No thanks," I scoffed. "I'm too honest for politics or the bar."

Landis' laugh made my shoulders drop a bit.

"You missed your calling, then," he said. "You would have made persuasive closing arguments as Defense Counsel." He glanced at his crotch, and then back to me. "I still think you have potential, though, as a personal bodyguard."

I reached into my coat pocket and pulled out a card. "My rates are reasonable. Call me anytime."

No, I didn't think he ever would. I wanted to drive a point home: I'm not intimidated.

"For the love of the game, Commish," I said over my shoulder as I started to leave.

"And what if I change my mind?"

There was a playful lilt in his voice, but I really didn't feel like dicking around anymore. One last thing I still needed to do in this case, and just thinking about it made my heart sink.

I stopped at the door and, again over the shoulder, replied, "What secrets do you keep, Judge Landis? And do you want to keep them secret?"

This time, I think Landis noticed the clock.

Okay, so I'd saved the institution of Baseball. Now it was time to save a man's soul.

CHAPTER TWENTY-ONE

To Thine Own Self, Be True

I checked my watch again. I do love the game, but by the Fates, I hate the smell of locker rooms. Balmy nights huddled in muddy trenches smelled nicer than these places. One more time, I checked my pockets to see if I had any of that alcohol that numbed up my sense of smell, or maybe a forgotten stick of *rubenna* root. I had neither on me ten minutes ago. Not fifteen minutes before then either. My sigh echoed lightly around me as I glanced at the time again. I saw Coach Barton make the call. I knew he was on the way. I had to relax.

A door opening pushed me back into the shadows. If he had been looking my way, he would have probably caught sight of me. He was heading right for his locker which, when you looked at it, really wasn't a locker. It was just an open space amongst a row of other spaces, all of them keeping the various uniform odds-and-ends of the Baltimore Mariners.

Stuff left here, provided it wasn't too valuable, would be safe. But what would someone breaking into a locker room deem as "valuable"? More to the point, what would a *fan* breaking into a locker room deem as "valuable"? It might make your stomach roil harder than catching a whiff of Orc shit. Sweaty socks, athletic supporters, and undershirts were all fair game to the fans, and revered as highly as baseball jerseys.

Jerseys would be harder to fence, though. If you were to steal anything truly valuable, you could incur the vengeance of other fans.

Still, you would want to be careful if you did leave anything behind here. From the way this player was checking his locker, he was thinking he hadn't been. Now he was starting to sweat a bit.

This situation was bad enough. Why make it torturous?

"It's not there," I said.

Eddie Faria turned around. He was looking too high to see me at first. When he spotted me walking out of the shadows, his head jerked back slightly. Then those baggy eyes of his widened as I held up the Pendant of Coe, passed it to the other hand, and let it sway.

"You," the pitcher finally whispered. He then pointed to the pendant. "That's mine."

"No, it's not," I replied. "It's not yours. It's not mine, either. And if you make a move for it, you're going to really, really regret it tomorrow."

He was thinking about it, but he could see that I wasn't bluffing. He also knew what the pendant in my hand was capable of.

Faria straightened up to his full height, sucked in the paunch, and snorted. "And why would I regret it?"

"You've already been accused of a lot of things you didn't do. Do you want to continue that streak and get in bed with a group of murderers?"

Eddie blinked. I wondered if this time he was so damn desperate to hang on to this illusion, he wasn't going to put it all together. Come on. Say it ain't so.

"Murder?"

"Murder. Grand larceny. Fraud. I'm telling you, the laundry list is long and it's nothing less than impressive, and you don't really need to be affiliated with these guys. In fact, you've got a real shot to walk away from all this, unscathed." My grip tightened on the chain in my hand. *How long have you been using this? How much damage has it done to you?* "You don't need this kind of heat again."

Finally, the pitcher took a seat on the bench, running the past season through his mind. He had been trying to look the other way for so long; that much I could see. The fact that someone outside of Trouble knew about his lucky charm, and knew what else this lucky charm was capable of doing, lifted the weight of both this world and Acryonis off his shoulders.

"You got to let it go," I said gently. "This has to be in your sight and you've got to let it go. The more you want it, the longer you stay connected. The longer you stay connected, the worse it's going to get for you."

He nodded, exhausted.

I could still catch a faint whiff of electricity over the ingrained stench of body odor. "What do you want?" I asked.

The pitcher took a deep breath and finally said, "I miss Katie. I told her I was on the road with a special exhibition team. Pay's been good so she didn't mind, but it's been empty because…"

"Because she can't see you play."

"Yeah," he said, his eyes welling up slightly.

I asked again, "What do you want?"

"I want to go home," he answered, his voice dry and cracking. "I want to be me again."

The tingling in my hand ceased, the scent of electricity dissipated, and Eddie "Shadow" Faria began to change in front of me.

His paunch drew inward, not of his accord but naturally. The face lost its sagginess, those haversacks under his eyes disappearing while his chin and nose lengthened, high cheek bones replacing the roundness that once had been there. A transformation like this would have apprentices or unwilling victims to a transformation spell howling in pain, but Eddie—or the guy that had called himself Eddie—seemed to be lost in a sweet euphoria.

The change slowed until finally it stopped. His wardrobe had not transformed with his face or body, and now the clothes seemed to hang on him.

I dropped the pendant into my coat pocket and brushed my hands together. Not sure why I felt the need to do that. Maybe it was that old Acryonis magic making me nervous.

"Shoeless Joe," I said, sticking out my hand, "it was a real thrill to see you play."

Joe scoffed. "With whatever that thing is, I got to wonder how much of what was out there was really me."

"All of it," I assured him. "I'll skip the details, but what this thing does depends on the desires and wants of its wearer. Your desire wasn't to be the better ball player or even to play on a championship team. Your desire was to play, and that desire was so intense that the pendant created a near-perfect disguise for you."

"Near-perfect?"

"You didn't notice, Joe, how everyone's attitude changed around you in the diamond? Other ball players saw it. Saw you—Shoeless Joe Jackson—on the pitcher's mound, at Home Plate. No one said anything, because if anyone had the right to be out there playing, it was you.

"Maybe Trouble had just enough respect for the sport to also see through your disguise, and that was how they figured out you had a 'lucky charm' that you always wore every time you played."

Joe swallowed hard. "I was practicing for a game. Semi-pro. No real cash to talk about. Strictly for the love of it, you know?"

Oh yeah, Joe, I know.

"So I get out to the park early, just to walk around, get a feel for the place. By the pitcher's mound, there that thing was. I was pretty anxious about this game, as I am about every game, and I thought, 'Why not? Good luck charm couldn't hurt.' When I put it on, I knew something was different, but I didn't notice it until the coach was asking me to my face who I was. At first I thought he was just kidding me, you know? But then I could tell he really didn't know."

I chuckled. The coach didn't recognize Shoeless Joe because he apparently wasn't an equal. Sometimes, magic can be brutally honest.

"So I figured I'd play under a made-up name, see if people would appreciate me for what I loved to do, not because of what happened…"

Shoeless Joe knew the game. He loved the game. I also knew, though, that he was coming from a simple background. He was street smart, a Grand Wizard when wielding the magic wand from Louisville. But he was also pretty naïve in how the world worked, and how things beyond it worked.

"I started to play again, started to get some attention. That was when I was approached to be a Baltimore Mariner. Brand new team, fresh start—it was what I wanted."

That was how magic worked. "You wanted to play while the guys around you wanted to win. Not just the guys on your team, but the other team as well. You all are brothers, and that's why I didn't see through your disguise. Not right away, anyway."

Joe looked at me for a second, noodling that one through, then continued. "Well apparently, Sledgehammer figured out there was something to my good luck charm. Not sure when he figured it out, but he did. He threatened to call the Commish, make it all stop. I asked him what he wanted, and that's when we made this arrangement. I'd loan him the charm, and then pick it up the next day."

"Your signal was Archie, right?" I could see the pictures in my head clearly. "I was looking at some photos and noted that the night before every robbery, he would wear his hat backwards. That was the drop signal for you, right?"

"I was supposed to leave it in my locker, tucked behind my jersey top. They'd…" Joe paused. He was beginning to piece together that he was, in fact, a silent member of Sledgehammer's crew. "They'd do what they do, and then I'd pick up the piece the next day like there wasn't a problem."

I walked over to Joe and took a seat next to him. "When did you figure out what they were doing?"

Joe shook his head, screwing his eyes shut. "I saw pictures in the paper of what happened at that jewelry store, and that was 'my lucky charm' kind of weird. When Shuffle was killed, I figured something was up."

He fell silent as we sat there, the rain just audible outside. We both stared ahead at nothing in particular. I was trying to commiserate with this fallen legend sitting next to me, but nothing I could say would really help. Shoeless Joe had found himself in a tight situation for the second time in his life. I wasn't blaming him, of course, but would he really understand how magic—at least, the magic of Acryonis—worked? Even my understanding of sorcery had its limits, and was perhaps tainted a bit with personal opinion and a smattering of bitterness at how it had cost me everything I knew as home. Joe was not really up on the supernatural, so all I could do was assure him his game was unaffected by the pendant. I'd done that. Nothing more was left to be said.

Or, maybe something was. "So," he asked me, still looking ahead. "What happens now?"

I looked up at him. "This is the good part, Joe. You go home."

He blinked again. "Just like that?"

"Just like that. Safe passage. Go home to Katie. I've got Landis basically closing up shop on the Mariners. You might have been enjoying a great season, but you were the only one. The 'good luck' your charm was generating was affecting your teammates, and the stats were probably not as honest as they would have been if you ever forgot to wear the Pitcher's Pendant."

Joe laughed. "Is that what it's called?"

"Well, by someone I know," I answered. "So you all are heading home later tonight. Back to Baltimore. The League is going to handle this as an owner thing, which really isn't that far from the truth, and the team—sans Trouble and yourself—are stepping down to the Minors.

"But the Commish doesn't know you're involved. To him, you're just another Mariner. I wasn't around for that Series, but I've read enough about it to know you don't need or really want that kind of attention a second time. I came up with an alternative for Landis, for everybody, and for you. Take it."

Joe looked around us, and smiled. He was taking in every detail of the locker room, committing the dim, smelly place to memory. To him, this place was as much a part of the game as the diamond itself, the four bases contained within it, and the cheers of the crowd.

My own smile faded away as I grew conscious of the Pendant of Coe in my pocket. What had this magic done to him? He must've been exerting a lot of effort, will, and desire to make his illusion happen. All this "bending of nature" shit came with a cost, and magic didn't care if you were a Dwarf, an Elf, or one of the greatest ballplayers to grace the game.

I gave Joe a friendly pat on his forearm, and then hopped down to leave.

"Hey, pal," he called out to me.

"Yeah, Joe?"

He was looking through his locker one more time, just gathering any belongings he'd left there. "How did you figure out who I was?"

This was something else I had liked about Shoeless Joe when I'd read up on him. The guy was clever. "It was your alias. Faria. From *The Count of Monte Cristo*. An epic tale of redemption."

Joe whistled. "I didn't think *anybody* would pick up on that. My Katie was reading that book to me when I cooked up this whole idea of getting back into the game."

"The sooner you get home," I said, turning to leave, "the sooner you can find out how it ends."

Du-shaw me raishia de Fates für me earnst, I prayed silently as I watched Joe pack up his things. He was ready to head on home.

EPILOGUE
Stealing Home

The rain was still coming down pretty hard. Trying to pick up a cab was going to be about as much fun as performing dental work on a hydra with halitosis. I stood in the alcove for a few minutes, looking around for the nearest diner I could duck into for a quick phone call.

Honk-honk!

My head jerked to one side and there she was: My ride. I knew the car well enough, and I also knew this was no chance meeting on a rainy afternoon. He was there to pick me up. Holding my Stetson down by the brim, I pulled the raincoat closer and made a fairy-line for the car. The door opened and, without looking in first to acknowledge the sole occupant of the limo's cabin, I hopped in.

"Thanks, Al," I said, taking off my hat and tapping it free of excess water. I figured he wouldn't mind the floor getting a little damp.

"Don't mention it, Small Fry," Capone chuckled.

The car started rolling just as I took a seat. What could I say that wouldn't sound like a bad set-up from an incompetent court jester? *Hey, Scarface, what brings you to Wrigley?* I did not really want to state the obvious, nor did I want to walk in the rain. This was a free ride (to where, I had no idea!), the limo was warm and dry, and I was not going to refuse Al Capone anything.

Well, almost anything. The Pitcher's Pendant was growing heavier and heavier in my pocket. The last time Capone was this close to a talisman there had been a lot of death and destruction.

Now here we were in his limo. Close quarters. Just fucking lovely.

"I'm telling you," he finally said, looking out through the curtain of rain water, "I don't think that second game is evah gonna get played, you know dat?"

"Maybe it's best it shouldn't, seeing as how good those Mariners are."

"Awww, come on, Short Stuff," Capone huffed. Was he actually chiding me? "Now is dat any way for a Cubs fan to talk? Huh? We got to have a little faith in our Cubbies."

"Well, you know how this game goes, Al," I said, not taking my eyes off him. "Anything can happen."

"Especially when you're talking with the Commish, huh?"

My bushy reds raised slightly on that question.

"Nah-nah-nah, I don' got anyone on the inside. I jus' saw him leavin' while I was waitin' fa' you."

"And is that why your boys didn't frisk me before letting me in here with you?" I asked. "I didn't think it was because you cared about letting me get out of the rain."

"Well, we're like friends, you know?" he chuckled. This was a definite change from the last time we talked here at Wrigley Field. "I mean, you're not an acquaintance, 'cause on account of dinnah. Den dere's the ballgame and jus' enjoying the afternoon. We're not, what I would say, *good* friends…" Capone paused in his assessment, and then nodded. "We're *like* friends."

Nice to know between "good friend" and "a problem needing a remedy" there's a middle ground with just enough room for a four-foot-one private dick. Maybe not a comfortable middle ground, but far more comfortable than eight to the ticker.

I felt the grin across my face. "And I bet, seeing as we're *like* friends and all, you're wanting to have a little chit-chat about one of your *good* friends." I leaned forward in my seat. "Or was Miles Waterson more of a business acquaintance?"

"Now, Short Stuff, what makes you t'ink I'm hobnobbin' with those upper-crust types, huh?" Capone shook his head, very disappointed in me. "Nah, nah, nah, you're sma'tah than that. I mean, you're the private dick and all."

"Oh now I think you have a lot more in common with the upper crust types than you give yourself credit."

His brow furrowed. "How so?"

"Well, there are a lot of stuffed shirts in the opera house, but I'm thinking it's the man in the box seats who knows what those big ladies in the bodices are pounding out. When the composer's Puccini or Verdi, who are the upper-crust turning to so they can get the deeper meaning behind the story?" I then motioned to him, a warm smile accompanying the gesture. "You, Big Al. Why? Because you speak the language."

"You t'ink?" Al gave a few grunts as he pulled a stogie out of his coat pocket.

A quick snip and strike of a match later, he took a few puffs, causing the flame to flare. His face was now shrouded by pearly-white smoke until his hand cut through the haze, clearing the air between us. I suppose it was good I didn't mind the smoking.

Then again, this was his limo. I assume anyone complaining would be left at the closest street corner…while the car was still in motion.

He took another drag before adding, "Never looked at it like that, Small Fry. Not that I would really be in the same business as Mistah Waterson."

"Yeah, that's the only flaw in this hunch of mine. Something tells me you and your Catholic upbringing really don't have a tolerance for Miles' chosen…lifestyle."

The gangster twitched uncomfortably, his face scrunching in distaste. "Well, let's imagine for a minute I was associates with him. I could still do business so long as he kept that bit outta it. So long as we kept it to business—provided we was *doing* business ta'getha—I wouldn't really care where that fag dipped his wick."

I nodded slowly. Let's see if he'd confirm it. "Not a big hit at your brothels, was he?"

"Nah, dat's where I figahed it out." He shuddered again. "Jus' ain't right."

You had to love Capone. A man of many contradictions.

"I bet you want to hear all about what happened the night I went over there, don't you?"

"Well, when you showed up like that on Mista Waterson's doorstep, wearing that backpack ya wore las' time you were at da docks, I was wonderin' if you were expecting somethin'…ya know…funny. Like las' time."

No, Al, there was nothing remotely funny in what I saw that night at Waterson's.

"Den I read in da' pay-pahs about Miles goin' all cracked in da' head, butcherin' dose guys from Baltimore. Now dat's bad business."

"But still your business, right, Al?"

Capone glanced around him, as if the rhythm of the rain, a noise from the street, or part of his limo's décor triggered a group of gray cells. Well, see, here's da t'ing, Short Stuff—breakin' inta' places, murder, foolin'people out of their hard-earned money, and this high society type is all behind it? Ya' really t'ink I'd be mixed up in business like that?"

"Like I said before, Al," I replied, my smile never faltering. "You speak the language."

He slowly turned the stogie in his mouth, taking a drag from it before removing it from his lips, his gaze managing to pierce the cloud of Havana's finest between us.

"Waterson was Chicago royalty. He was smart enough to put this operation together, but he needed a resource in the Underworld that had the connections. Connections that would get him out of Chicago, maybe even get him set up with a nice villa overseas. When Waterson got working with Sammy Saint, I'm sure he followed the few low-level connections Saint made while in jail. Guys like Waterson know it's the serfs that lead to the lords, the lords that lead to the princes, and the princes that lead to…" My voice trailed off as I motioned, again, to Capone.

He nodded, his frown deepening as he scratched his chins. "Dat's a pretty big hunch dere, Shorty. I mean, yes, Waterson was an associate. He was quite the purveyor of fine jewelry," he stated, wiggling the pinkie that sported a fine gold ring decorated with brilliant diamonds.

I took a quick whiff from where I sat. Yeah. The real thing. Miles was, most definitely, a very smart man.

"But if Waterson did dis here t'ing with the robberies," he continued, "why would he wanna do business wit' me?"

"Al…" Now it was my turn to chide him. "Al…what's with the humility? You're Alphonse Capone. I think that is saying more than enough."

He gave a few chuckles and turned his gaze back to the world outside the limo. "Yeah, well, that is touching for you to say, Baddings. Very touching." He glanced at the cigar, seeming to contemplate the ashes at the end of the smoke. Then, "In dis business you claim Waterson and I were dealing in, when he comes ta' me with this—*propasishun*—you think he tells me how he's pulling these jobs?"

"Well, *in this claim*, Waterson probably eluded to his crew being exceptionally talented, nothing more." I sat back, pulling out my travel pipe and a pouch of weed. "You would buy that, I think, until you see me at Wrigley Field. If I am involved, then maybe this business arrangement might be one of those *funny* business arrangements." Bowl packed, I asked, "You got a light, Al?"

Something impressed him in my gumption, asking the Crime Boss of Chicago to light my pipe like some kind of palace page. The match made a hard *scratch* before its flame kissed my pipe.

"Thanks," I said once the taste of the weed reached me. "Now, back to the hunch, I'm thinking seeing me at the ballgame was not as big of a surprise as seeing me show up at Waterson's when that manager was murdered."

The cigar just stopped shy of Capone's mouth.

"I'm *like* friends with you. I doubt if you have your *good* friends followed, do you?"

Al smiled a smile I didn't particularly care for. "You don't know me as well as you t'ink, Baddings," and the cigar was back in his mouth, that pig-grunt of a laugh softly setting a cadence.

"But a guy like Waterson was stuck when he started this caper, a caper that would catch everyone with their breeches down. The con of cons. A string of upper-echelon crimes all leading to an incredible case of fraud, bailing him out of a financial maelstrom."

"Mail-*what*?"

I swallowed hard. Here we go again. "Maelstrom. A giant whirlpool that pulls you down."

"*Mail*-strom," he repeated. "Damn, I t'ink I like dat one bettah dan 'flout'."

"Be careful though." I said, taking a puff from my pipe. "M-a-e-l-s-t-r-o-m. Those first four letters might trip you up."

"Thanks for da tip," he returned with a nod.

"Waterson needed resources he didn't have: Underworld networks, interested parties in stolen goods..." I puffed out a few smoke rings. "...and maybe a clean-up crew, for those pesky loose ends."

Capone's expression didn't change, didn't flinch.

"And that's why this prince ventured into the Thieves' Den: to obtain resources. Waterson was playing with fire, and he knew it. Had he pulled off this con, I think you might have caught a bit of heat. Maybe not the full blast from the dragon's mouth, but enough heat to singe those bushies over your eyes." I replaced the pipe in my mouth. "Provided my hunch is right."

For a minute—maybe longer—Al and I just enjoyed the ride through rainy Chicago. Wherever we were headed, we were taking the long way. We must've passed Mick's twice as we were driving around town. The quiet in the cab wasn't as unsettling as knowing that one of the Nine Talismans Capone was looking for was in my coat pocket.

"So," Al began, first to break the silence again, "in this hunch of yours, was fire the only t'ing Waterson was playing with?"

I summoned that face I wore at the tables when my hand was so bad it would make an Ogre turn around and wonder who farted. "I went to Waterson's expecting trouble, and I got shown the servant's exit. That's probably why your boys never saw me leave.

"I think here's where my hunch is flawed. If Waterson was getting a hand from you, he wouldn't have panicked like he did, snapped hard, and gone on a rampage. I think he saw the corner he painted himself into and completely lost the marbles." Let's score some coin from my lord and master here. "Either that, or he allied himself with Moran; and like the typical Mick that he is, Moran backed out of the deal. Left out to dry, Waterson butchers his crew and then goes for the insanity plea."

Capone grinned at that. He reached in front of him and rapped his knuckle against the glass between us and the driver, and sat back, his chuckle now audible. "You...*yoooooouuuu*...dat's good, Baddings. Very good. Great hunch, but nothing concrete you can take to da courts, huh?"

"Nah, just a hunch," I assured him.

The car was slowing. Well, what do you know...

"Thanks for the ride back to my office," I said.

"Don't mention it."

I opened the door to leave, but Capone's voice stopped me.

"Hey, Baddings, I meant what I said: We are *like* friends. You may not be a *good* friend, but I still got respect for yah. Jus' wanted you to know..." His cigar was pointing up to my office window. "...I didn't have anyt'ing ta do wi' what's going on up dere."

I looked up to my office window. Jerry was staring back at me. My eyes immediately returned to Capone.

"I swear," he said. "Not. A. Thing."

Public Enemy Number One wasn't lying.

The car pulled away a few moments after, and I bolted for my office building. Steps. Not waiting for the elevator. With each landing, I felt the Pitcher's Pendant. Not for a minute did I expect that this case was over and done with. The talisman I now had on my person was going to be a magnet—a very powerful one—for bad things. Until I gave it a special treatment like I'd given the Singing Sword, this case was still as wide open as a sea monster's maw.

I reached my floor and still wasn't breathing hard, even when I reached my open door. The smashed glass littering the floor stopped me cold. My eyes slowly came up and I saw what was supposed to be the waiting area, and it looked the way it would if Miranda had exploded into some kind of blood-rage. Papers were scattered everywhere. Potted plants were overturned. My skin was crawling as I thought about the poor son-of-a-bitch that had torn through here. Yeah, sure, I felt just a hint of pity for him. My pity was for what he was going to face once I found him.

"Billi!"

Miranda was in the doorway leading into my office. I could see behind her that it was in worse shape.

My desk had not been overturned, but it might as well have been. The drawers were out. The floor and the area rug I'm used to using as my pitcher's mound were now covered in a layer of case notes, photos, and stuff that I had filed away. Meticulously. In a system that worked beautifully. For me. For Miranda. And it had taken us two days to get everything set up the way we wanted it!

Someone was going to...wait a second...

Sniff-sniff. No. Was that—?

"—my eyes playing trick on me," Jer's voice popped into my head, "or did I just see you get out of Al Capone's limo?"

"I guess Al's looking to earn some extra cash where he can."

I groaned when I spotted my picture of me and the Babe, face down on the floor. Gingerly, I turned it over. The spider-web crack refused me a better look at the print. Hopefully, there was no damage.

"Mindy called me when she saw the door had been opened."

My mouth opened, but Miranda was already answering the question. "I wanted to see if we could get a few bills settled, so I came back to the office for them, and when I saw the door open I headed over to the library. Borrowed their phone. Made the call."

"Thank you, Miranda," I carried my prized picture over to my desk as if it were a fallen soldier being taken to his final resting place with full colors and procession.

"I don't think anything's missing," she continued, "apart from the petty cash. And now, well…"

Jer tipped his hat back, shaking his head. "I'm really sorry, Billi. This could have be—"

"This wasn't a break-in for cash, Jer," I muttered, staring at my battle axe, war hammer, and broadsword. "Of all the things in this office, you two have to admit that my survival gear is the most valuable stuff here. Or at least, looks like it."

My friend walked up to the battle axe and leaned in close, close enough to make it hum.

"Billi?" Jerry asked.

"Nah, you're fine, pal," I said. "The hum is a warning though."

"Hmmm…" He backed away after a moment and scoffed, "You're not big on dusting, are you?"

"Only way to be sure if anyone's messed with my things," I huffed back.

"So they ignored the décor because..."

"Because they knew it's charmed," I finished.

"Charmed?"

"What he means, Jer…" interjected Miranda. I turned to see her glancing between Jer and me nervously. Shit, that's right, he doesn't know. "…is that he's got those antiques of his wired. Special security measures. He calls them good luck charms, for making sure his weapons don't suddenly disappear."

"Right," Jer said, his tone hardly convincing.

He wasn't buying Miranda's cover and I should have been paying closer attention to what I was saying, but my attention was on my bookcase instead. *Sniff-sniff-sniff*. Yeah. Whoever the user was, their spell settled here.

"They weren't after our petty cash." *Sniff-sniff*. From the sharpness in the scent, I'm guessing... "Miranda, Jer, look inside any place that you could hide something—an overturned waste can, floor of the coat closet, drawer in an end table. You'll find every dollar of the office kitty there."

Now alone in my office, I went to the bookcase. It swung open easily.

"Billi!" Miranda ran back into the office, her face practically glowing as she held up a modest wad of greenbacks. "It was under the waste can like you said! How did you know?"

"Good detective work, Mindy, come on," Jerry answered. "I mean this is what he—"

"No, not good detective work," I said, looking at the empty cubbyhole in front of me. I should have left it at home. It would have been safer there. "The party responsible for this kind of crime wouldn't steal money. It's against their nature."

I felt Miranda's hand on my shoulder. "Billi, I'm so sorry."

My hand absently went to the Pitcher's Pendant still in my pocket. They came in here looking for a talisman of Acryonis. They left with My *World Book* (which Miranda had brought back here while I spent the afternoon out at Cog Hill) and personal journal. I don't know what scared me more—the fact that a portion of my personal life from Acryonis was now somewhere out there in Chicago, or the fact that this thief was in search of one of the Nine Talismans.

I still had the Pendant of Coe. Hardly comforting, but it was something.

"So, Billi, what do you want me to do?" Jer asked.

"Start picking stuff up. Just close your eyes as you do. This is private stuff." I then turned to Miranda. "And you—stand up. We've got some work to do. Get this office back in order."

"But what about your big book?" I could see Miranda becoming unhinged.

I smiled and placed a single kiss on her cheek. "One mystery at a time," I assured her, trying to block that smell of electricity around me. "One mystery at a time."

About the Author

photo by J.R. Blackwell

Tee Morris began his writing career in 2002 with the award-nominated, historical epic fantasy, *MOREVI: The Chronicles of Rafe & Askana*. He followed up that success in 2004 with *The Case of The Singing Sword*, the first of *The Billibub Baddings Mysteries*.

2005 introduced Tee to podcasting, a medium that has earned him a name as one of its pioneers. Podcasting *MOREVI* led him to co-founding Podiobooks.com, and co-writing *Podcasting for Dummies* from Wiley Publishing. He currently hosts *The Survival Guide to Writing Fantasy* and is now podcasting the *MOREVI* books in anticipation for his next novel, *Exodus from MOREVI: Book Two of The Arathellean Wars*.

Find out more about Tee Morris at www.teemorris.com.

3853368

Made in the USA
Lexington, KY
01 December 2009